The Last Midwife

The Last Midwife

SANDRA DALLAS

St. Martin's Press

New York

THE LAST MIDWIFE. Copyright © 2015 by Sandra Dallas. All rights reserved. Printed in the United States of America. For information, address St. Martin's Press, 175 Fifth Avenue, New York, N.Y. 10010.

www.stmartins.com

Library of Congress Cataloging-in-Publication Data

Dallas, Sandra.
   The last midwife / Sandra Dallas. — First edition.
      pages ; cm
   ISBN 978-1-250-07446-1 (hardcover)
   ISBN 978-1-4668-8614-8 (e-book)
  1. Midwives—Fiction.   2. Infanticide—Fiction.   3. Murder—Investigation—Fiction.   4. Colorado—Social life and customs—19th century—Fiction.   I. Title.
   PS3554.A434L37 2015
   813'.54—dc23

2015017976

Our books may be purchased in bulk for promotional, educational, or business use. Please contact your local bookseller or the Macmillan Corporate and Premium Sales Department at (800) 221-7945, extension 5442, or by e-mail at MacmillanSpecial Markets@macmillan.com.

First Edition: October 2015

10   9   8   7   6   5   4   3   2   1

To Beulah Glessner,

Glendon Schultz,

and Pansye Powell,

three extraordinary teachers

who made me a writer

ACKNOWLEDGMENTS

A couple of years ago, over lunch in New York, my editor, Jennifer Enderlin, suggested I write a book about a midwife. Oh, yuck, I thought. I don't want to write the details of childbirth. I could barely remember my own experience. After all, it had been forty-five years since my second daughter was born. But Jen has an unerring sense of what works. And she understands my writing. So I began researching midwifery.

Since my novels are set in previous time periods, I thought I might set this one, if I wrote it at all, in nineteenth-century Colorado. So along with medical accounts, I began rereading Colorado history, and one day I remembered a poem about a midwife in Summit County, Colorado. The poem is "In Those Rude Airs" from *The Tenmile Range* by Breckenridge poet Belle Turnbull. I had known Belle when I lived in Breckenridge in the early 1960s. She was a retired schoolteacher who lived with her novelist roommate, Helen Rich, in a log cabin on French Street. She drank whiskey neat and kept a mirror on the living room ceiling over her chair so that she could study herself when she grew bored with conversation. Then in her eighties, Belle was a sweet lady, but her poetry about mountain people was tough and hard edged. She captured the independence and tenacity of unsentimental folk who lived through winters at 10,000 feet.

As I reread the poems in *The Tenmile Range,* I realized my book would not be about midwifery but about a midwife who was part of the Tenmile, a woman who understood the ways of mountain-bred folk. Midwifery would not be the theme of the book but a part of it, just as quilting is a thread that runs through so many of my other novels.

So thank you, Jen, for your idea, and thank you, Belle, for giving me a love of mountain women. I am enormously grateful to William Hansen, who generously supplied me with material on nineteenth-century law and court cases involving midwives and murder and answered questions on early Colorado legal matters. I'm indebted to attorney and author Wick Downing, too, for providing additional legal help, and to Wick and Arnie Grossman for their support and encouragement. My thanks to Ann and Stan Moore in Georgetown for medical information and to Hansa for information about medicinal herbs.

As always, I'm grateful to my wonderful agents, Danielle Egan-Miller and Joanna MacKenzie (thanks for the title, Joanna) at Browne & Miller Literary Associates, and to my family—Bob, Forrest, and Lloyd, and to Dana and Kendal, the reasons I know childbirth is worth it.

Never along that range is ease:
Things are warped that are too near heaven

—BELLE TURNBULL, "FORWARD"

The Last Midwife

One

Dawn broke across the Tenmile Range in fiery slashes of red—flaming streaks the color of blood. Sunrise was always violent in the high country. There were no pink-edged clouds or pale patches of lavender. Such softness wouldn't be right in that raw landscape where men in their stampede for precious metals churned up the mountain streams until they were trickles of water through mounds of yellow waste rock, and scraped the thin topsoil from the land, leaving it naked, bare of anything that grew.

Tired as she was, Gracy Brookens stopped her buggy to admire the sweep of color that crept over the dark humps of mountains to the east and cast light onto the tips of the peaks with their honeycombed drifts of snow from last winter—or the winter before. It was past starshine now, and the red slashes were edged with gold richer than anything that ever came out of a

Tenmile mine. Swatches of blue the color of columbines seeped into the red. The glory of the sky told Gracy there was a Holy Spirit in that land of greed and struggle, particularly on a morning when she had just birthed a baby in Mayflower Gulch. Not that she needed convincing. The birth of a baby was proof enough. Every baby, she believed, was a miracle of God.

The infant had been a tiny thing, no bigger than a gray squirrel, most likely conceived in a mountain meadow, born in a hewn-log cabin with nary a window and only a dirt floor for him to crawl on. He'd be bred in the trees and rocks of the mountain peaks, like any other wild thing, brought up by the girl and boy who were only half grown themselves, young as Gracy's Jeff. It wasn't an easy life ahead. The baby had been born to poverty, would know disease and death, harshness and cold before he was grown, and likely, he wouldn't have much book learning. But he'd have love. Those two who formed him out of themselves had love enough to sell.

Gracy smiled to remember how the boy had hovered around his wife. Most men didn't want a thing to do with a lying-in. Once the labor pains started, a man usually taken out, rushing off to the mountain edge where he couldn't hear the screams. A man would find a bottle and sit with his friends, talking big, feeling he'd already done his part. Starting the baby had been up to him, but birthing was a woman's job. No need for him to be there. After the child was delivered, the father would amble back, chest out, brash, bragging about the fine young thing he'd whelped, as if he'd done it all himself, saying every now and then, "Well, God!"

But this new father was different. He'd come himself for Gracy, had run all the way down the mountain for her, run back and reached the cabin even before she'd arrived in her buggy. Then he'd refused to leave. Gracy didn't want husbands in the way, although at times she thought the men ought to know what their pleasure cost their wives. It would do for them to hear the cries, the calls for help, and to know the pain. Still, men got in the way, were clumsy in their attempts to help, offered her advice, as if she hadn't already delivered hundreds, maybe thousands, of babies and lost only a handful. She remembered those infants who hadn't taken a breath, some named, most not. She remembered the women who died, too. Every one of those deaths was an ache on her heart, a dark shadow. But it was the ones who lived that Gracy always kept in her mind as she coached a woman in the delivery. The baby who'd been born that day would live. Gracy knew that by his lusty cry. She didn't know what he'd been named, did not know the names of the boy and girl, either. She'd never seen either one of them before that night, and there hadn't been time for introductions. It was that way sometimes.

The boy had stayed by his wife's side, rubbing her back and whispering words of love as she twisted in pain and begged Gracy to make the baby go away. It hadn't been such a long labor, but the girl was wore out even before the time came for her to push. The boy, too. She was too young, too much a girl for childbirth, and the boy had promised he'd never again put her through such pain. Gracy had smiled at that. It was never a promise to be kept.

When the pains slacked off, the boy built up the fire and heated more water. He warmed the soft rags set aside to swaddle the baby, even offered to make tea for Gracy. The thoughtfulness touched her. She'd wanted a cup and half thought to say yes before she remembered how poor the two of them were. The tea was dear bought and should be saved for the girl.

"We've no money to pay you," the boy said. "But I noticed your cabin needs chinking, and I'm right smart at it. There's nary a breeze that comes through these logs." He nodded at the walls made of logs squared off and fitted tight, chinked with mud and burro dung, and tried not to sound proud. "And she knows where the best raspberries grow. We'll bring you a pail come raspberrying time. Or a pie. She makes it better than anybody, that one."

Gracy wondered where they'd get the money for the sugar, but she said, "Pay enough," and indeed, it was better than what she got from some. Cash money, even the two dollars she charged for a birthing, was hard to come by, and she didn't always receive it. She'd have attended the girl anyway, of course. You couldn't turn down a mother, especially one giving birth to her first. So Gracy might have told the boy she didn't expect anything from him, because they didn't have anything. The bed was spread with balsam for a mattress, and a stove had been fashioned from an oil drum. Still, those two wouldn't take charity. Gracy would have to warn the women in her Swandyke quilting group about that. They'd want to help, to bring their broth and stews, their tiny quilts and shirts. They would mean well. But they'd have to be humble. They'd have to say it would be a kindness to take the soup off their hands for they'd made too much and it would spoil. And it would pleasure them to see that blanket wrapped around another baby, would make them remember when their own were young. Would you bring us that joy? Oh, those two wouldn't take a thing if they thought it was charity.

When Gracy had lifted the sheet that was draped over the girl's legs, the boy had glanced away, ashamed as if it wasn't right to look at his wife like that.

"Ah, now," Gracy had said. "The baby's crowning."

"What?" the boy asked.

"Crowning. It means you can see the head. It's coming now. Look you."

And despite his reluctance, the boy had sent a sideward glance between his wife's legs and stood transfixed.

"Push," Gracy ordered, as the girl struggled and gripped the iron bars of the bed, the only piece of furniture in the room that was not made by hand—the boy's hand, most likely. The bed was old, the bars twisted, the brass on the knobs worn off. They'd probably found it in a deserted cabin or at the dump. "Push."

The girl pushed, her face contorting, sweat pouring off her body. She twisted, rattling the newspapers that had been spread beneath her on the bed.

The boy gripped his wife's arm, tears running down his cheeks. "Come on, honeygirl," he whispered. He glanced at Gracy, but she paid him no attention.

"Push. Oh, you're doing a fine job. You're such a good girl," Gracy coached.

"It hurts," the girl had whimpered. But she didn't ask Gracy to make it stop that time.

"Again," Gracy said, and the head popped out. "There it is. Oh, you are doing finely, the best I ever saw. You are made for babies. Push again."

The girl clutched the bars of the bed and gritted her teeth, and the baby's shoulders emerged.

"Once more," Gracy said, and the baby slipped from the girl's body. Gracy caught it in her worn hands and raised her head to smile at the new mother.

"Is my wife all right?" the boy asked.

Gracy liked that about a man, when he asked about his wife even before he'd looked to see if the baby was boy or girl.

"She is fine. She will be a strong mother."

The girl raised her head and asked, "The baby?"

"A boychild. A perfect boychild," Gracy said as she held the tiny thing in her hands, wiping it with a cloth. Reaching for the strong linen thread that lay in the basin of hot water, she'd asked the boy, "Would you like to tie it off, the cord?" She didn't always ask, but the boy had been so loving. He would be a good father.

He dipped his hands into the hot water, soaped them up, rinsed and dried them. Then as Gracy folded over the cord, the boy wrapped the linen thread around it and cut the cord with a pair of silver scissors shaped like a stork. Gracy wrapped a belly band around the infant and started to put him into the wooden box that would serve as a cradle, but instead she said, "You hold him whilst I care for your wife." She handed the baby to the father to hold while she wrapped the afterbirth in newspaper and set it aside. The boy could burn it in the fireplace, or maybe he'd bury it. Some did. They said it made roses grow. When all was finished, Gracy asked the girl if she knew about nursing.

"I reckon I do. Ma had eleven, and I was the oldest but one."

Gracy nodded, then told the girl what to do if her milk failed to come in, gave her advice on caring for herself. She set a packet of herbs on the table and asked the boy to make a tea of them for his wife. Was there someone who would help? she asked. Her sister would come, the girl said, from over the range. The sister had had a presentiment and sent word she'd arrive just after sunup. Until then, the boy said proudly, he would take care of everything.

"You'll do finely then. I'll stop by later on to make sure everything is all right," Gracy said. She picked up the soiled rags, the ones the girl herself had set aside for the birthing. She'd launder them and bring them back. There were no sheets on the bed, just a striped tick filled with dried meadow grass with newspapers spread over it. She crumpled the papers and handed them to the boy to throw into the stove, then told him to freshen the grass in the tick when he had a minute.

He offered to hitch the horse to the buggy, but Gracy told him to stay where he was, and he turned back to his wife. Gracy could hitch that old horse in the dark and often did. She gathered her things and slipped through the doorway. Outside, in the false dawn as she hitched Buddy, the gray horse, to the buggy, she wondered if those two even noticed she was gone.

The way near the cabin was steep, not even a washboard road but a slip of a trail, impassable for a buggy in winter and treacherous even in summer. But Buddy was sure-footed, would know the way home if she fell asleep.

Gracy leaned back against the seat now but did not think of sleeping. It had been a good birth, an easy one, although the girl wouldn't think so. Gracy wondered what number it was. She should have kept track of the babies she'd delivered, but she hadn't. She didn't even remember the number of ones who had died, and she thanked God this wasn't one of them.

A little brightness came into the sky now, the sun lighting the tips of everlasting snow on the farthest peaks, shining on the late crimson-tipped Indian paintbrush and tiny yellow wildflowers that shone like drops of molten gold in the green carpet of grass. It was a sunrise that seemed to last forever. Gracy passed a spread of stalks with bright pink blooms, the flowers the women called summer's-half-over. She'd seen them in the moonlight the night before and would have stopped to pick a bouquet for the girl, but she hadn't wanted to waste the time. She wouldn't pick them for herself, because she had flowers at home.

Gracy was good at growing things, making them thrive— flowers and babies, although not her own. She and Daniel had lost too many, poor halfway-built things that had grown inside her for only a few weeks or months. Those who had made it hadn't lived long. One had died at four weeks, another at two months. Emma, though, had lived four years, and Gracy had thought the girl was safe, perhaps because she wasn't Gracy's own flesh and blood but a weak baby given to her because the mother had had too many others to raise.

But Emma wasn't safe. She came down with a fever, coughing until her throat and tongue were bloody. In her delirium, she grasped Gracy, but her tiny hands could not hold on. So Gracy caught up the child in her strong arms and held her through the night, until the child crossed over. Gracy was bowed down with grief then. Sweet Emma was as much a part of the woman as if she'd given birth to the girl herself. The child already knew the names of herbs Gracy collected and would have been trained up to follow in Gracy's footsteps as a midwife and healer. Of all of the babies given to her—her own and the sickly castoffs— only Jeff had thrived, born more than sixteen years before. Gracy was almost fifty then. The irony of it, Gracy thought. Jeff had come along when she'd given up on ever mothering a child again. And he was the one who had lived!

The heavens lightened, and the red streaks softened, filling the sky between the mountain ranges with color. The sunrise never failed to thrill Gracy, especially in the mornings when she was returning from a birthing. Babies, it seemed, liked to be born in the dark. She stopped the buggy at the overlook, Buddy waiting patiently, for the old horse was used to Gracy's fits and starts. She tightened the shawl around her, because even in midsummer, the nights were cold, and she shivered as she got down from the carriage and peered out over the valley, across to Turnbull Mountain. The morning light shone on the glory holes that pitted it, their golden waste rock spilling over the hillside.

She could make out the miners climbing up to the Buckbush and the Tiger for the morning shift. She saw a prospector with his burro make his way across the mountain, headed for somewhere along the Tenmile Range. He might have been Daniel, but

Gracy knew he wasn't. Daniel would be gone a week or two, maybe more, and he'd said the night before when she had been rousted from bed that he wouldn't go until she returned. He wouldn't just leave out without a good-bye.

He'd come home from prospecting the week before, his pockets filled with ore to be tested. The assay had shown promise, and Daniel had said he thought this would be his strike. He said that every year, and he always believed it, never more so than now when their days were growing shorter.

Silver had been discovered over the mountains in Leadville in 1875, five years earlier, and although the Tenmile was gold country, Daniel now hunted for both metals, hoping to find blossom rock, which was what they called an outcropping of ore. He worked the mines on Turnbull Mountain in the winter, but come summer, he was off. Gracy kept her thoughts to herself. She would not dash his hopes that the next strike of his pick would open up a gold or a silver vein, just as she had never lost hope that each of the babies she'd borne would live. And there was hope. Each of them had struck gold before.

Turnbull Mountain came alive now, the night silence broken. She heard the call of men as the late shift came down off the trail. The miners had made it through another night and would be wanting their glass of beer. Gracy was used to seeing men drunk after shift, even when that shift ended at sunrise. From far away came the muffled sound of a dynamite charge and the rhythmic thumping of a stamp mill.

She watched the red streaks in the sky fade to magenta and amethyst and thought again about the young family in Mayflower

Gulch, thanking God the birth had been a good one. Over the years, Gracy had watched too many women die. She thought then of the woman on Potato Mountain who had given birth to her fourth early in the summer. She had three others who were still toddlers at her feet. The birthing had gone well. Gracy had tied the cord and handed the baby to the mother, then gone to call the father. When the two returned, the mother was dead. Had the woman's heart given out or had Gracy done something wrong? she wondered. She wished she could explain it to the husband, who now had four little ones to care for. But she didn't know what had happened. That death and all the others over the years had begun to weigh her down, made her wonder if it was time she stopped delivering babies.

Gracy shook away the thoughts of death as she climbed back into the buggy and flicked the reins. "Time to get home, old horse," she told Buddy, going downslope now. Gracy was tired. Her shoulders hurt, and she hoped Daniel would rub them for her. His fingers were strong, and he would knead her back the way she kneaded bread dough, pushing out the kinks. He'd fix her tea and toast, too, and then she'd put on her nightdress and sleep. Gracy was grateful she could almost always sleep. Later, she might get out her scraps and piece a quilt for the newborn baby, maybe ask one of the women in the sewing group to join her, for there was nothing a woman liked more than making a baby quilt.

As she rode through Swandyke with its buildings scattered along feather-stitched streets, Gracy nodded at each person she passed. She didn't recognize some of them, but she was aware that everybody knew her, so she didn't want to offend. The horse knew where to go, and without Gracy's prodding, Buddy made his way to the livery stable. He'd been standing in the cold all night and deserved his rest, too, Gracy thought, as she stopped the buggy inside the stable. She was glad the hostler was there. He would unhitch the wagon and feed Buddy for her.

Gracy gathered the birthing rags and the bag she always carried with her and got down from the buggy. "Hello, Earl, I'm back," she called to the stable boy. "Buddy could use a good rubdown if you've the time."

Earl was in conversation with three men, but they stopped talking when Gracy spoke. The men walked toward her.

"These fellows want to see you, missus," Earl said.

Gracy searched her mind. She couldn't recall any babies due just then. But there were always women back in the gulches who didn't call for her until the pains were on them. Well, it couldn't be helped. Worn out as she was, she would go to them. God always gave her strength, although for how much longer, she didn't know. She tired more easily now, and she seemed to dwell more on the hardships of birthings, the pain, the deaths. Those were other reasons she'd begun to think her time as a midwife might be over. Perhaps it was time for someone else to birth the babies, although there was no other midwife in Swandyke. She was the last one. She hadn't mentioned quitting to Daniel yet, but it was on her mind.

She waited for the men to reach her, and then she frowned. She knew them, and none was in need of her services. In fact two of them, the undertaker and the doctor, would have let their wives die before they called for her. She couldn't imagine what they wanted.

"Missus Brookens," the third man said. She liked him better than the other two, liked him almost as much as she did Daniel. He was the sheriff, John Miller.

Gracy frowned at the "missus." "Why so formal, John?" she asked. She glanced at the two men behind him, angry men who would dance on her grave, and wondered if mischief were afoot.

When the sheriff did not answer but only cleared his throat and looked around him, Gracy said, "Be quick about it. I've just attended a birthing in Mayflower Gulch and need my sleep."

"The baby live, did it?" the undertaker snarled.

Gracy gave a slight nod.

"Well, ain't it the lucky one."

"Ignorance," the doctor added. "Midwifery's naught but ignorance and superstition, if you ask me."

Gracy did not reply to the insults. She wasn't surprised by them. Instead, she asked, "John?"

"I don't like it, don't like it a bit, waiting for you like this, like you was a scoundrel, but it can't be helped."

"What can't be helped?"

He kicked at the straw on the floor of the stable and shook his head. Then he looked square at Gracy. "I got to arrest you for murder, Gracy."

"Murder?"

The sheriff nodded.

Gracy shook her head. What the sheriff said made no sense.

"What are you talking about, John? That baby was breathing as much as you or me when I left him a couple of hours ago. He's no more dead than . . . them." She nodded her head at the undertaker and the doctor.

"I'm not talking about that one. It's the Halleck baby, the boy born four days ago. Jonas Halleck brought him to the undertaker last night."

Gracy stood frozen a moment, grasping the buggy wheel to steady herself. How could that baby be dead? He was fine when she left him the day after he was born. Had she done something wrong, missed a problem she ought to have seen? Was the death her fault? She was more aware than anyone that she was not infallible. Babies had died before, and she feared sometimes that it was because she didn't know enough to save them. A baby she had delivered in Nevada had seemed all right, but an hour after she left him, he was dead. He'd turned blue and died, the mother had said. Gracy'd always wondered if she had stayed, if she hadn't been anxious to get home before a blizzard obscured the trail, could she have saved the child?

She hadn't delivered the Halleck baby but had been sent for a day later when the infant began choking. Jonas Halleck himself had acted as midwife. He told Gracy the baby had come too quickly, that there hadn't been time to send for her. He was an educated man, wealthy by Swandyke standards, and his wife had come from quality. People in Swandyke respected him.

Still, Gracy had never liked him much. Daniel had worked at Mr. Halleck's Holy Cross Mine that last winter and had been let go, told there was no need for him anymore. Mr. Halleck had accused Daniel of high-grading, but that wasn't the reason. Daniel had complained about shoddy materials used in the mine and a buildup of gas.

"I expect he named it the Holy Cross because he thinks he's Jesus Christ hisself," Daniel had said.

Gracy hadn't thought about all that when she'd learned the baby was in distress. She'd rushed to the Halleck house and been shocked at the sight of the baby. He was struggling to breathe. It was good she'd come, because there was mucous in the infant's mouth and he was choking. But Gracy had cleared it, and the baby was healthy when she left him. Mr. Halleck had done a poor job of tying the baby's cord, so she'd retied it with her stout linen thread. She'd checked the boy over, looked into his eyes, listened to his heart, and pronounced him as fine as if she'd delivered him herself. "I guess you could take my job from me if you'd a mind to do it," she joked. But none of them laughed, not Mr. Halleck, his wife, Edna, nor the daughter, Josie.

And then Mr. Halleck had said Gracy was not to tell anyone about the baby, that he had grand plans to announce the birth himself. It had been a strange request, but then everything about the birth was off.

Edna had retired from society weeks before, claiming ill health, and Josie had stayed at home to care for her. Nobody had suspected Edna was pregnant, but then some women were like that. Probably Edna, being highborn, considered it unseemly to be in public once her pregnancy showed. That was what Jonas Halleck said, at any rate.

Now, Gracy shook her head. In fact, her whole body shook.

There was no way she could have hurt an infant. "That baby was breathing fine when I left him, but sometimes it happens, they just die. I don't know the reason." It had always bothered her that God would reach down and snatch away a life. She didn't understand it. "Maybe it was pneumonia," she said. "It's common enough in the high country."

"It was not pneumonia," the doctor snarled.

"No. Then it was just God's will."

"Not that, either," the doctor said.

Gracy turned to observe him—Richard Erickson, Little Dickie, people had called him when he was young. He was a small man and not just in stature. He'd gone away to medical school, then returned to Swandyke just that summer, full of himself and his medical knowledge. He'd told the women they ought to have a doctor attend their birthings, that Gracy was no better than a witch with her herbs and her salves and all her soothing talk. But the women ignored him, and he resented that. The mothers had gone to Gracy for years, and they didn't see a need for a man with all his fancy learning. His shiny metal instruments scared them. Gracy could have worked with the doctor. There were times when Gracy would have welcomed a trained physician, times when the baby was turned or too big to pass through the birth canal. Or when there was something wrong with the infant. She lacked knowledge a doctor might have. But Little Dickie had made it clear that if the women went to Gracy, they shouldn't bother him if anything went wrong. Gracy wondered then if the young doctor resented that Mr. Halleck had sent for her instead of him.

"I'm sorry for the death, but babies just die sometimes. It isn't murder."

"Oh, it was murder, all right. I can tell you that," the doctor said. He started to continue, but the sheriff interrupted.

"Gracy, that baby was strangled," John said. "Jonas Halleck says you did it."

Two

"Strangled?" Gracy gasped, staring at the sheriff. She felt faint and took a deep breath to calm her body, which was flushed. "How can that be? Are you sure?" Heartsick, she grasped the buggy to steady herself. How could anyone think she had killed a baby, had done it on purpose? The idea sickened her.

"Did you think I wouldn't know?" the doctor asked. He raised his shoulders a little, trying to look taller, but he didn't succeed.

Gracy drew back at his scorn. Lord knew the town needed a doctor, had for two years, ever since the old one died. But did it need this one?

They'd had an understanding, the midwife and the old doctor. Gracy took care of childbirth; he was in charge of the town's health. Oh, she helped him when there was a mine accident, made the rounds of the cabins with him during the diphtheria outbreak, just as she called on him when there were complications with a birth or when something was wrong with a baby. But they knew their boundaries. Gracy wouldn't do surgery or prescribe medicines. She left cancer and broken bones and worn-out hearts to the doctor, just as he left the childbirth bed to her. He got nervous waiting around for a baby to be born, he'd said. He didn't have the patience to sit through the hours of labor and was grateful she took charge of all that. And he admitted the women were more comfortable with Gracy than with him.

But Little Dickie—Dr. Erickson, he'd insisted she call him, although he still called her Gracy—he'd said midwifery was based on superstition and old wives' tales. And he'd told Gracy she had no business taking care of sore throats and chilblains and fevers after the old doctor left. "There was nobody else they could go to. You'd expect me to let those folks die?" she asked the young doctor. She could have harmed them more than she'd helped, he replied, and Gracy scoffed, "But I didn't." She knew he resented the way sick folks still came to her with their ailments, even though she gently sent them to the new doctor. Folks didn't like him and complained he had no sympathy in him. He chided them and talked in medical terms they didn't understand. And then he charged them money and asked for payment right then. And he wouldn't take barter.

So she wasn't surprised that Little Dickie wanted to blame her for something. But murder? Gracy shook her head to show the outrageousness of it.

The sheriff glanced around the stable as if not wanting to confront Gracy. But finally, he raised his head and stared directly at her. "It was murder, all right. Strangled he was. There was a furrow around his neck and even a bit of the cord stuck to it."

"Could it have been an accident?" Gracy asked. Please, God, she thought. Let it be an accident.

"Not likely." The sheriff shook his head.

The undertaker, Coy Chaney, sneered. "Thought I wouldn't notice, did you? Thought when I put that little thing in a coffin, I wouldn't take a look at it. There it was, plain as day, a ring like ruby silver around its neck." The man glared at her.

Gracy blanched under Coy's gaze although she wasn't surprised the undertaker was against her, too. He'd been biding his time, waiting to get even, because he blamed her for the death of his daughter. But it was the man's own fault the little one had been born dead. Coy had gone to town for Gracy when his wife went into labor but stopped at a saloon to brag a little and let the boys buy him a drink. And then another. He'd gotten so drunk that he'd forgotten to fetch her. So it wasn't until the next day that one of his boys came to the cabin for Gracy. And by the time Gracy reached the Chaney house, the woman was all but senseless, and the baby was dead in her womb. It was another of those births that haunted Gracy, because the baby could have lived. The mother had lived, however, but only because of Gracy's care.

Coy didn't credit her for that, and he wouldn't take the blame for the baby's death. He wasn't that kind of man. Instead, he pointed his finger at Gracy. He claimed he'd awakened her before stopping at the saloon and told her to go to his wife. Gracy'd gone back to sleep, he said, had slept while his poor missus was moaning in pain in her bed, scaring the life out of their four little boys. Coy might not have been so angry if the baby had been another boy, but this one was a girl, and he'd never have another. The childbirth had left his wife unable to bear again. Folks didn't believe what he said about Gracy, not after Daniel let it be known that the undertaker had never come for her. But Coy stuck to his story, and after a time, Gracy thought he'd begun to believe it. And his wife, too.

"Little Dickie." The sheriff cleared his throat and started again. "That is, *Dr. Erickson* examined the body. He said there's no doubt the boy was strangled. It might have looked like an accident if the thread fibers hadn't been on his neck."

"A linen cord," the doctor added, "the very cord a Swandyke midwife uses." He pronounced "midwife" with distaste.

Gracy shook her head, still trying to accept that the baby was dead. "I doubt the cord I use is thick enough to choke a person."

"Then you must have wrapped it around his neck two or three times. Maybe more."

"He was alive when I left." She had checked him well, checked him twice over, in fact, then had pressed him against her chest, had felt his heart beat against her own.

The doctor cleared his throat. "So you say."

"And who's to say otherwise?"

"Jonas Halleck," Coy interjected, a sneer on his face. "And his wife and daughter."

Gracy stared at the man, incredulous. How could they say such a thing? Gracy felt a heaviness in her stomach almost as if she had swallowed a stone.

John stepped in then. "Jonas Halleck says you strangled that baby, Gracy, says you turned your back to him, but he was in the room. The baby was dead when he picked it up after you left. That's a powerful charge from a man like Mr. Halleck."

Gracy shook her head back and forth, as if to clear her mind of what she'd just heard. She was tired, more tired than she'd ever been, not from the exhaustion that came from being up all night with a woman in labor but a kind of senseless fatigue that was the result of incomprehension. "But why would I do that?" she asked. Why indeed?

"Meanness," Coy told her. "He fired your husband last winter, told him he was a useless old man who couldn't pull his weight, accused him of high-grading."

Gracy tensed at the memory. Mr. Halleck had had no right to say such a thing. Daniel had never stolen high-grade ore in his life. The charge had been unfair—and hurtful, because after Mr. Halleck spread it around that Daniel had high-graded, the other mines wouldn't hire him. But he hadn't high-graded. He'd only complained about conditions in the mine.

Daniel had looked for different work, but the only job he'd been offered was sweeping out the Nugget saloon. Gracy had been mad enough to chew nails. Daniel being treated like that was another reason she'd begun thinking it might be time to give up her midwifery. It wouldn't do for her to have her work when Daniel was at home doing odd jobs all winter. She could tell people she'd decided to call it deep enough. That was what the miners said when they quit a job. Together, they'd find a way to earn their living.

The hostler had unhitched Buddy but was hovering around,

waiting for them to leave so that he could spread the gossip. He'd left the buggy where it was, and Gracy leaned against the wheel, fearing her legs would give out. "I didn't do it, John," she told the sheriff. "A layoff isn't a reason to murder a child. You know yourself I wouldn't hurt a baby. My work is about giving life, not taking it."

Coy started to interrupt, but the sheriff held up his hand. "I guess that's up to a jury, Gracy."

Gracy ran her hand up and down a wheel spoke. "That baby was born on Monday. If I killed it the next day, why did they wait until last night—two days later—to bring it to the undertaker?"

The sheriff nodded slowly. "I never thought of that. Why's that, Coy?" he asked.

The undertaker cleared his throat. "Halleck said he buried it himself first, but his missus wanted it dug up and buried proper and wouldn't rest until it was in a coffin, a nice one. They bought one with brass handles and blue silk inside, even a blue silk pillow. It cost . . ." His voice trailed off.

"Them waiting all that time sounds a little odd to me, too. But still, Gracy, I got to arrest you," John said.

"You're taking me to jail?" Gracy stared at the sheriff, fire in her eyes. "There's a new mother up in Mayflower Gulch to look after. It's her first. And I have to launder these rags. She'll need them next time."

"Filthy rags!" the doctor said. "You should have told her to throw them out and use new ones."

"And I ought to have a driver and a coach-and-four to take me to the birthings. Where would that pair get new material?

They don't have two nickels to rub together. They don't even have the money to buy material for pillowslips. And there's nothing wrong with rags that are washed clean, dried in the heat of the sun, then warmed by the fire during the birth," Gracy told him. She turned to John. "She'll need looking after at least one time."

"I guess she wouldn't mind a real doctor attending her instead of a . . . what do they call you, a *sagehen*." Dr. Erickson sneered. "You do no more good than a prairie chicken."

Gracy straightened her back. "The Sagehen" had been her nickname and she was proud of being called that. Years before, a little girl who'd watched Gracy run across a meadow to attend a woman in childbed had said Gracy had moved apurpose, just like a sagehen protecting her young. The handle had stuck. So Gracy had been called that in Arkansas and then in California and Nevada and Colorado, too. Swandyke once had had a Granny Grace who delivered babies, but she'd been dirty and crude and drank too much. Folks hadn't trusted her. They liked calling her replacement the Sagehen instead of Granny Gracy, which was too close to the former midwife's name.

"You think that girl up there will spread her legs and let a man examine her, a man she's never even met? You think the word 'doctor' means a thing to her?" Gracy was indignant.

The doctor blanched at Gracy's crudeness. Even the sheriff was a little taken aback.

"Well, what do you think childbirth is? You think babies are plucked out of the ground like gold nuggets? Birthing is hard work for a woman, bloody work. You ought to know that. How many babies have you delivered, Dr. Erickson?" she asked Little Dickie.

He cleared his throat. "In school, we studied—"

"Ha! In school. You learn how to soothe a mother who's never known there was such pain and wants you to stop it? Or one that doesn't hear her baby crying the minute it's born and fears it's dead? You know what to tell a woman with ten kids when she begs you to put a stop to childbearing? Or what to say to her husband when he's ready to have a go at her a week after the birth? Do you?"

The men wouldn't look at her, and the doctor didn't answer. Gracy gave a bark of a laugh and turned to the sheriff. "Go ahead and throw me in jail, and if something happens to that young girl, it's on your soul. There's others out there that's going to deliver, too. You tell them why I won't be coming. You tell them to fetch the doctor over there and see what happens. Let him bear the pain and the guilt when a baby fails to take a breath or a young mother barely out of girlhood dies in childbirth."

"Well . . ." The sheriff seemed to struggle with himself. "I got to accuse you of murder, but when you put it like that, I guess there's no reason to lock you up."

"I can take care of the women," the doctor said. "Good, proper medical care, not herbs and ointment and incantations."

"Incantations like 'push'?" Gracy threw at him.

"Gracy's right. They won't go to you." John paused and added under his breath, "I know my wife wouldn't have."

"If you don't lock her up, she might taken out," Coy put in.

"And go where?" John asked. "I know Gracy Brookens 'bout

as good as I know anybody. She won't leave those women behind with nobody to take care of them."

"Well, she ought to. There's real medical help in Swandyke now."

None of them seemed to pay attention to Little Dickie, even the undertaker.

"Like I say, they don't want some sawbones," John said.

Gracy had had enough. She set her jaw and said, "I'm going on home. You decide you want to drag me off to jail, you come get me, John. Or you can come along now, and I'll fix us a boiler of coffee. It's been a long night, and I don't want it to get longer. You, neither. No telling how long you've been here waiting for me."

The doctor and undertaker started to protest as Gracy walked out of the stable, but John held up his hand. "I'll be responsible for her. I guess I've known her longer than you two, knew her even before she come to Swandyke, and she won't run off." He started for the stable door, calling, "You wait up, Gracy. I'll walk you home."

"I don't like it. I don't like it at all," the sheriff said, as he took the bundle of soiled rags from Gracy, letting her carry her birthing bag. "You got to know, Gracy, it's not my doing." When the Sagehen didn't reply, he continued. "But I talked to Mr. Halleck last night, after Coy come to me. He said he didn't see you put the cord around the baby's neck, but the baby was dead after you left. He said you put the baby in the cradle with a blanket over it and said to let him sleep. He thought at first the little thing had died its own self, but then he saw that mark around its neck. His wife and daughter said you did it, too. So what else could I do? It's not like Mr. Halleck is some drunken miner. He's just nearly the most important man in Swandyke. I don't have any choice but to arrest you. I'm bending the law as it is by not locking you up." He sounded as if he were talking to himself instead of to Gracy. "But I couldn't put you in jail, not a lady like you. Elizabeth would have skinned me for it. If I was to lock you up and she was here, she'd take dinner to you every day—*my* dinner. The other folks in town, they'll be right with her."

But not all of them, Gracy thought. She had enemies. There were men who hated her because she knew they beat their wives or took them by force when the women weren't yet recovered from childbirth. That was their right, they told her after the women complained to her and Gracy confronted the men. It was rape, plain and simple, she said, and the husbands replied it was no such thing. How could it be when they were married?

There were women, too, who resented Gracy, because she wouldn't abort the babies they didn't want, couldn't help them stop the pregnancies—couldn't because the methods she knew about worked only some of the time. There were failures, and more than one woman whose belly swelled blamed Gracy, whispering that the Sagehen had been false because all she cared about was the dollar or two she got for delivering a baby. Some women blamed Gracy because their babies hadn't lived. They couldn't accept that the deaths could be God's doing, or worse, their own fault. They couldn't bear that guilt, and so they blamed

Gracy. And she blamed herself for not knowing enough to keep the babies alive.

The sun was up now. Daniel would have eaten breakfast, would have set out a plate for her. She wished they could have eaten together, eaten hotcakes with sorghum, bacon cut thick the way he liked it, a dish of applesauce. She would have told him about the Halleck baby. Not everything, of course. But how sweet it was, as sweet a baby as Jeff had been. She felt a sting in her heart when she thought of Jeff. She missed him so. She thought again of Daniel and how she'd have told him about that young couple in Mayflower Gulch, how they hadn't a thing except love and how she thought that just might be enough.

She and Daniel had been like that when they were young, with nothing but love and hopes to carry them forward. They had farmed, but Daniel was restless, and they had left out for California when the first news of gold came to them. They'd thought they'd get rich and would pick up nuggets right out of the stream. Gracy had even packed an extra apron to collect them. Thinking of that foolishness made her smile.

They didn't find the nuggets or any other gold in California, but Gracy worked as a midwife to keep them in beans and salt pork, and she'd loved it. There was no greater joy than the first cry of a newborn, no more beautiful smile than that of a mother beholding her baby only a minute old. That was reward enough for Gracy. She was paid in gold dust, in firewood and sacks of nuts. She hadn't known how much Daniel resented her work back then, resented that she didn't need him, and hated that she was the one who provided for them when his gold pan turned up only dirt and gravel. Daniel had been a wanderer back then, like Jeff was now. Her son had been gone the better part of a year, and she wondered where he was. Jeff had been half boy, half man when he left out, and was likely more man now, she thought. Her hands ached to touch him, to pat his shoulder, to smooth his hand. She thought of how when he was a boy, he'd climb into her lap when he was tired and rest his head against her breast.

Now Daniel would be waiting for her, patient, for he knew a baby came in its own good time. Gracy never hurried a little one, never used the forceps in her bag unless the mother or child was in danger. She'd likely find her husband smoking his pipe, sitting on the bench he'd fashioned from aspen trunks, placed just so it caught the morning sun, a jackknife in one hand, a whittling stick in the other. Maybe he'd have picked a bouquet of her flowers and put them into the milk jug on the pie safe. Or perhaps he'd found a handful of pale green aspen leaves and placed them on the table for her. Daniel was thoughtful that way, and she needed his thoughtfulness now. She needed Jeff's, too, but she wouldn't have it, not now.

The sun was up, the day already warming, and Gracy could see the flowers that surrounded her house from a long way off, the blue delphinium reaching almost to the top of the windows, the poppies red as fire, daisies spread out in front of them like a petticoat, butter-and-eggs, their pale yellow blooms like little faces. She grew more flowers than anyone in Swandyke. Those flowers, Daniel had said once, they brought her more business than an advertisement in the newspaper. But she hadn't needed any advertising, because she was the only midwife around. If you wanted someone to birth your baby, you called for the Sagehen. She smiled at the daisies, for she loved a daisy more than any other flower, and even on that terrible morning, they lifted her spirits.

Daniel was indeed on his bench, set in an aspen grove, staring out at the mountains. "That's a right nice place to sit of a morning," the sheriff said when they caught sight of Gracy's husband. John was trying to make conversation, just as if it were mail time and he was waiting for a letter.

Gracy nodded but didn't reply, and they were silent until they reached the house.

Daniel stood, looking puzzled. "John, I take it as a kindness, you walking Gracy home. I'd have been there myself if I'd known when she'd get back, but I've learned you never can tell." There was a hint of a question in his voice, as if asking what was going on. Then he turned to Gracy, "You all right, honey?"

Gracy didn't answer, just stared at her husband, a look of such agony on her face that Daniel asked again what was wrong.

"Daniel, there's been an awful thing. Now you know I think the world of Gracy, and most everybody does—" the sheriff started.

"Oh, Danny," Gracy interrupted. "They think I killed the Halleck baby. Jonas Halleck says . . . and his wife and daughter . . ." She shook her head and began to cry. Gracy didn't cry often, and she didn't cry well. Her body shook with great heaving sobs. She laid her head on Daniel's chest, and he put his arm around her awkwardly, for they were not a couple who showed their affection in front of others. He thumped her on the back with a hand as big as a chicken hawk.

The sheriff turned away at the display of emotion.

"That true, John?" Daniel asked after a time, and the sheriff nodded. "Well, then, that's as stupid a thing as I ever heard. God, hell! Everybody knows Gracy's about bringing a baby into the world, not snuffing it out."

"Don't you think I know that?" the sheriff asked. "It's just that that baby was strangled—I seen the body myself—and Jonas Halleck said it was Gracy done it."

"And you'd take the word of a self-righteous—"

"Can't help it. I don't decide right and wrong, but I got to abide by the law. That's my job."

"What's going to happen?" Daniel asked.

John thought a moment. "Halleck says she killed his boy, and Mrs. Halleck and the girl, Josie, agree with him. So there's an accusation of murder hanging over Gracy, and if it was anybody else, they'd go to jail. There'll be a hearing when the judge comes to Swandyke to find out if she's to be charged formally. We don't have a full-time judge, you know, just one that holds court once a month or so when he's here. He'll decide if there's enough evidence to make a formal charge of murder or maybe manslaughter against Gracy. If he does, then there will be a trial the next time he comes to town."

"Ain't nobody in Swandyke will find her guilty," Daniel insisted.

The sheriff shrugged and said, "I'm hoping you're right.

You'd have to look from Genesis to Revelations to find somebody who'd speak ill of her."

At that, Gracy took a gulp of air and rubbed her eyes with
her hands. "Oh, there'll be some—some like Coy Chaney and
Little Dickie. I bet they're already spreading it about that I murdered that baby. And if you say a thing often enough, people'll
believe it."

"Well, I don't, and I know you better than anybody," Daniel
said. Then he frowned at the sheriff. "Shame on you, John, for
going along with this. You know she'd never hurt a soul."

The sheriff put up his hands. "I don't have no choice. I didn't
lock her up, though. You got to appreciate that. Anybody else
would have, you know."

Daniel scoffed. "Well, don't that beat all. You give yourself
credit for not locking up the best woman in Swandyke and an
innocent one at that." He put his arm around Gracy and held
her so tight she couldn't breathe. "You going to make her stay
to home? You'd have to tie her up, you know."

"The girl in Mayflower needs checking on, and the Tucker
woman's had some pain. I'll have to go to the other side of Rich
Mountain if she needs me," Gracy put in. "That all right with
you?"

"What'd you do if I said no?" the sheriff asked.

"Go anyway."

"I figured such. Just don't brag on it to Coy Chaney or that
doctor, will you?"

Gracy nodded. Daniel relaxed his grip, and Gracy all but fell
onto the bench.

"I guess you need your sleep," John said. "I don't know how you stay up all night at your age. You must be near seventy." When Gracy didn't reply, he added, "Well, maybe sixty. It's time you gave this up."

Gracy nodded. It was what she had been thinking. But who would replace her if she did?

"I'll be going then." John started for the trail, then stopped. "Don't you worry none, Gracy."

"What do you mean, 'don't worry'?" Daniel asked, anger in his voice. "Of course she'll worry. Somebody says she's a killer, and she's supposed to forget about it? Go on with you, John," Daniel said, throwing up his hand.

The couple watched the sheriff disappear, then Gracy asked Daniel if he wanted to hear what had transpired.

"Not until you sleep," he said. "It can wait. I know it's a pack of lies anyway. I'll just give your back a rub so's you won't wake up stiff." He began to knead Gracy's shoulders, kneading out the tiredness.

Gracy sighed as the soreness left her back. "Aren't you taking out for the high country?" Gracy asked after a bit, remembering that Daniel had planned a prospecting trip. "Looks like you got that burro all ready to pack." She nodded at the animal grazing near the house.

"And leave you here alone to face this? What do you take me for?"

Gracy gripped his hand, which was gnarled, two fingers misshapen where they had been caught with a gold pick. She was too overcome with fatigue and emotion to answer. Daniel had never in his life canceled a prospecting trip. But then, she'd never been accused of murder.

Sleep was always easy to come by for Gracy. More than fifty years of birthing babies had conditioned her to sleep whenever she had the chance. This morning was no different. Despite the silent tears running down her face, she spent only a moment fingering the worn patches of her quilt before she was asleep. The sun was just slipping onto the west side of noon when she awakened, sleep enough for a midwife. She rose and washed her face and went into the kitchen to prepare dinner. She fried up potatoes and made salt pork gravy to pour over bread. It wasn't much, she thought, but Daniel was never a picky eater. "My favorite dinner," he'd said often enough, "is what's on my plate."

They ate at a table Dan had made. He was a good carpenter. The furniture in the cabin wasn't fancy, but it was sturdy, built to last. Gracy had made cushions for the chairs, sewed them from indigo calico that was faded now. Things faded fast in the thin mountain air where the sun was too bright—bright blue the worst, but it was Gracy's favorite color. She liked a blue better than any other hue, so her cushions were bleached indigo, her curtains the color of columbines, her Bear Paw quilt on the bed pieced from blue and white scraps. Her scrap bag was filled with all shades of the color, and on her ride down the mountain that morning, she had thought she would piece a quilt for the new baby from them. She didn't make one for every newborn— she didn't have the time—but the young couple could use a quilt. She'd thought to piece a quilt for the Halleck baby, too, to show her love for it in the work of her hands.

Eating was serious business, and the two didn't talk until Daniel was finished with his plate and had cut an extra slice of bread, which he used to mop up the grease in the frying pan. "I been to town whilst you were sleeping."

"And?"

"As you'd expect, everybody's talking about you. You got to know they would be."

Gracy nodded. She had barely touched her dinner. "What are they saying?"

"Well, most people think the world of you, honey, but like you said, there are some . . ."

"I'm not surprised."

"I am!" Daniel said the words with a little too much emphasis. Then he glanced at Gracy's plate and asked, "You going to finish that? I'll eat it if you don't. No sense it going to waste."

Gracy handed him the plate.

"The worst of them is Coy Chaney. He says you ought to be run out of town."

"If they don't hang me." Gracy looked glum.

"Now, nobody's talking about that."

"I don't know why not. That's what you do with murderers." Gracy was by nature cheerful, had awakened cheerful to the bright sunlight and the soothing blue of the room, but the conversation had turned her glum.

"Nobody thinks you're a murderer. At the most, it was an accident."

Gracy jerked up her head. "Do you believe that?"

"No, of course not," Daniel said quickly. "But maybe you ought to think about saying that, to get it over quick. Wouldn't make no difference. People understand accidents."

"I'd never admit to that," Gracy said. "Nobody'd ever come to me again. There's women out there that would die if I didn't tend them." She considered that a moment, wondering what they'd do if she quit them. Wondering, too, if she'd have a choice about quitting.

Three

It was what God had intended her for, Gracy believed, this borning of babies, this creation of life. She saw God's face in every one of those children she delivered. A baby's first cry was the sound of angels' songs. No matter how long and difficult the labor, no matter how the mother moaned from the pain and the tearing, praying and cursing, Gracy knew joy at the sight of the baby's body pushing into the world, felt exhilaration as she caught the tiny living creature and held the soft, wet flesh in her hands a moment longer than was necessary. And she passed that sense of wonder on to the mother, exclaiming over the fingers and toes as tiny as birds' claws, the eyelashes thin as thread, the button of a nose.

It was not the money or the gold dust or the barter items that sent Gracy over icy trails, that drew her out of sleep-warm quilts at midnight to face cold and howling blizzards. She went where she was called because she knew a woman needed her, because new life waited for her. And so she gladly hitched her horse to the buggy or climbed onto a mule, riding astride like a man, her medicine bag tied to the saddle, hiking up mountainsides when the slopes were too steep for horses.

Late at night, she would wake to footsteps on the stones that led to the house. She was as sensitive to them as a mother to her baby's cry. Even before she heard the knock on her door, Gracy was out of bed, fastening her dress, her feet searching for her shoes.

"I'm sorry it's so late," the man would say.

"No trouble. I've been thinking her time might come tonight and could hardly sleep for the worry of it," Gracy would reply, wrapping her cloak around herself, picking up the bag that was always ready, cutting a chunk of bread to slip into her pocket, since she did not know when she would eat again.

"I wanted to wait till morning to fetch you, but she hurts so." If it was the first time, the man would twist his hands together, a look of anguish on his face, taking steps toward the door as if that would hurry Gracy. Even when he had come for her before and had a houseful of children, the man would be anxious, troubled. Men in those mountains were used to pain, a skull torn open by a rock fall, a hand crushed in an ore chute, fingers frozen in an ice storm. They knew how to ease the hurting. But childbirth bewildered them. There was nothing they could do to end the pain. And at the bottom of a man's confusion was the fear that his wife might die, that he would lose the person he loved most in the world, only to be replaced by a mewling piece of flesh. What would he do with it?

Gracy would reply, "Then it's good you came. No sense to being noble. Even if her time will be a while yet, she'll need someone to hold her hand, make sure everything's all right. I don't mind being rousted out." And she didn't. She was bothered more when the call came late, when she didn't arrive until the baby crowned.

Gracy kept her bag next to the door. She would go through it after each birth, washing or replacing what had been used so that she was always ready. If Daniel had slept through the knocking, Gracy wouldn't wake him. He'd know when he rose in the morning and found her note that she had gone and might be away two or three days. She never knew how long the lying-in would be. The knocks from husbands or neighbors, or even small children, came so often that Daniel was as used to them as the din of the stamp mill crushing the ore across the valley. And so he often slept on while Gracy roused herself and slipped out into the cold. When Emma and then Jeff were small, Gracy had awakened Daniel so that he could take the children to the neighbor lady who cared for them while Gracy tended her women. Daniel had fussed when Emma was a baby, said him being a man, it wasn't right he had to care for a child that way, even for the few hours. But Emma had died, and late in life, when Gracy thought there'd never be another child, Jeff had come to them, and Daniel was so grateful to her that he sometimes stayed home to care for the boy himself. But of course

Jeff was grown and gone off, and the couple was alone in the house—incomplete without their son.

Gracy knew from the time she could first remember that she would be a midwife.

The granny woman who'd catched her in a cabin in the Arkansas hill country had taken a fancy to Gracy. Gracy's mother had already given birth to ten children and was worn out by the time Gracy came along. There was still a child at her breast, born barely nine months before and not enough milk for two little ones. At first, Gracy's oldest sister, Orlean, cared for the infant, putting her finger into the milk pail and letting Gracy suck it. But Gracy did poorly, and when the granny woman came around to check, she snatched up Gracy and said the baby would die if she didn't get something more to nourish her.

"There's naught I can do for her. Take her," Gracy's mother said, thrusting her hand at the puny baby. And so the old granny woman had scooped up Gracy, wrapped her in one of the clean soft cloths she carried in her bag, and taken her home. She fed Gracy with warmed goat's milk and raised her up. "Prettiest baby I ever saw," she told Gracy over and over again, but she was given to saying that to all the mothers of new babies. The truth was, Gracy wasn't a pretty baby and wasn't pretty when she grew up, either.

Nabby, the midwife's name was, had never married, never known herself what it was like to push a baby into the world, like the hundreds she had delivered. But she knew how to care for

Gracy and how to love her, too. Gracy had learned from that, learned that you didn't have to give birth to a child to give it a mother's love.

Gracy grew up in a log cabin filled with dried herbs hanging from the rafters and bottles and jars of ointment and salves and concoctions lining the shelves. Before she could read, Gracy had learned how to mix the medicines Nabby used, had accompanied the old woman on her missions of mercy. She'd seen babies born, sometimes coming so easily that all that Nabby had to do was hold out her arms to catch them. But Gracy'd also seen the complications, the babies wedged crosswise or coming into the world feet first. She'd seen babies born dead and one so deformed that Nabby refused to show it to the mother. But Gracy saw, and it vexed her. She never stopped wondering why God created such beings. "God don't make no mistakes," Nabby told her, but Gracy wasn't so sure.

Nor did she understand why bearing children had to be painful. She asked Nabby about that, but the midwife just shook her head. "The Bible says in sorrow thou shalt bring forth children, and some say that means a woman has to pay for Eve's sin. But I never held with that. There's plenty of wickedness that men done in the Bible, and it don't mean men today pay for it." She thought over Gracy's question. "Others say suffering makes a woman love her children, but that ain't true neither, for it don't explain why I love you." Nabby shook her head. "I guess God knows why there's pain, but He ain't told me. I think it would be easier to plant the seed in the ground and harvest the baby come fall, but then there'd be no need for me."

Sometimes when a mother needed Nabby's attention, Nabby handed the baby to Gracy to care for. Or Gracy tied the cord and then used Nabby's stork scissors to cut the lifeline between mother and child. Those were special moments for little Gracy, and while still a child herself, she had come to feel a sort of ownership of the babies she helped birth.

Gracy's world was not all births—and occasional deaths—however. Nabby paid Orlean a dime every month to take Gracy to school. "Ignorance! It's a terrible thing to grow up not knowing," Nabby had explained when Orlean escorted Gracy to school the first day.

The Arkansas schoolhouse Nabby sent Gracy to wasn't far, and Gracy could have walked to it by herself, but Nabby insisted that Orlean accompany her and paid the sister the money. Gracy chafed to think she was not allowed to attend on her own. But then she realized that if Orlean didn't take her, Orlean couldn't attend school, that Nabby really was paying Orlean to go to school herself, an opportunity none of their brothers and sisters had. From Nabby, Gracy learned about such kindnesses, and like Nabby, she was quick to extend them. She shared the bounty that came from Nabby with her family, and apparently did so with the old midwife's approval. If Nabby saw that the dress she'd made for Gracy was being worn by Sabra, her next older sister, or that the store-bought candy ended up with Gracy's brothers, she didn't comment. When you give someone a gift, it's theirs to do with as they would, Nabby taught.

There had been no stigma to Gracy's being given away. Times were hard, and plenty of children in the Arkansas hills were placed with relatives or friends when there was no room at home for them. And so Gracy went back and forth between the two families. But it was Nabby's house that was home to her.

The midwife's cabin was the place where she learned how to cook in an open fireplace, to smoke venison, parch corn, and dry apples and pumpkins. She learned the signs of nature, which phase of the moon was best for planting—root vegetables in the dark of the moon, aboveground vegetables in the light, corn under a full moon, and never plow on Good Friday or lightning will strike the crop. Pound a nail into a fruit tree that doesn't bloom, and it will bud out. Never grow ivy. Only mean people grow ivy, Nabby insisted.

Gracy learned to spin and weave and to quilt. Next to birthing babies, Gracy loved quilting best. She would sit in Nabby's rocker on the porch, stitching the pieces of fabric together, making shapes of the scraps left over from Nabby's dressmaking or the pieces cut from usable parts of worn-out clothing. Nabby pieced together the shapes to form stars, for a star was her favorite pattern. Stars were comforting, just like the stars in the sky that guided Nabby through the night to some far homestead. Starting a quilt on Friday brings bad luck, Nabby told her as she showed Gracy how to cut out the shapes, and remember the dream the first time you sleep under a new quilt for surely it will come true.

And of course, Nabby taught her to deliver babies.

Gracy'd birthed the first one when she was just ten years old, and she had been so frightened that she'd almost refused.

Lucy, a girl from school who was no bigger than Gracy

herself, had come to the cabin to fetch Nabby. "Ma's in a bad way and Pa ain't no help noway. Tell Granny Nabby to get up over the hills," Lucy said. But Nabby wasn't there. She had gone miles away to deliver another baby, leaving Gracy behind, because it was a month for school, and Nabby didn't know when she'd return. Gracy would need hours to find her, and when she did, she wasn't sure Nabby would leave. The woman the midwife was attending was a first-time mother and might not be strong enough to survive the birth, Nabby had confided to the little girl when she left. Black Mary, Lucy's mother, already had a brood. Black Mary was what they called her to distinguish her from the other Marys who were her kinfolk, because her hair was as dark and glossy as a raven's wing. And because her moods were as black as the inside of a barrel.

"Black Mary knows as much about it as Granny Nabby," Gracy told the girl. "After the first five or six, it's just like shelling peas." She'd heard Nabby say that often enough. "You tell her Granny will be along as soon as she comes home."

"But Ma's hollering like I never heard her before. If Granny don't come, who'll catch that baby? My brother ain't fittin' for it. None of us kids is."

Gracy shrugged. "I can't help. Granny isn't here."

"Then you come," the girl said.

"Me? I'm not a granny woman. I can't deliver Black Mary's baby any more than a cat can," Gracy told her with a laugh.

"But you delivered babies before. I heard tell of it."

"Not by myself. I only help Nabby."

"You have to come. I never seen nothing but a chicken lay-ing eggs. Is that how it is?"

Gracy smiled to think of women sitting on nests of eggs like broody hens. It would be some easier if they could give birth that way. In fact, Gracy'd once asked Nabby why babies couldn't just be hatched. "Hard-boiled or fried up?" Nabby had asked by way of reply.

"Come on, Gracy. Ma's most out of her head. She rears and bucks. What if she dies?" The girl shuddered.

"I got no bag, no scissors," Gracy protested. The idea of de-livering Black Mary's baby by herself scared her out of her wits. She gripped the back of a chair in case Lucy tried to pull her out of the cabin. "There's other women you can get to help. What about Aunt Sarah that lives west of you?"

"She's gone to visit her sister, and Ma wouldn't let Old Betty that lives by the creek in the house for fear she'd put a spell on her."

"Even to deliver a baby?"

"Ma's stubborn. She'd rather die than let them tend her. Only Annie Laurie's there, but she's no more help than a yellow dog. All she done was give Ma a hot footbath. I guess I know more than she does, because the baby don't come out of your foot. Annie Laurie's the one sent me to fetch Granny Nabby. You got to help, Gracy. Ma and the baby dying, that'd be on you."

Gracy looked out the window, hoping she'd spot Nabby com-ing home, but the trail was empty. She wondered if Nabby had stopped somewhere to pick a bouquet of flowers or drink a glass of buttermilk. Maybe she should run down the trail and see. But she knew Nabby wouldn't dawdle when Gracy was home by herself. Likely that baby hadn't been born yet.

"Come on," Lucy said.

Gracy glanced at the pie safe where Nabby kept her doings— her salves and lotions, the soft clean cloths. Nabby would want her to help, she decided at last. So Gracy found a flour sack and began to fill it. "I don't have instruments, no forceps. Nabby took them. And I don't have the stork scissors," she said, going to the bench where Nabby kept her knife.

"We got a knife already," Lucy said.

Gracy knew it was likely a frog sticker, and that wouldn't do for cutting the cord. So she slipped the knife Nabby used to cut the herbs into the sack. Then she stopped to sharpen her school pencil and leave a note for Nabby. Perhaps the other baby had already arrived and Nabby would return in time. Gracy should have hurried—Nabby would have—but she held back, moving slowly, so that Lucy had to tug at her arm. Maybe if she lingered, Gracy thought, Black Mary's baby would already be born. But that was not a thought Nabby would have had. It would shame Nabby, and so Gracy began to hurry.

She followed Lucy down the trail and across a meadow and over two hills. She could hear Black Mary screaming from pain before she even spotted the cabin. When the girls went inside, Black Mary was lying on the bed, thrashing and hollering.

"The baby won't come out. It's stuck-like. I've been trying to help her, but I don't know what to do," Lucy's brother said. He knelt beside his mother, sweat running down his face, wringing his hands. He was a stringbean of a boy, puny as a newborn kitten, but he had nice hands, big hands, Gracy noticed. He nodded his head at Annie Laurie and said, "She's not worth much."

Annie Laurie sat beside the bed muttering. "There's something wrong. I never helped at a birth like this. I ain't knowing what to do. No I ain't. It's up to the Lord, not me."

"She wouldn't help," the boy said, "just kept saying it over and over like that, that it was up to the Lord."

It was not up to the Lord, however. It was up to Gracy. "Let me see," she said, her own hands shaking. She clasped them together so that no one would see and tried to act confident, the way Nabby did. "She's had others. It shouldn't be so bad." If those words coming from a ten-year-old sounded pompous, no one seemed to notice.

A kettle of water hung on a crane in the fireplace, and Gracy asked the boy to pour some into a basin. He did so, and Gracy took a piece of lye soap from her sack and washed her hands. Most folks wouldn't think that necessary since Gracy's hands weren't dirty, but Nabby had a notion that dirt could cause an inflammation, and so the midwife and her small assistant always insisted on cleanliness.

Gracy told the boy to pour out the water and replace it with fresh, and when he did, she slid her knife and a length of twine into the basin, wishing she had the forceps, but Nabby had taken them. "Hang these cloths by the fire to warm them," she ordered, taking a bundle from her sack and handing it to the boy. She sounded confident, although she wasn't. Then she went to Black Mary.

"Where's Granny Nabby?" Black Mary demanded. The pain had eased and she scowled at Gracy.

"She'll be here directly, after she delivers another baby," Gracy said, hoping she sounded more confident than she felt.

"Then whyn't you get Granny Alice? A little girl like you ain't knowing what to do."

Gracy shuddered, because Granny Alice was a dirty old woman who wouldn't wash her hands even if she'd been out pulling weeds. She spat tobacco juice on the floor and was known to make a dent in a jug of corn liquor while attending a mother. Sometimes she passed out from the liquor and was no help at all.

"Gracy's Granny Nabby's girl. She knows," Lucy said.

Black Mary started to protest, but a pain hit her and she cried out.

"I'll examine her," Gracy said, and she knelt on the floor beside the woman, who was laid out on an old quilt that had been covered by layers of newspaper. She lifted the petticoat that served as the woman's nightdress, hoping to see the baby's head emerging, but instead, there was a foot, and Gracy gasped. "The baby's turned. It has to be righted." She'd seen Nabby do that a dozen times, but her shoulders slumped and she wished again that she had not come. She wasn't a midwife. How could she do this by herself? What if the baby died, or Black Mary? Everyone would blame her. They'd shun her and maybe Nabby, too.

"Is Ma going to die?" a little child no bigger than a willow switch asked.

And then it hit Gracy like she'd been smacked in the face with a tree branch that Black Mary's life and that of the baby really did depend on her. Maybe the Lord had sent her. She took a deep breath, and calmed herself. She smiled at Lucy and said everything would be all right, saying it the way Nabby did. She glanced at Annie Laurie and told her to rub Black Mary's back and wash her brow with cool water. Best to keep the woman busy because she would only get in the way.

Gracy knelt down beside Black Mary again and parted the woman's legs. A pain seized Black Mary, and she strained, arching her back like a cat's. "Don't push, Black Mary," Gracy said. "I got to get this baby righted before it comes out."

That birth was something people in the hills talked about for years, how a ten-year-old girl delivered a baby that was breeched. Gracy reached into the womb with her child's hands and turned the infant a little. Then when at last Black Mary couldn't hold back the baby any longer, Gracy eased it along the birth canal, tried to slide it out by the feet, but they were too small and wet to hold on to. So she grasped them with a cloth, and out that baby came, sliding into Gracy's hands. "A girl, Black Mary!" Gracy announced. She stared at the wonder of the infant in her hands, then bound the cord and cut it. She held out the baby to Lucy, telling the girl to rub it with the oil Gracy had brought, while she dealt with the afterbirth. She wrapped it in a piece of newspaper and handed it to the boy. "Salt it, then plant it under a tree," she told him.

"And be careful Old Betty don't know where it is, for she'll dig it up and put a hex on Black Mary," Annie Laurie said, speaking for the first time since Gracy had begun attending the mother.

Gracy nodded. Nabby didn't believe in such things, but many of their neighbors did, and Nabby did not want to offend, so she always smiled and said it made sense to treat the afterbirth with caution.

The boy looked at Gracy as if to ask whether he should follow Annie Laurie's instructions, and Gracy said it wouldn't hurt. He shrugged his thin shoulders and gave Gracy a wry smile, and she knew he no more believed in the danger of afterbirth than she did.

Out of necessity, other girls in those hills might have tended their mothers in childbirth, when no woman was available. But no girl had come as a granny woman, had taken charge as if she were a regular midwife, had birthed a baby that might have killed its mother and itself. Lucy told it about what Gracy had done, claimed she had saved the lives of Black Mary and the baby, whom they named Marjorie, and maybe she had. The little midwife became a wonder, and the curiosity of it embarrassed her. She cared only about Nabby's praise, and the old woman was quick to give it. "You learned well, girl. You came when you was needed, and you helped. That's all a body can ask," Nabby said, and Gracy knew Nabby would have praised her even if Black Mary or her baby had died.

But they hadn't. Gracy did not know how long she worked with Black Mary. Time meant nothing to her. She didn't know that the sun set that day and the sky darkened and was lit by stars. She wasn't aware her shoulders ached and her back near broke in half. Not until the baby was safe in her arms did she glance up to see Lucy, her brother, and the others gathered around the bed.

She smiled at them, and they laughed and clapped with joy. And Gracy felt a joy so great it was as if she herself had given birth to the child. The feeling was not pride. It was a kind of radiance, like the burst of a sunrise, that warmed her soul. She knew then that she had the gift.

When all was well, Gracy handed the baby to Black Mary, who smiled at the child-midwife. Some with a houseful of children might have wished the baby hadn't survived, but Black Mary grinned at the infant and said she was God's blessing, brought to life by the youngest midwife in a hundred miles. Black Mary had never been more than five miles from her cabin door, and she figured the end of the earth wasn't much more than a hundred miles away.

Granny Nabby never arrived. When Gracy was satisfied the mother and baby were all right, she took up her things and started for the door. The boy stopped her on the porch and handed her a dime. "It's all we got," he said, "but it's due you. We don't care to be beholden."

Gracy thought to tell the boy to keep the money, because she didn't care if she was paid. The happiness she felt was worth more than a dozen coins. But she wanted to save his pride. So she took the dime and wrapped it in a rag and put it into her bundle. Later, she punched a hole in the coin, threaded it on a string, and wore it around her neck.

Four

The pounding on the door woke Gracy from a deep sleep. Had the person been banging for a long time? It wasn't like her to sleep through a knocking. Maybe she was getting too old. She slid her feet into her shoes and glanced at her bag. She had not replaced the herbs she'd used in Mayflower Gulch and tried to think what would be needed. Her supplies were neatly stacked in the pie safe, so it would take only a minute to gather the replacements. Gracy's dress was not on the hook near the bed, and she realized she had not taken it off after she and Daniel finished dinner. Her troubles, the melancholy she felt about her work, had tired her so that she'd gone back to bed after dinner, sleeping fully clothed.

Now, as she made her way to the door, she wondered who could be in labor. The Richards girl up on Turnbull Mountain wasn't near her time, but Richards women weren't reliable. One sister had been a month early by Gracy's reckoning, while the other had been a month past due. Or maybe it was the woman two streets over who had just moved down from Middle Swan. Gracy hoped it wasn't Mrs. Tucker. She did not want to have to hitch up her buggy and drive over a rocky road that afternoon—or evening. Was it already evening? Gracy wasn't sure what the hour was.

The cabin was dark and cold, but then it often grew chilly in the afternoons when the rains came. The storms on the Tenmile were harsh, not like the gentle rains Gracy had known in Arkansas, rain that fell so softly you could stand outside with your head raised to the heavens and feel as if an angel were washing your face. The Tenmile rains came down in torrents, sharp and cold, and they chilled a person to her bones. The water gathered in the range high up, then rushed through the gullies and canyons. You could drown on a perfectly nice day if you were caught in a flash flood down below.

Gracy had seen it happen. A girl was playing in a gully once with not an inch of moisture in it when a rush of water from a cloudburst came down toward her, sweeping her up and carrying her a mile away, before she lodged in some willows. Men had looked for her for two days before they found her floating among the willow branches, her hair spread out around her, looking like a princess from a fairy tale.

Gracy had been among the searchers, hoping against hope that the girl had washed up on a sandbar and was waiting to be rescued. Usually the searchers were men, but the mother had begged Gracy to help. The child would be chilled, maybe feverish.

Or her leg might be broken, the mother had pleaded. Gracy prayed the woman was right, but she knew there was little chance the girl had survived. Still, she went with Daniel and the other men, because the child reminded her of Emma and she couldn't bear the sorrow of losing another golden girl. She and Daniel plodded through the bushes until they came to where the water from the gully flowed into the creek. The child's body was half a mile downstream.

Daniel lifted the girl out of the water and laid her on the ground. Her dress was nearly torn off, and her arms were bruised, twigs in her hair. But her face had not been touched, and when the mother saw her, she said God had performed a miracle, that her child was only sleeping. But she wasn't. She'd drowned a minute after the flood waters snatched her, Gracy thought. She helped wash the child and lay her out for burial, thinking the girl did indeed appear to be sleeping. Lying in the coffin, her small hands neatly folded over her breast, the poor thing looked as if she could sit up and rub her eyes and ask what she was doing there. Emma had been like that on her deathbed, white and still, her hair about her face like curls of sunshine.

Gracy had to hold the mother back while the men lowered the small box into the grave, then shoveled dirt over it.

"Stop them. Don't they see she's not dead," the mother cried to Gracy.

"She's crossed over," Gracy said.

"She's not. God wouldn't do that to me. He took the others, but he let me keep her."

Holding the sobbing woman, Gracy found herself thinking

she ought to have known some way to revive the child, and for a moment, she was filled with guilt. She wondered, as the mother did, why God was so hard on women. She remembered her own babies, born before their time, living only a few hours, and the ones given into her care because they were too sickly to live. And she thought again of Emma. "God don't make no mistakes," Nabby had told her, but He did. Emma was proof.

The dead child's mother was not right in her head after that. She had spells. She took to sitting outside the schoolhouse, telling passersby she was waiting for her daughter, saying the girl was old enough to attend school now. Once, Gracy saw her in the store buying cloth to make a dress for the girl. But people paid little attention because such behavior wasn't unheard of in the isolated mountain towns. Other women went crazy because of the loss of their children from accidents or pneumonia. Or their minds gave out just from the loneliness, from the harshness of life on the range. Life could be warped that close to heaven, Gracy knew.

The knock came again, and Gracy pulled herself out of her thoughts. She was too much taken with melancholy that day. She opened the door and said, "John?" and for a few seconds she was confused. She had expected the pounding to have come from someone who needed her help with a birth. The blessedness of sleep had wiped the memory of her trouble from her mind for a few moments. But now it came back as she recognized the sheriff at her door: He had accused her of murder, the murder of the Halleck baby. Gracy stared at him for a time as she gripped the door and remembered the death of the infant.

"You going to make me stand out here in the rain?" the sheriff asked at last.

"I forgot my manners," she said, opening the door wide. She glanced behind John at the rain that came down hard, splashing through the jack pines onto the rocks and filling the washtub that she had forgotten to hang on its nail on the cabin wall. When the rain was done, the flowers would bloom brighter than ever and there would be designs of pine needles under the trees. But now, the sky was black with the heaviness of the moisture, and mist rose like smoke from a dynamite blast on the mountainsides. A flash of lightning lit up Gracy's can pile an arm's throw from the door, making the tin shine like silver.

John stamped the water off his boots and came inside, flapping raindrops off his hat onto Gracy's braided rug.

"I don't know where Daniel's got to," she said.

"He's down to the Nugget, drunker than Independence Day and spoiling for a fight. I ain't seen him like that for a long time, maybe not since Nevada."

Gracy smiled then to remember how the least little thing could set Daniel off when he was young, how he seemed to relish a brawl. John hadn't been much different.

When they first came west, Gracy and Daniel had settled in California, where Daniel panned the streams. But too many men crowded the banks, and the pickings were poor, so after a few years, the two had packed up and moved to Virginia City in Nevada, where Daniel worked a claim. They'd met John there.

He had been married then. His wife, Elizabeth, had been a bit of a thing, too fragile for the life of a mining camp. The harshness of it had bewildered her. She hadn't understood the brightness of the sun or the land that was ugly from mining. Elizabeth was all but helpless at times, and Gracy, strong and resilient, adored her. The two women made an odd pair, Elizabeth tiny and pink with hair the color of a sunflower, Gracy bigger, taller, rougher, her skin wrinkled from the sun, hair like dried weeds. But they had been as close as sisters, glad for the company of each other in that bawdy town, glad for a chance to quilt and gossip about the wealthy ladies who were no better than themselves except that they had money. Those women shook their hands in the air to make them white and bloodless before opening the door to visitors, Elizabeth had told her, and they called for carriage and driver when they were only going next door. The two had laughed together at such foolishness.

Elizabeth died in childbirth—and the baby, too. Gracy had attended Elizabeth, and she thought John would blame her just as she blamed herself for the deaths of his wife and child. But he didn't. After Gracy explained it to him, he understood that Elizabeth's birth canal was too small, that the baby had no way out.

"I don't care about the boy," he told her, all men sure that the first child would be male. Elizabeth had been in labor more than a day and was near dying with the pain of it. "By the living God, save Elizabeth, Gracy. You have to save Elizabeth, even if you got to kill the baby."

Gracy couldn't do it. She couldn't crush the skull of the fetus, couldn't bring herself to kill the life that was about to emerge. She anguished over it as much as John did. Only after she realized that the baby was dead, had strangled himself with the cord, did she force herself to crush the tiny head so that the body could emerge. But it was too late for Elizabeth. John's beloved wife lingered a day after the birth, John and Gracy at her side, Daniel pacing the walk outside the cabin, as he did when Gracy herself was in labor, for he could not abide a sickroom. When Elizabeth awoke for a minute and inquired about the child, John told her the boy was fine. Gracy turned away for fear Elizabeth would read the grief in her eyes.

Elizabeth smiled, and it was over. She did not take a deep breath or use her last ounce of strength to sit up. Only after a moment did Gracy realize her friend no longer lived, and she felt the sorrow of it descend on her. Sometimes it seemed as if the burden of each death was added to the others until she was bowed under the weight of dead souls.

John's grief was a terrible thing to behold. He mourned worse than any man Gracy had ever seen, tearing his shirt to pieces, howling like a coyote, cursing God, cursing the gold that had lured him to Nevada, cursing everything but Gracy. In his sorrow, he held on to her, knowing that Elizabeth had been precious to her and that he and Gracy were joined together in their loss.

Gracy believed John never got over the death of his wife. He had been a sober man, quiet, abstemious. But all that changed. He worked his claim only to get enough gold dust to spend on liquor, and he was drunk for two years. He turned mean and took on anyone who would fight him. That was because he wanted to die, Gracy thought. But he didn't. Instead, he was hauled off to jail now and again, locked up long enough for him to sober up. But once released, he'd start all over again. His clothes became rags, and he rarely bathed, smelling worse than a backhouse. Gracy and Daniel were hard-pressed to defend him or even be his friends, but they were loyal. They stood by him.

And then one day, John came to the little house in which Gracy and Daniel lived and presented himself. Gracy almost didn't recognize him. He'd gone to the bathhouse, then got himself shaved, his hair cut, and he'd bought a suit of clothes. Gracy wondered if John had found religion, but he didn't explain himself, and he wasn't partial to church, so she didn't think so. He announced he was going to Colorado to start over, and wouldn't Daniel and Gracy go with him?

Gracy was anxious to leave Virginia City by then, to put the past behind her—to start over after what had happened there. It would be best for her, for Daniel, and especially for Jeff, who was four. Virginia City with its gossip and temptations was no place for the boy to be raised up. Gracy loved her son fiercely and wanted to protect him, just as she hadn't been able to protect Emma. And so she told Daniel they were leaving, and not more than a month later, the three adults and Jeff traveled east to Colorado. They settled in Swandyke, but they didn't stay together long. After her vagabond life in California and Nevada, Gracy wanted to put down roots in Swandyke—it would be best for Jeff, she'd said—and Daniel was willing. But John was restless. He grew bored with the poor leavings in his gold pan in Swandyke and left out, making the circle of the mining strikes—Georgetown, Central City, Leadville.

Gracy and Daniel lost touch with their friend until he showed up in Swandyke again. His wandering days were over, he told them. And so was his search for gold. He'd be happy with a steady job, and so he'd been hired as sheriff. He was old for the job, but nobody else had wanted it.

Gracy always thought John would find himself another wife, but he was not interested in women, other than those who worked in a house at the end of the path around the back of Turnbull Mountain. He had his needs, Gracy thought. He never mentioned Elizabeth, never spoke of whether he missed her, never indulged in recollections, and Gracy and Daniel did not bring up her name. Some men, like some animals, mated for life, and maybe John was like that. When anyone asked John whether he had a wife, he answered with an abrupt, "No." Since it was poor manners in those mountains to inquire too deeply about a man's background, people let it go at that, assuming John had never married. But Gracy thought he still mourned his wife, and she wondered if he felt he would betray Elizabeth if he found another woman.

John had not come to talk about the past, Gracy knew when she opened the door to him that day, letting in the chill of the rain. He stood on her rug, water running off his hat, while Gracy waited for him to tell her his reason for being there. He slapped his hat against his leg, but he had already shaken off the drops of water. At first, he refused to look at her, glancing around the room instead, searching for something that would take his attention. But the house was plain. There were no pictures, no gewgaws, nothing to catch the eye.

John would have come to talk about the murder charge against her, because he was not one to stop by for gossip. There could be no other reason for the visit. Maybe he'd changed his mind about not locking her up and had decided to take her to jail. Gracy wished Daniel were there. She could ask John to wait until Daniel came home, but if her husband had been drinking, he would be angry and belligerent, quick to defend her even at his age, and just then, Gracy did not need that.

"What is it, John?" she asked after a time.

"You got coffee?" he asked.

"None made, but it's no bother to fix it. If you'll build up the fire, I'll get the water." She hoped Daniel had taken the lid off the water barrel so it could catch the rainfall.

"No need."

"There's bread," Gracy said. Like John, she wanted to put off a talk that was inevitable. "Wheat bread. I'll have a slice myself. I couldn't eat my dinner. I guess it's near suppertime."

"Going on evening. You can't tell the time with the rain. It's darker out there than the inside of a bobcat."

"It is that." Gracy needed to eat. She hadn't put a thing into her stomach since the little she'd eaten with Daniel that noon, but she made no move for the larder.

The two were silent for a moment. At last, Gracy said, "Sit yourself."

"I guess I will if it's agreeable."

Gracy nodded. "It is."

John looked around, then lowered himself into Daniel's chair, a big chair that had been fashioned from logs, the bark removed and the wood polished to the color of amber. "You made this place real homey," he said.

Gracy nodded but didn't reply. The sheriff hadn't come to talk about the cabin. She went to the table and busied herself with the wick of the kerosene lamp. She struck a match and lighted it, and the lamp sent a honeyed glow over the room. Then she sat down across from John, in the chair that Daniel had made for her, one that matched his own but was smaller. The heaviness of the day weighed her down.

The two were silent, John looking around the room, Gracy staring at him, until she couldn't stand it. "Out with it, John. Why have you come? Are you taking me to jail?" She took a deep breath and let it out.

He shook his head.

"I don't blame you for it, this charge against me, you know. You didn't accuse me of anything. It was Jonas Halleck said I did it, and Coy Chaney and Little Dickie." She paused and gave a small smile. "You didn't have a choice but to charge me."

"I know that. Jonas Halleck can be a devil-root, but he's an important man in these mountains. I had to listen to him, especially when Coy and Little Dickie"—he spat out the last name—"backed him up."

"I know you did." She paused. "What is it then?"

John's eyes stopped on a shelf where Gracy's books were lined up—*The Matron's Manual of Midwifery and the Diseases of Pregnancy*, *Dr. Chase's Recipes or Information for Everybody*, and the Bible. All were worn, for Gracy consulted each one often. Then he cleared his throat and mumbled, "Elizabeth came to see me last night."

"What?" Gracy thought he'd used Elizabeth's name by mistake, or else she'd heard wrong.

He nodded. "Elizabeth. She visits me sometimes, when I'm troubled. We talk." He glanced at Gracy, then looked away quickly, his face flushed.

"She comes to you?" Gracy asked, not understanding.

He nodded. "You'd think she'd come when I was asleep, but she don't. I'm always awake."

"She's come before?" Gracy had heard of people dreaming they'd connected with the dead, but that was all it was—dreams. This was strange. Maybe John's grief had touched his mind.

"When I need her. Or sometimes just to visit. She says the boy's all right. He's growed now. She named him Charlie."

Gracy leaned back in her chair and put her hand to her mouth, too astonished to say anything. Women in childbirth sometimes saw things—a mother who was long dead standing by the bedside or an angel flying up near the ceiling. She herself had seen Nabby beside her the night Jeff was born. But such visions always ended when the pain stopped. Was John possessed?

He stared at the floor, then glanced at Gracy, the corners of his mouth turned up a little. "I know you think I'm crazy. A person would. And I'd appreciate it if you didn't pass it along, even to Daniel."

Gracy nodded. She'd kept secrets before, even from her husband.

"The boy's growed like I say, but Elizabeth, she hasn't aged. She's still fresh and pretty as a buttercup." John grinned for a minute, then caught himself and frowned. "I know you think I've turned strange, a big man like me and sheriff to boot. I wouldn't want it knowed around about this. Folks would think I was foolish."

"No. I keep things to myself." Of course she would not repeat what John told her. If people knew their sheriff had truck with his dead wife, they would think he was indeed touched, and maybe he was.

John leaned back in the chair, making himself comfortable. "I wasn't going to tell you about her, but she said it was all right, that you'd understand."

Gracy nodded, although she didn't understand at all.

"The first time was in Virginia City," he said suddenly. "You remember. I was all tore up after she died and wanted to kill myself, only I was too much of a coward. I figured maybe I'd get somebody else to do the job for me or else drink myself to death. I near did get shot dead once or twice. Then Elizabeth came to me, told me I shamed her by acting like that. If I got liquored up and killed in a fight, she and Charlie didn't want nothing to do with me. Maybe you didn't know Elizabeth could be like that, sharp if she had to be, and she surely was that when she come to me the first time. She told me I had to clean myself up and get out of Virginia City, start over somewheres else."

"I remember when you sobered up," Gracy said. "I thought you'd got religion. Then I decided you hadn't, that you'd just woken up."

"It was Elizabeth."

"And we all came to Colorado. Did she tell you to do that, too, to take Daniel and me with you?" Gracy almost laughed at herself, talking about such foolishness.

John shook his head. "No, she leaves the way of it up to me, just like when she told me to come back to Swandyke and I got to be sheriff. She said you and Daniel might need me one day."

"And that's why you're telling me this?"

"No." John glanced over at the table and said, "Maybe I'll have me that piece of bread now. Talking sure does make me hungry."

Gracy remembered she was hungry, too, and got up. She took out a loaf of bread only a day old and a dish of butter, then found a glass of wild raspberry jam she'd made from pickings up on Potato Mountain. Using her butcher knife, she cut two slices of bread and buttered and jammed them, then handed one to John. He ate it in three bites before Gracy could sit down. So she offered him her own bread.

John shook his head. He waited until Gracy had eaten, then leaned forward in the chair, taking her hands. "Elizabeth said I had to help you. Maybe she knew those years ago that Jonas Halleck was going to say you killed his baby and that was why she sent me back to Swandyke." He nodded his head up and down.

"Help me?" The conversation was getting stranger and stranger.

"That's what she said."

"You already kept me out of jail. What else can you do?"

"I can get you out of Swandyke."

Gracy was shocked. "You mean send me to the jail in Middle Swan or Breckenridge?"

"No, I mean, get you out of the country altogether." He stood up and walked to the window, looking out at the rain, then returned to the chair, holding on to the back of it. "I mean I could take you to Denver, say you should be locked up there in case somebody wanted to hurt you, you know, like Jonas Halleck might want to get the men at the Holy Cross so riled up, they'd hang you."

"They wouldn't do that."

"I know it, but I could say I was afraid they would. So I'd take you down below." John paused and sat down. "Then I'd see that you and Daniel got on a train for Chicago or Independence or even California. I'd say Daniel must have had it all figured out and was just waiting for a chance to help you escape." He paused. "Maybe you could join Jeff."

Gracy felt a sting in her heart at the mention of her son. He'd been gone eight, nine months now, and she missed him every day. Daniel was blustery, but Jeff had a quietness in him. He could sit with her and look out at the splendor of the mountains turning blue at day's end, and she knew without his saying a word that he sensed a peacefulness. Still, he was destined for something more than the Tenmile, this child God had given to her. He would seek a life beyond the range, perhaps become a doctor, for he loved to hear her talk of the women she tended. He had kindness in him, Gracy thought. Perhaps greatness, too. She hoped he still did. "I don't know where he is. How'd we ever find him?"

"He'd find you. He won't be gone forever."

"Maybe. Maybe not." Gracy thought a minute. "You'd expect me to run away?"

John nodded.

"You'd lose your job, maybe get arrested yourself. Then what would become of you?"

"You and Daniel stood by me after Elizabeth died. I owe you."

Gracy shook her head. "No you don't. Not like that. I couldn't let you do it. Besides, if I ran off, people would think I was guilty. How would I clear my name? John, I didn't kill that baby. You believe that, don't you?"

John didn't answer. Instead, he stood and walked about the room again, picking up the tin of lucifers and examining them. Then he turned and faced Gracy. "You don't know how serious this is. Coy and Little Dickie have spent the day spreading it around that you strangled that baby, and they've got some folks convinced. Now, I have it in mind you'll be charged with man-slaughter, and that's why I didn't lock you up, which I'd have had to do if you faced a murder charge. I think the justice of the peace'll agree when he comes around week after next. But if he charges murder, I won't have any choice but to put you in jail. If you're convicted, you could spend out your years in jail. Or hang."

Gracy took a deep breath and squared her shoulders. "No-body would hang me. I delivered most of the babies in these mountains. There's not a soul would find me guilty." She sounded defiant.

John just stared at her.

Gracy squirmed a little. "Well, I guess there are some that don't like me. But why would I do it? Why would I kill that innocent little thing?"

"Jonas told me you had your back turned to him and was working over the boy, that he was crying. Then he wasn't, and when Jonas picked him up out of the cradle later on, he was dead. It's his word against yours."

"Did you see the baby?"

"I did. I saw the bits of string, too." He thought a moment. "Leaving's the only way I can think of to help you. You ponder it."

Gracy leaned back in her chair, closing her eyes, her fingers worrying the coin she always wore around her neck, the one Black Mary's son had given her so many years before. Was she guilty of something? Maybe that baby had died a natural death, died because she didn't know enough about medicine to see that something was wrong. That would make her guilty, maybe not in a court of law but in her own heart.

Perhaps John was right. Maybe she should leave. Swandyke was the best home she'd known since she left Arkansas. She wasn't sure why she loved it so. Swandyke was not a pretty place. The cabins were made of logs, many with the bark still on, some unroofed because the builder had moved on before the house was finished. Jack pines surrounded the houses, blocking out the sun, and the only decoration was the can piles. Streets were muddy ruts and crooked, impassable in winter when the snow drifted above the windowsills or blocked the doors, snow so deep a person could drown in it. Winter lasted nine, ten, eleven months. She'd seen it snow in Swandyke every month of the year. In winter, the cold sifted through the logs of the house where the chinking had been knocked away, and Gracy hung quilts over the window to keep out the chill, but nothing seemed to warm the cabin.

As if to make up for the long winters and thin springs, the short summers were glorious, the wildflowers pretty as sunrise, the aspen in early fall bright enough to blind a person. Birds flitted through the trees, bluebirds and mountain jays like bits of sky that had fallen down. There never was a sight so pretty as the sun setting over Turnbull Mountain, sending its last rays to light the firs and turn the eternal patches of snow white as a baby's christening dress. Gracy couldn't imagine being any place but Swandyke in the summer.

But it was the people who meant the most to Gracy. There were the gold seekers such as Daniel, who worked the mines in winter, but come snowmelt, they left out for the mountains, their burros loaded down with picks and shovels and enough supplies to last until the first frost, although coming home a time or two because they couldn't stand the loneliness. Most of them never found blossom rock, but they never lost hope. Not a one of them but believed he'd strike it rich someday, that the next swing of his pick would show ore. That was Daniel, vigorous as the Lord Harry, telling Gracy he'd be back with a gold mine. He'd buy her a diamond ring and a silk dress, and she'd be a lady. "Maybe we'll go to San Francisco and live on top of a hill," he'd say.

"I live on top of a mountain. Why would I settle for a hill?" she'd reply, knowing in her heart she had nothing to worry about. But not for the world would she say that to Daniel.

Gracy loved the women, mountain-hard, strong, knowing like her that come fall, they'd be no better off, but they let their husbands hope, watched as the men packed their burros, sent them off with smiles and cries of "Save me the biggest lump of gold." But what a woman really thought was maybe he'd find a little gold this time, enough to go back home, to go back where they'd come from, where rain was warm and the wind didn't howl its loneliness.

They watched the men out of sight. Then the smiles faded, and the women sighed as they turned to each other, wiping their eyes with their aprons. "There he goes, one jackass following another, not the sense to call it deep enough," a woman would say, pointing with her chin at her husband walking behind a burro. Or "I still got coffee." Or "He was too anxious to be off to eat his breakfast proper-like, the mining fool. Come for pancakes. He always wants them thick, but I like them thin, spread out in the pan like lace." They built lives without men, gathering rose hips for jam and fishing the beaver ponds with each other. Women friends weren't as demanding as husbands. A woman could stay abed in the sleep-warm quilts until the sun rose and breakfast on raspberries. Still, they were incomplete by themselves, and they joyed when their men returned after three or four weeks, saying they needed supplies but knowing they needed their families more. When frost came, the women would stand outside, shading their eyes as they looked for shapes on the mountains, thinking maybe this time there really had been a strike but knowing there hadn't been, knowing, too, that they would live out their days in the timberline country.

Most of those women had come from elsewhere and remembered life when it was easier. But there were also the young women, mountain bred like the girl in Mayflower Gulch to the harshness of life high in the Tenmile. They didn't know anything else. They loved the high country, and when they went below, their lungs filled up with the heavy air. They couldn't breathe unless they could see mountains. They were the ones who wouldn't call for Gracy until their labors were on them. She'd scold them for not seeing her sooner so she could make sure the babies were coming along all right. But they'd laugh and say it was only a baby. So the pain of labor seemed to come as a surprise. They thought they knew pain, but they didn't, and it confused them. Of course, they forgot the pain of childbirth, as all women did. Later, they would laugh at themselves, say they were foolish for crying and shouting.

When they came to town, they'd call on Gracy, show off their babies. Gracy would admire them, say how much they'd grown, say who wouldn't be proud? She felt a kind of ownership of each one, ushering them into the world as she had.

She couldn't leave them, Gracy thought, coming back to her senses. She couldn't leave the women and the children, the children yet to be born. They needed her. They might die without her. But how long could she carry on? Would they come to her now that she'd been accused of murder? She'd thought just that morning on her way home to Swandyke that it might be time to call it deep enough. But maybe now it wouldn't be her choice. Maybe they'd stop coming to her. But not just yet.

There was another reason Swandyke was precious to her. They'd been a family there, she and Daniel and Jeff. She'd raised the boy in those mountains, watched him grow into a strong young man, lusty as his father but made of finer stuff.

And so she shook her head back and forth at John. "I can't go," she said. "I won't go. That's all there is to it."

John nodded. "I told Elizabeth you'd say that. I guess I know you better than she does." He rose and slapped his hat against his leg. "If they find you guilty, we can talk about it again, see what I can do. I won't let you hang—or go to prison, either. I promised Elizabeth."

"You tell her I appreciate what she asked you to do," Gracy said.

"I'll do that." John started for the door.

"If Elizabeth knows everything, she knows I didn't murder that child."

"I know it, too. But I'm not the one you have to convince. You've got to get a jury to believe you didn't kill Edna Halleck's baby." When he opened the door, the wind grabbed it out of his hands. Rain blew into the house.

Gracy didn't pay any attention to the weather. "Say that again, John."

He frowned. "I said you have to get a jury to believe you didn't kill Edna Halleck's baby."

Gracy shook her head back and forth, and then she said softly, "I do not believe that Edna Halleck was the mother of that boy."

Five

John turned around and stared at Gracy, as the wind blew rain-drops into the house. He closed the door. "What's that?"

Gracy nodded slowly. "I said I'm not sure Edna Halleck gave birth to that baby." She dipped her chin to emphasize her words.

"Then whose baby was it?'

"Whose do you think?"

John frowned. "Josie Halleck's?"

Gracy nodded. "That's my bet. I can always tell a mother, and I'm thinking Josie birthed that boy."

"But how can that be? Mr. Halleck said it was his wife's. Josie and Mrs. Halleck were right there when he told me, and they didn't say otherwise. Why would he lie?"

"Why would you think?"

John thought a moment. "Well, Josie don't have a husband."

"No, she doesn't. She's too young for marriage, and almost too young to have a baby, too."

"She is that. She's a poor excuse for a girl—sullen, scared of her own shadow, and not too choosy about who she nuzzles up to. At least, that's what they say at the Nugget."

"I believe she has been mistreated."

The two stared at each other a minute before John said, "I guess I will have that cup of coffee."

He went to the fireplace and added a few sticks of kindling to the ashes, then blew on them. The fire flared up, and when the kindling caught, John added larger pieces of wood. Gracy used a dipper to fill the heavy iron teakettle with water from the barrel, then dumped a handful of roasted coffee beans into the grinder and turned the crank. As she did so, she looked at herself in the mirror over the dry sink, wondering if being accused of murder had made her look different. Not that she could tell, because the mirror was all but useless. It was old, and much of the silver backing had worn off. The rest was crazed. Gracy could have gotten a better glimpse of her face in a beaver pond.

She hadn't seen herself in a good mirror in two or three years, and it was even longer since she'd looked into a full-length one. She wondered if she'd put on weight. Probably not. Her clothes still fit. She was big, tall, and heavy-boned, but she was still gaunt, mostly angles—elbows and knees and hipbones. Maybe it was a good thing she couldn't tell what she looked like. What purpose would it serve to see how old she'd gotten, how stooped? Besides, it didn't matter anymore. There'd been a time when she'd longed for a young girl's look, soft and downy, had resented the sharpness of her body, the length of it. She'd looked into the mirror back then at her lank hair, which was now still smoky dark in places but mostly gray, had thought if she were small and yellow-haired, men might find her attractive, one man anyway. She'd studied her faded calico, her flapping sunbonnet, and wondered how she'd look dressed in satin, cut low, her hair swept up in curls, an emerald necklace. Like a pig with earbobs, she'd thought, like the fool she was. But that had been a long time ago. Now she was content with herself, and Daniel was, too, bless him.

Still, Gracy wondered if she had changed—changed since she'd seen the Halleck baby a few days earlier, looked at it and knew as she did that Josie was his mother. She leaned closer to the mirror and decided her face wasn't any different, not yet. There were a few more laugh lines around her eyes and her mouth, but her eyes were still bright.

Gracy shook her head, disgusted with herself. Here she was dreaming in the mirror when she'd been accused of killing a baby. She finished grinding the beans and dumped them into the coffeepot, and when the water in the kettle steamed, she poured it over the grounds, leaving the pot on the stove to keep hot while the coffee steeped. She took down the cups and deep saucers, proud that one cup still had its handle and that the saucers were only a little chipped.

When the coffee was ready, she poured it, then handed a cup to John, pointing to the sugar bowl and the glass spooner filled with silver spoons, her one extravagance. The spooner had turned purple from the sun, and the spoons inside gleamed, for

Gracy polished them often. They had been gifts, the first from Nabby, given as a wedding present, others from Daniel, one from Jeff, two or three from women in payment for Gracy's doctoring. The fanciest had belonged to Elizabeth, and Gracy wondered if John recognized it, but men weren't taken with that kind of sentiment. Most likely, John had forgotten he'd given it to her.

Taking the coffee from Gracy, John sugared it, then poured the liquid into the saucer to cool. After a minute, he raised the saucer to his mouth and drank. "You always did make a decent cup of coffee, Gracy."

She waved away the compliment. "Coffee's coffee." But it wasn't, and she savored the remark. Her extravagance was coffee, made from rainwater when it came or, when it didn't, from creek water hauled from above the mine workings, and good beans that Daniel had roasted that morning, before she came home. She left her own coffee in the cup and sipped it, then sat down at the table with John. "Tell me what the Hallecks told you about the baby," Gracy said.

The sheriff had taken off his coat, because the fire had warmed the cabin, and sat in his shirtsleeves, leaning forward on the table. "Jonas claimed he'd delivered the baby because it came too fast to call in you or Little Dickie. I already told you that. He said they got to worrying that next day that something was wrong, so he sent Josie to fetch you. Jonas said you worked over the baby, said it was all right. He didn't pick it up for a time after you were gone, and it was dead. That's what he told me."

Seated across from him, Gracy pushed the kerosene lamp aside, then looked down at her hands. "That wasn't the way of it. Not the way of it at all," she said softly. "The baby was born Monday last, four days ago, like you said. I put it down in my book the next day, after I saw him. I always do that, because the babies have to be registered and I didn't know if the Hallecks knew that. There's parents that get the date mixed up. You have a mother saying it was on the second of the month, and the father says the third, because the baby came just after midnight. I remember one time a baby's father swore his boy was born on Christmas Day, when it was really New Year's. Imagine . . ." Gracy's voice trailed off as she realized she was wandering.

"So the Halleck kid was born Monday," John said, "not that it matters much."

"No, not much." Gracy reached over and turned up the wick on the lamp. Full night had come on. She shook her head back and forth as if to remove cobwebs in her brain and said, "I got off the point. It wasn't Mr. Halleck sent for me. It was Josie. She came to the cabin and pounded on the door. Daniel was out, and I was sitting here with my piecing. I thought she must be a man come to get me for his wife, and I remember looking around for my bag. But it wasn't any man. It was Josie, and she was scared to death. Her hair was down, and she was so weak she had to hold on to the door to keep from falling. She had a look to her like she'd been chased by the devil. And she had the look of just giving birth, too. She said to come quick, that there was a baby, and something was wrong. She was afraid he would choke to death."

"She didn't say it was hers."

"No, not then, not ever. Lord knows how she was able to leave that house in her condition to come to me. At first, I thought maybe I was wrong about Josie giving birth, that maybe she was just frightened and wild-eyed. After all, I hadn't seen Edna in a long time, so the child most likely was hers." Gracy stared into her coffee, at a shimmer of oil on top of the liquid. "It wasn't until I got to the Halleck house that I knew something was off."

"How's that?"

"Edna and Mr. Halleck weren't expecting me. He hadn't sent for me at all. Josie had fetched me on her own. I don't know how that could be, but maybe they were worried enough about that baby not to notice Josie was gone. Edna was in her nightdress holding the baby, muttering to it, Jonas yelling at her to do something. I could see the baby was having a hard time of it, so I took him from Edna. The poor thing was choking. There was something stuck in his throat—mucous, like I said. I cleaned it out, and then he was fine. When I was sure of that, I checked him over and retied the cord, because Jonas had done a poor job of it.

"When he found out the baby was all right, Jonas started strutting around as if he'd just struck a vug of solid gold, saying he had a son and heir. He told me he was going to put part of the Holy Moses in the boy's name and raise him up to be just like himself. I never thought that baby wasn't safe."

"A man will talk like that."

"Yes, and so will a mother. But there was no joy in either of those women. Edna was standing there solemn as Judgment Day, wringing her hands, and Josie was in a daze. I thought they were just worried about the baby, but when I picked him up, I knew something else was wrong. I can look at a baby and know who sired it. It's a gift, you might say. But like I said, I can tell the mother, too. There's times when a woman will try to fool you, but I always know. So I was sure Edna hadn't given birth. It was Josie. When I studied the girl, I saw again that she had the look of a new mother. She was clutching her hands so hard her fingers were white, and fidgeting, looking from the baby to me and back. She couldn't stay still. She reached for the baby, but Jonas slapped her hands away." Gracy shook her head at the cruelty of it. "I said I ought to examine the mother, make sure she was all right."

"Did you?" John looked surprised.

Gracy pursed her lips. "You'd have thought I'd suggested something indecent, because Jonas Halleck told me I'd examine Edna over his dead body. I looked at Edna then, but she was staring at the floor and wouldn't say a word."

"So you didn't examine her?"

Gracy gave a mirthless laugh. "You think I'd throw her on the bed and rip off her nightdress?"

"I see your point."

"And you didn't examine Josie, either."

"Of course not. I wish I could have. She's small and young, not more than fourteen. She might be all tore up. I don't know how she birthed that baby."

"I don't suppose you know who the father was. You said you could tell."

Gracy hesitated. "I expect the father could have been anybody. Poor kid up there in that big house, the lonesomest place on God's footstool, with a rabbity mother and a father meaner than winter."

"You don't think her father . . ." John couldn't finish the question because the awfulness of it overwhelmed him.

Gracy knew what he meant. "It happens." She looked away. Thinking about the baby's father pained her.

"Mr. Halleck's a pretty big man in these mountains, although I know you don't like him. Is that because of Dan?"

"Partly. But it's what the power does to him, too."

"There isn't a man with more of it in Swandyke, and he wants you to know it. You think he mistreats his wife and daughter?"

Gracy looked away. "I wouldn't be surprised."

"Is she simple, the girl?"

"I don't think so, but her mind's addled in some way. I'm told she wanders around."

"She's not proper. I can tell you that. She goes into the Nugget. I saw a miner in there buying her whiskey once and had to tell her to get on home. I warned him if Mr. Halleck caught him cozying up to Josie, he just might find himself at the bottom of a glory hole. I tell you, Gracy, I'm not surprised she got herself in the family way."

For a minute, Gracy traced a design on the oilcloth on the table, then she looked up and continued. "Mr. Halleck left the room for a minute, and I thought Edna might tell me then that the baby was Josie's. She knew I could see it. But she's not a talking woman. I suppose she fears her husband too much."

"She wouldn't be the only one afraid of her husband." John

stood and went to the fireplace. Using his shirttail, he lifted the coffeepot, pouring more liquid into his cup, and when Gracy held out hers, he filled it, too. Then he made a great to-do about adding sugar and pouring the coffee into the saucer, where he let it cool. "If Josie was the mother, it's odd nobody in town knew about it. Folks've got eyes, and they like to gossip."

Gracy nodded before she answered. "I can tell you Edna hasn't been seen in a month or two or three. She hasn't been at quilting circle or even at church. Mittie McCauley remarked on it last week, said she wondered where Edna had got to. I thought a little about it then, because Edna had let it out that she was ailing, which is what a woman like her will do if she's pregnant. Edna's not like the rest of us that don't have a choice and have to go about our business when we're as big as an ore bucket. Edna's a wellborn lady, and that kind would as soon dress naked on the street as be seen with a swollen belly. And of course, I hadn't heard a word about Josie. If I'd paid more attention, I would have figured Josie was staying home to care for her ma. Those two have been shut up in that house for weeks. So there's no reason folks would think Edna wasn't the one to give birth."

Gracy took a sip from the cup she had left on the table, the coffee cold now, as she thought back. She said slowly, for she was not a woman to betray a confidence without reason, "Last time I saw Edna, she and Josie came to me for salve for Josie. Edna said the girl was bruised from falling down in a glacier bed. But I saw Josie's black eye and the welts on her back and knew they weren't from any fall. More likely, they came from a horsewhip."

"Whose?"

Gracy shrugged. "They didn't say. My guess is they were too afraid."

"What's Edna Halleck like?"

"You don't know her?"

"I've been to the house on occasion but never heard her speak. I called on her this evening, but she didn't say a word, just nodded when I asked her if you'd killed the baby. Josie did the same thing. Of course, Jonas was there. He wouldn't let me talk to them alone. "

"No, he wouldn't. But even when her husband's not there, Edna doesn't have much to say. When they first came here, she was a lively sort, and Josie was as sweet a little girl as you ever saw, bright as a gold nugget. But over the years, Edna's got kind of beat down, you might say. She still plays the lady. When Bible circle meets at her house, she brings out a tea set fit for a queen, solid silver it is. Serves up the tea in china cups thin as a butterfly's wing." Gracy glanced down at her own chipped cup and shook her head. "Always sponge cake or chocolate pudding in cups not bigger than a thimble." Gracy smiled at the memory of such extravagance.

"The Hallecks have the nicest house in town," John observed.

"They do at that, but there's something I don't like about it. That house is always closed up, only a little light through the shutters. Too prim for my taste, like it's frozen, and not a speck of dirt. Edna keeps it that way herself. All that money and never a servant. She does the work, says her husband doesn't like people underfoot, that a maid would steal them blind. Only thing he'll allow is to send out the laundry." Gracy stopped for a moment, feeling talked out. "One more thing, she's a Bible reader, always talking about the Lord's will and how He punishes people. Myself, I believe in a joyful God, one that gives us flowers and sunrises and men like you and Daniel. But Edna, her God sits up there in judgment, making people pay for their sins, and she believes in a plenty of them. I hate to think how poor Josie is being punished for fornicating."

John was about to ask another question but there was a noise outside, a rattle as if someone were throwing tin cans down the mountainside. Maybe it was the old dog Sandy, but he would have gone with Daniel. A bear, Gracy told him. One had been wandering around the cabin with her cubs. She warned John to be careful when he left. He didn't want to get between a mother and her young ones. Bears or humans, it didn't matter. A mother would protect her young.

"Is that what Edna did? Punished Josie for getting pregnant? Could she have strangled the baby?"

Gracy thought that over for a long time. "I've wondered ever since this morning, when you told me what happened, who would have done it. Of course, it could have been anyone— maybe someone from outside even—but I don't believe that, because Mr. Halleck wouldn't have blamed me. There are three people who could have strangled that baby. Josie's too timid, and Edna's too afraid of her husband."

"That leaves Mr. Halleck."

"But why would he do it? He was proud of the boy." In fact, the man had been almost giddy with joy, and Gracy had thought then that the baby wouldn't have such a bad life. He would grow up rich, get an education, inherit a mine. It was more than most boys had—her son, Jeff, for instance. She thought a moment. "Maybe it was an accident? But how could you put a cord around a baby's neck by accident?"

"Do *you* think Mr. Halleck did it?"

Gracy nodded. "There isn't anybody else. I think when he settled down, he feared somebody would find out who gave birth to that baby, that maybe I'd let it out. Do you think that's why he blamed me?"

"Maybe." John shifted in his chair. "You know, Gracy, I think it's best that we don't say who the baby's mother was. I ought to put down what you said with the other evidence I have to turn over to the prosecutor. After all, I'm the sheriff, and it's my job. But I'm thinking there's no proof, so it would be like passing on gossip. And if we're wrong, we could ruin a young girl's life. So let's just keep it between us."

Gracy nodded and peered at the liquid in her cup. Better to keep everything about that baby secret, she thought. If folks knew Josie was the mother, they'd be awful interested in the father. Josie didn't need that speculation.

"I think I told you he buried that baby back behind his house, laid it in a dynamite box and dropped it in a hole in the ground," John continued. "He said Mrs. Halleck made him dig it up, maybe the only time she ever stood up to him. She said God would punish them if that baby wasn't buried in sacred ground, said she was going to get a preacher whether Halleck liked it or not. Maybe Halleck figured he would go to hell if he left the baby there. Old Halleck's a Bible-thumper, too."

Gracy raised her coffee cup to her lips and drank. The cold liquid made her feel better. She liked a cup of tea, particularly when she was tired. But coffee, now that was a drink to make the blood course through your arms and legs. She wished she had a bit of cream to add to it. They'd kept a cow in Virginia City for a time, but Swandyke was too high up for a cow, too cold. Besides, who would milk it if Daniel was away on one of his prospecting trips and Gracy got called out for a day or two? Still, she missed pouring cream off a jar of milk and spooning it into her coffee, missed churning her own butter, too. She had to buy it at the mercantile, and that place charged jewelry rates. John nudged the sugar bowl toward her, but Gracy shook her head. Sugar ruined a good cup of coffee. Nonetheless, she picked up her spoon and stirred the unsugared liquid, thinking.

After a time, Gracy set the spoon in the saucer and looked up at John. "Edna is a Bible woman, and it would sit hard with her if that baby didn't have a Christian burial. Most likely, she taught Josie about the Bible, and the girl would have wanted a proper service for the child, too. The two of them must have insisted, and maybe Mr. Halleck was afraid somebody would find that grave, and that would be worse than admitting there'd been a baby."

John thought that over. "Mr. Halleck isn't a man to take orders from a woman, much less his wife, and you said she was beat down. I imagine he can thump her pretty good, the girl, too."

Outside came the sound of tin cans rattling again. Maybe Daniel had come home and fallen into the pile. He was none too steady when he drank. And he wouldn't be holding his liquor well, because it had been a long time since he'd been on a bender. Gracy went to the door and opened it, but the night was black, and there was no sign of Daniel, no sounds of a dog barking. The bear again, she told John, or maybe the wind had blown hard enough to rattle the cans. Then she saw a shape in the dark, a man, and she thought some miner must have been drunk and fallen into the can pile. She stood a minute to let the cold rid her of the tiredness before she closed the door and went back to the table. "I don't know where Daniel's got to."

"I'll see to him when I leave," John offered.

"I'd be grateful." She thought back to what the two had been talking about. "There are times when a woman will stand up to the worst kind of beating. Maybe Edna threatened to take the baby to town herself if Mr. Halleck wouldn't do it. And Mr. Halleck was afraid Coy would see the boy had been strangled and blame him. So he came up with the story about me. But I don't understand why anybody would think I'm the guilty one."

"Don't you?"

Gracy had been staring into her coffee cup, and now she looked up quickly. "No I don't. How can you ask it?"

For a moment, John studied the oilcloth. Then he stood and walked around the room, stopping at the fireplace where he stared into the coals. "Here's what I think, Gracy. Like I said before, if you get charged by a judge, it ought to be manslaughter. I don't suppose you know about the law, do you?"

Gracy shook her head.

"If you kill somebody in a fit of passion, it's not murder; it's manslaughter."

"Passion? What passion?"

"As I see it, you could have been so angry at Mr. Halleck for what he did to Daniel, charging him with high-grading and keeping him from working in any of the mines, that you wanted to get back at him. You didn't plan it. You just acted, wrapped a cord around the baby's neck to strangle it."

"But that's not what happened," Gracy protested. "You don't believe me, do you?"

"Of course I believe you. But I know you've helped a girl or two who didn't want to be pregnant. Some say that's murder, too. You performed an abortion, maybe more than one."

"I won't say I did, and I won't say I didn't. But even if I did, it's a different thing. That's not a living baby." She nodded to emphasize the point. "I will tell you I've sent girls to that doctor in Central City who advertises she specializes in diseases peculiar to women." She looked at John fiercely. "Remember Ruth Bond that froze to death right outside her cabin? Her death was no accident. She was pregnant. That's why I can't slam the door on a girl who doesn't want her baby."

John turned from the fire and stared at Gracy, startled. "I thought Ruth missed the trail, got confused with all the snow swirling around. I remember I told you it was a shame the way she died no more than five or ten feet from her own door."

"She was carrying a baby, and it wasn't her husband's. Remember, he'd been in prison for a year or more? She told me she'd been raped by a miner from the Tiger, and I believed her. She'd been beat bad, and when I examined her after that, I could see she was tore up. She knew there was a baby started and asked

me to get rid of it, and I wish I'd done it." Ruth's death was another that made Gracy feel guilty, that added to the load of re-
morse she carried.

She watched John leave the fireplace and walk around the
room again, stopping to pull back the curtain and stare out into
the blackness. "John, that manslaughter idea you came up with,
me killing the baby, is that what you think happened?"

"I told you I didn't," John said. "But I expect a prosecutor will
say that at the hearing. Here's what'll happen, Gracy. First there
will be a hearing with a judge and a prosecutor to determine if
you're to be charged. The judge is a circuit rider, going from town
to town, and he'll be in Swandyke week after next. So that's when
the hearing will be held. The prosecutor presents evidence, but
you're not allowed to open your mouth at the hearing. If the
judge finds there's enough evidence to charge you, he'll set the
trial for the next time he's here, a month or so from now. That's
when you'll have a chance to defend yourself."

Gracy waved her hand as if to dismiss the idea. "No matter
what I thought of Mr. Halleck, I wouldn't kill the boy, because
he's a child of God. You ought to know that."

John opened his mouth to say something, but just then, there
was a pounding on the door. "That must be Daniel," he said.

"No, why would Daniel knock?" Gracy asked, and went to
the door, opening it to find a man standing there, rain dripping
off him. "Ben sent me for the Sagehen," he said.

Gracy frowned, because she couldn't see the man's face in the
dark and didn't know who he was.

"I'm Davy Eastlow. Ben Boyce's wife, Esther, she's having her baby. Best you follow me."

Now Gracy knew the man. She smiled. "I'll just be a minute. Let me get my bag. John, thanks for the company," she said, as if the sheriff had come on a social call. Gracy hummed a little, gathering the clean cloths she would need and putting them into her bag. She scribbled a note to Daniel, then reached for her cloak, which was hanging on a peg. She felt a familiar thrill. A baby coming, and someone needed the Sagehen. The conversation with John seemed to slide off her, and she thought of the birth of a Boyce baby instead of the death of the Halleck infant. She grabbed her bag and started for the door, stopping to smooth Daniel's pillow on the bed. He'd be coming home tired, maybe drunk, and would be wanting her there. She wished he wouldn't have to sleep alone that night.

Six

All the tiredness left Gracy as she scurried down the trail to the stable, Davy Eastlow leading his horse a few steps behind her, the sheriff watching from the doorway, shaking his head but making no move to stop her.

There was nothing like a child to be born on a night that was fresh with rain, stars shining now, to lift Gracy's spirits. She would think about the Halleck baby later. Right now, a woman needed her. Gracy was lighthearted, as if a burden had been lifted from her shoulders. She wondered how many more times she would feel this happiness. But she wouldn't think about quitting now, not when there was a baby waiting to be born.

"You want to ride my horse?" Davy called. Without turning, Gracy waved him off. Stepping fast, she could walk to the stable in less time than it would take her to mount the horse and fasten her bag to the saddle. "Earl, I'll be needing my buggy," she called to the stable boy. She'd told him that hundreds of times, and the boy knew to hurry. He led Buddy out of the stall and hitched him to the buggy, then helped Gracy climb in. Davy tied his horse to the back of the vehicle and sat in the seat beside her, reaching for the reins. Gracy batted aside his hands and said she would drive. The horse wouldn't respond to anyone but her, she said, which wasn't altogether true. But they'd go faster, surer, if she handled the reins.

"We're going to Mayflower Gulch," he told her, and Gracy smiled to think there were two births in two days in the same part of the Tenmile. Maybe the two babies would grow up to be friends. Perhaps if this one was a girl, she might even marry the boy who was a single day older. Maybe she would be like Emma, knowing about herbs. The midwife could teach her healing, and one day she would follow in Gracy's footsteps. The old woman smiled at the possibilities, then shook her head. What foolishness. She was getting soft. Still, they were nice thoughts.

"When did she start her labor?" Gracy asked. She wished she could remember Mrs. Boyce's name.

"Esther," Davy said, as if reading her mind. "Esther just said to get the Sagehen. I don't know about such."

Of course he didn't, Gracy thought. An old bachelor like that. How would he know? Still, he lived with the Boyces.

Gracy remembered the scandal of it. Ben Boyce and Davy Eastlow were already in Swandyke when Gracy and Daniel moved there. The two men weren't young then, maybe forty. They trapped in Mayflower Gulch, beaver and fox and weasel, built a cabin in an aspen grove, the trees so thick you could hardly

walk through them. Gracy had stopped there once with Daniel, and had found it clean and neat as her pie safe. She hadn't
expected that from a pair of old bachelors. The two men had
scurried around their cabin, proud to have guests. Ben had
ground the beans for coffee, while Davy put on the water. Then
they'd taken a black currant pie from the window, a pie still
warm from the stove, and cut it into four pieces. Gathered the
currants themselves, they'd said, and Gracy marveled that two
bachelors would have the patience to pick enough tiny berries
for a pie. It had been a good pie, too, as good as if Gracy had
made it herself, and she had said so.

"It's Davy does the cooking. See there, we got a cookstove,"
Ben had said. "He keeps up the house, too. I tend the garden
and hunt. We eat pretty good."

When she left, Gracy had seen the garden, the lettuce, the
rows of turnips and radishes. How did Ben keep the wild animals from the produce? she wondered. She was lucky if the deer
and the rabbits left enough of her own garden behind for a
meal or two.

"Those boys might as well be married," Daniel had said.

"They get along better than most couples we know." Gracy
had agreed.

But then, last fall, Ben had come home with Esther, him old
enough to be her father. There had been talk about where he'd
gotten her. The postmaster said Ben had received an awful lot
of letters from back East, and he reckoned Esther was a mail-
order bride. Another speculated that Ben had gone to Denver
and gotten drunk and woken up to find himself married. But most

agreed Esther had worked in a dance hall over in Kokomo. Ben never said, nor Davy either. It was Daniel's theory Ben had baited her with a fox skin red as the sunset, red as Davy's hair, loaded her onto a sled warm with wolverine pelts and taken her to Mayflower Gulch.

There was talk about Davy, too, some saying he should move on, give the couple a chance. But the cabin was half his, the trapping, too. The men had been together too long to be separated. "She'll be to hell and gone before she parts them," Daniel had predicted. Others agreed. Give her a year, they said, maybe less. She wouldn't last out the winter, snowed in with two old men, her young like she was, pretty as candlelight. She'd go back where she'd come from once the thaw came. But she hadn't. Gracy had seen her in town and knew the reason. You couldn't go back to a dance hall with a swollen belly like that.

"You're the Sagehen," Esther had said. "I'll send for you when my time comes."

"I ought to check you now, make sure everything's all right," Gracy had told her.

"That's silly. What could be wrong? It's only a baby." She'd smiled the dreamy smile of first mothers. "I hope my time's in midsummer when the flowers are blooming. If it's a girl, I'll name her Rose for the wild roses around the cabin. If it's a boy, well, I guess he'll have his father's name. But I'm hoping for a girl. There's already too many males in that place." Gracy had met her in the mercantile where the girl was buying bullets. "Ben's taught me to shoot," she said in explanation. "He says I'm a natural-born at it, could shoot a wildcat through the eye."

"It's a skill to have," Gracy replied.

"I help him trap," she added, lowering her eyes as if she'd been caught bragging. "But I'd rather shoot an animal than trap it. Being caught in a trap's a hard way to go. In a trap, you'd know you was dying, and you'd lie there thinking about it, watching your blood flow out. I wouldn't want to go to my eternal jubilee that way."

Now as Gracy sat beside Davy in the buggy, she asked about Esther. "Does she cook?" she asked.

"She'll do," Davy replied.

"She said she hunts."

"She did, but it's not a woman's place. Ben takes care of the hunting."

Gracy wondered what Esther did in that cabin all day long. "I expect she's a breath of fresh air. When I met her in town once, she talked about the wild roses."

Davy didn't reply, and they rode in silence under the wet firs. Gracy could abide a silence, but she was curious. Of course, what was between the three of them wasn't any of her business, but that didn't stop her "She's a pretty girl. Sweet, too, it seems. I met her only once, so I can't say I know her."

Davy turned to the side and looked at the night.

The moon was out, and Gracy was glad because that made it easier to see the trail. If Davy didn't want to talk, that was all right with her.

"They say you murdered a baby," he said abruptly, turning back to Gracy.

Gracy took a deep breath as the image of Josie's baby came

back to her. "Yes, they say that, but I didn't kill the baby." When Davy didn't reply, Gracy added, "If it makes a difference, I'll turn around. You can fetch the doctor."

"I never had any use for doctors," Davy said. "Besides, Esther don't want him, says he thinks he's too good for her, the way he looks down his nose at her, like she's not worth a continental. He's got no call to treat her like that. It ain't his business where Esther come from . . ." Davy's voice trailed off. "No, she won't want him. She said to fetch you, even though I told her what's said in town about you murdering a baby and all. I heard it this morning when I went to the mercantile to buy her a can of peaches. She had a craving for them. I didn't know I'd be back in Swandyke so soon again. She'd said the baby weren't due yet."

Davy shut up then, as if he'd talked himself out. He didn't speak again until he pointed to a turnoff and said, "Go left there and stop where the trail starts up. We'll have to walk because there's no room between the trees for the buggy. Esther wanted to make a road to the house, but me and Ben wouldn't allow it. We don't want company. It ain't far now." He got out of the buggy and untied his horse. Gracy took her bag and followed.

She saw the cabin in the moonlight shining through the aspen trunks that always reminded her of bones, smoke curling out of the chimney, as pretty a sight as any she ever saw. A smaller replica of the cabin, new-built, stood a few rods away. That must be where Davy lived now, Gracy thought. Of course, it wouldn't be right, the three of them living in a one-room cabin. She wondered if Davy resented having to leave. But that wasn't her business, either, and she put thoughts of the odd trio out of her mind as she scurried to the dwelling.

Davy was ahead of her and he flung open the door. "I brung the Sagehen," he said. He stood in the doorway, staring at the bed, and Gracy had to shove past him to enter the room.

Esther lay on a quilt, her legs spread, while Ben stood at the end of the bed, his face red and wild. "It's coming out. I'm not knowing what to do," he said.

"That's my job. Move aside," Gracy told him, hurrying to the bed and setting her bag on the floor. She glanced down at Esther, then grinned. "Why, you hardly need me at all, Mrs. Boyce. That baby wouldn't wait. It's almost here." She turned to the men. "Get me hot water fast so's I can wash up first."

Davy grabbed the teakettle off the cookstove and poured water into a basin, water so hot it almost took the skin off Gracy's hands. She worked quickly, putting on her apron, washing her hands, then nudging Ben aside. "You're doing a first-class job, Mrs. Boyce—Esther, is it? It's almost over. Oh, yes, you're doing finely. The baby's halfway born. Now you push hard with the next pain." Just in time, Gracy positioned herself to catch the baby, because in a moment, Esther groaned and pushed, and the baby fell into Gracy's hands.

"A boy!" Ben said. "By Dan, Davy, she's give us a boy."

If she'd been paying closer attention, Gracy might have thought it odd that Ben would announce the baby's sex to his partner instead of to his wife, but Gracy was too busy with the baby to notice. "You hold him," she said, handing the infant to Ben. "I didn't have time to get out my scissors." She placed the baby in Ben's hands while she opened her bag and took out the scissors, linen string, and clean cloths. Dipping the string in hot water first, she thought of the thread that had been around the Halleck baby's neck. But she shook the thought out of her head and bound Esther's son's cord. She handed the silver stork scissors—the very scissors Nabby had left to her—to Ben and told him to cut. Fathers who cut a baby's cord seemed to bond a little better with them.

Ben did as he was instructed, then grinned at Davy. "Lookit there. We got us a son."

"He's yours all right. Dark like you, and he's got your ugly chin," Davy said.

"I'd hoped he wouldn't, but he does, don't he?"

Gracy ignored the bantering as she turned to Esther. The baby had come so fast that she had barely looked at the woman. Now when she studied Esther's body, the nightdress pulled up, Gracy frowned. She placed her hand on Esther's belly and gasped.

At the sound, the two men glanced away from the baby. "What's wrong?" Ben asked.

"There's another'n in there. Mr. Boyce, your wife is going to have twins."

"Another?" Ben asked, confused.

"Sometimes it happens." Gracy turned to Esther. "Mrs. Boyce, you get yourself ready. There's a second baby about to be born. It'll be easier than the first."

"I don't want—" Esther started to say, but a pain seized her. And in a moment, a second boy emerged into Gracy's hands.

This one was smaller, lighter, with ears flat against his head and downy hair the color of fireweed—the color of Davy's hair—and Gracy's hands shook as she held the infant. She could almost always tell who the father was. It was an odd thing, but she knew the minute a baby was born if its father wasn't the woman's husband. She never let on, of course, never told. So there were fathers out there taking pride in children sired by other men. Knowing at the birth who had fathered a child was a skill Gracy sometimes wished she didn't have, like now, although anybody could see who'd fathered this second boy. It was a rare thing, twins, each one sired by a different man. Gracy had read of it in a book, although she'd never seen it herself, not that she knew of, at any rate.

She stopped as she pondered what had taken place in that cabin, was still so long that Esther asked what was wrong. Nothing, Gracy told her. The baby was as healthy as the first one. She'd only gotten a tear in her eye and had to push it away. She started to hand the boy to Davy but stopped and told Ben to give his partner the first infant so that he could help her with this baby's cord.

Ben didn't say a word, just stared at the boy as he followed Gracy's instructions. She had no time to study the men because there was the afterbirth to deal with. And she needed to examine Esther to see if she was all right. "Two boys. Two healthy boys," Gracy told the new mother. She ordered the men to turn away while she helped Esther out of her nightdress and into a clean one, because the first was covered with blood. Then she remade the bed with a fresh quilt and helped Esther to lie down again.

Usually when there were twins, Gracy tied a string around the wrist of the first one to show who was older, but there was no need for that here. "There now," she said. "I expect you want to hold your boys." She took the red-haired baby from Ben and handed him to Esther, then gave her the darker infant. "I think you'll have milk enough for two, but if you don't, just send Davy to tell me. There's a woman in Swandyke had a stillbirth, and likely she'd make a wet nurse." It wouldn't matter to Esther that the woman wasn't married, Gracy thought, or that she'd worked at the Red Swan on Turnbull Mountain. That would be the least of Esther's problems.

Esther took the two babies, one in each arm, and cooed to them. If anything seemed strange, she didn't remark on it. "This one," she said, nodding at the red-haired infant, "he's named for you—Benjamin. We'll call him Benny." She smiled at her husband. "The other . . ."

Gracy held her breath. Surely she wouldn't name the other boy for Davy.

"His name is Thomas. That's my brother's name. Tommy. I always favored it."

Gracy sighed a breath of relief when the second child was named, then busied herself with applying the bellybands and cleaning up. She wrapped the afterbirth in newspaper from her bag and handed the package to Davy with instructions to bury it under one of the wild roses Esther loved. "Do it now," she said, nodding at the door, and Davy went out. After the door closed, Gracy turned to the stove, and taking out a tin of catnip tea, she made a cup for Esther, adding a little sugar. The tea would help bring on the new mother's milk, and she'd need plenty of it with two babies. Things were already tangled enough without bringing in a wet nurse. When the tea was made, Gracy set it on the bureau beside the bed.

The cabin was warm, well chinked, which was a good thing for the babies, what with summer on the downside. On the dresser were stacks of baby clothes, flannel diapers. A cradle made from pinewood, sanded and burnished until it was the color and sheen of honey, was beside the bed. They'd need a second cradle, but for now, both babies could fit into one. Gracy opened the safe to find it filled with food, two loaves of bread resting on a towel. Esther must have baked it the night before, maybe when she couldn't sleep. Or perhaps Davy had made the bread.

The baby—the first one, anyway—had been anticipated, planned for, loved, Gracy thought. Now what? What did that red-haired baby mean? What had happened between the two men and the woman, and what would happen now? Would Davy move out, maybe take the second boy with him? Perhaps Esther would leave, threatened and forced out by her husband. Blood, like water, boiled too quick at timberline. But where could a dance hall girl with two babies go? Or perhaps the three adults would go on as before, pretending that nothing had happened, that both of the babies were Ben's. Not many people made it to the trappers' cabin, so perhaps no one would suspect the babies had been fathered by two different men. Maybe the red hair would turn dark. Sure, and maybe next year the sun would melt the snow before June, Gracy thought.

Well, what was to be was up to the three of them. Gracy couldn't do anything about it except worry and keep her mouth shut, and she knew how to do both. She finished her work and packed the soiled nightdress along with her own apron in her bag. If Davy did the washing, he wouldn't want to scrub out the childbirth. Gracy would bring the laundered items with her when she returned. "I'll be back," she said, "I want to make sure everything is all right." But how could it be all right?

Neither Esther nor Ben seemed aware that Gracy was leaving. She went to the bed and gazed at the infants, both mewling, curling their little hands around Esther's fingers. Gracy smoothed the red down on Ben's head, hair thin as frog's hair, then picked up her bag and went through the door, shutting it quickly to keep out the cold air. Davy was sitting on the bench outside when she emerged. He rose, saying he'd see Gracy to her buggy. She nodded, wondering if he did not want to go inside and face Ben.

"Do you need me to take you home?" he asked.

Gracy laughed. "I guess I see better in the dark than a raccoon. I know this trail. I'll find my way." But maybe she *should* ask him to take her home. Perhaps she should get Davy away from the cabin for a time, give Ben a chance to love both babies? Davy's being there would complicate things. But then it already had. The three would have to face their situation, and perhaps it would be better if they did so right off. If Davy was going to leave, he ought to go now, find another cabin and set his traps before winter came on. But would he go? After all, both men had adjusted to Esther. Perhaps they could adjust to the idea of one of those babies being fathered by Davy. Maybe there'd been an arrangement. Gracy knew strange things happened in a lonely mining camp. She didn't judge.

"I best go in. Somebody'll have to fix supper. There's been so much bother, I ain't had time to think about it," Davy said.

"Bother" wasn't the way Gracy would put childbirth. Still she said, "Isn't she the lucky one! Most fathers—most men, that is—they aren't a hand at cooking. Expect their wife to climb off a childbed and fix the victuals. But Esther can sit there like the Queen of Turkey with you to do the cooking." She leaned forward and said, "She ought to stay in bed ten days after giving birth to *two*. Feed her beef tea if you can get it."

Davy nodded.

"My, isn't she the lucky one with two men to take care of her," Gracy said again, although she wasn't sure there was much luck around that place.

Davy didn't reply, just handed Gracy into the buggy. He reached into his pocket and took out a gold coin.

Gracy protested the pay was too much.

"I guess you get double for birthing two babies," he told her.

"It's only a little more work than one."

"We're obliged," he said as he untied the reins from an aspen tree. He stared at the leather straps for a long time. "I guess folks will talk, won't they?"

"They won't hear anything from me. That red-haired baby isn't any of my business." There, she'd said it out loud.

"There'll be others that'll think it's their business." He

handed the reins to Gracy. "You know, Esther said she had a sister with red hair."

Gracy stared at Davy for a moment. "I was thinking someone in the family might." And then she muttered to herself, "Well, God!"

The sky had clouded over, blocking out the stars and the moon now, and the night was black as a grave, Gracy realized with a sudden shudder. Usually, she liked the night, the dark enfolding her like a quilt. The horse knew the way home, and she could drowse a little if she wanted to. But the births at the trappers' cabin weighed on her mind. She remembered another time she had birthed twins, a boy and a girl. Both were healthy, but when Gracy went back to check on them a few days later, the girl was dead. "I'm glad," the mother told Gracy. "I got five others, and I can't take care of them and two babies besides. My husband says best the boy lives, because a girl ain't worth much." Gracy had pondered whether the mother had killed her own child. Or maybe the father had done it. The mother had gotten pregnant again not long after that. She'd asked Gracy to perform an abortion, but Gracy, knowing how weak the woman was, said it might kill her and refused. Later, the woman stumbled over a cliff and died anyway. An accident, her husband said, but Gracy wasn't so sure. The man disappeared, and the children went to an orphan home. And Gracy had asked herself if the risk from an abortion had been worth the certainty of death from a fall?

Now, thinking of both women who'd borne twins, Gracy was

uneasy. The blackness didn't help. The pine trees were dark shapes dripping with rain, hiding wild animals. She wished she could have brought Sandy with her, but he was with Daniel. The dog generally stayed behind anyway, because Gracy never knew how long she'd be gone and she didn't want to worry about feeding him.

Gracy roused herself. She was not easily frightened. She'd driven through dark nights before, and in blizzards to boot. This evening was summer cool but warm enough so that she was comfortable wrapped in a cloak and the quilt she kept in the buggy. It was the not knowing that bothered her, not knowing what had gone on in that cabin and what would happen now, she told herself. Should she do something? Tell the sheriff? But what was there to tell? And what could he do anyway? It wasn't a crime to have babies by two different men. A sin, maybe, but not a crime, and sin was commonplace in a mining town. Besides, maybe Esther really did have a red-haired sister. But even so, Gracy was sure Davy had sired one of the babies. She could tell.

The wind blew through the pines, making a soft moaning noise that Gracy always found comforting, only now it added to her anxiety. Then came a rustling that made her start. A deer or an elk in the wet leaves, she told herself. But there were bears, too, and mountain lions. After the old doctor died, Gracy had been called to attend a man who'd been attacked by a lion, the side of his face scratched to the bone, one eye gone, his chest tore up, his arms and legs broken. It had been a horrible sight, and Gracy felt it was a blessing he'd died. She shivered to think a lion could be stalking her, that she might be laid out on the trail, bleeding and broken, maybe dead without a chance to say good-bye to Daniel. He wouldn't be able to go on without her. Gracy's thoughts were always of Daniel, even years before, when he'd broken her heart.

The horse caught the scent of something and picked up speed, running nervously, and Gracy had to hold him back with the reins. Gracy felt an evil about that didn't have to do with the folks in Mayflower Gulch. Perhaps she should go back and ask Davy to take her home. But how would she explain herself? They would think her a silly old woman. Besides, how could she go back? There was no place on that narrow trail to turn a buggy. She'd have to walk, and that would make it mighty easy for a lion. Gracy tried to laugh at herself, but she couldn't. She couldn't help the feeling that something was out there, something ominous.

She wasn't a timid woman, but she had had those feelings before. Nabby had told her to trust them because they came with the gift of healing. She had had a premonition once in Arkansas about a baby Nabby had delivered. Gracy had helped with the birth, and it had gone fine. The baby was healthy, and so was the mother. But after the two midwives left, something gnawed at Gracy. She couldn't sleep that night, and the next day she told Nabby she had had a presentiment. So the two returned to find the woman in agony from puerperal fever. They stayed with her for a week, placing cold cloths on her head and a flannel bag of hops soaked in hot vinegar on her abdomen, mustard poultices on her feet and thighs. "You saved her life. If we'd come back even half a day later, we'd have lost her," Nabby told Gracy after the fever lifted. "You have a gift."

There were other times Gracy had had presentiments, like that night in Virginia City. She had tried to ignore it, but she couldn't. It had been too strong.

Gracy was sure the feeling now had nothing to do with the two babies. It was about her. She was in danger. She reached behind the seat and took out the pistol she kept there. It was loaded, and she knew how to shoot. She stared into the darkness ahead of her, thinking it must be a panther, because they were more stealthful than bears. She wouldn't hear it until it sprang onto a horse—or onto her. Gracy shivered to think of the animal's claws raking into her back, his teeth sinking into her neck. She shook her head. She no longer held the reins to keep the horse back but urged him on. She wished she had left the whip in its socket, not because she wanted to use it on Buddy but as protection. But she never whipped a horse and had left the whip behind.

Perhaps the force she felt was a man. Gracy hadn't never been afraid of the miners. They knew the Sagehen, knew her because she had attended their wives and sometimes even nursed them. No one in Swandyke would hurt her. Still, there were men who were not quite right in the head, who would rape, even murder a woman alone.

She urged the horse on, slapping the reins on his back. He was old and did not move fast, but he picked up the pace, as if he, too, sensed danger. She wished the clouds would lift, that the moon would light the way, but the moon was covered, and the trail was black. She thought about the road now, whether there were ruts and rocks. She hadn't paid attention when she'd ridden with Davy Eastlow to the cabin.

Then far off in the distance, she saw a light like a lantern, and another and knew that Swandyke lay just ahead. She let up on the reins and sank back into the seat. The fear had been for nothing. She had indeed been foolish.

Just then the horse stumbled, and the buggy hit a log that lay across the road, a log that hadn't been there when she had passed through on her way to Mayflower Gulch. Gracy grasped onto the side of the buggy, but she was too late, and the vehicle swerved and went up on one wheel. Gracy flew out of the buggy, and her head hit the log. She rolled off the road and sank into unconsciousness, her last thoughts of Jeff, the infant she had warmed with her love from the moment of his birth. And of Daniel—of Daniel in his youth, Daniel strong and handsome as a racehorse.

Buddy ran on, the buggy bouncing behind him, leaving Gracy a dark shape in the dirt, as still as the night around her.

Seven

Daniel was Black Mary Brookens's son, and he had watched as Gracy at the age of ten midwifed her first baby. She didn't see him again for a dozen years, not until Lucy, the daughter who had fetched Gracy to attend Black Mary that day, birthed her own child.

By then, young as she was, Gracy already had delivered her share of babies, although when someone sent for her, she deferred to Nabby, saying, "She's the midwife. I'm only her assistant." Nabby was getting along in years, however, and had turned frail, and like as not, she would tell Gracy to go herself and attend the mother. "I'm not good for nothing but sitting in the chimney corner," she'd say, waving her hand toward the door. Of course, times when she suspected the birth would be difficult, Nabby went along, but even then, she instructed Gracy instead of doing the birthing herself.

Folks knew about the girl who had delivered Black Mary's last child, knew her to be a midwife blessed by God with a special gift. So they didn't fuss when Nabby sent Gracy instead of going herself. Lucy didn't ask for Nabby, however. She sent word she wanted Gracy to attend her, sent the sister Marjorie, the one Gracy had birthed twelve years earlier, to fetch her. "Lucy trusts you more than God Hisself," the girl said, and Gracy, flattered, didn't mind the blasphemy. In fact, she didn't always trust God.

Although the two young women lived far over the hills from each other, Gracy had kept up with Lucy, knew she had married, knew she'd lost a halfway baby the year before when she was out picking pole beans. Granny Alice, a midwife on Lucy's side of the hills, had attended her. Perhaps Lucy blamed the woman, which was why Gracy had been called for this time. Most likely it was not Granny Alice's fault. God often called home a baby who wasn't perfect instead of letting it suffer, although not always. He let a plenty of misformed ones slip through His fingers. Gracy reminded Him of that in her prayers.

Lucy would be afraid there was something wrong with this baby, too, and Gracy would have to reassure her. Lucy would blame herself if she lost another child, would think she was cursed, which could make her go strange in her mind. That meant this birth had to go well. Gracy hoped for Lucy's sake— and for her growing reputation as a midwife—that the baby would live, that it would be normal.

The sister, Marjorie, scooted up onto her mule. Gracy handed up her bag then climbed onto the mule herself, and the two rode bareback, through a meadow, over the hills, and down into a hollow. It was near dark when they arrived, and Gracy wondered if the baby might have gotten there ahead of them. After all, it had taken two hours for Marjorie to ride for Gracy and for the two to return to the house.

But that had not happened. The cabin was crowded. Black Mary stood at the end of the bed, two of Lucy's sisters on either side, one wiping Lucy's brow with a damp rag, the other rubbing Lucy's back. An old man, Black Mary's husband, rocked beside the fireplace, a pipe in his mouth, a jug on the floor beside him, calm as if the woman in the bed were doing no more than taking a nap.

Then Gracy glanced at the man standing next to Black Mary's husband, a young bull calf with hair the color of ginger and shoulders as broad as a roof beam. And hips! Gracy always did like hips in a man. He slouched against the cabin wall, staring at her with eyes the smoky blue of a bluebird. He was Lucy's husband, Gracy thought, and one to give a wife trouble. She almost shivered as she caught his look, him standing there as proud as the Lord Hal, a smile on his lips. Oh, he was the kind of man who could claim a girl's heart as easy as picking a flower, but one who'd bring her heartache. Lucy would be hard put to keep him at home, a man like that who could make a girl feel she was the Queen of Turkey, but a man who would be tempted, who would stray. He could put his wife in her grave. Gracy looked at him a little too long before she went to the bed to examine Lucy.

"You men get along now," Gracy ordered. Her voice sounded weak to her, and she cleared her throat to put more authority into it. The ginger-haired man was Lucy's husband and none of her business, and lucky for that Gracy was. For a second, Gracy wondered what it would be like to kiss him. "You men go outside," she repeated, her voice stronger.

At Gracy's orders, Black Mary's husband stood, then reached down for the jug. "Come along, boys. We don't want to be here nohow."

"But I'm Lucy's husband," a man sitting beside the bed said. Gracy had not noticed him until then, and she stared.

"I can't leave her now," he added.

"I thought . . ." She turned to the other man.

"That's our brother Daniel," Marjorie spoke up.

"You seen him before. He was there when Ma birthed Marjorie," Lucy said from the bed.

Gracy turned and stared. She remembered him now, remembered him as a runt, a boy hardly worth noticing. As if knowing what she thought, Daniel grinned and tilted his head a little. "I guess we'll be outside," he told her. "You come get us when she's done."

He glanced at the dime Gracy wore around her neck. She'd pierced it with an awl and threaded a leather string through the hole and had worn it until it was almost a part of her. Now she remembered that Daniel had given her the dime, her first payment as a midwife. She'd thought it would bring her luck, which was why she never took it off. The last fingers that had touched it so long ago were his, she thought. Daniel lowered his eyes to take her in, then went out the door, Gracy staring at his hips as he left. If hips is what you want, then hips is what you'll get, Nabby had told her.

Just then a pain seized Lucy, and Gracy turned to her and all but forgot the young man who had made her quiver. Nothing was more important than the baby.

She put the man out of her mind as she asked Marjorie to fetch a basin of water and then took out the clean cloths she'd brought and gave them to another sister to warm by the fire. She examined Lucy and told the girl that the baby wasn't ready to be born just then. "Don't push yet. It's too early," she instructed.

The women in the room knew what to do. Women always knew, Gracy thought. They kept the fire going so the cabin wouldn't get cold. They cooed to Lucy and one sang hymns in a voice as sweet as a mockingbird's. Marjorie placed an axe under the bed to cut her sister's pain. Black Mary massaged her daughter's arms and legs, while the others pulled up chairs and talked in low voices. Every now and then, Lucy's husband opened the door and peered inside, but Black Mary told him, "Not yet. She's got a lot more pain ahead of her. You think about that next time you're wanting to rut." Black Mary turned to those inside. "All men's good for is keeping up the species." The women laughed. They were earthy people, devoid of refinement.

Gracy was one of them, and she wasn't. She was born into a family like this one, but she'd been raised by a woman who'd gone to school, who'd insisted she speak and act properly. Still, the ways of the hill people didn't bother her. She liked to sit with the women while they made their remarks, joking about their men.

Women came together best at childbirth, Gracy thought. They forgot about chores that needed doing and worked to aid and comfort one of their own through her pain. They joyed together at the birth and sorrowed together when something went wrong.

She turned to see that an old woman had seated herself in the vacant rocker and taken out her piecing. Was there a woman in those mountains who didn't carry bits of material in her pocket, a precious needle pinning them together? Gracy herself brought her quilt pieces to a childbed, although she rarely had time to sit and stitch. Nabby had taught her to quilt, and as with most things she taught, Nabby had insisted Gracy do it right. Nabby's cabin held no heavy quilts made from big squares cut from men's britches. The old woman insisted her quilts be pretty, made from good fabric, the pieces uniform, put together so that the corners were square. And the stitching! Nabby had stitches as fine as a baby's eyelashes. She taught Gracy to sew the same way, with small, even stitches, and perhaps that was why when Gracy had to sew up a cut, the jagged edges of skin came together perfectly, her stitches as uniform as the ones on a quilt.

Gracy had started her quilts when she was just a tot of a girl, using Nabby's patterns—stars mostly. But after a time, she dreamed up her own designs. She took her patterns from leaves and plowed fields and the shapes of clouds. Nobody she knew made such quilts. Other women thought Gracy's quilts strange, but after a while, they came to like them. They fingered the abstract lines that represented rows of corn and the shapes that were goats and chickens. If Gracy had been a prideful woman, she would have preened over those quilts. But she was not taken much with self-worth and shrugged off the compliments.

Now she took a moment to peer at the old woman's quilt

square, a nine-patch made from faded material salvaged from worn-out clothing. "For the baby," the old woman said. "I am some behind because there was a baby born last week and one the week before. I am hard-pressed to keep up."

"You are Black Mary's mother," Gracy said.

The woman shook her head. "Lucy's husband's mother, come to bear witness to my grandson's birth."

Gracy grinned. "A boy, then."

"Of course. First one in our family's always a boy. Name'll be King David. My son's Jesse, and King David's the son of Jesse."

"Does Lucy know that?" Gracy asked.

"That's the way of it. Ain't her business."

"Oh."

"Saw you looking at Daniel. Best to keep away. His kind'll tear your heart out and stomp it flat."

"I don't know him. I haven't been over in these hills much since Marjorie was born."

"You will. There's something draws you two together. I saw it. You could no more stay away from him than you could stop birthing babies. Same with him. There's just things that are. You and Daniel's one of them."

"That's foolishness," Gracy said, her face red as she turned back to the woman on the bed.

"Maybe so, maybe not. Myself, I think it's better to have a love so great it breaks your heart than a little one that brings no pleasure. The Lord'll make you earn your sorrow with that one. He'll keep you to a hardship. You will set out with bright anticipations, but you are doomed to disappointment and will have a dreadful time of it." She sighed and muttered, "No Cross on earth, no crown in heaven."

It was only his hips, Gracy thought. She had a weakness for hips. That was all.

Gracy lost herself then in caring for the young woman on the bed. She put her thoughts behind her to tend the mother and babe, tend them wholeheartedly. The baby came quickly now, and when she caught him with hands still as small as a girl's—a boy, as the grandmother had prophesied—she was as happy as if she'd given birth herself. She studied the child a moment, checked him over before she put him into Black Mary's out-stretched arms.

"Is he . . . is he all right?" Lucy asked from the bed. Her face was flushed, and she was covered with perspiration.

"Of course he's all right," Black Mary thundered, before Gracy could answer.

But Lucy had addressed the question to Gracy and waited for the midwife's reply.

"He is at that," Gracy said. "He's as perfect as sunrise."

Black Mary tied off the cord and reached for Gracy's scissors, and when Gracy nodded, Black Mary cut the cord, then handed the baby around, while Gracy tended to the new mother. When all was done, Gracy took the baby back and handed him to Lucy. "See for yourself," she said. Then she whispered, "Better name him quick, before your husband does."

"I favor Abner," she said. Lucy held the baby against her breast, then looked around the room. "Where's Jesse?"

Black Mary offered to fetch him and threw open the door. "Best come in. See what you wrought, Jesse," she called.

The father rushed into the room, then stopped and gazed at his son.

"A boy," Black Mary told him.

Jesse tiptoed to the bed and smiled at his wife, who showed him the baby.

"King David," Jesse said as he touched the top of the baby's head with his finger.

"I favor Abner," Lucy told him.

"King David's the son of Jesse."

"Abner's the son of Lucy," the new mother said stubbornly.

"I always thought King David—"

"You name the next one. And you give birth to him, too, give birth through your ear. Them that has the baby names it," Black Mary told Jesse, fire in her eye. Lucy nodded. She was her mother's daughter.

For a moment, Jesse stared at his mother-in-law, then muttered, "Abner. Abner's the son of Jesse."

Gracy was amused at the exchange, thinking Lucy would do all right. The women in that family were a strong-minded lot. Maybe the men were, too. She glanced around the room. Old Man Brookens, Lucy's father, had come back inside, but Daniel was nowhere to be seen. It was just as well, she thought. She didn't want a bullheaded man. Besides, the old woman by the fire had talked foolishness.

Gracy gathered up her things. There was no need to stay longer, since Lucy had her mother and sisters to look after her. The new mother was healthy, would be out of bed long before the ten days of confinement were past. Maybe it was a good thing. In her place, Gracy wouldn't have stayed abed for even more than a minute. She laughed to think of herself lying on a quilt for days after childbirth. "I'll be going now. I'll come back in a few days, but if you need me before then, you send Marjorie for me," Gracy said.

The others barely noticed she was leaving, and Marjorie made no move to go for the mule. Gracy would have to walk. But she was used to it, even after a night spent with a woman in labor. She was young and healthy, and she loved the air in the hills, the wind that thrashed the leaves like a woman in labor, the flowers along the road, bright as colored glass. Besides, sooner or later, someone would come along and offer her a ride. She went out onto the porch and stared at the mountains that were black against the dawn light. It wasn't unusual for her to leave as the sun came up. Dawn was her favorite time of day. God birthed the world then, she thought. She stepped down off the porch, and as she did so, someone grabbed her bag.

"I'll see you home," Daniel said.

Gracy, startled, hadn't expected him to be there. "No need," she said. "I can walk it."

"I expect you can. I expect you can do most anything you set your mind to, but it's far off, and the mule's getting lazy. I'm a good hand with mules. Horses, too." He paused, and Gracy thought he might have smiled at her, but it was too dark to see. "I don't reckon Jesse paid you, did he?"

"It's all right. Maybe they'll send a jar of honey. The honey up here is awful good."

Daniel snorted. "Honey. That's no pay for a night's work." He reached into his pocket and took out a five-dollar gold piece and handed it to her.

"It's too much. I never got paid five dollars in my life."

"But you got paid a dime once." He reached up and touched the dime hanging from Gracy's neck, then left his hand there, warm against her flesh.

"The dime means more than the five-dollar piece," she said. "It's the one you gave me, you know. I expect you had to work maybe a month—maybe a year—to earn it."

"I thought you'd want more. I thought you'd throw it back to me."

Gracy looked up at Daniel, and his hand fell away. "It's the first money I ever earned, the best I ever earned, too. It gave me my calling."

"I guess you won't want to be anything but an old granny woman then," he said, teasing. "There aren't many fellows who'd want to take to wife a woman who'd put other people's kids before him."

"He'd have to understand, although I wouldn't want a man to feel second place."

"It'd take an awful big man for that."

Are you such a man? Gracy wanted to ask. But she was silent. A question like that would have been pert, would have shown she had a fondness for Daniel. Besides, she was not one to flirt, never had been. While the girls she had grown up with were already married, already mothers, Gracy had never had a way with men. She was too straightforward, too brusque. She was never fond of silly talk. Oh, boys had asked to walk her home from church. They had stopped by Nabby's cabin a time or two, asking if Gracy needed help chopping wood. But she had pointed to the woodpile she'd stacked cabin-high and said she was fine. They'd suggested a walk up the hillside to where the azaleas bloomed, but she'd nodded at the azaleas beside the barn and said she could see the blossoms from where she stood. Nabby had smiled and warned Gracy she wasn't likely to catch a husband by turning down courting. But Nabby had never married, and Gracy saw no need for a husband for herself. He'd only get in the way of her calling.

"You could do both," Nabby said. "No reason not to. Plenty of midwives are married."

"I don't know of a man who suits," Gracy replied.

Now, as Daniel helped her onto the mule, Gracy wondered if he would suit. He climbed up in front of her, and Gracy leaned against him, one arm holding her bag against her leg. Maybe he would, she thought. But it was likely he was doing no more than playing with her. He was as handsome a man as she'd ever seen, a man who could have any girl. Why would he choose her? She'd become a tall, bony woman, thin, her skin the color of white clay. Well, she did have nice legs, she told herself, better than most girls, trim ankles and slender calves. But it wasn't likely Daniel would ever know it—or any man, for that matter. The old woman was wrong. A man as striking as Daniel would never choose her. She would have to guard her heart.

They rode along easily, neither feeling the need to talk. Every now and then, Daniel pointed to a ridge of mountains that was lavender in the early light or a white-tailed deer hiding in the trees. He nodded at a burning bush and told her Black Mary called it hearts-a-bustin'-with-love. Once he stopped to take in the sunrise, a glorious sky with pick clouds edged with purple. Gracy'd never known a man to appreciate a sunrise like that.

"Makes me wish I was a painter," he said.

"Are you?"

Daniel shook his head. "But I've seen paintings, big ones."

"Where?"

"Oh, I've been here and there. I don't intend to spend my life farming these hills."

"Where would you go?" Gracy had never been more than twenty miles from Nabby's cabin and had never thought of leaving Arkansas.

"I've been to Kentucky and Georgia. I even went to the nation's capital, and I have in mind to make it to New York. I've seen buildings as tall as that pine tree."

"No," Gracy said in awe. She couldn't imagine such a thing.

"You ever thought of going someplace else?"

"I would like to go to Washington City and see President Jackson."

Daniel turned around and glanced at her. "You know who the President is then. Most girls don't."

"I've been to school. I never saw the sense of being stupid."

"No, I don't suppose you would."

"You're leaving Arkansas then?" Gracy hoped he didn't sense the disappointment in her voice.

"Oh, not just yet. But someday."

The bag was awkward, and Gracy switched it to her other arm. Would she ever leave? It wasn't Arkansas that held her so much. It was her work. And Nabby. She could be a midwife anywhere, but Nabby was old and tired. She needed caring, and Gracy wouldn't leave her. All she was she owed to Nabby. She smiled to herself. This was foolishness. Daniel was giving her a ride home. He wasn't asking her to go away with him. Gracy rarely had such silly thoughts, only sometimes late at night, walking home after a birthing, one in which the father shared his wife's pain, sat by her side and wiped her tears and cried a little himself. Those times, she dreamed of a home, a cabin chinked so tight the strongest wind couldn't get through, a chimney that didn't smoke, maybe a cookstove; she'd heard of them. There would be children, one of them a girl who would learn the skills of a midwife. All those dreams had been vague, however. There was no man's face in them. And there were times when Gracy thought that like Nabby, she would never marry, for she had not fancied any man.

Now, Gracy leaned against Daniel, felt his strong back warm through his shirt, felt her heart beat harder, and she wondered if that was love. She put her arm around him to steady herself, and Daniel placed his hand on top of hers. They rode along in the warm air, along a trail that was dappled with sunlight, not talking until they reached Nabby's cabin. Daniel jumped down off the mule and turned to help Gracy, but she had dismounted on her own. She should have waited for him to help her, she thought, but there was no need for a man to do for her when she could do for herself. She didn't know the ways of a young girl; she had been born old.

She thanked Daniel, then thought to ask if he would like a drink of water. When he nodded, she went to the water barrel and brought back the dipper. Daniel drank his fill, then handed the dipper to Gracy, who finished it.

"There's side meat, and I could make pancakes. I wager you haven't eaten since Lucy took to her bed."

Daniel grinned. "I'd like that."

Hiding her own smile, Gracy turned, but Daniel took her arm. "There's something else I've a mind to ask you," he said.

"Ask it."

"You know how to read and write?"

Gracy nodded.

"Teach me."

"You need learning, then?"

"I do. I have a fierce desire to know."

Slowly, Gracy nodded. So that was what he was after, not Gracy herself, not courtship, but reading and writing. She felt a flutter of disappointment, but she would not deny him. She herself had been so anxious for knowledge that she couldn't refuse someone else with the same desire. Only later did it occur to her that Daniel could have found a teacher on his side of the hills.

———

They married in the spring.

When Daniel asked, Gracy told him she wouldn't leave Nabby. The old woman had a lump in her breast the size of a walnut and was almost too frail to get out of bed.

"I'll wait," he said. "I'll wait if you'll promise to leave when it's over. I'm not of a mind to stay here."

"I have my work. I wouldn't want to give it up," she said, thinking no man would put up with the conditions she demanded.

"I wouldn't have it any other way. It's how I met you."

When Gracy told Nabby, the old woman said, "You go on. You can't save me. Don't wait for me to die."

Gracy refused.

"You don't think I'm making a mistake, do you, marrying him?" she asked Nabby once.

Nabby studied the young woman she had raised from a baby, looked at the thin face she loved and saw that it had softened, saw the way Gracy's eyes shone and she held her head high. Maybe she thought to warn her that Daniel would break her heart. She could have said such love would have its sorrows, that with love, Gracy would take on unhappiness, an unhappiness so great it would bow her down. But maybe it was Gracy's only chance at love. Nabby didn't want Gracy to be alone, her womb barren, not fulfilled like the wombs of the mothers she tended. Nabby herself had never had a man, but she had had Gracy, and that had been enough, more than enough. "No, I don't think he's a mistake," Nabby said. Then she warned, "But guard yourself well. When the time comes, and it will, remember that the sin is his."

Gracy did not understand, and so she did not heed the words then.

They stayed in Arkansas nearly a year, living in the cabin with Nabby until she died, within the week leaving for Kentucky—and later Illinois and Iowa. Then came word of gold discovered in California, and Daniel said that was where they would make their fortune.

Gracy did not put up a fuss. She loved the Midwestern farm where they lived then and the women she tended. She had hoped Daniel would settle there for good. The Bible said a woman's duty was to follow her husband, however, and besides, a part of her knew it was best to move on. They would start fresh, for by then, Gracy knew the sorrow Nabby had warned her about, the trouble the old woman, Jesse's mother, had prophesied, knew it even better than either of those women had warned.

Eight

It was Daniel who found her not long after sunrise.

The horse and buggy had returned to the stable without Gracy, Daniel told her later, wheel spokes broken out, reins dragging in the dirt. Earl, the stable boy, not taking the time to unhitch the horse, had rushed to the Brookens' cabin and pounded on the door.

"I was asleep," Daniel explained to Gracy, then looked away when he added, "I'd gone on a high lonesome."

Gracy knew that was unusual for him. Long ago when the promises had been made, one was that he wouldn't drink anymore. He'd backslid on that one. Not often. But sometimes the occasion called for it. Like that day. Gracy forgave him, because she knew you couldn't expect a man to hear that his wife was being charged with murder and not want to ease the pain.

"Earl came for me," he explained. "I'd thought someone was

knocking for you, but it was Earl there to tell me the horse had come back with the buggy and there was no sign of you. I told him to saddle a horse for me." Gracy imagined Daniel riding to her, riding fast. Even at his age, Daniel was a fine horseman, and folks would have stopped to watch as he sped past.

When Daniel found her, Gracy was lying in a ditch, unconscious, and she did not come to her senses until she heard a dog bark and then hurried footsteps. She curled into herself, thinking someone had come to hurt her. And then she heard Daniel's voice.

"Gracy!" he whispered. His voice was low and full of anguish. "Gracy! Are you all right? It's me. It's your Danny." He dropped down beside his wife, who lay facedown in the dirt, her cloak covering her like angel wings. "Gracy," he said once more. He knelt on one knee and gently turned her over, while she moaned a little. "Well, God!" he said when he heard her. "You're alive. Are you hurt bad?" he asked.

Not quite conscious, Gracy did not reply right away. She heard her husband's voice through a fog, felt him brush her hair from her face, knew he wiped away the dirt. He touched the lump on her head caused by the fall. Daniel felt her arms and then her legs, and Gracy moaned because one leg was twisted under her. She stirred a little and lifted her hand. "It hurts," she muttered.

"Be still," he told her. "John Miller's behind me, and Little Dickie. I told Earl to fetch them. They'll be here in a minute."

"The buggy . . ." Gracy muttered. "It tipped. Is Buddy . . . ?"

"Buddy made it to the stable. He's all right." Daniel reached for Gracy and held her, and despite the pain his embrace caused, she was glad.

"What happened?" she asked.

"There's a log in the road. It must have fallen off a wagon. I expect the buggy hit it."

"She all right?" a voice asked.

Gracy felt Daniel whirl around.

"Didn't hear you, John. I can't tell. She's had a bad fall, hurt her head, and her leg's twisted. I best get her home. Will you go back and bring a wagon?"

"No need. Earl says Little Dickie'll be on his way in one. I said to tell that doctor it was a matter of life and death and to hurry up or he'd have the town to face. He'll be along directly."

"'Bliged."

"She conscious?"

Daniel nodded. "Gracy, John Miller's here," he said in a loud voice, as though Gracy had lost her hearing. "I believe she's in some pain," he told John.

"Nothing me and you can do for her, I guess, till Little Dickie gets here. He's three removes from an idiot, but he's the only doctor we got." He paused, then said, "Dan, we ought to move that log before somebody else gets hurt."

"I'll be right here," Daniel whispered as he made a pillow for Gracy with his coat, then covered her with her cloak. "You watch over her," he told Sandy.

Gracy heard the two men grunt as they rolled the log to the side of the road. Then John said, "I wonder how that log got there. It's big enough for a mine timber. Must have fallen off a wagon, maybe going up to the Princess of India mill." He stopped, frowning. "But that don't make sense. The Princess is off Shirt Tail Canyon. You don't take the Mayflower Gulch trail to it. Nobody comes this way, just a few people that live on this side of the gulch. I bet not more than five or twelve use this trail in a day."

Gracy was fully conscious now, and she listened to the two men talk.

"That ain't no log. It's a tree," Daniel said. "Lookit there. Somebody's felled it a-purpose to lay across the road. You can see the stump over there and the hatchet marks on it. Whoever did this hacked off the branches so's you'd not notice it in the dark."

"Who'd do that?" John asked. The two men stared at each other for a time, and the sheriff answered his own question. "Maybe somebody who wanted to hurt a person coming down the road in the dark." Then he asked, "Do you think someone was after Gracy?"

"Why would anybody want to hurt her?"

"Maybe a man that thinks she killed a baby." John had lowered his voice, but he still spoke loud enough for Gracy to hear. She wondered if the two men knew she was listening.

"She never," Daniel said.

"You believe that, and so do I, but there's others . . ." He glanced down the road, hearing the sound of horses. "That'll be Little Dickie."

But it was not. Two men loomed up in the gloom of the trees, riding fast. When they saw Daniel and the sheriff, they stopped. Daniel faced them, his hands clenched. "What are you doing here?" he growled.

One of the men held up a hand and said, "Whoa, now, Brookens. Earl at the stable said the Sagehen's missing. We come to help," he said.

"There's others that'll search," the second man said. "We'd feel awful bad if something happened to the Sagehen."

Gracy tried to sit up so that the men could see she wasn't dead and raised her hand in a gesture of thanks.

"Mrs. Brookens is all right. She's here, just where we found her," the sheriff said, nodding his head at Gracy. "The dog's watched over her whilst we moved the log. It was in the middle of the road. Her buggy must have run into it and tipped. You know anything about that?"

The two riders glanced at each other. "Of course not," one said. "Probably a freighter dropped it."

"There isn't any reason for a freighter to be along here. Most likely somebody cut it down and not long ago, maybe just an hour or two," the sheriff said.

"Why'd he leave it like that?" the second man asked.

The question hung in the air, and none of the men answered it. They stared at each other until they heard a wagon and turned to see Little Dickie. Gracy turned to him, too.

"'Bout time you got here," John said.

Little Dickie ignored him as he climbed down from the wagon. "You found her?" he asked Daniel.

Daniel led him to where Gracy lay and knelt beside her.

"Move out of the way, then. I'll see to her," Little Dickie said in a voice that sounded almost arrogant.

Daniel held up his hand, stopping the doctor. "You be gentle. You hurt her, you answer to me."

"And me," John added.

"I'm a doctor. I don't hurt people," Little Dickie said. He reached into the wagon for his medical bag, then squatted down beside Gracy. "Mrs. Brookens," he said. His voice was high-pitched, and he lowered it. "Gracy. It's Dr. Erickson. Can you hear me?"

Gracy had slumped down and didn't answer, and John asked, "Is she gone up?"

"No," Little Dickie replied. "I shall use all of my medical skills, and they are considerable. She will be all right."

"God, hell! I hope you're more than book smart," Daniel thundered.

Little Dickie sniffed, then examined Gracy, touching the bruise on her head, feeling her limbs, stopping to examine her twisted leg. "Might be broke. Get her in the wagon," he said, and Gracy thought he sounded hopeful. Daniel and John lifted Gracy and carried her to the vehicle. Daniel climbed in and took the reins. "I'll drive. You tend her," he told the doctor.

"You know where my place is?" he asked.

"We're not going to your place. I'm taking her home," Daniel told him. "She won't want to wake up anywhere but her own bed."

"But—"

"Do like he says," John said quietly. "You don't want to rile him."

Daniel drove slowly to keep from jarring Gracy, but he couldn't miss all the holes and rocks in the road, and Gracy moaned from time to time as the buggy hit obstacles. John followed, leading Daniel's horse, the two men riding behind him. They passed other riders who had come to help, who called, "Earl says the Sagehen's hurt. Is she all right?" Daniel didn't answer them, but John said they were taking her home.

"We'll pray for her," one man said.

"Already done that," Daniel muttered.

Gracy, lying in the bed of the wagon, her cloak covering her, caught the words, and her eyes watered. Daniel was not a praying man. Then she heard her husband mutter, "If it please you, God, sir . . ."

"What's that?" Little Dickie asked.

"Mind your business," Daniel said.

In town, people stood along the road, a few with bowed heads, others staring. One man muttered, "She's tried to run away, has she?"

"Shut your mouth," a woman told him.

He shrugged. "That's what you do when you're guilty."

"Who says she is?"

When the procession reached the Brookens cabin, Daniel and John lifted Gracy out of the wagon and carried her into the house, laying her on the bed.

"I'll fetch you a basin of hot water," Daniel told the young doctor. He knelt beside the fireplace, added kindling, and started a blaze.

"I'll get her out of her clothes," Little Dickie said, and Daniel said no. Nobody but he would undress his wife.

"I can do it," Gracy whispered.

"I'll wait outside," John said. It was clear that the sheriff did not want to remain in the room while Gracy was being examined.

"You go, too," Little Dickie told Daniel.

"I'm staying."

"You'll just be in the way. I'll wager your wife doesn't want men around when she's delivering a baby."

"Come along. We need to talk about that tree," John said.

Daniel was stubborn. "You go. I'm staying." He stood beside the bed and unbuttoned Gracy's dress. She could have done it more easily herself, but she wouldn't stop Daniel from helping her. Then he held the garment, still warm from Gracy's body, smoothing it with his hand, as if the dress were Gracy herself. She was a little ashamed then of the dress, faded from too many washings, and worn. The material was so thin in places that Daniel could have poked his finger through it. The collar had been white, but it was gray with age and had been mended, and more than once. Daniel had forgotten her bonnet, so Gracy reached up and removed it. The bonnet was old, too, worn and faded from the sun. She had trimmed it last year—or was it the year before?—but the new ribbons were wrinkled and the color washed out.

The doctor began to examine Gracy, and Daniel went to the

other end of the room, as if embarrassed. After a time, John came back into the cabin. "I'm real sorry," John said. "I hope she's all right. I can't think what we'd do without her. Gracy's the only woman I admire as much as I did Elizabeth."

"She's the best woman . . ." Daniel couldn't finish, and Gracy, lying on the bed, reached out her hand. But Daniel had turned away.

"I'll go back to that tree, check the axe marks now that the sun's out, see what I can find out," John said. The doctor had gone to his wagon for something, and the two men raised their voices a little, and Gracy could hear them clearly.

"Everybody in Swandyke's got an axe. You can't tell one axe mark from another."

"You're right about that. But maybe there's something else I can find. Might be he dropped something—a button, a cigar."

"You think this was done a-purpose to hurt Gracy? You thinking somebody wanted to kill her, then." Daniel lowered his voice but not enough.

"I do."

"Who? There's nobody would do such a thing."

"One man."

Daniel looked at the sheriff.

"Jonas Halleck."

Daniel shook his head back and forth as he considered the name. "You think he really believes Gracy killed that baby?"

"Of course he don't believe it. I bet he done it himself. I can't prove it, though."

Daniel turned away for a moment as if collecting his

thoughts. "If it was Halleck felled that tree, he should have made sure it killed her, because Gracy doesn't scare."

"No, I don't," she muttered.

"You know that, Dan, and Gracy there knows it, and I know that. Jonas Halleck don't." He paused. "My guess is *he* didn't put that tree there. Most likely, he was in the mine office with somebody to vouch for him. He sent a man to do it."

"But you can't prove that, either," Gracy muttered.

"No, I can't. But I'll try." The doctor returned to the room, and the sheriff was quiet. After a moment, he went out, leaving the door open. Daniel sat down in his chair and stared at the bed until there was a soft knock on the doorjamb.

"Somebody's been at your tin can pile, Mr. Brookens," a voice observed.

Gracy raised her head off the bed. There had been too much activity in that can pile. It was just outside the window, and Jonas Halleck must have sent someone to snoop. She recognized the woman and smiled. "Hello, Mittie," she called. The woman was Mittie McCauley from her quilt group.

"I heard you been hurt. You all right?"

Daniel answered for Gracy. "Dr. Erickson says so."

"Oh, Little Dickie. I'd rather Gracy tended me any day. He's learning proud."

Gracy glanced up at the doctor, who heard the remark and reddened. She was glad when Daniel replied, "Maybe he's not so bad."

Mittie held out a plate to Daniel. "I brung you an apple cake.

It's all I had, but Gracy's been good to me, so I wanted to bring something. I expect before the day's out, you'll have enough food for a week."

Daniel nodded. Then he said in a loud voice to Gracy, "Mrs. McCauley's brought you a cake."

"I came to sit up with her," the woman said.

Daniel shook his head. "No need," he said firmly. "I'll do it."

"She's my friend," Mittie insisted. Then she added, "This thing about the Halleck baby . . ."

"What about it?"

"I don't believe a word of it. But there's others. Folks out there's willing to believe the worst of a person, and some of them are women Gracy's been good to. I just feel like I ought to be here, to stand up for her. I wouldn't want her left alone for fear—"

"Nobody'd hurt Gracy!"

The woman shook her head. "Looks like maybe somebody already tried."

When Little Dickie finished with Gracy, he pulled a quilt up to her chin and told Daniel and Mittie they could go to her.

"I gave you a scare," she whispered.

"She shouldn't talk," Little Dickie said. "She hit her head bad, and she'll have to stay in bed a week."

"Oh, bosh!" Gracy muttered, then sank back into the pillow as if the words had been too much for her.

Little Dickie ignored her. "Her leg isn't broken, and that's a miracle I'd say, but it was twisted around and it'll hurt her for a time, maybe a long time. Maybe forever. She can take laudanum if the pain gets bad."

"I never took opiates in my life, and I won't start now."

"I put ointment on the bruises and cuts—"

"Kerosene works fine," Gracy said.

"You let her rest," Little Dickie told Daniel. "I'll come back this evening and check on her."

He stood and made for the door, but Gracy called to him and he stopped. "I'm obliged, Dr. Erickson. I'm grateful for your care. Maybe I wouldn't have made it without you."

The doctor stood a little straighter and nodded.

"I'll pay you now," Daniel said, reaching into his pocket and taking out a coin. "Is that enough?"

"It's enough." Little Dickie took the money and smiled a little. "Wish everybody was so prompt in paying." As he opened the door, he asked Daniel in a low voice, "You find out who cut down that tree?"

"The sheriff's working on it. You got any ideas?"

"Me?" The doctor appeared flustered and shook his head. "How would I know?"

"You seemed to have a powerful hate for Gracy yesterday."

"And I saved her life today," he replied, picking up his bag and leaving the house.

When the doctor was gone, Daniel asked Gracy, "You think Little Dickie might have saved your life?"

Gracy smiled. "No, but what harm does it do for him to think it?"

"You're a good woman," Daniel said, and sat down on the edge of the bed. Mittie, as if finding the conversation too personal, went to the dry sink and busied herself.

"You really think somebody tried to kill me?" Gracy asked.

Daniel thought a long time, then sighed. "I don't know, honey. Your buggy hit a tree that was laying across the road. I don't believe it was there by accident. I think somebody cut it down so's you'd hit it. John thinks so, too."

"Somebody tried to scare me?" She shivered a little, glad Daniel was there to protect her but wishing Jeff were, too. He'd been her protection ever since he was a little boy and had thrown rocks at a mean dog to scare it away from his mother.

Daniel nodded.

"Or kill me?"

"Maybe so."

"But they didn't." Then she teased, "Are you awful glad, Danny?"

Daniel clasped her hand. She thought he wanted to tell her he loved her, but Daniel wasn't much for such talk. Besides, Mittie McCauley was in the room. It didn't matter, however, because Gracy knew.

Nine

Mittie McCauley came every day, bringing soup, a loaf of bread, a bit of cobbler made with the last of the raspberries on Potato Mountain. At first, Daniel growled. After all, he could take care of his wife. But the young woman brightened Gracy's day, and besides, Mittie's offerings varied Daniel's cooking, giving them something to eat besides fried meat and potatoes. For this, Gracy was thankful.

Mittie did more than bring food. She washed out the rags Gracy had used birthing the twins in Mayflower Gulch and spread them over bushes in the sun to dry, mended Gracy's dress, which had been torn in the fall from the carriage, tidied the cabin. Perhaps best of all, she brought Gracy scraps of fabric in her favorite blue, and the two sat in the sun piecing.

Mittie herself was like a bit of sunshine. Gracy remembered

the first time the girl had come to the cabin, five, maybe six years before. Gracy had looked out the window and seen her staring at the house. She was slight but wiry, with sun-bleached hair and sunburned skin. She reached down and picked up a tin can that had fallen onto the trail and pitched it on top of the pile.

The girl looked determined. She stood for a minute or two, staring at the house, her hands at her sides. She took a few steps, then stopped as she continued to stare. Then, determined, she walked to the cabin, straightened her back, and knocked. When Gracy opened the door, the girl said in a rush of breath, "I need your help." And then she seemed to wilt, as if the words had taken all her strength. She clamped her mouth shut and seemed about to turn tail and run off.

Women had come to Gracy before like this, had stood on her doorstep, mute as moles, thinking she could guess what they wanted, and sometimes she did. She stepped aside and gestured for Mittie to enter the cabin, knowing it wouldn't do to prod. The girl would tell her in time or she'd make some excuse for calling, maybe say she'd come for the borrow of a spool of thread, and then leave without ever revealing what she wanted.

After a time, when her visitor didn't mouth a word, Gracy said, "I recollect you now. You're Mittie McCauley, aren't you?"

The girl was startled. "How'd you know?"

"I remember you from the church quilting. You took stitches as small as mustard seeds."

The girl smiled her pride. "I am vain about my quilting."

"You have good reason to be."

Mittie didn't respond, and Gracy waited until Mittie said again, "I need your help." She twisted her hands and opened her mouth, but no more words came out.

So Gracy at last asked, "You're having a baby, and you don't want it?"

Ever since Gracy had become a midwife, women had approached her and asked how to get rid of babies growing inside them. Gracy always listened. She offered comfort, told each woman that another baby wasn't so bad or that the young man who'd gotten her pregnant was ripe for marriage and all she had to do was tell him her condition. Gracy didn't judge, because she knew a woman had her reasons for not wanting a baby. She might have too many to care for already or was sick and thought another might kill her, and without her, what would become of the little ones? There were those who hadn't any husbands, who'd been sweet-talked into lying with a miner or a traveling man who wouldn't own up to being the father. Unmarried, pregnant, a girl might be disowned by her family and thrown out with no place to go except to one of the whorehouses. There were indeed reasons not to have a baby, and Gracy had heard them all. She didn't want to abort the babies, not with instruments anyway; it went against her nature. But she was always sympathetic. If the women were insistent on ending their pregnancies, Gracy usually sent them to the woman doctor in Central City, the one who advertised her specialty was treating women who were "irregular."

Some of the women were too poor to afford a real doctor, however. Or they couldn't get away to Central, for their husbands or families didn't know about the babies, and what excuse could a woman use to disappear for a day? So Gracy gave them lady's mantle or squaw vine, which were recommended to bring on a woman's monthly, but the herbs mostly didn't work.

A few women were so desperate they threatened to kill themselves. Those were the ones who troubled Gracy the most, the ones who were on her heart, even years later. It wasn't right, Gracy taking a baby like that, she who had lost so many herself. But it wasn't right, either, to risk the life of a mother too run-down to care for the children she already had or destroy the future of a young girl barely past puberty who'd fallen for a sweet talker. One or two times, Gracy suspected, the baby had come about because a father had lain with his own daughter. Those were the ones Gracy ached over, the ones that made her wonder if God intended His gift to her to be used for death as well as life. She never talked to Daniel about what she did, never talked to anybody. After all, it was against the law for a midwife to take an unborn baby. But the law didn't care about women the way Gracy did.

Sometimes she felt the Lord didn't care, either, else why would He make childbirth such a danger to women. Why did He let women die when He could have told Gracy how to save them? Why did He seem to let his wrath settle on her when a mother or a baby died?

Mittie stared at Gracy a long time, then shook her head. "Oh, no, ma'am." She put her hands over her mouth. "Is that what you're thinking, that I want to get rid of a baby?"

Gracy waited.

"I would never do that. Ever. I'd rather die than kill a precious baby. I came to see you for the opposite reason."

Gracy frowned, not understanding, and Mittie said in a rush, "I want a baby in the worst way. I've tried and tried, tried for eight years, and I'm barren as a molly mule." The girl let out her breath and hugged herself. She was too embarrassed to look at Gracy, and she used her foot to worry a tin can lid nailed over a knothole in the floor.

"Oh, my dear," Gracy said, and reached for the girl's hands. "I know the sorrow, know it myself."

"But you've got a son."

"Yes, and it took a long time before he came to me. I lost so many before him." She wished Mittie could know the joy she'd had when Jeff smiled at her the first time, a toothless, wet grin, or came running into the cabin to tell her about his first day of school. He brought her the earliest columbine each spring, and together, they would smooth it flat and press it in the Bible. Even when Jeff was older, his face would light up when he came through the door and saw his mother.

Mittie looked up, and Gracy could see her visitor was beyond girlhood, with worry wrinkles around her eyes. "Can you help me? You see, I got a good husband, but he's about fed up with me," Mittie said. "I worry he'll taken out on me. He wants a son something fierce. What if he leaves me for somebody who can give him one? Then what would I do?"

"Have you ever conceived?" Gracy asked.

The girl looked embarrassed. "No, ma'am."

"Then maybe the fault is his."

Mittie's mouth dropped open. "How could that be? He's a man."

"It happens."

"Well, I never heard such a thing, and Henry—he's my husband—he'd tell me I was crazy to say such." She smiled a little. "He's a big old fellow and likes his time in bed. The very idea!"

Gracy nodded. She knew men believed they could not be at fault, but if a wife never even got pregnant, it was possible her husband was the reason. Gracy knew of too many times when a woman was "barren" with her first husband but fecund with her second.

Mittie leaned forward and said earnestly, "You're the Sagehen. You know all about babies. I thought you'd give me something so's I could have one. Ain't there some way? Ain't there?" She thought a moment. "Do you think somebody put a spell on me?"

Gracy had grown up with spells and incantations. She didn't really believe in superstitions, although she didn't run afoul of them, especially the ones about quilting. She never started a quilt on a Friday, just as Granny Nabby warned her, for a woman who did so wouldn't live to finish it. She always wrapped a quilt around herself when it was finished, for good luck. And there was a time she'd been pleased when she broke her needle while quilting with her friends, because it meant she would have the next baby.

But she did not believe that burning flowers brought death or that a wedding after sundown meant the couple would be unhappy. And she especially did not believe that one person could cast a spell on another.

Still, she knew others accepted such things, and Nabby had explained that it was enough just to believe. A woman who was sure a cat walking across her sickbed meant death, might just give up. A man who woke up with the moon shining in his face could make himself turn crazy. It wasn't that the superstitions were true, it was that the mind could make them so. You couldn't just dismiss them. You had to give a cure. So Nabby once told a girl who believed she had boils because she'd been bewitched to burn a hair of the woman who'd put a spell on her, at midnight in the dark of the moon, and the boils would go away. And they had. When Gracy asked how Nabby had known the antidote, Nabby said she hadn't but had made it up on the spot. So Gracy took such beliefs seriously.

But before Gracy could answer the girl, however, Mittie said, "I guess I don't believe there's any spell on me. Who would do such a thing? I ain't got any enemies, and Henry, why, he's just a big old bear everybody loves."

"So you want—"

"I want a herb, a potion, something that'll get me with child," Mittie interrupted. "Ain't you got something?"

Gracy sighed. That was it, of course. The girl wanted some magic concoction. Gracy was a believer in herbs. Black pepper sped up labor, and sometimes wild yam prevented conception, although not often enough. Hot ginger brought on menstruation.

But first, she would talk to the girl, ask her if there were other problems. She led Mittie to Daniel's chair and told her to sit. Then she took her own place and leaned forward, her hands grasping Mittie's. "Sometimes the act isn't done right," she began.

Mittie stared at Gracy, confused at first. When she understood, she glanced away, her face red. "It's not worth talking about."

"Yes, if you truly want a baby, it is." Gracy paused. "There's the makings for coffee if you'd like a cup. I already built a fire. It's no trouble to heat the water and grind the beans."

"No, thanks to you. I had my coffee already this morning."

"Tea, then?"

Mittie shook her head.

"So be it." Gracy squeezed the girl's hands and said, "There's men that practice what's called withdrawal. Now mostly that's done to keep from having a baby, but sometimes men have other reasons." A wife had once told Gracy that her husband did that for fear she'd rob him of his strength. "Do you understand what I'm asking you?"

Mittie nodded and squirmed in her seat. "That ain't the problem. We're fine that way."

"And you don't wash yourself right off?"

"I lie there still as a log so's all that will go up into my womb." Mittie was so embarrassed that she hunched up her shoulders and stared over Gracy's head, not looking her in the face.

"I had to ask," Gracy said. "You see, there's some with strange notions, and seeing as I don't know you . . . how would I know . . ." Her voice trailed off as she smiled at Mittie.

"I guess you do have to ask, but me and Henry, we're all right that way. It's just something in me that won't get a baby started, and I heard about you . . ." Mittie looked Gracy in the face.

"Have you tried raspberry tea?" Gracy asked.

"I've drunk so much raspberry tea my skin almost turned red. Ain't there something else?"

Gracy nodded. She went to the pie safe and took out red clover and explained to the girl how to take it.

And so Mittie had taken it for weeks, months even, but the red clover hadn't caused her to conceive. Later on Gracy gave her alfalfa and then nettles, but they didn't work, either. Over the years, each time either one of them heard of a remedy, Mittie would try it, but nothing caused the young woman to conceive. Eventually, Gracy talked to her about adoption. There were so many babies and young children who needed homes. But Mittie was adamant. "I want my own baby. I couldn't never love somebody else's like my own."

Gracy had come to love the young woman, had thought Emma would have grown up to be like her, and indeed, at times, the two were almost like mother and daughter. They shared a fondness for quilting and Bible reading, and Gracy had hoped the girl might learn about the herbs, about midwifery, although she wasn't sure Mittie was bent that way. Gracy grieved for Mittie's plight, just as she had once grieved over her own.

Now, the two sat outdoors a few days after Gracy's accident, stitching in sunlight that sifted through the jack pines. "I believe I have my strength back, although my leg still bothers me. It wasn't broke, only twisted, and I limp a bit," Gracy observed.

"I'm lucky there weren't any babies born this week. But I expect the Richards girl will deliver anytime. I best be ready."

"She gave birth yesterday," Mittie said, then looked away as if she shouldn't have blurted out the news that way. She paused as she placed one quilt piece on top of another, not looking at Gracy.

The old woman put down her needle. "She didn't call for me? She must have thought I was too ill, but I could have gone to her. Richards women have an easy time of it."

Mittie turned her head to stare at a squirrel that was hollering.

"Did her sisters help with the birthing?"

Mittie looked directly at Gracy then. "She sent for Little Dickie."

"Dr. Erickson? Rebecca Richards told me she'd as soon give birth by herself as have him do it."

"She must have thought you were too poorly to come."

Gracy glanced at the quilting in her lap. "Or she thought I might harm the baby. Is that it?" Gracy looked squarely at Mittie. They were not women to hide a truth, to sugarcoat and coddle and put a better face on a thing than it deserved. "What are they saying about me, Mittie?"

The young woman put down her own sewing, smoothing it with her fingers. She took her time, glancing down the trail as if she'd heard footsteps. Then she looked at Gracy. "There's some that say you done it."

"I know that. There's been talk at the saloon. Daniel told me."

"I mean among the women."

"Edna Halleck?"

"I haven't heard her say it, haven't seen her in fact, but it might be that's where it started. At the mercantile, there was some saying they wouldn't trust you. Effie Ring said she'd always suspicioned you after she lost her girl last year."

Gracy thought that over. Effie Ring's baby had come too soon, and thank the Lord, because the poor thing had been born with deformed arms. Effie had begged Gracy not to tell anyone, even her husband, and she hadn't—hadn't breathed a word. She'd buried the infant behind the Ring cabin, buried it under the columbine. Effie had blamed herself, said she was a sinner because she'd lusted after a miner at the Tiger, although the two had never done anything more than kiss. Gracy had replied that sinning had not a thing to do with it. The Lord didn't punish women by hurting their babies. Besides, what was wrong with admiring a figure as handsome as a fireman and doing a little flirting?

Gracy was aware, however, that knowing a secret could create an enemy. She hadn't thought Effie would turn against her, but maybe the woman regretted that Gracy knew so much. Perhaps Gracy shouldn't have been surprised. "Are there others?" she asked Mittie.

"Coy Chaney's wife."

"That one's to be expected."

"Maybe one or two more."

Gracy didn't ask their names. She sat for a long time, her sewing in her lap. It hadn't been a week since the Halleck baby was murdered, and yet some already had found her guilty, blamed her for the sorrow that made her ache as much as it did Josie Halleck. "I've been thinking it might be time to give up my work." There, she'd said it out loud.

Startled, Mittie raised her hands to her face. "Not deliver babies? Why, you're the best there is. The only one there is. You're the last midwife. What would women do without you?"

"There's the doctor."

"I wouldn't let him deliver my baby. I wouldn't at all."

"I've already been thinking about calling it deep enough," Gracy said. She didn't tell the girl the real reason, that she could no longer take the burden on her heart of the hardships, the deaths of women and children that were part of childbirth. Instead, she said, "With Daniel not working in the winters, he's home by himself and lonesome. I got to think about him."

"Does he want you to quit?"

Gracy shook her head. "I don't know. I haven't told him. I've only been thinking about it. But maybe it's not for me to decide. Maybe nobody'll want me after this."

"I'll want you."

Gracy almost said it wasn't likely Mittie would ever have need of her that way, but such a remark would have been cruel. Gracy only smiled and said, "I wouldn't quit *you*."

"What are they saying about me in town?" Gracy asked Daniel that night after supper. The two sat in their chairs facing the fireplace, the cabin lit only by the dying fire and the glow of a kerosene lamp.

He shrugged. "Oh, you know how folks love to gossip. Men's as bad as women. I wouldn't put much worry into what a drunk miner or two says."

"The women are talking, too. Mittie told me."

Daniel pounded his fist on the arm of his chair. "She shouldn't have."

"Yes, she should. I need to know."

"Then you ought to know that mostly, folks don't believe you killed that baby, despite what Jonas Halleck says."

"Does anybody think *he* did it?"

Daniel pondered that. He leaned forward in his chair and began to unlace his boots. "There's aplenty that don't like Halleck, but it wouldn't be a good idea to speak against him. You remember when he accused me of high-grading? Quite a few came to the house to tell me they knew I didn't do it, but I don't recollect anybody saying it in public. There's not many would want to bring down the wrath of Jonas Halleck."

"Worse than the wrath of God," Gracy said.

Daniel pulled off his boots and stretched out in the chair. "Truth of it is, Gracy, and I know you want it told to you straight, I haven't heard a soul say Mr. Halleck did it—except for John Miller. And that's a strange thing, because John's doing everything he can to find evidence against you."

"That's his job."

"Well, it's a mighty poor job if it means trying to put you in jail. After all you done for him!" Daniel reached for a tin of paste and a rag and started oiling a boot.

"Time for you to get new boots. You've worn those since we

came here." Gracy picked up the second boot and began rubbing the oil in with her fingers. "I'd rather have John Miller gathering evidence instead of somebody who doesn't know me. At least he'll be fair. It's worrisome that Jonas Halleck might be trying to get some of his people to talk against me." She got up and went to the pie safe for a rag, then sat down again and began to polish the boot. "Like I said, some of the women have already turned on me."

"And after all you've done for them, too!" Daniel set down the boot, disgusted, and looked at Gracy.

"Oh, there were always a few who didn't like me, but it seems there's more of them than I knew. Mittie thinks Edna Halleck might be behind it. I'm not so sure. She's a good woman. Maybe Mr. Halleck put her up to it."

"I sure wish Jeff would come home. Maybe he could help."

Gracy stared at her husband. "Jeff?" She wanted her son close, all right, had wanted it every day since he'd left out. He always managed to make her smile, to feel whole, despite her sorrows. Still, maybe it was best he was away. She didn't want him caught up in her troubles.

"Might be he will."

Gracy jumped at the sound of another voice that came through the open doorway, and Daniel said, "God, hell! Who's there?"

"It's only John Miller," the sheriff replied, stepping into the room.

"How long have you been standing there listening in?" Daniel asked.

"Just a minute."

"Well, I hope it was long enough for you to hear me say I thought you weren't much of a man, trying to find evidence against Gracy like you're doing."

"What do you think a sheriff's supposed to do? I got to get the evidence against Gracy if it's there. That's what I'm paid to do."

"That's what Gracy says, but that don't hardly make it right."

"You'd rather one of Mr. Halleck's men handled it? That's who'd be appointed sheriff if I left. You know I'd quit if it would help Gracy, but I'm helping her more by being sheriff."

Gracy put her hand on Daniel's arm to still him, then said to John, "There's coffee, fresh made an hour ago."

"Save it for breakfast."

Daniel didn't rise, didn't offer John his hand. Instead, he gave the sheriff a surly look and asked, "What are you doing here, trying to find more lies about Gracy?"

The sheriff regarded him a moment, then reached out his hand to the dog and let Sandy sniff it.

"Dog doesn't know the difference between friend and foe," Daniel said.

"You're the sorriest old leather belly I ever met up with. You don't know when a man's come to help. It's a wonder Gracy puts up with you."

Picking up the coffeepot, Gracy went to the fireplace and set it in the coals. "I guess I could stand a little coffee myself. I'll get a cup out for you in case you change your mind, John. Daniel?"

Her husband grunted, which Gracy decided was a yes.

"How can you help when you're trying to turn up something bad about Gracy?" Daniel asked. He picked up a sack of tobacco and pinched enough for his pipe before he held out the bag to John, who shook his head.

"First off, I brought the name of that lawyer fellow I told you about, Gracy—Ted Coombs. I already sent him a copy of what I turned up. I copied out the coroner's report for him, and I haven't even give it to the prosecutor yet. I thought I'd let you have first crack so you'd know what you're up against, although I expect it's against the law for me to do. It puts a hard point on it, me being sheriff and trying to help a friend, too." He stared at Daniel, who dropped his eyes. "Dan, you know I'd do anything in the world to save Gracy," he said.

"I know," Daniel said softly, filling his pipe, then lighting it.

"What did you turn up?" Gracy asked. She used the hem of her apron to lift the coffeepot out of the fireplace, then poured the black brew into three cups. "I should have made fresh. You deserve it," she said, handing a cup and saucer to John. He poured the coffee into the saucer to cool, which made Gracy wonder why she'd heated it in the first place.

"There are folks saying bad things about you. I won't deny it. You want me to tell you or not?"

Gracy sat down in her chair and took Daniel's hand, then nodded. "We've been talking about that."

"The way I see it, there ain't much hard evidence. What it boils down to is your word against Jonas Halleck's. He's not liked much, but folks respect him for being rich and smart, and plenty will believe him. He said he was there when you done it. He didn't see you tie a string around the baby's neck, but he said you were the last person to tend that baby before he picked it up dead. Couldn't nobody else have done it but you. That's what he says."

Gracy nodded. She knew all that.

"You believe that, John?" Daniel asked.

"I've told you what I believe, but it don't matter. It's what a jury'll believe, and you'll likely get a miner or two from the Holy Cross on it if you're not careful. Not many folks would want to call Jonas Halleck a liar. He's too powerful."

"I checked that baby over before I laid him in his cradle, and he was sleeping when I left. That's the God's truth." Gracy remembered how she had held the baby tight against her chest before she set him in the tiny bed, then had let her hand linger on his cheek, reluctant to turn away, not knowing if she would ever touch him again.

"I know that," John told her.

"What else do you have?"

There was the testimony Coy Chaney and Little Dickie Erickson would give, he said, but Gracy already knew about that. Then John cleared his throat. "This will surprise you, Gracy. Georgia Simmons and Pearlie Evans both say they suspected you of killing their infants."

If the charges surprised Gracy, she didn't show it, not at first. She thought that over for a long time, before she replied, "Georgia's husband works at the Cross. Pearlie wanted me to give her something . . ." Gracy didn't finish, because she didn't talk about the women who had come to her to terminate their pregnancies.

Pearlie Evans had asked Gracy to perform an abortion because she'd gotten pregnant one summer when her husband was away prospecting. Pearlie was sickly, and Gracy had told her the abortion might kill her. The woman had been as mad as a yellow jacket and swore Gracy hadn't the right to say no. The baby had come early, and nobody was the wiser. Gracy thought Pearlie had gotten over her anger. Now it was clear she hadn't.

"There's men, too," John said. He picked up the saucer and held it to his mouth. "I don't put much store in what most say, seeing as how they work at the Cross. But Boston Chowder don't work there, and he says you got a temper that beats all."

At that, Gracy chuckled. He had indeed seen her temper, seen it when Gracy told him he'd have to keep away from his wife for six weeks after she gave birth. The man's name was Barton Crowder, but he was so mad at Gracy that he'd spit out a mouthful of milk punch, and Gracy had said it looked like Boston chowder. The story had stuck, and so had the name. She should have had better sense.

"Can those men testify? What they say doesn't have anything to do with the Halleck baby," Daniel asked.

"No, it don't, and I believe they can't be called. What they talked about doesn't have a bearing, as they say, on the case against Gracy. Still, it depends on the judge. You better hope you get a judge who isn't in debt to Jonas Halleck." John slurped the rest of his coffee and rose. "That offer's still open, Gracy."

Daniel frowned. "What offer's that?"

"One I wouldn't take," Gracy replied, and then thought she might have been wise to consider it.

Ten

"Are you sure you feel like quilting today?" Mittie asked Gracy.

"Of course I do. When did I ever not feel like quilting?" Gracy shoved a half-finished quilt block into a flour sack, along with her needle and scissors and scraps of material. She moved slowly, because she still hurt from her fall.

"I mean going to quilting. Maybe you hadn't ought to come."

Gracy tied the ends of the sack and started to drop it into her medicine bag. She almost never went anywhere without the bag, even to quilting, not since Marianna Martin went into labor one afternoon right there at the quilt frame. "*I* know what you mean," she told Mittie. "You're afraid Edna Halleck will attend, maybe Josie, too, and there will be a set-to."

Caught, Mittie looked down at her toe and scraped it back and forth over Gracy's braided rug. "I don't want you to have to hear mean things."

"I might as well get used to it. There will be plenty of mean things said if there's to be a trial. The hearing is next week."

"What's a hearing?" Mittie asked.

"It's where the prosecutor gives the judge all the evidence the sheriff collects against me. I guess Jonas Halleck and Coy Chaney will have their say, and maybe Little Dickie. Then the judge decides whether there's enough to put me on trial. The thing is, at the hearing, I won't be able to say a word. I'll have to wait until the trial to defend myself."

"That sheriff's been going around asking about you, asking about things you done, asking about *gossip*. He ought to be ashamed of hisself."

"He doesn't have any choice. He's the sheriff. That's his job."

"I told him to get out of my house."

It was nice having friends, loyal friends who stood up for her, Gracy thought. Mittie was one, and there would be others, although perhaps not as many as she had once thought.

Gracy decided not to take the medicine bag after all, since as far as she knew, no one who'd be sewing that day was pregnant She left the bag in the pie safe and slung the flour sack with her scissors and needle and scraps of fabric over her shoulder. "If I don't go to quilting, women will say I'm ashamed to show myself. They'll talk about me even more. I don't much want to face them, but it's best I get it over with. It'll only be worse if I wait. I've spent too much time to home as it is."

Mittie didn't seem so sure. She set a slow pace as they made their way to the church, where the quilting was always held, stopping two or three times to ask Gracy if the walk tired her, for the old woman limped badly, despite the walking stick that Daniel had made for her from the trunk of a young aspen tree, stripping the bark and polishing it until it looked like ivory. Once, Mittie stepped off the trail to admire a patch of butter-and-eggs that were a creamy yellow in the soft morning, and another time she picked a perfect aspen leaf off a tree, held it up, and remarked that it looked like a heart. She could trace around it and make a pattern for quilting, she said.

Gracy knew the girl was dawdling, and at last she told her, "Best to hurry it up, Mittie. If we're late, we won't find a place around the frame to sit. Is there a quilt ready for us or are we going to work on our own piecing? Maybe I should have brought Daniel's stockings to darn."

"Nancy Culpin's got her quilt set in. She asked for the borrow of my frame. I don't look forward to the quilting of it." She sent Gracy an accusatory look. "If you'd stayed home we wouldn't have to work on it."

"I'm fit as I'll ever be," Gracy said, although her face was still badly bruised, and the limp was worse than when she'd started out.

They stopped at the churchyard to open the gate, then put the wire loop over the fencepost to keep the gate shut. The women were careful to do that because the yard was filled with flowers, not that a shut gate would keep animals from eating them.

The quilters were just then taking places around the frame

when Gracy and Mittie entered, and their chatter stopped, except for a remark one woman said to another under her breath.

"They don't say nothing out loud, just whisper," Mittie said to Gracy, whispering herself.

Nancy Culpin looked startled and said she hadn't known Gracy was up to quilting. "I thought you'd be at home being dilatory," she said.

"Nobody ever accused the Sagehen of laziness," Mittie defended Gracy.

"No, no. I'll have to find another chair. I didn't expect you." Gracy caught the long look Nancy gave Mittie, not sure whether Nancy was put out that Mittie hadn't told her Gracy would be there or annoyed that Mittie hadn't kept Gracy away. It would be as awkward an afternoon as she had ever spent.

She looked around at the dozen women, relieved that neither Edna nor Josie Halleck was there. Gracy had thought she might have to excuse herself if those two attended. Still, one of Rebecca Richards's sisters was present, along with Effie Ring. Pearlie Evans was there, too, and she wouldn't look Gracy in the eye. Gracy knew both Effie and Pearlie had spoken against her. The air in the room seemed as thick as smelter smoke, and Gracy thought perhaps Mittie had been right, that she shouldn't have come. But she had, and she was determined to stay. Walking out would only make things worse. She stiffened her back as she gripped the walking stick.

"Take chairs," Nancy told the women. "Thread you a needle and commence." The women sat and removed their needles from their sacks or under their collars or hems or wherever they kept them. None of the women was so rich that she owned needles enough for an entire sewing circle, so each brought her own. Some were lucky to have even a spare. Nancy reached for an emery bag and pushed her needle in and out more times than was necessary. Gracy didn't know whether she was nervous to see what the women thought of her quilt or because Gracy had shown up.

Gracy took a chair near the center of the quilt and turned to Rebecca Richards's sister Martha Richards, thinking how nice it would be to have a sister to quilt with—or a daughter. She'd once thought she and Emma would quilt together when the child was older. In fact, Gracy had already taught her to stitch a seam and had kept the little girl's work folded up in a paper in the bottom of her pie safe.

Rebecca and her sisters were married, but nonetheless, they were always referred to by their maiden name. Gracy took a deep breath. She hoped she could take the sharpness out of the air. "How's Rebecca doing? Did she have a boy or a girl?"

Martha was startled and looked down at the quilt in the frame, rubbing her hand across a red square. "Well, it was a girl. They named her Rebecca and call her Becky."

"About time," Gracy said with a smile. "After two boys, who wouldn't want a girl! And Becky. It's a name to live up to. I'll wager she's as pretty as her mother."

"Oh, she is, prettier even," the other sister said.

"And her labor, did it go easy with her?"

"That baby just popped out. Dr. Erickson said he never saw a baby come so quick, claimed it was the easiest baby he ever delivered . . ." Martha's voice trailed off as she realized she'd admitted Rebecca had sent for the doctor instead of Gracy. She looked down at the quilt in front of her.

"How many's he delivered?" Mittie asked. Gracy smiled to herself as she wondered if the others had caught the sarcasm in Mittie's voice.

"Two," Martha said, "including Rebecca's."

At that, the women laughed, and the tension eased a little, although not much. Even Effie Ring smiled, Gracy noted. Mittie had sat down on one side of Gracy, and Effie was on the other, because her chair was the only one left when Effie reached the quilt. She had slid the chair as far away from Gracy as she could, and Gracy could feel the distance between them as if it were a gulch.

"Is Rebecca in need of anything?" Gracy asked. "I'd have taken her some soup if I hadn't been stove up."

"Oh, she has every little thing already. Our mother saw to that. Mother cannot rest content if there is a cent left in the house."

"She bought Rebecca a sewing machine, a washtub, and a silver spoon," the second sister added.

"A sewing machine!" one of the women marveled. "Why, we wouldn't need a quilting if we had a machine that sewed."

"My husband said he'd buy me one, only it would make me a shirk," Effie said.

"Not that he ain't a shirk hisself," someone muttered.

The women settled in, and the afternoon took on a familiar hum, as the quilters gossiped and talked about their children, the weather, whether the ore was running out at the Tiger Mine. After the early tension, Gracy felt more at ease.

Following a silence, a woman observed, "This is a good place to quilt. Plenty of room for a frame."

"A better use for this place than on Sunday, I can tell you," another said in a low voice. "Sunday last, the Reverend Frome preached so long you could have gone across the water on a ship by the time he finished."

"Where is Salome Frome?" Mittie asked after the preacher's wife.

"She doesn't stitch. She reads novels. He says it disgusts him. But she will not stop reading novels, and he will not quit smoking."

"I believe that is called a compromise," Gracy said.

Then someone asked Gracy if she had heard from Jeff. "I expect your troubles will bring him home."

The unexpected mention of her son jolted Gracy. Jeff's presence would indeed be a consolation, although he wasn't likely to come. She and Daniel hadn't heard from the boy since he left out. So he wouldn't know about the Halleck baby. She'd let folks think that Jeff had gotten it in his head to see the world, but she suspected they had gossiped that his abrupt departure was something more. "He's not one for writing. And I expect he moves around some. I'm not sure just where he is now," she said. Jeff had said he wouldn't write, but still, Gracy had hoped he would. She needed that little bit of contact from him.

The women let that answer satisfy them and did not inquire further. They were silent again until someone remarked, "Such a beautiful top." It wasn't, Gracy noted, and that was the reason she did not look forward to stitching on the quilt. The design was only a Nine Patch, the colors clashed, and some of the fabric was so worn out it wouldn't survive more than two or three washings. And Nancy Culpin was not known for her fine stitching. The sashing was askew, and the pieces in the blocks didn't fit properly. But not for the world would one of the women criticize Nancy's quilting. There was nothing that insulted a woman more than to say her stitching wasn't perfect.

"That purple next to orange, it looks like sunrise," Gracy said. The others murmured agreement, although the colors together looked as bad as a dog's dinner.

"It's just like nature. Why, look at the flowers over there by the altar, red and orange and pink together. I believe the Lord likes every color," Nancy said. "Did you ever see so many flowers for a burying? Some got sent up from Denver on the stage."

"I never seen so many folks at a service," another woman observed.

"Well, they didn't care so much about that poor baby passing from death into life eternal as they was curious. There's not been but one murder in Swandyke since I came here, and when you think it was a baby killed by a midwife, why, a funeral will draw folks like a fat lady at a circus," Effie said.

Gracy shuddered. She couldn't help herself. Nancy said, "Effie!"

"Oh . . . I . . . oh . . ." She turned to Gracy. "Oh, aren't I the little goose. I forgot you were here."

The others glanced at Gracy, then looked away.

"There's too many folks not minding their own business," Mittie observed.

"I've been told there's a hearing next week, and that's everybody's business. You know I didn't mean anything by what I said," Effie remarked, but Gracy knew better. What's more, she knew the others in the room did, too.

"No, none of us mean it, Gracy," Nancy insisted. "We'll have to ask you to forgive us, treating you like you murdered a baby when I for one know you'd do no such thing. You'd think we hadn't known you for ten, fifteen years. I'm ashamed I haven't called on you." She took a few sloppy stitches in her quilt.

Some of the others nodded in agreement, but not all, and they included Effie. She yanked her needle through the quilt so hard that the thread broke.

"Effie?" Nancy said.

"I don't know no such thing. There's a baby dead, and Edna Halleck said Gracy did it. I never knew Edna to be a liar."

Gracy kept her eyes on her needle, although her hand shook.

"And I never knew Gracy to be anything but healing," Nancy said.

"Did Edna say she saw Gracy kill that baby?" Mittie asked.

The women were silent, thinking. "I never heard her *say* it," Martha said.

"Well, she didn't deny it. It's the same thing. Besides, Coy Chaney said she told him Gracy done it," Effie said.

"Oh, Mr. Chaney," Mittie said, waving her needle, as if to dismiss the man's words.

Effie didn't reply, just licked the end of her thread and pushed it through the eye of her needle. She knotted the other end of the thread, then took a stitch, pulling her needle through the fabric and scraping it against Gracy's arm, drawing pinpricks of blood. "I heard Edna and Josie agreed with Mr. Halleck that Gracy killed the baby."

Gracy barely felt the scratch. She was staring at her own needle, which had dipped down through the quilt sandwich of top, batting, and backing, and up again. She stared at her shaking hands, the gold wedding ring nearly worn through. Her hands were thin, the skin loose and veins prominent as worms, and they were rough and dotted with dark spots. Old hands. She thought of those other hands, smooth as a newborn's, the nails trimmed, the gold ring with a faceted stone that glittered like fire. A diamond, she supposed it was. She roused herself, wondered why her mind had brought that up just then. Perhaps it was to block out Effie's words. She didn't know how to respond.

"There's plenty of men out there that agree Gracy's guilty," Effie finished.

"Plenty of men that was never in a room where a woman gave birth. What would they know?" Mittie asked.

"Besides, men agree with Mr. Halleck or they clam up. That man could make discord in Eden," Nancy told them. She stood and said it was time to roll the finished end of the quilt over the edge of the frame to expose an unquilted portion. So the women got up and stretched to get the kinks out of their backs and turned to small talk. One said it was a shame they couldn't sit outside in the churchyard and quilt, the weather being so good. Why, come winter, they'd look back on that fine day and be sorry they'd wasted it.

"A day's never wasted when we're quilting," another said.

Nancy came over to Gracy and whispered, "They don't dis-esteem you. They are just uncomfortable with this squally busi-ness."

"You are given to kind remarks," Gracy replied, grateful for the unexpected support from Nancy. The woman had never been a close friend, and Gracy was surprised Nancy had sided with her. Others, some of whom she had considered friends, would not be so kind. Marianna Martin, whose baby Gracy had delivered in that very room years before, had not said a word. She had been Gracy's good friend and was much admired by the others.

The women sat down at the quilt and began to gossip once more. Gracy didn't pay them much attention until one announced she had seen Swede Olson's wife on the street, looking like she had a ham under her coat. "I expect she'll be calling for the Sagehen shortly."

"Why, she hasn't been married six months," a woman said sourly. "I saw her talking to that young doctor, so maybe you won't have to do for her, Gracy."

Gracy didn't respond. The pregnant woman had come to her months before, begging Gracy to end her pregnancy, saying she didn't want to marry such a man as Swede, who was foul-mouthed and taken with himself, although he was handsome as a racehorse. Gracy had given her herbs, but they hadn't helped, and now Gracy felt responsible for the young woman marrying a man she didn't love.

Others who might have been her patients would seek out the doctor now. Perhaps she wouldn't have to make that decision about whether she would continue as a midwife. The murder charge was destroying the reputation she had spent years building. Fewer and fewer women would come to her until there wouldn't be any at all. So she would not die in her boots. Instead, Gracy would empty out her medicine bag and put it away. The births would fade in her mind, although the deaths she would always remember. She would think about them as she stitched out her days, an old dotty thing piecing quilts for brides and for babies that others delivered, wishing she could make one for a grandchild, but not for herself, for she and Daniel had enough quilts to last.

"Well, I for one wouldn't want anybody else to attend me. I'd have my husband deliver my baby before I'd go to that doctor who thinks so kindly of hisself," a woman said, and the others laughed. "Of course, that ain't no thing for you to worry about, Gracy, me being an old peahen."

"It's the thought that counts," Mittie spoke up.

"Is there going to be a trial, Gracy?" a woman asked.

Suddenly, the women were still. There wasn't so much as a cough or the sound of a needle squeaking through the fabric. Gracy herself stopped quilting and stared at a piece of yard goods so worn you could see clear through it. Why would anyone use old material like that? she wondered. She turned her mind back to the conversation and slowly looked up, wishing the talk had moved away from her. "I can't say for certain," she said at last. "It will depend on what happens at the hearing. If the judge decides there's enough evidence against me, he'll order a trial. Sheriff Miller's collected evidence—"

"The idea!" Nancy interrupted, but Gracy held up her hand.

"He has to. Like he says, it's his job. My guess is he's got enough for a trial. And if the judge agrees, then the trial will be held the next time the court's here in Swandyke."

"Well, won't nobody find you guilty," Mittie said.

"But if Jonas Halleck says . . ." one of the quilters muttered, letting her voice trail away.

"That man's heart is as cold as a banker's," Mittie broke in.

"Maybe Edna will stand up for you, Gracy," Nancy said. "Maybe she'll say it was an accident."

"You think she'd defy her husband?" Martha asked. "I'd as soon put my hand in a snake's mouth as do that. And Edna . . ." She shrugged, and women nodded. Edna would melt in front of her husband just like a dish of butter left in the sun.

"What about Josie?" Nancy asked.

"Now there's your goose," Martha scoffed.

"She's an odd one, all right. She wanders. I've seen her up toward Mayflower Gulch, all by herself. Now what's she doing up there?" a woman Gracy did not know asked.

"And she don't like to quilt."

The women smiled. What better proof was there that something was wrong with the girl?

"Maybe she did it, Gracy. Did you ever think of that?" Nancy suggested. "Maybe she didn't like having a brother."

"Not Josie. She's too kindhearted. I know she took home three baby rabbits after a fox got their mother, raised them until Mr. Halleck turned them out," came a reply.

"Her mind might have snapped if her father bragged to her about finally having an heir, somebody he'd leave the Holy Cross to one day."

"It'll be out of ore by then," Marianna said, speaking for the first time. The others laughed.

Nancy ran her hand over the quilt, smoothing it. "He never had any use for Josie, treated her worthless."

"It's funny Mr. Halleck never talked about that baby until after it was dead. Did anybody ever hear him say he was hoping for an heir?" Mittie asked. "I never heard of him saying it until after he brought the baby to Mr. Chaney."

A woman at the end of the quilt looked up and remarked that Mr. Halleck had never been heard to say his wife was pregnant. "You'd think he'd be a-braggin' about it."

"Maybe that's Edna," Martha said. "You know how she is, hiding like she done so's nobody'd know she was pregnant, so nobody'd know what she and Mr. Halleck were up to. She'd like to believe you picked babies off a tree, like plums." The others laughed at that, and one woman muttered, "I'd a lot rather pick plums than sleep with Jonas Halleck." They were earthy women, and Edna Halleck's fastidious ways made them uncomfortable.

Mittie made a knot and nipped off her thread. "Well, I'd hide out, too, if I'd done the thing with Mr. Halleck."

"Time to turn," Nancy said, getting up. "I brung a surprise. I brung gingerbread because I know I'm a better cook than I am a quilter."

There were a few protests, the women saying that Nancy was a fine quilter, but they knew she was not. They were grateful for a chance to get away from the frame for a minute. Nancy cut the gingerbread and handed around the squares. There were no plates or forks or napkins, and one woman said she'd get a pail of water so they could wash the crumbs off their hands. After all, they wouldn't want to soil Nancy's quilt.

The woman went outside for the water while the others chatted and picked crumbs off their hands and their bosoms. The door opened, and Gracy, her back to it, paid no attention until she realized the others had grown silent. She turned around.

Edna Halleck stood in the doorway, Josie behind her. Edna looked around the room, dropping her eyes when she came to Gracy, but Josie stared at the midwife. The girl's face was drawn, and when she raised her hands to her mouth, her fingers tightened into fists. Despite Josie's haggard look, Gracy could see that the girl was beautiful. Gracy had never paid much attention to Josie until that day in the Halleck house when she had examined the baby, and now she noted that Josie had hair the color of clotted cream, so pale it was almost white, and it set off her black eyes and fine nose and wide mouth. Gracy had never seen such coloring. The girl was small and slender, with tiny hands and feet. Any man would have been drawn to her, one anyway. Gracy thought of the baby, which did not look like the girl but instead had been the spit of his father. She wanted to hold Josie to herself, just as she had Josie's baby, but she kept her hands to her sides.

"Oh, I did not know about the quilting," Edna said. "I thought to bring back some flowers, to press . . ." She did not look at the women when she spoke but instead kept her eyes on the quilt.

The silence in the room was as loud as the stamps in a mill, and Edna's words hovered in the air. The women shifted their eyes to each other, sending furtive glances at Gracy and then at Edna.

Gracy herself did not know what to do, what to say. She should have been prepared for Edna, thought it out ahead, practiced some words in her mind. But she felt numb. She stared at the woman for a long time, but after that quick glance, Edna would not look back at her. "Edna . . ." Gracy said at last.

Edna looked up then. "Gracy . . . I . . . Gracy . . ." she said. "Oh, the sin of it!" She raised her hands to her face, but she did not cry. She seemed to steel herself, then turned and fled while Gracy wrapped her arms around her body to keep from shaking. She had hoped Edna might have said something, perhaps broken down and admitted she'd seen her husband strangle the baby.

Marianna Martin yanked her needle from the quilt and picked up her scissors and hurried after Edna, and Gracy knew she had lost Marianna. Another woman followed. So did Pearlie Evans.

Josie stood in the doorway, transfixed, her eyes on Gracy. Then suddenly she came to her senses. "Our baby's killed," she said, and bolted.

Eleven

The courtroom was packed for the hearing, not just with men but with women, too. Women rarely came to court—they never sat on juries, of course, and only on occasion did they attend trials or hearings. It wasn't seemly, even in a small mountain town that often ignored convention, for women to gather in a foul courtroom. So that morning they sat primly, uncomfortably, straight backed with their hands clutched together, while men sprawled in wooden chairs and on benches and even took over the rocking chairs in the jury box, since this was only a hearing and not a trial. The trial would come later, after a judge determined whether there was reason to formally charge Gracy. Every so often a man stood to offer a woman his seat, because while conventions could be done away with, manners might not.

A burly miner, with a beard nearly to his waist, gave up his seat to Mittie McCauley, who nodded her thanks and perched on the edge of the chair. The seat was in the front row, and the miner walked heavily to the back of the room, where he leaned against the wall. Although a spittoon stood nearby, he spat tobacco juice on the floor, splattering it on his white beard as he did so. The beard was already stained with the brown stuff.

The room was stifling, even with the windows open, and smelled of cigar smoke and chewing tobacco—and sweat, for the bathhouse charged twenty-five cents, and who needed a bath just to attend a hearing? Here and there a woman held a handkerchief against her nose, but most were used to the smells and didn't notice them. Nor did they pay attention to the noises of men spitting, jawing, joking. The courtroom was a commotion until a clerk seated at a desk in front pounded a mallet on a piece of wood with the power of a stamp crushing ore in a mill, startling the audience into silence. In a few seconds a judge in a black robe emerged from a door, and the clerk ordered everyone to stand up.

Those in the courtroom glanced at the judge briefly but saved their stares for Gracy as she followed the judge into the room, drawing a few glares as well as smiles. The injuries from her carriage fall were not yet healed. Her face was bruised, and she still limped a little as she clutched the heavy walking stick Daniel had made for her.

Gracy was startled to see so many people. She faltered and grabbed the arm of the man beside her to steady herself. He was her attorney. Until John Miller insisted on it, she had not thought to hire such a man. She had never been in a courtroom before and knew nothing about trials. At first, she'd thought she would merely tell what had happened in the Halleck cabin and that people would believe her. They would decide whether her version was more credible than Jonas Halleck's.

John had disabused her of that idea not long after he'd offered to help her escape, however. "You need a solicitor. You need him bad, Gracy. The prosecutor is a rough fellow who will dig up every bit of trash he can find about you, whether it's true or not. He will call you a murderess, and so will men like Coy Chaney and Little Dickie Erickson. And you know how powerful Jonas Halleck is in Swandyke. Folks may not like him, but they respect him."

Gracy thought that over—after all, John was more knowledgeable about such things than she—and finally nodded. "I could hire old Andy Hawkins. He's as good as we've got on the Tenmile Range." Hawkins handled mining claims and property disputes, and he'd arranged a divorce for a woman whose husband had run off with her silver spoons.

"He's old and dotty," John replied.

Gracy shrugged. "He's also all there is."

"You need a good lawyer, someone from Denver."

Gracy shook her head. "That'll cost. Where'll we get the money to pay for a Denver lawyer? Andy will have to do."

John had taken her arm then and turned her to face him. "Maybe you don't really understand, Gracy. You could be charged with anything from manslaughter to murder, first-degree murder if that prosecutor has anything to say about it. He'll play Ned with the truth. You could go to jail. You might even hang."

He let the words themselves hang there. He'd said them to her before, but this time she listened.

"You get a decent barrister and let me worry about paying him," John told her.

"Blamed if I'd let you do that."

"I owe you a debt. You were Elizabeth's friend."

"You owe me nothing. Elizabeth died. I can't ever forget that. She died because I couldn't save her, and so did the baby." Elizabeth's death was among those that haunted Gracy most. She might have saved the woman if she'd been willing to kill the baby, but she hadn't been, and so both of them had died.

"You did everything you could for her. Besides, when things were down for me, you stuck. You and Dan stuck."

"You did the same for me."

Neither of them wanted to think of those times, and they broke their gaze.

"She'll tell me to do it, Elizabeth will. She's a fondness for you even after all this time, Gracy."

"Has she talked to you about it yet?" Gracy could hardly believe she was having this conversation about a . . . a ghost.

John shook his head, and Gracy was about to say that if Elizabeth "visited" him again, he should tell her Gracy paid her own way. Still, Gracy understood that John would be hurt she if didn't accept his aid, even though it smacked of charity. Giving help could be harder than receiving it. So she nodded her thanks. "A loan," she insisted. "I'll repay."

"I know of a good man in Denver. He's young, but I've seen

him at work. He's been up here in the courtroom a time or three, and he knows mountain folks, knows they want respect, so he doesn't talk down to them or use fancy words. I'll arrange for him." He added a final word of persuasion. "Jeff would want you to have the best defense."

Yes, he would, Gracy thought. She remembered a time when a drunken miner had stumbled on the street, knocking her down, and Jeff had defended her. He'd taken a swing at the man and done a pretty good job of it, too, although he was only ten years old.

And so Gracy walked into the courtroom that morning on the arm of Ted Coombs, a man dressed in corduroy and rough wool who did not look much different from the miners in the room. He was clean shaven, but his hair was rumpled like that of the men around him. He had told her to hold her head high and smile the smile of the innocent.

The smile faded as Gracy saw the crowd. She knew she was a curiosity, but she hadn't expected the courtroom to be jammed. Many in the audience were familiar—men who had come to fetch her in the night when their wives were in labor, here and there a woman whose baby she had delivered, a few girls who had approached her in time of trouble. There were people she knew in town, women from the church, men who had prospected with Daniel. But others were strangers, and Gracy wondered what business they had in the courtroom that day. Surely they had not come to see her. But in her heart, she knew better. The talk at the quilting had taught her that. Besides, she'd seen the looks people gave her as she walked past them, noticed the abrupt end to conversations when she entered the store, even the church. She was someone they knew who had been accused of murder, and a woman at that. Gracy Brookens was a novelty, an attraction, just like the freaks in a sideshow. The hearing must have cleaned out the saloons, because a woman likely to be charged with murder was a sight more interesting than even a drunken fight.

She glanced at Mittie in the front row, a quilt square in her lap to still her hands, and smiled. Mittie grinned back and made a steeple with her hands as if to tell Gracy she was praying for her.

Gracy's eyes searched the rest of the room. Daniel wasn't there, she realized, with a start. She frowned as she looked about. He should be there. The lawyer had said Daniel couldn't walk with her into the courtroom, but he should be in one of the seats—in the front row, for that matter. Folks would take stock by the way he looked at his wife. Now what would they think if her own husband wasn't in the courtroom to see her through the hearing?

She turned to whisper a question to Ted, to ask had he sent Daniel away? Perhaps Daniel had gone on a high lonesome, but that wouldn't be like him. He'd sworn off drink years ago, although he'd backslid now and then, had done it the day Coy Chaney accused Gracy of murder. He'd gotten drunk at the Nugget then. Still, Daniel wouldn't have taken a drink that morning. He wouldn't let her down like that. Maybe he'd gotten into a fight. He still had fists as tough as chunks of ore. John could have taken him to jail. But John was right there in the front row, looking solemn, since it wouldn't be proper for the sheriff to smile at her.

As she walked to her seat, Gracy scanned the courtroom again, looking for her husband, and then the door opened, and she looked up to see Daniel enter the room, his hat in his hand, his face red as if he had been running. She smiled at him, and then the smile turned into a look of joy as she spotted the young man behind her husband. "Jeff!" she mouthed, and her son grinned back at her. "You found him. You called him to us, Daniel," she whispered. She felt an overwhelming happiness at the sight of him. Gracy held out her hands as the two men walked toward her. "My son," she told the lawyer, then squeezed her son's hand so hard that he winced. She would have hugged him, but it wouldn't have been proper, right there in the courtroom. Gracy wanted to know where he'd been, how he was, but just then, it was enough that he was there.

Ted shook hands with both men. Then he stared at two miners seated in the front row, stared so hard that they got up and moved to the back of the courtroom, freeing up their chairs for Daniel and Jeff. Father and son sat down next to Mittie.

Gracy wanted to ask how Jeff had known to come home, how Daniel had found him, but Ted led her to a table and told her to sit down. She eased herself into the chair and sat, back erect, staring at the judge, who had his own mallet and pounded it, silencing the murmurs that had begun when Gracy entered the room.

The judge was not a local man. He was a circuit rider, going from camp to camp and holding court in courthouses or meeting halls or even in barrooms. He held court in Swandyke every four weeks or so. Gracy smiled at him, but he did not return the smile, and she felt foolish. She clasped her hands on the table and stared straight ahead.

"Gentlemen—and ladies," he added, clearing his throat. "We are here to consider charges against this woman." He nodded at Gracy. "This is not a trial. It is a hearing to determine whether there is enough evidence for a trial. I brook no outbursts. I warn you to be quiet and observe proper decorum, or I'll eject you from the courtroom." Then he added for those who did not understand his words, "Quiet, or out you go. Understand?" There were nods and a few murmurs.

"Mr. Doak, are you ready?" the judge asked.

"Yes, Your Honor." A small man who was narrow between the eyes, which made him appear untrustworthy to Gracy, stood up. She had never seen him before, had not noticed him when she entered the room, but she realized he traveled with the judge and was the prosecutor. Ted had warned her that convicting a woman of murder would add to his stature, so he would be relentless.

The man walked to the center of the room and looked over the audience, smiling at them. "Ladies and gentlemen—" he began, but the judge cut him off.

"We're not here for a trial, Mr. Doak. We are here to determine whether murder charges will be filed against this woman"—he glanced down at a paper in front of him—"Gracy Brookens. Is Gracy your baptismal name, Mrs. Brookens, or is it Grace?"

Gracy glanced at her lawyer, who nodded at her to answer. "It's Gracy, sir," she said.

Her voice was so low that the judge leaned forward and said, "Eh?"

"Gracy," she said in a louder voice. "Gracy Harriett Brookens."

Doak turned and smirked at her, as if there were something obscene about the name. He reminded Gracy of a weasel, and she wondered again how anyone could have confidence in what he said. But as if knowing what his client was thinking, Ted sought to disabuse her of the idea. "Don't sell him short, Mrs. Brookens," he muttered. "He's tough as granite. I've seen him work. He doesn't like to lose, and he doesn't do so often."

Doak walked to the judge's bench. "Your Honor," he said, smiling in such a way that Gracy suspected they were old friends. "It is my solemn duty to ask for charges against this Mrs. Gracy Harriett Brookens of Swandyke, Colorado, for the heinous murder of a newborn baby just two weeks ago."

He paused and lifted his chin at the gasps in the courtroom. Although everyone there knew Gracy was likely to be charged with the murder of an infant, people were nonetheless shocked at hearing the words said out loud.

"A murder so vile, so ungodly that I hate to speak of it in the presence of ladies," he continued.

"Then don't," the judge interjected. "This is a hearing for an indictment, Mr. Doak. You can save the rhetoric for the trial."

Ted jumped up. "Your Honor, I object to the assumption that there will be a trial. We are here for the purpose of deciding whether there is enough evidence for a trial, and I for one believe there is not."

"Yes, I'm sure you do," the judge said. "But you are quite

right. Our job here is to determine whether to prefer charges. And Mr. Doak, you will watch your language."

"Of course," the prosecutor said in a voice that sounded as if he were thanking the judge.

"And Mr. Coombs, you are not a participant in this hearing, so I expect you not to interrupt. If your client is charged, you will have your say later. Today, only the prosecutor gets a turn." He turned to the courtroom. "Let me make it clear again that the evidence Mr. Doak presents will determine whether we proceed with an indictment. If we do so, then Mrs. Brookens will have the opportunity to defend herself at trial." He looked around to make sure everyone understood, then nodded at the prosecutor to continue.

"Your Honor, it is the belief of the prosecution that Mrs. Brookens was called to examine the Halleck child and was so distraught at seeing the happiness it brought its father, a man she had reason to hate, that she strangled the poor little thing."

Again there were murmurs of horror.

"This woman, this Gracy Brookens is a backwoods witch doctor who employs the crudest techniques in her practice as a midwife. There was a time when she was the only one in Swandyke who could deliver a baby. As you will see, the town now has a competent doctor. But Mr. Halleck, being a kind and compassionate man and knowing Mrs. Brookens is the sole support of a worthless husband—"

At that, Daniel jumped up. "You got no call—" he began, but the judge pounded his gavel, and Jeff pushed his father back into the chair.

Gracy was stunned and turned to Ted. "That's not right. Daniel's a decent man."

"We'll have our turn," Ted whispered back. "The more outrageous the things he says, the easier it will be for us to poke holes in his case." Ted patted her hand, and they turned back to the prosecutor.

"As I was saying, Mr. Halleck is as good a man as ever lived, and to his everlasting sorrow, this woman was called upon to examine his child. We will now present the evidence."

He read Coy Chaney's name off a list, and the man who was mortician as well as coroner walked to a chair beside the judge's bench and sat down.

"Stand while we swear you in," the judge ordered.

Coy jumped up, embarrassed, while a few in the courtroom snickered. He swore to tell the truth and was told to sit back down.

"Tell us how you first saw the baby in question, the Halleck baby." The prosecutor nodded at Coy.

Coy swallowed and seemed shy, perhaps because of the crowd in the courtroom. "It's all wrote down in that report I made. Can't you read?"

Doak smiled, as if that were a good joke, and said, "We'd like you to tell us out loud."

Coy took a deep breath and steadied himself. "I'm the undertaker. And the coroner, too. Jonas Halleck brought that baby to me to be buried. I could tell right off there was something wrong."

"And what was that?"

"Well, the baby had been buried already, shoved in the cold ground in a dynamite box, not one of my good coffins that I sell cheap, if you're in need of one."

"Yes, well, I don't need one, thank you." Doak thought over the words and looked confused. "You say the baby had been buried before?"

Ted smiled at Gracy, because it was obvious the prosecutor hadn't known about the first burial.

"Yes, sir, he told me he planted the body right off, but his wife couldn't abide it not having a proper burial, so he dug it up and brought it to me."

"Mr. Chaney," the judge interrupted. "You can testify only to what you know personally, not what someone told you."

"Well, can't I testify to what he *personally* told me?"

"No, you may not."

"And will you describe the baby to us, Mr. Chaney?" Doak said.

"Well, it was a boy. I could tell that right off by the little button on him."

A few men smirked at the remark. One even let out a laugh, and the judge tapped the gavel to silence him. "This is not a matter for humor."

"The baby's neck," Doak prompted. "Tell us about the baby's neck."

"Oh, that." Coy raised his head and looked around the courtroom, smiling a little as he saw that everybody was watching him. "There was a red mark going all around his neck, and I seen a bit of linen thread caught on it like what the Sagehen uses. I knew right there that baby had been strangled. Knew she done it, too—Gracy Brookens. Her always so high-and-mighty and not getting there in time to do what she's supposed to. My daughter'd be alive if that woman'd come sooner. Didn't have nothing to do with my stopping for a drink. I wasn't never drunk that night."

"Confine your remarks to answering the questions," the judge admonished. "Your personal life is of no concern to this court."

The prosecutor paused until all eyes were on him, then asked in a dramatic voice, "And what makes you think that Mrs. Brookens strangled the baby?"

"I recognized the thread. Nobody else uses linen thread that way, uses it to tie off a baby's cord. I seen that on a baby that died once, seen it used on his belly." He glanced at the judge, then said quickly, "Besides, Mr. Halleck told me she done it."

The judge pounded his gavel, but Coy had already spoken his piece and sat back, satisfied.

"Thank you, Mr. Chaney. That's all for this hearing. I believe, Your Honor, that Mr. Chaney has established that the baby was strangled and with a thread or cord known to be used by Mrs. Brookens."

Coy looked disappointed at being dismissed. He sat a moment longer as if hoping there would be more questions, but when the prosecutor made a scooting gesture with his hands, Coy got up from his chair and started down the aisle. Just as he reached Gracy, he said, "I hope you hang."

The judge banged his gavel again. "Enough of that talk, sir."

"Too late," Coy mouthed to the room.

Doak waited until Coy found a seat and then he called, "Richard Erickson. *Dr.* Richard Erickson," and Little Dickie walked to the front of the room and was sworn in.

"You are a medical doctor, not a quack," the prosecutor began, glancing at Gracy. She stiffened, knowing the word "quack" was meant for her. "Tell us your medical background."

Little Dickie raised his chin and began to recite his educational accomplishments, the professional organizations to which he belonged, and his experience. Gracy noted that he didn't have much to say about his experience.

"You are a *medical* doctor, a trained medical doctor, then?" Doak asked.

The judge leaned over the bench and said, "Enough, Mr. Doak. The court accepts that this man is a doctor."

"I was just making sure."

"You did. Go ahead."

"You examined the murdered baby," Doak said, drawing out the word "murdered."

"I did."

"Tell us about him."

Little Dickie cleared his throat, then described in great detail the condition of the baby, using language so technical that only Gracy had an idea of what he was talking about. The doctor seemed to enjoy his performance and prolonged it more than was necessary. Finally, the judge said, "Mr. Doak, would you like to ask your witness to state that in English?"

Little Dickie gave a disdainful smile and said, "I concluded the baby died of strangulation a day or two before he was brought to me, strangled with a length of linen string."

"Well, you should have said so and saved us all time," the judge told him.

"I am just being thorough."

"Too thorough," the judge muttered. "There is other business before this court today. Move it along, Mr. Doak."

The prosecutor dismissed Little Dickie and then announced, as if he were calling forth President Grant himself, "My last witness is Jonas Halleck."

Gracy had not seen the man since the day she'd examined Josie's baby, and her hands shook as she turned to stare at him. Jonas refused to catch her eye.

Looking important, he walked slowly to the front of the room and raised his hand, saying, "I do," when the clerk swore him in. He rubbed his hand across his face, and Gracy thought he might have been drinking. His nose was red, and his eyes were glazed. She'd never heard that Halleck was an imbiber, but that might be the reason Edna was in the temperance society. You never knew about vices that took place behind closed doors.

"Tell us how you saw Mrs. Brookens strangle the baby," Mr. Doak said.

"We haven't established she did. Rephrase your question," the judge ordered.

Before the prosecutor could speak, Halleck said, "I saw her do it. She held that baby with her back to me, working over him, and then she laid him in the cradle. And when I went to pick him up later on, he wasn't breathing. There was a red ring around his neck and what was left of a piece of string, too."

Gracy glanced at Ted. If her back was to Mr. Halleck, how could he say he'd seen her strangle the baby? Ted caught her eye and gave a faint nod.

But Doak had seen the contradiction, too, and he asked, "If she turned away as you said, how was it you saw Mrs. Brookens murder the infant?"

Halleck had spoken softly before, but now his voice rose. "I saw her hold the baby. I saw her turn her back to me. And when next I picked up my son, he was dead. If that isn't seeing, what is?"

He stared at Doak so hard that the prosecutor muttered, "Indeed, sir, what is?" Flustered, Doak studied his notes, then asked. "You know Mr. Brookens, Mr. Daniel Brookens, husband of Mrs. Brookens. Is that correct?"

"It is. He was in my employ. I fired him."

"And why was that?"

"He's too old. Besides, he high-graded. Mining isn't charity work."

"And you think maybe Mrs. Brookens strangled your baby because you fired her husband?"

The judge interrupted, saying what Halleck thought was of no consequence.

Halleck ignored him. "What other reason would there be? She is a hateful woman."

"I think we've heard enough," Doak said. "You are excused,

Mr. Halleck, with the sympathy of the court over the loss of your precious son."

Halleck didn't stand up, however. "What about you?" he asked Ted. "Aren't you going to question me? I've gone up against you shysters a time or two. I'm not afraid of you."

"This is a hearing. The defense doesn't have a say. He'll have that right at trial," Doak answered. The prosecutor thought that over and added slyly, "*If* there is a trial, and I believe there will be one." He grinned at the judge, who didn't return the smile. He watched as Halleck returned to his seat. Then addressing the room instead of the judge, Doak said, "That's all the evidence I need to present."

"Won't Edna have a say?" Gracy whispered to Ted

He shook his head. "Sheriff Miller talked to her—and to the daughter, too—and they nodded when he asked if you'd killed the baby. But they wouldn't talk to him. I tried to speak with her, but she wouldn't see me. Her husband's all but got her locked up." Then he whispered, "What you told me about her daughter, I guess the sheriff didn't tell the prosecutor. I bet Doak doesn't know she might be the mother."

The judge glared at Ted to be still, then turned to the prosecutor. "You were saying?"

"I believe we have established that the Halleck baby was murdered and that the evidence points to Mrs. Gracy Brookens as the killer. I ask that you prefer charges against her, that you charge her with murder in the first degree."

"She never—" Daniel yelled.

The judge banged his mallet, while Gracy turned to look at

Daniel, who had risen in his chair as he spoke. "I will have no outbursts," the judge said.

"She's my wife. I know her better than anybody, and I know she never did such a thing," Daniel insisted.

Jeff pulled his father down and said loudly enough for Gracy to hear, "Be still, Pa. You don't do her any good speaking out that way."

There were a few mutters in the courtroom. One man said, "You tell him, Daniel," while another called, "She ain't no killer, not her." A woman called, "No!"

Gracy barely heard the cries of support, as she stared at the judge, hoping he would say a charge of murder against her was nonsense. But she knew that wouldn't happen. After all, three men who had testified had said just the opposite. She gripped Ted's arm, her fingers digging into his flesh as the judge gaveled the room to silence.

"Murder is a serious accusation, and this court does not take it lightly. Mrs. Brookens is a respected member of the community," the judge said.

"We haven't established she is any such thing," Doak said quietly.

"Don't interrupt, Mr. Doak. Mrs. Brookens's reputation is well known, not only in Swandyke but across the Tenmile."

Gracy relaxed a little.

"However," he said, and Gracy's shoulders slumped. "However, it appears from the testimony of Dr. Erickson and Mr. Chaney that someone murdered that baby. Mr. Halleck has accused Mrs. Brookens. There is no physical evidence she committed the crime. It is his word against, presumably, Mrs. Brookens's. So I believe it is appropriate to take this case to trial. I do not believe that this is first-degree murder, however. If Mrs. Brookens did it, then it was a crime of passion—manslaughter. You have your indictment, Mr. Doak. Trial will commence the next time the court meets in Swandyke. I expect that to be in four weeks, maybe sooner."

Gracy slumped against the back of the chair. The reality of the manslaughter charge hit her every bit as hard as if she had been chunked on the head with a piece of ore. She put her hands to her face, her fingers pressed against her eyes to keep from crying. She'd be ashamed if anyone saw her cry.

She started to get up, but Ted held her down. "We're not through yet," he whispered.

Doak was speaking to the judge. "We ask that Mrs. Brookens be jailed until the trial," he said.

Gracy turned to Ted, her eyes wide. "There's women due. I can't deliver their babies in jail."

"Your Honor," Ted spoke up. "I believe I have a say in this matter. As you yourself said, Mrs. Brookens is a respected member of this community. There are women whose babies are about to be born, and incarcerating Mrs. Brookens would do them a great disservice. You would punish them more than the defendant."

"There's a doctor can deliver babies," Doak argued.

"I don't want Little Dickie," a woman called, and the courtroom laughed.

"I'll make sure she's here for the trial," John Miller said. Gracy sent him a grateful look.

The judge thought a moment. "I don't see any reason to lock her up, Mr. Doak. It's on you, John. You make sure of her appearance."

The sheriff nodded, glancing at Gracy, who remembered how he had urged her to disappear. There weren't many who were such good friends as Mittie McCauley and John Miller, even though he had gathered evidence against her.

"That's all for this case," the judge said, looking down at a paper in front of him. "Next we got a man suing the owner of a dog he says took off with a pouch of gold dust." The judge smiled. "We'll take a minute, since I expect most of you didn't come to hear that case."

People got up then, scraping their feet, muttering, here and there expressing an opinion about the outcome of the hearing. Gracy stayed where she was, however, too stunned to move. "I'd hoped . . ." she said.

"We got just what we wanted," Ted told her.

Gracy didn't understand. "I'm charged with murder."

"With manslaughter, not murder. That's a much lesser charge, easier to defend. After those three men spoke out against you, the judge had to do something. We just have to prove someone else might have killed the baby."

"Jonas Halleck."

"My money's on him."

"But how do we prove it?"

"We don't. We just cast enough doubt that you did it, enough so that at least one juror votes you not guilty. I believe we can do that."

"Mr. Halleck has his hates. You could see that on his face when he looked at me. I believe he'll have a way of getting men on that jury who'll vote to hang me."

"It's my job to see he doesn't," Ted said, but he didn't sound as confident as Gracy wished.

Twelve

Gracy was mute as she and the lawyer followed the crowd outside. She could see Daniel standing a few steps away; he was angry and agitated as he stood in the sunshine, taking in huge gulps of air.

These charges against his wife, they were all a mistake, Gracy heard him say, his voice loud with scorn.

Jeff gripped his father's arm as he searched the crowd for Gracy. "Ma needs us. Come along, Pa."

Daniel nodded and said in a voice loud enough for Gracy to hear, "She was right glad to see you. Surprised, too."

"You didn't tell her I was coming?" Jeff's voice rose above the murmur of the crowd.

"Didn't know for sure you really were, not after the way you taken out. I didn't want to disappoint her if you didn't show up."

"You knew I would."

"Did I?" Daniel shrugged. "I wouldn't have thought you'd run off that way. God, hell!"

Gracy hurried toward her husband and son. At seventeen, Jeff was a slimmer, taller version of his father. No one could doubt that Jeff was Daniel's son. The boy had Daniel's handsome face, his broad shoulders, his hips, but his brown eyes were the color of Gracy's. Well, almost. They had bits of amber that Gracy's didn't have. The flecks made his eyes sparkle like shards of quartz in the sun.

Just as Gracy reached the two, someone grabbed Daniel's hand and said, "It's a crime, them charging her with murder. My missus thinks a heap of yours after the Sagehen sat through two nights with her. I don't hardly believe she'd have made it if Mrs. Brookens hadn't been there. You let us know can we do anything."

Others murmured their support and slapped Daniel on the back. But not everyone, and a miner said in a loud voice, "That's the murderer's man."

Daniel punched the fist of his right hand into the palm of his left and stared at the miner who'd insulted Gracy. The man backed away, and Jeff grabbed his father's arm and steered him to Gracy.

She watched them approach, her back straight, her lanky body in the dark dress black against the shadow of the courthouse. After Gracy's dress was ripped in the buggy accident, Daniel bought her a new one, red, the bright color of fireweed, and she had exclaimed over it. But Ted had said her black merino—her Sunday dress—would be better for a courtroom, even though the room would be as hot as a frying pan inside, and so she had worn the old dress, a garment that had been old when Jeff was a baby.

People stopped talking then, and the silence was eerie, so quiet that Gracy heard the song of a lark bunting and the swish of a squirrel as it scampered up a pine tree. Most people looked openly at Gracy, curious, although a few pretended not to stare and glanced at her from the corners of their eyes. They were watching, waiting to see if she said anything they could repeat, something they could gossip about. A woman clapped, and a few others took it up. It was their way of supporting her. Still, Gracy thought the display odd, more like people clapping at the end of a minstrel show. That was what the hearing had been, and the trial would be worse, a show, an entertainment, something for people to watch and snicker over.

Daniel saw Gracy, and the two of them smiled at each other, the laugh lines beside her mouth and eyes deepening. Then she turned to Jeff and held out her arms. It was an unusual gesture, right out there where people could see. She had never kissed Daniel except when they were alone, and when he took her hand once as they were walking along a street, she had snatched it back, embarrassed. She didn't show her emotion with her son, either, not in front of people. But right then, Gracy didn't care what people thought. She hugged her son, and he hugged back, just as he had when he was a boy.

"Son," she said, her eyes glistening with tears.

"Hello, Ma," he said as he pulled away, grinning. "You're still pretty as ever."

Gracy couldn't help but laugh at that. She was aware she'd never been much to look at, but in Jeff's eyes, she knew, she'd always been beautiful.

"You can't keep out of trouble when I'm not around to look after you, can you?" he asked.

"Seems not," Gracy said. She used her arm to wipe away the tears. Her eyes watered more now, although she still didn't cry much. "I never saw a sight in my life that looked so good as you there in the courtroom with your pa. Why, it was almost worth getting into trouble just to have you home."

"Oh, it wasn't worth that much."

"No." She shook her head. "But it's good to see you just the same. Where've you been?"

"Oh, here and there, everywhere. I went out west, back to Virginia City."

"I figured you would." She put her hand on his shirtfront, feeling the warmth of his skin through the fabric.

"I didn't like it so much as Swandyke."

"No, you wouldn't. There aren't mountains there like the Tenmile, and I know you love a mountain with snow as deep as your head in winter and aspen trees with leaves the color of green apples in the summer. The mountains out there are kind of dry with sun, and puny, as mountains go."

"And you and Pa weren't there."

"There's that, and you're a good boy to say so."

Jeff looked around and saw people watching them, leaning close to hear what he and his mother were talking about, for many were curious about why the boy had disappeared the year before without a word to his friends. Jeff stepped back from his mother. "We got time to catch up later."

Gracy glanced around and took her son's meaning. "Best to go on home now," she said.

She took a step, but a woman gabbed Jeff's arm and welcomed him home. Then Jeff exchanged words with a young man his own age, and by the time the talking was done, the crowd had dispersed, leaving only those with business at the courthouse.

A man came up to Gracy then and said, "Mrs. Brookens, if you don't mind, I'd like to get your side of the story." He didn't introduce himself, because Gracy knew him as Joseph Grossman, the editor of the *Swandyke Clarion*.

"My side? I've got no side. Only the truth."

"She has nothing to say," Ted Coombs said, coming up beside Gracy.

The man started to protest, but instead he turned to Daniel. "What about you, Dan. What do you think of all this?"

"It's a goddamn shame—"Daniel began.

Ted cut him off. "He's got nothing to say, either. Ask me your questions. I'm Mrs. Brookens's solicitor."

"Well, then, what do you have to say about it?"

"I say it's a disgrace to charge this good woman with the crime of killing a baby. A poor child is dead, and Mrs. Brookens had nothing to do with it. Why would she do such a thing? Anybody can tell you there are venal men who are trying to blame Mrs. Brookens for the death of the infant. They have a powerful hate. I suggest you look to her accusers, sir."

"You think one of them did it?"

"You'll have to ask them. That's all for now. I will be pleased to talk to you after the trial is over and Mrs. Brookens is acquitted of this crime. Until then, she has my instructions not to discuss the case. I'll make it hard on you if you speak to her again."

The editor looked alarmed. "But what if my wife goes into labor? She isn't due for more than a month, I reckon, but the Sagehen knows that up here in the high country, babies come anytime."

Ted chuckled. "In that case, you have my permission to contact her, but if you ask her about the trial, I'll instruct her to return home."

"I doubt she'd do that," the editor said.

Gracy smiled. "You don't have to worry about that, Joe. I'll be there for your wife. I just won't answer your questions."

"Much obliged." He started to turn away, then spotted Jeff and held out his hand. "Say, aren't you the Brookens boy? Come back to stand beside your ma, have you? Where've you been? Maybe the Sagehen isn't the only story here."

"I been farther west, looking to find a gold mine." Jeff grinned.

"Any luck?"

"Not yet."

"That's no story."

"Come along, boy," Gracy said. "We'll go back to the house. You coming, too, Mr. Coombs?"

Ted excused himself, saying he had to get back to Denver. He'd be up in a few days to talk to Gracy, confer about the witnesses, plan a strategy. "Don't you worry, Mrs. Brookens. There's not much of a case against you." He said that in a loud voice.

Gracy only nodded and turned to Jeff. The sight of her son was the best thing in the world to take her mind off the manslaughter charge. They set off, Jeff between his parents the way they had always walked, not talking, because there were stragglers on the street. They turned down the trail to the cabin, and Jeff kicked aside several tin cans lying in the path. "Something's been in your can pile, scattering everything," he said.

"Somebody sent by Jonas Halleck to spy. Or maybe it's Coy Chaney," Daniel told him. "Someone's been skulking here at night, looking for trouble. I'll pound him if I catch him."

Jeff turned to Gracy. "You in danger, Ma?"

"No—"

"She sure as hell is," Daniel interrupted. "Somebody tried to kill her when she was out birthing the Boyce babies, felled a tree across the road where she ran into it. I'm thinking Jonas Halleck is behind that, too. They ought to put him on trial for trying to kill your ma. I told her no more babies till this is over, but you know her. She won't listen to me."

"Then I reckon I'll go along with her when she gets called out," Jeff said.

"Are you staying that long? You're not here for just a day?" Gracy asked. Her face softened at the idea. She'd bake him brown-sugar cookies and dried apple pie, his favorite fixings.

"I'll stay as long as you need me, maybe longer. I've been doing some thinking. I've got things worked out."

"I'm glad, real glad," Gracy said. "You tell us when you're ready."

She should have been mending, because Jeff had brought home clothes that needed it, but mending didn't steady her nerves like quilting did. So later that day, Gracy sat at the quilt frame that hung from the ceiling in the middle of the room. Daniel had made the frame for her when they moved into the cabin, designed it himself because the cabin was too small for a standing frame. It was a large square made of slats of wood and suspended from the ceiling by ropes, and it could be lowered when Gracy worked on a quilt, then raised to the ceiling to keep it out of the way. She had taken the frame down the day before to soothe herself, and now she sat down to quilt for a few minutes.

Gracy worked on her quilting until near dinnertime, then pulled on the ropes to raise the frame, but not before Jeff leaned over to view the quilt in progress. It was one of Gracy's "people" quilts, as Jeff called them, made up of crude fabric figures set into squares that had been stitched together. The quilt top had been placed on top of a batting and a backing and set into the frame.

"What's that you're working on, Ma?" Jeff asked.

"Just a quilt. Something to keep my fingers out of trouble." She tried again to raise the quilt frame, but Jeff held the ropes.

"Who've you got in it?"

Gracy shrugged. "Nobody, just people."

"I think that's me." He pointed to the figure of a man in front of a mountain. "Look, you made me a shirt out of that yard goods once."

Gracy shrugged, a little embarrassed. "You were never out of mind. Maybe I was making the quilt to keep you warm when you came home."

"You knew I'd come back?"

"Of course I did, son. The ties between us are too strong."

"You were right." Jeff studied the quilt. "Is that Pa in that square, with his gold pick?" He smiled at his father.

"Looks like."

"And there's Sandy, sitting right in the middle of what looks like the can pile." Jeff pointed to a square, then moved his finger to another. "And you, Ma. I can see you down there in the corner, holding a baby. Who's the baby?"

"Any one of them, I expect. I've birthed so many."

"It's not me, then?"

"No . . ." Gracy stopped. She moved Jeff's hands from the rope and raised the quilt. "It's not done yet, but there's no time for quilting with you here. I got to get to your dinner." She secured the quilt but didn't go to the dry sink or the stove. Instead, she sat down on the bench at the table and pointed to a seat in front of the fireplace, and said, "Take a chair." He sat down. "I need to know first how you came to be here," Gracy said to Jeff, leaning forward.

Jeff nodded. "I guess you got the right. It was John Miller wrote me."

"John?" Gracy was startled. "How'd he know where to find you?"

Jeff took a deep breath. "I couldn't write to you. I told you I wouldn't. I had to go off by myself, work things out."

Gracy nodded. Daniel had been a wanderer, too, before they were married.

"I asked John before I lit out if he'd write to me and let me know how you were doing. He sent me a letter the day that dead baby was brought in and told me I'd best get home."

"You knew about the baby, then," Gracy said.

"Yes, but I didn't know whose it was. Isn't Mrs. Halleck kind of old to have a baby?"

Gracy wouldn't tell him about Josie. She hadn't even told Daniel. Ted and John were the only ones she'd confided in. So she asked, "John knew where you were, and he never told us? Us worrying maybe you were dead or hurt?" Gracy's voice was filled with disappointment.

"I made him promise he wouldn't."

"That's not a promise meant to keep."

Jeff stared at the floor at a spot where a tin can lid had been nailed over a knothole. "Maybe not, but I said I wouldn't write him at all if he told you. I wanted to be by myself, figure things out without you explaining them to me. I was angry, too, didn't want anything to do with you for a time."

"You had no right," Daniel broke in. He had been standing in the doorway, listening. "You had no right to go off like that and bring sorrow to your mother. Wasn't right at all."

"And you, Pa, did you have the right?"

Gracy stood and went to Daniel, putting her hands on his shoulders, kneading the old muscles with her strong hands. "It's all right, Danny. We gave him cause. But he's back now. That's all that matters. We'll be a family again." She turned to her son. "I tell you, Jeff, you walking into that courtroom was the happiest thing I've ever seen. It's been the loneliest year of our lives."

"Not a year, Ma. Only two hundred thirty-seven days. I kept track."

"Two hundred thirty-eight," Gracy told him.

"That's if you count the first day. I don't, because I was sitting on Jubilee Mountain that day, looking down at the house, thinking, could I really go? I saw you come out of the cabin with my note in your hand, the one I wrote telling you I was going off. You looked around. But you didn't look high enough. You didn't see me."

"Would you have come back if I had?"

Jeff shrugged. "I'd have gone away sometime."

"I expect he's right about that, Gracy. There was just so much we could tell him," Daniel said.

Jeff stood and looked out the window, making it clear he was finished with the conversation. So Gracy moved to the fireplace, set kindling, then took a match to the wood, and it flared up. When she was satisfied the kindling was burning, she reached into the wood box for larger pieces. "I wasn't expecting you, so it's only what's left over for dinner. But I'll bake a pie for supper. There's currants I picked only yesterday, a whole pan of them."

"I guess I'd come home just for your pie, Ma."

"Oh, go on with you. I was never known for my cooking," Gracy said, clearly pleased.

Jeff went to the fireplace and took down a piece of ore that he turned around and around, studying it. The mantel was filled with rocks—ore samples and a peach can of gold nuggets smaller than the tip of a baby's finger. Then he asked his father whether he'd found a vein that last year. It was like old times, Gracy thought, the two men sitting, hefting ore samples, talking about gold prospects, while she hummed at her cooking, pleased to care for them.

She listened to them for a time, then turned to thoughts of the hearing at the courthouse that morning. It had been harder than she'd expected, people staring, smirking, as if she hadn't birthed almost every young'un in the room. But listening to Coy Chaney and Little Dickie Erickson talk about her as if she were the devil's wife had almost undone her. A time or two, she'd had to sniff back tears.

And if listening to the charges against her hadn't been enough, she worried about the young women who would need her when their time came. Would they trust her now? Would they go to Little Dickie instead? He'd be better than no one, but the women wouldn't like him. He was too brusque. He lacked sympathy and patience. He'd try to hurry the women along instead of waiting for nature's own time. So some women might turn to a sister or a mother to deliver their babies. And then what would they do if things went wrong? Gracy would never forgive her accusers if a baby or a mother died because someone believed Gracy was a killer and wouldn't send for her in time of need. And she would never stop blaming herself.

She couldn't worry about that now. There was the trial to

think about. The charges weren't going away as she'd hoped. She would be tried for manslaughter and maybe sent to jail. Ted Coombs was right, she knew now. The prosecutor would dig up everything she'd ever done wrong and throw it out there. Ted had asked was there anything he should know, something that would throw him off if he wasn't prepared for it.

Gracy shook her head. She took out a bowl and added flour and the mixings for biscuits. There was leftover stew in the larder. She could add a little water, more potatoes, and make it stretch. She'd cut some lettuce and wilt it with salt and vinegar. It wouldn't be a dinner to brag on but not such a poor one at that, most likely better than what Jeff had eaten the last two hundred thirty-eight days.

She stared out of the window at Jeff and Daniel, who'd gone outside to chop wood. They worked the way they had from the time Jeff was little. They bore such a strong resemblance to each other. Gracy had seen Daniel in the infant's face the first time she held him—the chin, the ears bent forward. Only a Brookens had ears like that. The hair, though, that was like his mother's. Even if it wasn't apparent to others, Gracy had seen the connection. She always did with a baby.

"You came home," Gracy muttered. Despite the events of the day, she felt a surge of happiness. Jeff had come to terms with things, she thought. They would go back to what they'd been. But no, Gracy knew. Things were different now. They'd never be the same.

Thirteen

Earl, the stable boy, took down the sidesaddle that hung on the wall and carried it to the horse. Gracy had come to the stable before dawn because she wanted to visit the babies, now nearly four weeks old, that she'd birthed in Mayflower Gulch. She would have called on them earlier, but her accident, the hearing, and Jeff's return had kept her away. Gracy wished she could take the buggy, which had been repaired, but the trail between the two cabins was not wheel-clear. Mayflower Gulch was closed in the middle, no way from one end to the other except on horseback. She would have to pick her way through the trees and across streams. If she took her buggy, she'd have to go down one trail and back, then take a second trail to the other cabin. So she'd asked Earl to saddle Buckshot, one of the stable's horses.

"No sidesaddle," she told the hostler. "I'll take a man's saddle. You ought to know that by now."

"I just thought you might want to ride like a lady. You know, with what's happened . . . what people will think . . ." Earl's voice trailed off.

It always surprised Gracy how folks looked askance at a lady who rode astride. There was no sense for a woman to have to sit in that uncomfortable sidesaddle position, her body half turned away and cramped, unable to dismount by herself. Where would she find a person to help her get off the horse at some lonely spot? She'd learned to ride astride in Arkansas, could race a mule with the best of them, even Daniel. She didn't hold with being trussed up in a sidesaddle. Despite what Earl said, she didn't care what people thought, not about the saddle she used, at any rate. She had a long ride by herself through the pines, and her comfort and safety mattered more than her reputation, tattered as it was now.

Earl shrugged and took down a second saddle and swung it over Buckshot, while Gracy went to her own horse, Buddy, and rubbed his nose as if to tell him she was sorry he wouldn't be going out that day. Then she mounted Buckshot, and Earl handed up her medicine bag along with a burlap sack that she tied to the saddle horn. The sack held jars of jelly, laundered cloths, and three baby quilts that Gracy and Mittie had made. They weren't their fanciest work. There hadn't been time for that, so they'd made string quilts. But they would keep the babies warm, and that was what mattered.

She headed off in the borning light, too early, she hoped, for anyone to see her. Riding astride like she was, with her bag and sack attached to the saddle, she didn't want folks to think she had left out. Besides, somebody out there might follow along and do her harm. There had been no more incidents since Gracy's buggy hit the log felled across the road, but Daniel worried, and so did Jeff now. More than ever, they—and the sheriff—were convinced the accident had been the work of Jonas Halleck.

Jeff had offered to go with his mother, and Gracy wanted him to. She couldn't allow it, however. New mothers had questions of a personal nature, and they wouldn't be honest with her if Jeff was along. What woman would ask Gracy how to treat cracked nipples or when to resume relations with her husband if a strange man was standing nearby? It was hard enough on the woman that her own husband might be listening. Besides, she wanted Jeff and Daniel to have their time alone.

As Gracy left the last cabins in Swandyke, the sun hit the peaks of the Tenmile Range, shining on patches of snow higher up. Snow had been in the basins since Gracy arrived in Swandyke and might have been on those mountains since the beginning of time. As the sounds of the stamp mill and the smoke of morning fires faded, Gracy breathed in the mountain air, took in the sharp scent of juniper, and thought this was a place that God had made. She'd loved the Colorado mountains from the time she'd first set foot in them. Now, she listened to the sound of wild things, the squirrels tsking at her, the birds pecking among the pine needles, a coyote or maybe it was a fox scavenging in the underbrush. This was where her heart dwelled, among the jack pines and the columbine and the pink summer's-half-over, dwelled there as much as it did in the cabin with Daniel.

If she were found guilty of the murder of the Halleck baby,

she thought, she would have to leave these mountains. She'd be locked up in a prison somewhere, in a cell where she'd never feel the sun's rays on her face, never see a one-flower gentian or a stalk of fireweed. She would die without the sun and the mountains, and without her to care for him, Daniel would likely die, too.

She'd been in a prison once, back when the war had just started. Daniel was for the Union, but he hadn't wanted to fight, knew too many Confederates to want to go to war against them. Gracy and Daniel had moved to California and then Nevada. It was the gold that called them west, but it was the war almost as much as the gold that made them stay. In California, there'd been tension between those who stood for the North and those for the South. Violence as well.

Daniel and another Union man had been attacked by three men who called them turncoats and cowards and shot Daniel's friend. Two of the instigators got away, but the third was arrested and charged with murder. Gracy didn't know him, but the next day, she was called upon to deliver his baby. His wife was sickly, and when she asked Gracy to tell her husband about his new daughter, Gracy couldn't refuse. She went into that jail, where half a dozen men were crowded into a single cell. The smell of unwashed bodies and human waste made her want to put her apron to her nose, and it was only with great effort that she didn't. The husband sat on a bunk, scratching the graybacks that infested his body. "Don't never tell my wife how it is here," he said. "I can't stand being locked up like this. I won't never see my daughter. I don't reckon I'll last long enough." And he didn't. He and another man were shot down while trying to escape.

She'd had her chance to escape, too, Gracy remembered. John Miller had given her one, but she'd refused to take it. Even worse than being locked up, Gracy believed, was the idea that if she ran off, people would believe she was a murderer. That would kill her soul every bit as much as it would die in a prison cell. She stopped a moment in an aspen grove, putting her hand against a leaf that quaked in the breeze. By the time the aspen turned gold, the trial would be over. If she were found guilty, she'd never see the colors change, never see the way the fallen leaves formed a carpet as yellow as the sun.

In a minute, Gracy nudged the horse along. She was in no hurry. She had a day to spend among the pines and the sage, but there was work to do. She rode to the edge of a meadow set among the high mountains and looked across it at a log cabin so low to the ground that she might have missed it if she hadn't known where it was. Smoke came from the chimney, and washing was spread over the bushes. Still, the camp was desolate, set almost at timberline, with only stunted trees around it, and Gracy wondered what those two—those three now—would do when the snows came. It wasn't much of a living up that high, Gracy thought, looking up at the saddle that connected two mountains. The boy worked a prospect, but judging from the sparseness of the cabin, he didn't take out much gold. Maybe they'd move into town, but Gracy didn't think so. Mountain-bred like they were, they'd feel closed in among other people, would sicken in the air thick with smelter smoke.

She called "Hello, the house" as she came through the gulch

and cut across the meadow, the horse Buckshot threading his way through the scrub.

After a time when there was no movement, she hailed the house again, and the boy came out of the door, putting up his hand to shield his eyes, for Gracy was against the sun. Then he called, "Come out, come out. It's the Sagehen's come calling." And in a minute, the girl emerged. They watched Gracy as she rode toward them, then stopped.

"Alight," the girl said, and Gracy dismounted, tying Buckshot to the hitching rail.

"I've come to check on the baby," she said. "Have you a name for him yet?"

"Isaac," the girl said. "Isaac's the son of Abraham, so we didn't have but one choice." That was the first time Gracy knew the father's name was Abraham.

"And she's Sarah," the boy said. "Funniest thing in the world, ain't it, me being Abraham and her Sarah."

"Like in the Bible," Sarah said, as if Gracy didn't already know.

"It makes perfect sense, then, to name the boy for Abraham's son," Gracy said. "Does he thrive?"

"Lively as a jackrabbit," Abraham said.

"He smiles," Sarah said.

Gracy smiled herself. Who was she to tell the mother that a baby that young only had gas bubbles?

"We got coffee that ain't been heated but twice before. Nice and thick it is, made just before my sister taken out for home.

She came and stayed with me all this time," the girl said. "We'd be honored if you'd have a cup."

And because Gracy knew it would be rude to refuse, she said, "I'd like that, if it wouldn't rob you."

The boy opened the door, which was attached to the frame with leather hinges, and they went inside that dark place.

"I take him outside when the sun's not hot on him. I don't want him to burn," Sarah said. "Abe's going to make a window, and next year, we'll have real glass in it."

Gracy went to the rough cradle and lifted out the boy, while the parents watched with pride—and a little apprehension, for the Sagehen might say that something was wrong. But nothing appeared to be wrong, and Gracy rocked the baby back and forth in her arms, taking in his sweet smell, which brought to mind the Halleck baby and, long before him, Emma and Jeff. They had smelled as sweet. She removed the knitted blanket and examined the baby, wondering as she did whether Little Dickie Erickson would take a day to ride into the mountains to examine an infant he'd delivered. It would be his loss if he wouldn't, for examining a baby you'd birthed, examining him when he was only weeks old and seeing him healthy and happy in the love of his parents, was one of the greatest joys Gracy knew.

Sarah held out her arms for her baby, and Gracy gave him up reluctantly. She understood how the new mother's arms ached to hold her son. When Jeff was little, Gracy had held him for hours at a time, studying the bright eyes and ears that stuck out like his father's, not bearing to give him up, even to Daniel. She had waited so long for someone to replace Emma. She thought Jeff would die if he left her sight.

"He thrives indeed," Gracy said, and the young couple relaxed.

"I got a plenty of milk," Sarah said. "I make sure to keep my hands out of cold water, but it's hard, what with me having to haul the water from the creek."

Gracy smiled but didn't reply. What did it matter if the girl believed her milk would dry up if she put her hands into cold water? It didn't hurt, and maybe it kept the girl's hands from being chapped.

Abraham went to the fireplace and removed the coffeepot, pouring thick coffee into three cups. It was the last of the pot, and Gracy wished she had brought along a sack of coffee beans for the couple. They went outside and sat on stumps, Sarah shielding the baby from the sun, and drank their coffee from tin cups that were battered from use.

"As good as I ever tasted," Gracy said.

"Better when it sits a day or two," Abraham remarked.

When she had drunk all of the black brew—there had been more in her cup than the other two, she noticed—Gracy rose and went to the horse and took down the burlap bag. "I brought you a little something for Isaac," she said, taking out the quilt. "It's not but a string quilt, but it will keep him warm and would please me if you'd use it." She'd wished she had some of Jeff's baby clothes, for likely the boy would need them in the winter cold. But she had given them away when they left Nevada.

Sarah ran her hand over the bright colors and exclaimed at the fabrics, the fine stitching. "Why it's new material," she exclaimed. "I never had a quilt but what it was made of wore-out clothes."

"I brought your cloths back, too, washed them up. And here's a little something else." Gracy reached into the sack for the chokecherry jelly she'd made that summer.

Abraham took the jar and held it up to the sun, which shone through the glass, lighting the jelly like a stained-glass window. He grinned at his wife and said, "We got chokecherries around here, but I forgot to buy sugar when I was to town, so we don't have no jam or jelly."

Gracy took that to mean the two hadn't the money for sugar, so she reached into the sack and took out the second jar, the one she'd intended to give to Esther Boyce. The Boyces could afford sugar, could afford it more than Gracy. "Why, lookit here. I believe I put in two jars," she said.

The boy and girl exchanged glances, and for a moment, Gracy was afraid she'd gone too far, that they would turn down the gift, thinking it was charity. The poorer mountain people were, the greater their pride. But the girl nodded, and Abraham said, "We thank you."

"Thanks to you," Gracy told them. "I do like jelly-making, and I've done so much of it this year that we won't eat it all up before next summer."

The three sat on their stumps without talking, the girl holding her hand over Issac's face to keep out the sun, Gracy thinking she could stay there all day, but the sun was high, and she did not want the young couple to have to share their dinner with her. Besides, she had another stop to make, one that made her apprehensive. She did not know what she'd find at the Boyce cabin. So she rose at last and said she must be on her way.

"You're the second caller we've had this week," Sarah said, as Gracy leaned over to smile at the baby. "The other's Josie Halleck."

"Josie?" Gracy straightened up. "What in the world is she doing up here? It's a long way from town."

"We're not so far from the Holy Cross. Josie goes there with her father, and when he's underground, she walks over here, done it for a year or more. We used to talk, and I liked the company. Now Josie just sits and stares at Isaac. I almost fear she'll snatch him away."

"She's an odd one, but she'd never hurt Isaac," Abraham added. "She never says a word, just sits and watches him. I expect one day she'll have her own young'un."

Gracy stared at the boy for a minute, realizing he knew nothing about the murder of the Halleck baby, didn't know there'd even been a baby. Maybe the couple wouldn't have been so welcoming if they'd known Gracy was charged with killing the infant. "Women love babies," she said at last.

"For a time, Josie didn't come around, and I thought she'd run off or maybe got married, even young as she is. But she's back. I like her, but she makes me uneasy," Sarah said.

Gracy gave her a questioning look, and Sarah glanced at her husband, who was untying Buckshot. She lowered her voice. "Abe says he seen her at the Nugget, says she brushed up against him once, and it near scared him to death. He said he didn't know what she was about, but I knowed."

She glanced at Gracy, who took her meaning and glanced at Abraham. "That one's too smitten to look at another woman."

"Truly?"

"You needn't worry. Besides, I think Josie just wants a friend. She's a lonely girl."

"I saw that myself."

As Abraham led Buckshot to Gracy, she peered again at Isaac, lifted her finger and let Isaac grasp it with his tiny hand. Gracy touched the soft skin on the infant's arm and smiled at Sarah. "He is a gift of God," she said, wishing she could say the same about the Halleck baby.

The day was a hot one, and the cool of the forest high above the side of the marshy gulch felt good after the heat of the meadow. Gracy, rocking back and forth on her horse, thought that it was God's day, the air clean, the breeze lazy, the sky free of clouds. It would rain in the afternoon—it always did in the high country—but there would be places for her to wait out a storm. She would find a cabin or a rocky overhang and shelter herself until the sun came out, then ride home through trees shining with wetness. Like the rest of the landscape, the rain was harsh and cold, no gentle drops of water like in Arkansas. It was as if the sky wanted to rid itself of its moisture, and the rain fell thick and cold. Perhaps the rain would not start until going on evening when Gracy was home.

Thinking of a storm, Gracy pushed her heels into Buckshot to hurry him along, but he was a lazy horse, and after a few quick steps, he slowed to a walk. She heard a rustling in the underbrush and glanced that way, thinking a fox might be there, but it could be a bear, too, and she should be vigilant. If she met with an accident, she might never be found in that remote mountainside. She could die there, her flesh eaten by scavengers, her bones scattered. She'd come across more than one human bone in her wanderings in the high country.

And then Gracy remembered the accident, the way her buggy had hit the log that had been dragged across the road. If someone were out to harm her, he would have an easy job of it in the timber of the mountain. She turned to study the growth near her, trying to pinpoint the sound, but everything was still. And then there was a flash of red near a honeycombed snowdrift left over from winter. Gracy thought it might be a clump of Indian paintbrush, but it was too late for paintbrush to bloom. Perhaps she should dig her heels into Buckshot, force him to hurry, but she was not one to shirk danger. So she called, "Who's there?"

No one answered. There was a stillness, not even the chattering of birds. Then slowly, an arm in a red sleeve reached out, and Josie Halleck rose from behind the underbrush.

"Josie! You startled me," Gracy said.

The girl didn't reply, just stared at Gracy with eyes so dark they were almost black. She was such a pretty thing, and Gracy could see how men—boys, too—would be attracted to her, would want to protect her.

Gracy didn't care to scare the girl, who was jumpy as an

antelope, so she didn't dismount, only sat on the horse and waited. She was used to waiting. Waiting was part of being a midwife.

The girl didn't move, didn't speak, only stood there staring at Gracy, her back as straight as a young aspen, ready to bound away. So Gracy slowly reached into her sack and brought out a round of bread. "I could share my dinner with you," she said. "I've a piece of cheese, too." She didn't thrust the bread at the girl, only held it in her hand.

Josie's eyes shifted to the bread, and Gracy said, "I wish I had some raspberries. I haven't seen any bushes up here. Maybe it's too high for berries. Would you be knowing about that?"

"It's too late," the girl said. She took the bread and sat down on a fallen log, and said, "Would you have some?" Asked it as formally as if they'd been sitting in the Halleck parlor.

Gracy dismounted and handed the cheese to Josie.

The two broke off chunks of bread and cheese, eating silently. Finally Gracy said, "I had a jar of jelly, but I gave it to Sarah and Abraham."

"The baby," Josie said.

"Yes, he's a pretty baby, isn't he?"

Josie turned to Gracy, but her eyes didn't focus. She seemed to be staring into the distance. "Our baby," she said.

Gracy had raised a piece of her bread to her mouth, but she slowly put it down. "What about your baby, Josie?"

"He's dead," Josie said. She stood and walked to a lichened granite outcrop. "Dead. I saw it. I saw the string." A sorrow as great as Gracy had ever seen came over Josie's face.

"You saw the baby being murdered?" Gracy asked. She went to the girl and held out her hand. "Who put the string around his neck?"

Josie shook her head, as if to shake away a vision. Then she turned to Gracy. Her eyes grew wide, and there was horror in them. "Oh, you!" she said. "You tried to help. But you didn't." She turned and rushed back into the woods toward the Holy Cross and disappeared.

Fourteen

Gracy waited for several minutes, hoping the girl would return. She called softly, "Josie. I want to talk to you about your baby." Her whisper did not go much beyond the pine trees in front of her. Each time she heard a noise, she turned, hoping Josie had come back. But the noise was only the breeze in the firs or a squirrel moving through the fallen pine needles. As hard as she looked, Gracy saw no sign of Josie's red dress.

She knew the girl was out there somewhere, hiding, her spirit empty, her arms aching to hold her baby. Gracy waited a long time for the girl before giving up. She could not call up Josie any more than she could summon a mountain jay. She would have to wait until the girl approached her again, and perhaps she never would.

Buckshot had been grazing, and now the old woman mounted the horse and kicked him into a walk, then into a trot. She had a mile to go to the Boyce cabin, and she had dawdled, first to sit in the sun with Sarah and Isaac and then again waiting for Josie. She thought for a moment of going home and visiting the Boyces another day, but there was a woman in Swandyke whose baby was due, one who had made it clear she still wanted the midwife to deliver it. Gracy had taken a chance being away for one day. She wouldn't risk another. And the Denver lawyer, Ted Coombs, had sent word he would be coming up. If Gracy didn't see the Boyce boys that afternoon, she might not be able to return for a long time, maybe never if a jury found her guilty.

The sun was on the down side of the sky, and except for the little bread and cheese that she had shared with Josie, Gracy had eaten nothing since breakfast. The berry bushes along the trail had long since given up their fruit to the birds and wild animals, and the few remaining were dry and juiceless. But what did it matter? That day would not be the first time she had gone hungry. Rarely during a labor did anyone in a house think to offer a bite to eat to the midwife.

Both families—the young couple and the Boyces—lived in Mayflower Gulch, but a rock slide had split the gulch in half, and Gracy had to climb the mountain to reach the other side. She prodded the horse up to timberline just below the hump, where the air was thin, the sun hot as a blacksmith's fire, where she could see as far as tomorrow. The wind sent up snowsmoke in the north-side mountain bowls of snow rills. Gracy looked at the scraggle of wind-whipped trees at timberline, at the damp places that were the streamheads of rivers below. She hurried the horse, thinking that Buddy and the buggy went faster than Buckshot, but they could not have made it through the trees or up to the timberline. She glanced at the sky, mindful of the clouds that had begun to gather over the range. With luck, she would be at the Boyce cabin before the rain came. She hurried the horse along, stopping only to let him drink the snowmelt of an alpine stream, drinking herself because the day was warm. She thought to pluck a bouquet of mountain marigolds from the sponge of the marsh to take to Esther Boyce. Their petals were as white as the patches of snow, their centers gold like mill tailings, but their stems were hollow as drinking straws, and without water, they would wither in minutes. Still, with two babies to care for, Esther likely hadn't time for flower picking, and most men didn't think of such things. So Gracy dismounted and broke off some stems of wild daisies.

She pushed ahead, riding through the gulch again. She had not gone to the Boyce cabin this way before, but she knew trail signs, and at last, she came across the familiar path that led to the Boyce clearing.

Only then did Gracy remember that her accident in the buggy had taken place on her way home from the birth of the Boyce twins, and it occurred to her that the two men might have had something to do with the log that had been felled across the road. But as soon as the thought came into her mind, she dismissed it. The men had been with her throughout the birth and after, and besides, what reason would they have for hurting her?

More troubling was Gracy's concern about what had happened in the trappers' cabin since the babies were born. Surely Ben realized that he had not fathered the second son. Had he beaten Davy for it, perhaps killed him? Gracy had not seen the men since the day the babies were born, and she had not heard that Davy had taken out, so likely he was still there. But after what was so apparent, how could the two men remain partners? Gracy dreaded the mood that must hang over that home.

Before she reached the opening in the trees that led to the cabin, Gracy made out the sounds of men felling a tree, a rhythm of two axes biting into the wood, the first axe making a dull thud, the second repeating it like an echo. As she rode into the clearing, Gracy heard the sounds of two voices as rhythmic as the axes, singing together the words of some old hymn she did not recognize, singing in harmony. Coming closer, she saw Ben and Davy working together, shirtsleeves rolled up, sweat running down their faces, as their axes bit into a pine that stood beyond the cabin. The tree was nearly sliced through, and Gracy waited until the men finished the cutting and set aside their axes to push over the tree. It crashed into an aspen grove, taking some of the slender white-bark trees with it. The two men grinned at each other and raised their fists in the air in a sign of triumph. If there had been a breach between them, it had been mended. Perhaps there was an understanding, had been one when Ben returned to the cabin with a wife.

Gracy knew of such things. She thought about two men back in Arkansas, brothers they were, who shared a wife. It was not remarked on. Perhaps Gracy was the only one who knew about them. She had discovered the truth of it when she birthed a baby at the cabin and heard the two men speculating which of them was the father. The wife heard it, too, and she begged Gracy to keep their secret, explaining she considered each one as husband.

The Bible allowed a man more than one wife, the woman said. Was it so wrong that she had two husbands? Gracy had kept still about it, because it was not her place to judge. Only God could do that. But Davy Eastlow and Ben Boyce were not brothers. So Gracy could not help but wonder what went on in that cabin in the darkness of night, how it had happened, and whether it was agreeable to Esther.

Gracy edged Buckshot into the clearing then, and the two men saw her and grinned. "I guess we should have yelled 'Timber,'" Davy called. "We didn't know there was nobody around."

Gracy thought that was a strange thing to say, because Esther and the babies must be around.

"Get you down off that horse, Sagehen. Did you see the size of that tree we felled? We were fixing to have a drop for our hard work. We got an extra cup," Ben added.

"Water'll do if you have it. I got to get home by nightfall," she told them. "I came to see the babies. I hope they're well."

The two men looked at each other, and as if realizing Gracy had come to see Esther, not them, they let the smiles fade. "Oh, the babies," Ben said. "They're fine. Make a lot of noise."

"Babies do. And Esther, is she fine, too?"

"As good as could be expected," Davy said, his voice dropping, as if his partner's wife were no concern of his.

It seemed strange to Gracy that Esther did not come out to greet her. The new mothers were always anxious to see her, to show off their babies, to brag about how well they thrived. But perhaps the woman was sleeping. Or tending to the infants. Gracy went to the bucket beside the door and scooped up a dipperful and drank, then filled the dipper again. The water was cold and clear, and she thought it must have been hauled from the spring not more than an hour earlier. "Tastes so good it makes me want to swallow my tongue," she said, then asked, "Is Esther about?"

"She's within," Ben said, gesturing with his head at the cabin, then turning away.

Gracy raised the latch and went inside. After the bright sun, her eyes needed a moment to adjust to the dark, and at first, she did not make out Esther, who sat against the far wall, on the bed, a baby in each arm. "I came to see the little ones—and you—to see if you are all right," Gracy said, wishing now that she had not given the second jar of jelly to Sarah and Abraham. The Boyce cabin was dreary, dark with not a single bright thing, not even a flowered dish, to add a bit of color. As Gracy moved toward the bed, she saw that Esther was looking unwell. She was listless, her hair scraggly, her skin the dirty white of old snow. "I brought you some flowers," Gracy said, holding out her handful of blooms.

Esther's mouth made an O, but she didn't say "Thanks to you," didn't say anything, in fact. "I'll just be about finding a jar for them," Gracy added, looking around until she spotted a whiskey bottle with its neck broken off, then filled it with water from the bucket outside. She set the bouquet on the table and said, "Flowers always make me happy." Esther didn't seem happy, so Gracy cleared her throat and asked, "How are the little ones?"

Esther shrugged and handed the larger of the two boys to the midwife, who unwrapped him and removed the bellyband. She checked for inflammation at the place where the cord had been attached, then looked into the infant's eyes, which were bright and clear as the water in the bucket. The boy was well cared for, clean and alert, and he made soft noises as Gracy ran her hands over him, noises that her Emma and Jeff had made when they were tiny. When she was satisfied the baby was all right, she wrapped him up and returned him to Esther. Then she examined the second boy, the red-haired one, who was smaller but just as healthy. "They do well," she proclaimed.

Esther still didn't say anything. She only clutched the babies in her slim arms, and when one whimpered, she held him to her breast, where he began to nurse.

"Your milk holds up?' Gracy asked.

Esther nodded.

"I've brought herbs to help if you think you're drying up."

"I have aplenty of milk," Esther said, speaking for the first time.

"That's good. I brought herbs for tea, too, to keep up your strength," Gracy said, getting up and going to the cookstove and removing a lid. The fire had dried almost to ashes, and Gracy fed kindling into it until it flared a little. Then she put in larger pieces of wood and watched until the fire burned bright before she replaced the lid. She carried the teakettle outside and filled it, noticing the men had disappeared. Nothing seemed quite right. In all her years as midwife, she could recall few fathers who didn't strut around the newborn, waiting to accept praise for the infant's size or looks, claiming the baby was smart as a nettle and sure to make a mark in the world. But Ben—or Davy, for that matter—didn't seem interested.

Back inside, Gracy placed the kettle on the stove and set about finding cups and measuring the tea into an ironstone pot whose handle was broken off. "It's the Lord's own day out there. Have you been about?" she asked.

Esther shrugged, and Gracy wondered if the woman had been outside at all since the babies were born. She sat down on the bed beside Esther and took the infant who had finished nursing, rocking him in her arms, smelling his sweetness. "This one is Ben . . . Benny, you must call him."

"I suppose." She was still a moment. "I mean yes, he's Ben, and I suppose we'll call him Benny."

They sat quietly until the water boiled, and Gracy busied herself making tea. She brought a cup to Esther, who did not move. So Gracy held the cup to the woman's mouth and said, "Drink." When Esther ignored her, Gracy said in a firmer voice, "Drink it everything up. The babies need your strength."

Esther reached for the cup with her free hand and sipped, spilling a little on her nightdress, which was already stained.

Gracy removed the cup from Esther's hand and set it on the table. "I'll leave the sack of tea behind. Drink you a cup every day." Then she took the woman's hand and rubbed it before saying softly, "There is a condition I've observed among some women after childbirth. I don't know what it's called. You feel you ought to be happy, but you aren't. You can't eat, and you don't want to move, only stay in bed. It's childbirth sulks, and women get it with good reason. You feel poorly from the labor and the birthing, you have the care of new babies, and you've got all your other work as well. And sometimes you've a husband who feels neglected and demands attention. The feeling goes away after a time, but until it does, you almost don't care to live. I believe you have it."

Esther turned and stared at Gracy.

"I've seen women in your situation who don't want their babies, who wish they'd never had them."

"I love my babies."

"Of course you do. But you're overwhelmed by them. Is there a woman nearby, someone you can talk to? Women understand these things. Men aren't much good at it."

"You're the only woman I seen since the babies was born."

"What about Ben and Davy? Do they take over your chores?"

"They keep me to a hardship." She thought that over. "Davy cooked before I came. Then I took over. They don't like it now when I don't cook their dinner, but sometimes I'm just too tired."

Gracy had a sudden thought. "Do they cook for you then?"

Esther shrugged.

"They take care of each other but not you?"

"They're partners."

"So are you and Ben," Gracy said. "I believe I should set him straight."

Esther flared at that. "Don't do it. Ben wouldn't like it." When Gracy didn't reply, Esther said, "Promise me."

Gracy finished her tea and took the cup to the dry sink and set it aside. "I fear for your health if you live on in this state."

"It's my own fault. They're partners. I shouldn't have come here. I didn't know how things stood."

Gracy scoffed. "You are man and wife—and parents. I believe that matters more than any partnership."

"I had my plans. Oh, yes . . ." Esther sighed. "It's the way things are."

"And how are they?" Gracy asked, sitting down on the bed again. She heard the sound of thunder outside, and suddenly the rain came, came down hard and fast and cold the way mountain rain did, bringing a chill to the cabin. Gracy thought to close the door, but the freshness of the rain overpowered the sour smell of the room. For a moment, she wondered if the men would come rushing inside, but after a time, she believed they had found shelter elsewhere.

Gracy's question hung in the air, and in a moment, Esther said, "Things are just what they are."

"You worked at Bessie Williams's house over in Kokomo," Gracy said. She had heard that Esther had been a prostitute, although she didn't know it for a fact, and if she was wrong, she thought the woman might tell her to leave, would put her out in the rain for the insult.

Instead, Esther said. "I guess it's known. I never hid it. Ben knowed, of course. It's where he found me."

"Things go on there . . ." Gracy did not know how to say it, to say that acts that would shock a Presbyterian could be commonplace in a parlor house.

But Esther took her meaning. "Is it so bad, two men? After

all, at Miss Bessie's, I had more than two in one night. I don't guess it's much different, things here . . ."

"But you hadn't counted on it."

"No," Esther said. "Like I say, I should have knowed. Ben told me he had a partner. But I thought it would be just me and him, that we'd have a proper marriage. We had a real wedding and a license. The girls cried, and Miss Bessie baked a cake shaped like a horseshoe with 'Good Luck' on it. Oh, it was real pretty. And Ben had his boots blacked and wore a tie, and he gave me this ring. He said it was his mother's." Esther held out her hand so that Gracy could see the band with the red stone on her finger. "Only truth is, it was Davy's mother's."

"So you became a wife to both of them."

"Not at first." The second baby gave a sharp cry, and Esther opened her nightdress to nurse him. When the infant settled down, she continued. "I thought we was just a married couple, but one day when Ben was out, Davy come on me. I told him no, but he said I was as much his as Ben's. He said that was why Ben had married a whore, so's they could both have me. They were partners and expected to share me, just like the wagon they bought and the traps. I said it wasn't so. I told Ben what Davy'd done, but he just laughed and said they didn't want two women around and figured one would do for both of them. It didn't matter if I was willing, because he was my legal husband and owned me. Besides, what could a whore complain about? I had it better here than at Miss Bessie's."

Esther rubbed the top of the baby's head, taking a strand of thin hair between her rough fingers. "I guess it wasn't so bad, the three of us. After a time I got used to it. We even had us some good times, and I got to thinking I was lucky there wasn't another woman here. They treated me all right. Maybe they even loved me a little. But after the babies came and I seen one was Davy's, I told Ben that was the end of it. I wouldn't shame my boys. I got standards. I might be a whore, but I got standards."

Gracy didn't know what to say. Instead of talking, she moved so that Esther's back was to her, and she began to knead the woman's muscles. Esther relaxed into Gracy's hands, moaning with pleasure. "It wasn't so bad before the boys was born. We had us a good time. But now everything's different. It don't sit right with them that I won't be a wife to both. So far, they've left me alone, but it won't be long."

"You could leave," Gracy said.

"And go where? Miss Bessie wouldn't take me back with two babies, and who'd want me in Swandyke? I guess I could go to Denver, but there's only one kind of work I can do, and I can't do it with my boys." As if anticipating Gracy's next question, she added, "I couldn't leave them here. Ben and Davy don't care much for babies. Oh, they was excited before they come, thinking, I guess, that babies took care of theirselves. Now, they complain of the crying and the smell, and say the boys are too full of ginger. They ain't never even picked them up. My babies would die without me. So you see, I got no choice." She looked at Gracy with empty eyes.

Gracy sighed. She remembered Esther saying she liked to hunt but didn't care for trapping, had said a trapped animal knew it was dying and lay there watching its blood flow out. Now Esther seemed trapped that way. Gracy'd rarely seen despair as bad as this, and like Esther, she had no answer for it. "Maybe you'd feel better if you got out of this cabin, went for a walk," she said, knowing that was no solution. Still, exercise might help Esther's mood, and she continued, "Davy said once you liked to hunt. Maybe you and Ben could go hunting. Deer meat would do you good. You could make a broth to build yourself up. You want to be healthy for the boys."

"I'd like to hunt, but who'd look after the babies? I can't leave them."

"No," Gracy said. She rose and went to the door and looked out. The rain had tapered off to a drizzle, and the sun was low down. She needed to be on her way if she was to get home before dark. "There's a woman, Sophie Kruger, lives on the way to Potato Mountain not far from here. I'll stop on my way and ask her to visit."

"Don't bother. I called on her once. She slammed the door in my face, said no fancy woman would set foot in her cabin."

Gracy smiled a little. She knew about the woman. Sophie Kruger had worked in a house herself, up in Middle Swan. But now she pretended she was quality. There were none so self-righteous as those who rewrote their past.

As Gracy stood looking out, she saw Ben and Davy come down the mountain toward the cabin. "Here's your husband," she said.

"Which one?"

Gracy smiled at the jest, then realized Esther was serious. "Both of them."

"I expect they'll want their supper." Esther didn't move.

"Let them fix it," Gracy said, turning to Esther, who smiled at her for the first time.

Gracy gathered her things then. "I'll come back to see how you are." She went over to the bed and put a hand on each baby, marveling as she always did at the downiness of their hair, the softness of the skin, the purity of their innocence. And in an impulsive gesture, for Gracy was not given to touches of affection, she put the back of her hand to Esther's cheek and stroked it. She wanted to say that God would find a way, but who was she to speak for the Lord? Besides, often enough, He hadn't found it convenient to listen to her. Instead, she said, "I'll pray for you." And then because that sounded self-righteous, she added, "Not that it will do any good, but it won't harm you, either."

The men came into the cabin as Gracy was packing her medicine bag. They didn't speak to the women, but only to each other. "Women sure got a way of dawdling," Ben told Davy.

"Lazy as winter," Davy replied. "Ain't no sign of supper."

Gracy was riled. "Did you forget how to cook? Fifteen years of batching, and you forgot, did you?"

Neither man looked at her, and Gracy wondered if she had only made things worse. "Your wife's ailing from childbirth," she told Ben. "Best to help her with her chores so she can save her strength for the babies." Then she turned to Esther. "I'll be back, make sure things are all right with you." She picked up her bag and went to the horse. Neither man offered to help her mount Buckshot.

Gracy had ridden half a mile before she realized she had forgotten to leave Esther's laundered nightdress and the baby quilts. The sun was close to setting, and if she turned back, she would not reach home before dark. But when had darkness kept her from going to the aid of a woman? She sighed and turned Buckshot around. The horse, as if knowing he was going in the wrong direction, slowed, then stopped, and Gracy had to kick him to move. She made her way back through the trees and into the clearing, where there was no sign of the men. Perhaps she had shamed them into making supper. She smiled at the idea. Her visit might not have been in vain.

She tied Buckshot to the hitching post and removed the bag containing the quilts. Then without knocking, she went inside. The men sat at the table, venison and potatoes on their plates. As Gracy entered, Ben forked a piece of meat into his mouth and wolfed it down. There was no plate set out for Esther, no food left in the skillet.

She took in the room—Esther sitting on the bed with the babies, just as when Gracy had left her, the two men hunched over their plates. "Where's Esther's dinner?" she asked.

Davy looked sheepish, but Ben was defiant. "Them that does the cooking eats," he said.

Gracy was never quick to anger, but the answer infuriated her. Esther had been forced to lie with both of them. She had gone through the pain of childbirth—twice, once for each man. Instead of cherishing her, the men punished her. Those two were as twisted as timberline trees. She grabbed Ben's plate and retorted, "Them as defiles a woman, don't eat at all."

The men, too astonished to react, only watched as Gracy thrust Ben's plate at Esther and ordered her to eat. The woman began to shovel the food into her mouth, gulping it down, while the men stared. Gracy waited until Esther was finished. Then saying, "You're not fit to associate with hogs," she picked up Davy's dinner, lifted a lid on the cookstove, and flung the contents into the fire.

Fifteen

When Gracy went up the trail to her cabin, she saw her husband sitting in the dark, on the bench in front of the house, with his knife in his hand, the dog snoring beside him. Gracy would have taken Sandy with her, but the old dog wouldn't have been able to keep up, so she'd left him behind. Now, the two of them waited for her, and just as the moon came up over Turnbull Mountain, Sandy's tail thumped, and Daniel jumped up to greet her. "God, hell! There you are, old girl," he said.

"Why, if I didn't know better, I'd think you were worried about me," she told him.

He gave her a hug in the moonlight, right there where anybody might see, and she hugged him back. "Maybe I was, just a little," he admitted.

"No need. I was on a horse that didn't move much faster than a turtle, and on horseback, I'd have seen any log Jonas Halleck's men felled on the road."

Neither of them mentioned that there were other ways she could have been hurt.

Daniel, embarrassed at his show of affection, turned brusque. "I got your dinner warming, probably burned up by now."

"Why, Danny," she murmured, and it was clear he was pleased at her words, although he looked away, looked down at the dog and patted his head, picked up a stick and threw it for Sandy to fetch.

Daniel took Gracy's medicine bag, and impulsively, he grasped her hand, Gracy thinking, what foolishness is this?

Later, at the supper table, Gracy told Daniel what had happened in Mayflower Gulch.

"You are not a hater," Daniel said.

"No, I'm not, but the hate came over me today like almost nothing I ever felt."

Daniel nodded. She knew he had seen her react like that once before. But it had not been hate—anger perhaps, more likely sorrow so profound that it had bowed her over in grief.

"I was so mad I couldn't help myself. I never should have taken away those men's dinner like I did. But I kept thinking they were not fit to knock at Esther Boyce's door. Most likely, I made things worse for her." Gracy paused. And then suddenly, her face lit up. "But I believe it was the first time Esther's eyes sparkled since the babies were born. It served those boys good and right."

"You see," Daniel said. "You did some good after all."

"Only for that moment. It's not possible to help her for longer than that. Nobody can do any good for the poor woman. I never saw a thing so hopeless as that cabin. What's to become of her? Where could she go? There's aplenty of things folks in Swandyke might overlook, philandering being one of them and maybe even working at a parlor house. But a woman with two husbands? Even the whores would turn their backs on Esther." Gracy thought that over. "Funny, if it'd been a man with two wives, folks would chuckle, say what a rare fellow he must be. But a woman?" Gracy shook her head. "I don't know the answer for it."

"The one boy looks that much like Davy, does he?"

"Hair the color of fire, brighter than any I ever saw, just like Davy's. Hands like his, too, the way they curl and the thumbs stick out, and green eyes the color of a beaver pond. Oh, yes, it's enough to be remarked on, Danny." Gracy cut off a piece of the chop that Daniel had fried. Daniel was used to Gracy being away, used to fixing his own meals, because he never knew when she would return. But that morning as she left, Gracy had said she'd be back at dark, and so he'd readied the fire and put out the chops, boiled the potatoes, then kept the whole warming to await her return. If the supper had been there too long and was overcooked, Gracy didn't notice.

Jeff wasn't at home. Gracy yearned to see him but didn't ask about him. She knew he had friends to see. Or he might have gone to the saloon, for he'd picked up the habit of drinking when he was away. He'd grown up during the time he'd spent in

Nevada. Well, it was to be expected. Maybe leaving Swandyke had been a grown-up decision.

Jeff had been more than sixteen when he left, almost a man then. No, Gracy, thought, he was already a man, although she hadn't known it. They couldn't have stopped him from leaving, because Jeff was stubborn. And where had he gotten that? Gracy smiled to herself at the answer. The boy was too much like his father. Their minds worked the same way. They were both determined. Like his father, Jeff was sturdy as a mule, his hands powerful, and he carried them as though they were a thinking part of him. When he assembled a piece of machinery or mended the broken wing of a bird, Jeff's hands seemed to tremble, as if they and not his brain were in control.

Maybe when this trouble over the Halleck baby was done with, maybe if Gracy were found not guilty, Jeff would go to the mining school down below, in Golden. Or he might just leave again. Gracy wished there were a way he could stay in Swandyke, but what was there here for him besides his parents? He would leave, but this time he would go with his mother's blessing.

Gracy tried her best to swallow the food Daniel had prepared, but she couldn't eat when she was upset, and she was worried— about the trial, the Boyce woman, the Boyce babies, even Josie Halleck. She knew Daniel was concerned, too, because she'd seen the half-dozen whittling sticks he'd left outside beside the bench.

Daniel looked at her across the table now. The kerosene light was soft on Gracy's face. Her hair, most of it as gray as a winter sky, curled a little over her forehead, and up close, it smelled like wood smoke, left the scent of smoke and sage on her pillow in the morning. Daniel'd never cared that she wasn't much to look at, she knew. He'd said there was something beyond pretty about his wife: the spirit that lit up her face, the way she carried herself with pride, the hands, gentle enough to coax a baby from a woman's womb but strong enough to grip an axe or a plow handle—or his arms in bed at night. She was a something, hardboned, tough in sinew, he'd told her, shivering at the way she held him. In all those years, he said, he'd never gotten over the wonder of her.

Gracy glanced up and caught Daniel watching her. "What are you thinking, old man?" she asked.

Daniel grinned at her. "I'm thinking I'm not such an old man yet." He reached across the table with his gnarled hand and gripped Gracy's arm. "Not too old at all."

Gracy's face lit up. "You are a sight to come home to," she said. Then she looked around and asked where Jeff was.

"Over to Middle Swan, maybe getting drunk. I expect he won't come home till morning."

"Is he home for good, do you think?"

Daniel shrugged. "He hasn't said."

"You haven't talked to him about it?"

Daniel shook his head. "What is there to say?"

"Does he trust us?"

"He loves us."

Gracy set down her fork, leaving most of her food untouched. "There is a difference," she said, "between love and trust."

"I know that."

"He'll get over it."

"You did, then?"

Gracy nodded. "Of course I did. You know I did."

"But you didn't forget?"

She shrugged. "I've tried."

"I'm sorry, Gracy."

She rose and picked up the plates, then scraped her dinner into the slop bucket. "It's not worth talking about. I don't recollect the Bible saying you had to do penance for the rest of your life."

Daniel got up from the table and went to the stove, pouring hot water into the dishpan. "You want to wash or dry?"

"Wash."

"You know your Bible, all right, more than any person I ever knew, except maybe my mother. And she couldn't read."

"Black Mary had it in her memory. It's a good thing to know."

Gracy handed her husband the washed plates and then the forks. She added the fry pan to the dishpan and scrubbed it, setting it by the fire to dry. Daniel carried the basin to the door and threw the dishwater onto the garden. In that dry place, no water was wasted.

"I believe I'll spend some time with the Bible this evening," she said, untying her apron and hanging it on a hook beside the stove.

The Good Book lay on the seat of her chair, and Gracy went over and picked it up. But Daniel took it out of her hands. "Later," he said, drawing her toward the bed. "Maybe later." Gracy smiled at him, thinking, *hips. He still has those hips.*

———

Dreams woke Gracy, and the memory of them would not let her go back to sleep. She went outside and brushed aside the wood shavings Daniel had left on the bench and sat down in the moonlight. How many babies had died? she wondered. How many women since that first one in Arkansas so many years before?

She thought of that young mother now, although she couldn't remember her name. Gracy hadn't been delivering babies for more than a year or two when a man came to the door asking for Granny Nabby. "You go," Nabby had said. "She's had half a dozen already with nary a problem." Nabby's legs were swollen, and Gracy knew it would pain the old woman to stand beside a childbirth bed. So she had picked up the medicine bag and gone through the night with the man.

The cabin stood in a field of purple asters, and Gracy had begged him to stop for just a minute so she could pick a bouquet. His wife would have something pretty to look at during her pain, she'd explained.

When Gracy arrived, she found the woman still in the early stages of labor. So between the pains, the two women talked.

"I am wishing for a girl this time," the woman said. "I love my boys, but boys grow up and cleave to their wives. A girl is a daughter forevermore, no matter where she goes or how many young'uns she has. I crave a daughter because all the others are boys." Gracy glanced over at a second bed, where a gaggle of little boys was sleeping in a pile, like puppies.

"You'd teach her to cook. And to sew, too," Gracy said, sitting on a chair beside the bed. She had examined the woman and knew the baby wouldn't come just then.

"And quilt. We'd sit on the porch of an evening with our pieces, stitching them together."

"It's as pretty a picture as there is," Gracy said, thinking one day she would have a daughter who'd sit on the porch with her and stitch in the late day when the hills turned blue in the fading light. "What will you name her?"

"Mary. I'll call her Mary. I had that name in mind since before the first boy was born. My husband says he knows it will be a girl, says I carry it different-like."

Hours later, the woman did indeed deliver a girl, and she and Gracy shared the joy. "Your boys have a sister," Gracy announced, as she held the newborn up for the mother to see. The woman's happiness stayed with Gracy for a week, warmed her until the father came by Nabby's cabin and said in a voice worn from sadness, "She's dead."

"No," Gracy said, sharing the man's grief. "She was such a sweet thing, your Mary," she said.

"'Twasn't Mary. My woman died. She got a fever and near about burned up from it. I buried her in the meadow this morning."

The man didn't blame Gracy. Childbirth was dangerous. Men knew that as well as women. But Gracy blamed herself. She should have told the man to send for her if the woman did poorly. She'd never lost a mother and couldn't help but wonder if she'd done something wrong, left a piece of the placenta in the womb, for instance.

Gracy grieved for weeks, until Nabby explained to her that

death was part of the cycle of life. You couldn't have birth without death, Nabby told her. You couldn't experience the happiness of delivering a perfect child without taking on the sorrow
of losing a mother or a baby. That sorrow would always remain
with Gracy, Nabby warned. The sorrows would build up until
sometimes the weight of them was almost too much. Gracy would
have to learn to bury them deep in her mind, to think instead
of the mothers and babies who lived.

And for the most part, Gracy had done that. But not always.
That very night the overwhelming grief had returned in her
dream of the woman so many years before. She carried the
memory of that dead mother and all the others like a sore. And
now she had added Esther's plight to that grief.

She looked out over her garden in the moonlight. She'd planted
daisies and hollyhocks and all the other flowers to bring her
peace. But she'd never planted a purple aster.

"I woke up, and you weren't there," Daniel said, standing in the
doorway. "I waited for you to come back to bed."

Gracy smiled to think how he must have moved over to her
side of the bed to keep it warm for her. But after a time, he would
have worried when she didn't return, so he'd gotten up.

"I thought you might be reading your Bible," he said.

Gracy shook her head. She had left the Bible inside.

"You want your shawl?" Daniel asked, because the air was
chilly and Gracy wore only her nightdress.

Gracy looked up at Daniel, dressed in his long underwear,

and shook her head. "Aren't we a pair, out here in our night clothes. Anybody seeing us would think we were daft."

He stood behind her, his hands on her shoulders. "You came out here to think, did you?"

"I couldn't sleep."

"You never can't sleep, Gracy. You still worried about the Boyce woman?"

"Her and all the others." Daniel knew how the grief came on her sometimes, and she didn't want to talk about it, so she asked, "What if they find me guilty? What if they send me away?"

Daniel tightened his grip on his wife.

"What if they lock me up in jail, lock me up so's I could never see you and Jeff again. What then, Danny?"

"They wouldn't do that."

"But they could. People I thought were my friends have turned against me. Women," she said, her voice a sad cry. She shivered and Daniel lifted her up, feeling the bones in her back. Gracy was never a fleshy woman, and she had lost weight in the last weeks. "Come to bed, old girl," he said gently, leading her back into the house.

Gracy patted his arm. "Not so old," she said, repeating his words of earlier that evening.

Daniel smiled. "We're still good together," he said.

Gracy smiled back, but the relief she had felt earlier in the night when they'd clutched each other in bed was gone. Her troubles had returned.

In the morning, Gracy sat outside again, this time with a soda biscuit in her hand, Daniel beside her on the bench, his knife stripping the bark from a stick. He was almost finished when they heard someone on the trail, and the old dog got up and wagged his tail. Some watchdog, Gracy thought. Was there anybody Sandy didn't like?

At first, she believed that Jeff had returned. So pushing the slivers of bark from the bench, she stood up, brushing the crumbs off her apron. But instead, John Miller came into the clearing.

"You're working hard, I see," John said, clapping Daniel on the back.

"There's aplenty of sticks out there that needs their bark stripped off, and I intend to do my duty," Daniel replied.

"A man's life ain't easy with work like that to be done—sticks to whittle, coffee to drink, sun to be sat in." John stood beside Daniel and was silent then.

"Did you come for a reason or just to rile me?" Daniel asked.

"A reason," John said. "I got the word this morning that the judge will be up here on Friday. He's set Gracy's trial for that morning."

"So soon?" Gracy asked.

John nodded. "Maybe it's best to get it over with."

"Maybe. Lift that cloud from our heads," Daniel said, smiling at Gracy, trying to put the best face on it.

But she didn't smile back. "We'll know in a week, Danny," she said. A week and she'd be free, Gracy thought. Or she'd be gone from him, perhaps forever.

Sixteen

The courtroom reminded Gracy of the country fairs she'd attended as a girl in Arkansas—festive and noisy and filled with commotion. She had thought things couldn't be worse than at the hearing, but they were. Now, just six weeks after the Halleck baby was killed, it seemed to Gracy as if people had come to a celebration instead of a trial, as if her own life were not at stake. The room was packed as tight as nails in a keg, with miners and mill workers, clerks and draymen and bums with nothing better to do than listen to Coy Chaney and Jonas Halleck and Little Dickie Erickson accuse Gracy of murdering a baby. The watchers lounged in the chairs, scratching and spitting, sometimes aiming their tobacco juice at the spittoons, sometimes not. A few of the men were dressed in suits. Gracy didn't know them. They were law clerks up from Denver come to witness the trial, Gracy's lawyer, Ted Coombs, explained to her. And newspaper reporters. Ted nodded at one man and whispered to Gracy that he was from the *Rocky Mountain News*, the major paper in the state.

"What's he doing here?" Gracy asked.

Ted took a deep breath and let it out. "This is big news, Gracy, a woman being charged with murder, and the murder of a baby at that. And the baby is the son of a prominent mining man. You and I, we're aware of what kind of man he is, but outsiders regard him highly, and so do a fair number in Swandyke. We're lucky the New York newspapers didn't send somebody to cover the trial." He glanced around at men in suits and paper collars, bowler hats hanging from the knobs on their chair backs, and added, "Maybe they did."

Gracy didn't care what people in New York thought about her, but she was concerned about folks she knew in Colorado, maybe in Arkansas. She hoped there were no reporters from back there. "The reporters being here, is that good or bad?"

Ted shrugged. "It depends on the judge. Some judges think it's their job to ask questions. If a judge likes to see his name in the papers, he'll likely talk too much, ask you questions himself, and argue with Doak and me. As far as I know, Judge Downing isn't an investor in the Holy Cross, but still, he'll treat Jonas Halleck with respect. We're lucky the judge isn't up for reelection, else he might turn this into a circus."

"Looks like it already is," Gracy said, turning to gaze through the open doorway at hawkers outside selling Cornish pasties and doughnuts and cups of lemonade One had tried to sell an apple to Gracy as she approached the building, then realized who she was and said, "Well, if it ain't the baby killer." That was what she was to people who didn't know her, Gracy realized—and to some who did.

Despite the fact Ted had told her earlier that the judge might exclude women from the trial due to the delicate nature of the charge—what mining town woman was delicate? Gracy had scoffed—a third of the spectators were female. Mittie McCauley sat in the front row again, next to Daniel and Jeff. The young woman had brought supper to Gracy three times that week, and that very morning, she had shown up at the Brookens's cabin at first light with a breakfast cake, made with cinnamon and brown sugar. There was a nurturing about Mittie that moved Gracy. It was a pity the woman had no children.

Gracy knew many of the women in the courtroom. Two or three smiled at her, and one woman waved the hand of a girl no older than Emma when she died. Gracy had birthed the girl. In fact, she had delivered most of the children there. The women had brought baskets with them, probably their dinner, since the trial was expected to last all day, maybe longer.

The people Gracy knew smiled at her and waved and made gestures of support, but not all of them. Effie Ring was halfway back in the courtroom with Georgia Simmons, Pearlie Evans, and two other women, all of them once Gracy's friends. They had turned against her. Little Dickie Erickson sat off to the side. He was dressed in a black suit and wore spectacles, which made him appear older, but only by a day or two. He stared straight ahead and wouldn't look Gracy in the eye. Next to him was Coy Chaney, who scowled at Gracy when she glanced at him, and behind them sat Jonas Halleck and his wife, Edna. Jonas kept his gaze at the front of the room. His face was drained of color. Gracy stared at Edna, who, like Gracy, wore black, but Edna would not look at her, either, only kept her eyes on her hands folded in her lap.

Gracy glanced around for Josie and realized the girl wasn't with her parents. For some reason, Gracy had expected her to attend the trial. After all, she was the mother of the baby Gracy was accused of murdering. What mother wouldn't be there? But then, who knew Josie was the mother? Jonas Halleck had claimed Edna was the mother, and who doubted him? Gracy had told only John Miller and Ted Coombs the truth.

She thought the trial might be too much for the girl, who was already fragile. Besides, the prosecution hadn't listed her as a witness—in her state, there was no telling what she'd say, Ted had explained. For that reason, he didn't plan to question her, either. Nor had Edna been listed as a witness, although the one time John had questioned her, she'd agreed that Gracy had killed the baby. "With Halleck testifying, Doak must believe he doesn't need her," Ted had speculated to Gracy. "Maybe he thinks she'd be sympathetic to you." Ted himself didn't plan to call Edna, either, for fear she'd accuse Gracy. He hadn't been able to question either woman. Jonas hadn't allowed it.

The courtroom was jammed now, with people standing along the walls and in the doorway. A few were outside, hoping others would leave so that they could push inside. Gracy hadn't expected so many people, and she felt fluttery inside. "Is it always this bad?" she asked Ted.

He shook his head. "Like it or not, Gracy, this is a big case. It's been written up from here to the East Coast. There are ministers in Denver preaching against you."

"They don't know me. They don't know what happened."

"When did that ever make a difference?"

Gracy was about to respond when the clerk pounded on his desk and told everyone to rise. "The Honorable Judge Downing presiding," he announced.

The judge came into the room, looking a little surprised—and maybe pleased—at the size of the crowd, then sat down, and when there was a murmur, he pounded his gavel.

"No need for a trial. She's guilty," Coy Chaney said in a loud voice.

The judge pointed the gavel at Coy. "One more comment from you, sir, and you will be ejected from the room." The judge glared at Coy, who glared back, then looked away. "Now if that is understood, we will begin jury selection."

"I know most everyone here," Gracy whispered to her lawyer, and indeed, more than one potential juror nodded and smiled at Gracy or told the judge she'd delivered his child.

The prosecutor, too, realized that Gracy knew many of the potential jurors. "I believe I must request a change of venue," he said when, by mid-morning, only seven jurors had been selected. Gracy remembered Doak well from the hearing less than a month before—hard and mean-spirited. "It is impossible to get an impartial jury in Swandyke. I believe we should move the trial elsewhere—to Middle Swan or to Breckenridge."

"Too late, Mr. Doak. You should have thought about that

earlier. We are going to begin this trial today—and here in Swandyke," the judge said "Now on with it, sir."

Doak nodded, as if he'd gotten what he'd asked for. The clerk called another name, and Gracy was startled to see Davy East-low stand up.

"No," Gracy muttered, and she whispered to Ted what had happened at the Boyce cabin.

The prosecutor asked Davy a few questions, then said he was satisfied.

Ted was not so quick to agree on Davy. "You know Mrs. Brookens?" he asked.

"She delivered my partner's boys."

Gracy listened for snickering but heard none. Apparently no one in Swandyke yet suspected that Davy was the father of one of those babies.

"You like to eat, do you?"

Davy looked startled and didn't answer, while the judge leaned forward and frowned. "What kind of question is that?" he asked.

"A perfectly logical one if you will indulge me for a minute," Ted replied.

"I'm betting the answer is yes. That's the way I'd answer it," the judge said. People laughed, and that time, the judge did not gavel them into silence. He glanced at the group of newspaper-men as if to see whether they'd written down his remark, then motioned for Davy to answer.

Davy didn't respond at first, just turned to stare at Gracy. "I reckon," he said after Ted prompted him.

"Venison?"

Davy shrugged.

"Is that a yes?"

People glanced at each other, not understanding what was happening.

"Get on with it, Mr. Coombs. This isn't a boardinghouse," the judge said.

"Yes, sir. Mr. Eastlow, is it true that Gracy Brookens came to your cabin to check on your partner's wife and found you and Mr. Boyce treating her shamefully? Is it true the two of you refused to care for her? Did Gracy Brookens throw your dinner into the stove because she objected to your treatment of Mrs. Boyce?"

People snickered again.

"Well?" Ted asked.

"That Sagehen had no right. Weren't my place to fix Esther's supper. She wants to eat, she can do for herself."

"With two newborn babies to care for?" Ted asked.

"Ben never should have married her. Them babies changed everything. We was all fine before they come along."

Ted started to ask another question, but the judge interrupted. "We haven't got all day, Mr. Coombs. I'm guessing you'll excuse this man for cause. Am I right?"

"Yes, Your Honor."

"I'd vote guilty," Davy said, before the judge told him to step down. As Davy walked down the aisle, men in the courtroom looked away, but women glared at him. Gracy knew that Swandyke folks would wonder about him now, would wonder about

Esther, too, and the babies. Perhaps she should not have told Ted what she had done with Davy's supper.

"Hurry it along," the judge said, and as if both the prosecutor and the defense attorney were tired of interviewing, the two men quickly agreed on five more. The twelve jurors sat down in rocking chairs in a boxed-off area that served as a jury box, sending up a racket of squeaks as they moved back and forth.

When the jurors were settled, Doak stood and walked over to the twelve. "Members of the jury," he began, "your duty is to find this woman, this Gracy Brookens, guilty of murder, the murder of a helpless baby."

Ted stood to protest, but the judge waved him down. "He can say what he wants. Your turn's next," he said.

"Mrs. Brookens—the Sagehen, as some call her—played God with the life of an innocent, a child not more than a day old. She appointed herself God and took his life."

Edna Halleck moaned, and people in the courtroom muttered and shook their heads. Doak apparently forgot what he was going to say and had to look down at a paper in his hand to find his place. He cleared his throat, and continued. "That baby was God's perfect child, the heir of one of our finest citizens."

He turned and pointed a finger at Gracy. "But that woman there did not want the baby to live. She had a grievance against his father, a man as beloved and respected as any man in this community. You see, Jonas Halleck had recently fired Gracy Brookens's husband, a man known to be shiftless, intemperate—and a thief!—and Mrs. Brookens was determined to get even."

Gracy glanced at Daniel and mouthed, "For shame." Jeff put

his hand on his father's arm, but Daniel didn't move. He sat stone-still, his head high. Gracy read the humiliation in his face.

"You see, Daniel Brookens is an old codger, too feeble to handle the work in a mine. There have been accidents"—Doak shook his head but did not explain—"and Mr. Halleck could no longer use him. I'll grant you Mr. Brookens had worked for the Holy Cross every winter for five, ten years, and he might have had a claim on that job. But he high-graded, stole the very ore that belonged to his employer. Mr. Halleck is a reasonable man, a Christian, but what mine owner would employ a thief? And a drunk!"

Gracy shook her head and whispered to Ted to stop the prosecutor. She knew Daniel hadn't high-graded. And he'd never been drunk on the job. Since Daniel'd made that promise in Nevada, Gracy could count on the fingers of one hand the times he'd gotten drunk.

"Now, I'll admit that was a sad situation, one that would cause difficulty in a household, but the Brookenses had a son who could help them, so they were not left destitute," Doak continued.

He kept on. "That wasn't good enough for Mrs. Brookens. She harbored a hate for Jonas Halleck, a hate so strong that she would do anything to get back at him. And anything included murder—murder of an innocent boy.

"She took a cord out of her medicine bag and wrapped it around the baby's neck again and again. Then she pulled and pulled until she pulled the life right out of that baby. She must have smiled at that as she laid the lifeless little body in the cradle, smiled to think of how she had stolen that family's happiness. She thought the Hallecks would believe the baby had died a natural death. And they would have if Coy Chaney in his wisdom had not observed the mark around the baby's neck and discovered the fibers of a cord used by a midwife."

Gracy, sickened, looked down at her hands and shook her head. How could anyone think she had done such a thing?

The prosecutor all but shouted then. "Folk remedies! Potions! Tonics! That's what midwifery is about." He paused dramatically after each word and nodded at the jurors. "Yes, such things exist even in a fine Colorado mining town like Swandyke. Why, Gracy Brookens is illiterate," he said. Gracy herself started to object. She could read, in fact, had read every word in the Bible, and more than once. But Ted touched her arm, and she kept still.

Doak listed so many foul charges that when the man was finished, Gracy felt dirty. Could people really believe she was as devoid of all godliness as he claimed?

"Our turn," Ted whispered, but he didn't stand until the judge said, "Mr. Coombs, do you have anything to say?"

"Yes, Your Honor," Ted said, rising slowly. "I just wanted to finish writing down all the lies Mr. Doak recited so I can answer them. First off"—he turned to the jury—"your job is not to find Mrs. Brookens guilty. Your job is to find out *if* she is guilty. It is to find out the truth. And when you know it, you'll return a verdict of not guilty, because Mrs. Brookens is innocent. The evidence will show that. She didn't kill a baby. She couldn't have."

"No," a woman muttered.

Ted paused to let the woman's utterance sink in. "There's not a one of you who doesn't know the Sagehen. You know her because she delivered your children, and if she didn't, you know her by reputation. She is a good woman who goes out in mountain blizzards with no thought of herself, when women need her. She is a midwife, a woman trained to deliver babies. And she does it for no more pay than a load of wood or a bucket of raspberries, maybe not even that, because she loves women. And babies. When has Gracy Brookens ever turned down someone who needed her? She is one of the finest women ever created under heaven. I know that, and you know that." He looked at the jurors one by one. A couple of them nodded. One scowled.

"Mrs. Brookens has delivered hundreds of babies along the Tenmile Range and lost only a handful. Some of those babies she birthed were weak in body or mind, but she never hurt one of them. In fact, there are a good many babies in this place—and women, too—who would have died without Mrs. Brookens. Gracy you all call her. That's what I'll call her, too."

Ted paused and drank from a glass of water on the table. "You know that for a time, Gracy was the only person on the Tenmile who could doctor you. So some of you went to her when you broke bones or needed a cure for chilblains or pneumonia. And you're sitting right here in the courtroom because she healed you.

"Now I'll agree with the prosecution that the Halleck baby may have been murdered." He paused. "Or maybe not."

Gracy jerked up her head at that, but Ted went right on. "If the baby was murdered, the murderer was not Gracy Brookens. By the time you hear all the facts, you'll know Gracy no more committed a murder than you did." He pointed to one juror. "Or you." He nodded at another. "Or you. Or any of you." He was silent a moment. "And you'll have a good idea of who really wanted that baby dead." He turned and stared at Jonas Halleck. The man did not look away but only stared back. "No, your job is not to find Gracy guilty. Not at all. It is to find the truth, and when you know it, you will return a verdict of not guilty."

Ted paused a moment, then glanced at Daniel. "Now, as to the charges of drunkenness and high-grading the prosecutor made against Mr. Brookens, Mr. Halleck never went to the sheriff with them. If somebody stole gold ore from me, I'd have asked for satisfaction. Wouldn't you? Mr. Brookens was not let go because he was a drunk or a thief. Oh, no. Daniel Brookens was fired because he complained about conditions in the mine. He complained about shoddy materials and a buildup of gas underground. Mr. Halleck, that 'beloved, Christian man,' didn't want to spend money making the mine safer. *That's* why Mr. Brookens was let go."

Ted started to sit down, then stopped as if remembering something. "Oh, and by the way, Mr. Doak, Gracy Brookens can read and write as well as you can." He held up a letter Gracy had sent to him. "And her handwriting's a good deal better."

People laughed at that, although none of the ones who found the remark funny sat in the jury box.

Ted smiled and sat down, and Judge Downing said, "Mr. Doak, you may present your evidence."

Doak smiled and stood up. Then he turned to Gracy. "Mrs. Brookens, I apologize for my error. I would not have thought someone so steeped in superstition could read."

"Your Honor . . ." Ted protested.

"Mr. Doak, that wasn't necessary," Judge Downing said.

Doak smiled, as if he and the judge shared a joke. Then he called his first witness—Coy Chaney. After Coy was sworn in, Doak asked him his occupation.

"Coroner and undertaker," he said.

"And you were the one who first discovered the Halleck baby had been murdered?"

"I was."

Coy was silent until the prosecutor said, "Well, tell us about it, man."

"You bet." Coy grinned as he glanced around the courtroom, although the grin disappeared when he looked at Gracy. "My guess is she done it," he said, pointing at Gracy. "Couldn't have been anybody else."

"Your Honor, Mr. Chaney is not here to guess," Ted protested.

"Quite right. The jury will ignore that. Mr. Chaney, you will stick to the facts."

But the damage had been done, Gracy knew. How could the men on the jury forget what they'd heard?

Coy, looking pleased with himself, sat back in his chair and told how Jonas Halleck had brought the baby to him to be buried, how he had found marks of a cord that had been wrapped around the baby's neck and fibers of the cord itself. And he knew the boy had been strangled. It was the same story he had told at the hearing, although he embroidered it with more detail and gave himself credit for discovering the murder. Once or twice Ted objected to something Coy said, but Gracy thought it was a

waste of effort. The jury had already heard Coy say he believed
she was a killer.

When Coy was finished, the prosecutor appeared satisfied,
and Gracy understood why. She'd suspicion her own self.

But Ted didn't look convinced when he stood up. "You are
acquainted with Gracy Brookens, aren't you?" he asked Coy.

"Oh, sure."

"And how is that?"

"Everybody knows the Sagehen."

"But you know her personally. She delivered your child. Is
that correct?"

"Did a poor job of it."

"And you hate her for it."

"I never said that."

"Oh, but you did. And you threatened to get even with her,
too, didn't you? I can call Mr. Asa Jackson and Mr. Jake Comfort from over in Middle Swan to the stand, if you like. They
heard you down at the Nugget."

Gracy leaned forward. She didn't know that. Where in the
world had Ted gotten the information?

"I didn't mean it. I was mad."

"But you did threaten to get even."

"I don't recall."

"Judge—" Ted began.

Judge Downing cut him off. "Did you say that, Mr. Chaney?
I will remind you that it is a crime to lie when you are under
oath."

"I guess I did."

"And do you want to give us the details of what happened to make you so angry at Mrs. Brookens?" Ted asked.

"Not hardly."

Before Ted could turn to Judge Downing, the judge snapped, "Well, do it anyway, and don't take all day."

Coy glared at Gracy. "She took her time getting to my house. The baby died, and my wife could have too, because of that old woman." He pointed at Gracy.

"And was Gracy late because you failed to call for her when your wife told you it was time to fetch her? Is that because you got drunk and forgot to collect the Sagehen?" Ted asked.

"Could have happened to anybody."

"No, sir. It could not. I will wager these gentlemen would not have done such a thing." He indicated the men in the jury box.

Doak objected, and the judge said, "Mr. Coombs, the jury is not interested in your speculations."

"I think I've established this man has good reason to bear false witness against Mrs. Brookens," Ted said, and returned to his seat.

"Next witness is Dr. Richard Erickson," Doak said, and Little Dickie stood up, stood up straight to make himself look taller. He walked to the witness chair, and head high, he stood in front of it while he was sworn in.

"You are a *medical* doctor, are you not?" Doak asked.

Little Dickie cleared his throat. "Indeed I am. I am a graduate of one of the finest medical institutions in the country. My knowledge is based on centuries of healing, not on *ignorance* and *superstition*." He spat out the words.

"Indeed, sir, and you have been certified as a physician by the state of Colorado."

"I have."

"Are midwives certified?"

"Of course not. There was a time when they might have been necessary, but today, there are real doctors to deliver babies. And we do not think much of midwifery. These mountains would be better if we had no more midwives. "

"Now, Dr. Erickson, you are here because you examined the Halleck baby after Mr. Chaney called you in, is that correct?" When Little Dickie nodded, the prosecutor continued. "And what was your conclusion?"

"That the infant had been strangled—strangled with the linen cord a midwife uses."

There were murmurs in the courtroom, and as if playing to the audience, Doak said, "You say it was the kind of thread a midwife like Gracy Brookens uses."

"I did."

"And you conclude that the child was strangled."

"Of course."

Doak continued to ask Little Dickie about the thread and the strangling, until Judge Downing said, "Enough, Mr. Doak. Thread's thread. This isn't a sewing circle."

But the prosecutor wasn't satisfied. Before he took his seat, he said, "I just want to make it clear, the Halleck baby was strangled by the sort of linen cord a midwife uses. Is that correct?"

"It is."

Then it was the defense's turn. Ted studied Little Dickie so long that the doctor squirmed. Finally, Ted said, "You have an impressive medical background, Dr. Erickson. How long have you been a physician?"

"Not long."

"How long is 'not long'?"

"I am just setting up my practice. I have been here since the start of summer."

"Two months then, maybe three. And how many patients have you had?"

"I wouldn't know."

"Oh, come, sir—hundreds, thousands, or"—Ted paused— "nine?"

"It takes time to build up a practice," Little Dickie sniffed.

"And is it true that five of those patients were referred by Gracy Brookens?"

"I wouldn't know."

Ted smiled. "But you do know that people in Swandyke would rather go to Gracy than to you, don't you?" Little Dickie started to protest, but Ted said quickly, "You have good reason to want Gracy Brookens to be the last midwife on the Tenmile, don't you?"

"I will not be insulted—"

"No, of course not," Ted said, then added sarcastically, "You are a doctor with the highest medical credentials. Tell me, Dr. Erickson. Did you examine the Halleck baby after it died?"

"I have said I did."

"And your conclusion was that he was murdered—strangled with linen thread." When Little Dickie nodded, Ted asked, "Did you consider any other cause of death? Could the baby have been dead before the cord was put around his neck?"

"Why would anybody do that?"

"That is not the question, sir. Could the baby have been dead before the cord was put around its neck?"

"I suppose."

"But you didn't examine him for any cause of death besides strangulation? So you would not know if he had died of natural causes?"

"The body was cold, stiff, dirt had sifted down on it. The baby had been dead and buried for a day or two!"

"And how do you know that?"

"Jonas Halleck told me . . ." His voice trailed off.

"So you don't know yourself when the baby died or what was the cause of death? Is it possible, sir, that the baby died on its own and someone put a cord around his neck to cast suspicion on Gracy Brookens?"

Little Dickie looked so confused that Gracy almost felt sorry for him.

"One more thing, Doctor." Ted turned to the jury and asked, "Do you yourself carry the linen cord that was found around the neck of the Halleck baby?"

Little Dickie's mouth fell open. "All physicians carry—"

"Yes or no."

Little Dickie shuddered. "Yes, but I didn't kill the Halleck baby."

"No, no, of course not." Ted gestured at Little Dickie to step down, then asked, "Oh, by the way, Doctor, how many babies have you delivered?"

"I am fully competent."

"How many?"

"Two."

After the defense lawyer took his seat, the judge looked around the courtroom, and said since it was well past the dinner hour, he would declare a recess. People filed out of the room, and in a few minutes only Gracy and her lawyer, Daniel and Jeff were left.

Jeff looked at his mother and smiled. He had his father's smile, and Gracy knew how that could melt a woman. It had always melted his mother. Gracy hoped he'd find a good woman, one who would understand him as she did Daniel.

Jeff came up to his mother and took her arm. "I think we did pretty good," he said, then turned to the lawyer. "Didn't we?"

Ted nodded. "Better than could be expected. But Jonas Halleck is next on the list, the prosecution's last witness, and him being so prominent, people will want to believe him. We will have to be careful."

Jonas did not testify that day, however. When court resumed in mid-afternoon, Jonas Halleck was nowhere to be seen.

"Where's your witness?" Judge Downing demanded.

"Your Honor, I beg your indulgence," George Doak said.

"Yes, I'm sure you do. Where is your witness, Mr. Doak?"

The prosecutor fidgeted. "This morning's testimony was too much for the poor man. He is indisposed. I ask you to give him time to restore himself to sanity. He will testify in the morning."

The judge was angry. "He what?"

Ted sucked in his cheeks to keep from smiling too broadly. Then he spoke out. "He means his star witness got drunk at the Nugget saloon."

Gracy herself could hardly keep from smiling. Jonas Halleck, that upright man, that beloved *Christian*, drunk at the Nugget! How could that have happened? And how did Ted know about it?

"Him not being here to testify, I believe the prosecution must rest its case," Ted said.

"I'll produce the witness tomorrow, sober as a judge." Doak seemed to consider his words, then hung his head. "As the expression goes. No offense, Your Honor."

"I object to the prosecution's request. The law guarantees my client a speedy trial. Why should she have to wait another day because a witness takes off on a high lonesome?" Ted asked.

"Quite right, Mr. Coombs. Why should she, Mr. Doak?"

Doak was silent, and for a moment, Gracy thought the trial would end there. The only evidence presented so far indicated the Halleck baby had been strangled with a linen cord, maybe even strangled after he died.

"We are dealing with a man under duress. He stopped for a drink. Just one. It is my belief somebody slipped a powerful drug into it and that knocked him out."

Ted scoffed. "Not likely."

"Quite likely. He had one drink. A grown man like Mr. Halleck doesn't pass out from a single shot of whiskey." Doak glared at Ted, then turned back to the judge. "I ask you in the name of all that is just to recess the court until morning. Manslaughter is a serious charge, and the dead child deserves justice. Mr. Halleck is an upstanding man, and none of us knows the truth as to why he is not here. If he is not in a condition to testify in the morning, I will make my closing argument," Doak said.

"I object!" Ted all but shouted.

"Yes, of course you do, and I do, too, but Mr. Doak is right. The charge here is so heinous that I believe the prosecution should be granted a little leeway. I had not planned to hold court tomorrow, it being a Saturday, but I see I must. Mr. Doak, make sure your witness is here first thing in the morning."

"He will be here," Doak promised.

Gracy was sure he would.

Seventeen

Mittie McCauley brought a stew to the Brookens cabin that night for supper.

"What'll your husband say, you always taking his fixin's to us?" Gracy asked.

"He's working the night shift. It's lonely at home with just me."

"Then sit you right down and eat with us," Gracy told her.

"I'd like that, being with a family. But ain't you got something to talk about?" She looked at the lawyer.

"Nothing you can't hear," Gracy replied.

So Jeff moved aside and made room for Mittie on the bench at the table, Gracy thinking it seemed like the young woman belonged there. She was a comfort. Gracy looked forward to a time when the two of them would quilt together again or go fishing in the beaver ponds.

"You think the prosecutor's got something up his sleeve, with Mr. Halleck not showing up like that?" Jeff asked.

Ted Coombs thought a moment. "I wondered myself, but I don't think Doak would dare pull a stunt that way. Besides, I can't think why he would. The judge could have called for closing arguments or dismissed the charge outright. I wish he had, but of course, he didn't. I imagine George Doak is sweating it out right now, hoping Jonas Halleck will be sober in the morning."

"Serves him right," Mittie muttered. "I don't like that prosecutor."

"I know Halleck is a drinking man, but I can't imagine why he'd let himself get drunk. And at the Nugget of all places," Daniel said. "Do you suppose somebody really did slip him something?"

"He was drinking next to a miner who seemed pretty interested in what Mr. Halleck was saying, even bought him a shot of whiskey and kept urging him to finish it off. Maybe he did put something in the drink," Jeff said.

"I wonder who it was," Daniel said. "I don't know anybody who'd buy Jonas Halleck a shot of whiskey."

"Tall man, young, but his hair was white, scar on the side of his face." Jeff gave his mother a sly glance.

Then Daniel and Gracy exchanged a look. Jeff had just described Henry McCauley, Mittie's husband. "Whoever he is, I'd like to shake his hand, and bake him an apple pie," Gracy said, smiling at Mittie. Mittie blushed, then turned away. The girl was trying to help in more ways than one.

"Halleck'll be sober in the morning. A man like that's not

likely to repeat his mistake," Ted said. He leaned back on the bench. "We almost had them. Another judge might have dismissed the charge against you, Gracy, but Judge Downing, he leans over backward to be impartial, and it didn't help that Halleck is somebody important." Ted paused. "The judge likes to hunt. My guess is he started the trial on Friday so he could spend the weekend here in Swandyke and go hunting. He'll look for a reason to adjourn early tomorrow. The jury might not get the case until Monday."

"How do you think it went?" Jeff asked.

Ted shrugged. "We got our licks in. But who knows which way the jury will go. They like you, Gracy. Still, it bothers them that a baby was murdered."

"But you said maybe the baby wasn't murdered, that that string might have been put around the baby's neck later on, after it died," Jeff said.

"I did at that," Ted replied. "But I don't know that anybody'll really believe it. Still, if they want to find Gracy not guilty, that just might give them a reason."

"Do *you* think that baby died by itself and somebody put that string on him to cause trouble?" Mittie asked Gracy.

Gracy looked at her plate. She'd tried to eat Mittie's stew so that the young woman would know she was grateful, but she hadn't any appetite. "It could have happened, I suppose, but why? Here's what I think: Jonas Halleck strangled that baby, then buried it. When he dug it up and took it to Coy for burial, Coy saw the mark around the boy's neck. Jonas had to blame somebody, and since I was the only person outside his family who'd seen the baby, Jonas blamed me."

"What's Halleck going to say tomorrow?" Jeff asked.

Ted thought that over. "He'll say the same thing he did at the hearing. He has to, because it's on the record, so he'd be guilty of perjury if he changed his story. I won't lie to you, Gracy. He's an important man, and he's a threat."

"He usually gets what he wants," Jeff said.

"You know him?" Ted asked.

Jeff nodded. "I met him a time or two. I can't say I liked him. He didn't like me much, either."

"Because of me?" Daniel asked.

Jeff shrugged.

"I'll try to trip him up, but he's sly." Ted paused. "Still, I believe when Gracy takes the stand, the jury will believe her." He turned to Gracy. "You'll be the last witness. People in Swandyke know you have a reputation for honesty."

Gracy opened her mouth to say something but changed her mind and remained silent.

Jonas Halleck did indeed show up sober the next morning, head held high as if daring anyone to charge he'd been too drunk to testify the day before. Edna Halleck walked meekly behind her husband, and like Gracy, she wore black again. Edna's dress, however, was black silk and in a new style, unlike Gracy's black merino, so old she'd once worn it with hoops. An air of sadness hung over Edna Halleck. Her life had been troublesome, probably from the time she married Jonas Halleck. Despite Edna's highborn ways, she had had it worse than others, Gracy thought.

Jonas walked up to the witness chair and sat down, preening, until the clerk told him he had to wait until he was called. He scowled and took a seat next to his wife, just as the clerk told everyone to stand and Judge Downing came into the room.

Gracy, at a table next to Ted, took a deep breath. She wished Jonas's testimony was over. She wished her own were, too. She'd been reluctant to testify in the first place, and now, after seeing how clever the prosecutor was and understanding that he could ask her almost anything, she'd all but made up her mind not to testify at all. She hadn't told Ted that. He would be furious, of course. But there were things she could not say. There was too great a chance the prosecutor would trip her up. Ted might trip her up, too, since he didn't know the whole of it. Maybe Jonas would talk all day, and she wouldn't have to make a decision until Monday. But in her heart it was already made. Now she had to wait only two more days until she knew whether she would be found guilty. And without testifying, her chances were not good. Gracy sighed as she watched Jonas Halleck sworn in. He was sure as a rooster, but maybe that would be his downfall.

"Mr. Halleck," the prosecutor began. "First, sir, my condolences on the loss of this precious child."

Jonas did not reply, only dipped his head as though the remark was due him. Judge Downing said, "Do you have any questions, Mr. Doak, or is this about niceties?"

The newspapermen smirked, and the judge smiled at them.

"Thank you, Your Honor. I do indeed have questions," Doak said. "Mr. Halleck, will you tell us everything you remember from the time Gracy Brookens arrived at your home the day your son was born?"

Jonas raised his chin imperiously. "I myself delivered the child, because it came so quickly. There wasn't time to call a doctor." He glanced at Gracy. "Or a midwife. The boy was in perfect health, but then he began to choke. So I sent for Mrs. Brookens."

Gracy shook her head back and forth and whispered to Ted, "He didn't send for me. Josie fetched me on her own."

"And she came," Doak prodded.

"Yes, to our sorrow. I thought it was an act of charity to employ her, since I had fired her husband. I knew they were in want and that the two dollars I paid her would help. As you said, I am a Christian, sir."

Gracy snorted, because she had never been paid any two dollars.

Doak glared at Gracy then turned back to Jonas Halleck. "And did she examine the baby?"

"Yes, she said he was in good health. And then she told me I had not tied the cord properly, so she took out her spool of thread and cut a length and retied it."

"What did she do with the thread?"

Jonas thought a minute. "She said the spool was used up and set it on the table."

"And later on, was it there?"

"Just the empty spool."

"And did you see her strangle your son?"

Jonas paused. "I turned away when my wife said something to me."

"You mean the baby's mother?"

Jonas was startled. "Of course the baby's mother. "

Gracy leaned over to Ted. "I told you that's not true," she whispered. "Edna didn't give birth to the baby. Josie did."

Ted nodded. He knew. Then he rose and said, "Judge, will you remind Mr. Halleck he is under oath, that perjury is a criminal offense."

"He does not need to be reminded of such a thing when he is telling the truth," Doak sniffed, before the judge could reply. Jonas gave Ted a hard look.

"If he's lying, you'll have your turn to question him," the judge told Ted.

"I will indeed," Ted replied, while Jonas continued to glare.

"Forgive us for the interruption, Mr. Halleck. I know it is difficult to talk about the murder of your own son. He was your only son, wasn't he?"

"Yes, my only son," Jonas repeated. Doak told him to continue, and Jonas said, "When I looked back, Mrs. Brookens was holding the baby, and he had stopped crying. She said he would sleep a while, and she put him into the cradle. Later on when I picked him up, he was dead."

Doak stopped and turned to the jury, shaking his head. Then he said, "Now, Mr. Halleck, at first you did not take that baby to the coroner, did you?"

"No, sir."

"Instead, you buried him yourself."

"My wife is a private person. She has not gone out in society for many weeks. No one was aware she was with child. I thought it would be best if people did not know a baby had been born and died. It wasn't anyone's business. So I buried it in the rose garden."

"And there came a time when you changed your mind?"

"Yes."

Jonas said nothing more, and the prosecutor had to prod him. "And?"

"My wife insisted the baby have a Christian burial, that he had to be buried in sacred ground. She was out of her mind with grief. So the next day, I dug him up and I took him to Coy Chaney. That's when I discovered Mrs. Brookens had murdered him."

Ted jumped up and protested that Gracy's guilt had not been established, and the judge told the jury to ignore Jonas's last remark. But it didn't matter, Gracy thought. Jonas had already had his say.

"And you swear every word of this testimony is true, Mr. Halleck?"

"I said it, didn't I?"

At that, a man snickered, and the judge banged his gavel. The courtroom was silent, and Gracy knew Jonas had impressed the onlookers, the jury, too.

The prosecutor sat down, and Jonas stood up.

"Mr. Halleck, I have a few questions," Ted said.

Jonas looked angry. "I've said all I intend to."

"Your Honor," Ted said.

"Sit down, Mr. Halleck," the judge ordered. "You are well aware the defense has the right to ask questions."

"Well, hurry it up. I have a mine to run." He remained standing.

Judge Downing banged his gavel and said, "You will return to the witness chair, sir, or I will throw you in jail until you agree to cooperate. This trial is already overlong because you failed to show up yesterday."

Gracy exchanged a glance with Daniel. If at first, the judge had sided with Jonas Halleck, he might have changed his mind. Ted had said Judge Downing would have taken Jonas's failure to show up in court the day before as a personal insult. Still, that didn't mean the judge was likely to favor the defense.

Jonas himself scowled but said nothing as he took his seat. Ted smiled at him, but he refused to smile back.

"First, Mr. Halleck, you say you are the father of the baby born in your cabin. Is that correct?" Ted asked.

"Are you impugning my wife, sir?" Jonas was indignant.

"I am asking, sir, if you are the father of the baby? Yes or no."

"Yes," Jonas muttered.

"I didn't hear you."

"Speak up," the judge added.

"The boy is mine."

"And your wife, Edna, is the mother?"

Jonas didn't reply. His eyes narrowed.

"Your Honor," Ted said.

The judge leaned forward, while people in the courtroom quieted, wondering what Ted was getting at. "Mr. Halleck?" the judge said.

"What right do you have to ask such an impertinent question?"

"Who is the mother of the baby born in your home?" Ted asked in a booming voice. He looked at the jury instead of Jonas.

"Your question is outrageous. Of course my wife is the mother of my son."

"Well, why didn't you say so in the first place?" Judge Downing asked him.

"Because it's a lie," Ted answered for Jonas. People in the courtroom started muttering, but the judge was so caught up in the accusation that he ignored the stir.

Now it was the prosecutor's turn to protest. "This is preposterous. We are here to determine who murdered a baby, not who its parents are."

"We are here to determine the truth, and Mr. Halleck is lying. This lie casts doubt on the rest of his testimony."

"There's no proof Mr. Halleck is lying," Doak said.

"Be careful, Mr. Coombs. Jonas Halleck is not to be trifled with," the judge admonished.

"The truth is for the jury to determine," Ted insisted, and the judge told him to go on.

"You say you are the father of the baby," Ted said. His voice was quiet, but so was the courtroom. "You also say your wife is his mother. But isn't it true, sir, that your daughter, Josie Halleck, gave birth to the boy? And it was Josie who ran for the midwife when the baby began to choke?"

At that, there were gasps in the courtroom, and a woman cried, "For shame." The courtroom was so noisy that the judge pounded his gavel for silence. But that didn't stop the mutters and whispers. Edna Halleck put her hands over her face and began to cry. Gracy glanced at Daniel and then at Jeff, whose eyes were wide, a look of horror on his face.

"Well, Mr. Halleck?" Ted asked.

"That's a damn lie." Jonas stood and pointed his finger at Gracy. "She made that up to save herself."

"You have already stated you are the father, so isn't it true," Ted continued, "that you murdered that baby yourself, because the mother was your daughter? You killed him because you feared Gracy Brookens would tell?"

Doak jumped to his feet. "Your Honor, this is shameful. The defense lawyer has besmirched the reputation of one of our leading citizens. There is no proof of such a foul deed."

"Mr. Coombs?" the judge said.

"Of course there is. Gracy Brookens will testify as to its mother."

Doak scoffed. "Well, how would she know? She wasn't there when the baby was born. She'd make up any lie to keep from going to jail."

By then, the noise in the courtroom made it difficult to hear. Women covered their faces with their aprons or clutched each other, while men turned away, glancing about, not sure whether they should smirk or show their disapproval. "It couldn't be," someone yelled. "Nobody would do that," said another. But Gracy knew Josie had given birth to that baby. She knew who the father was, too.

The judge himself appeared stricken at the charge. For a moment, he simply stared at Jonas Halleck. Then he came to his senses and gaveled the room to silence. "We'll have no more outbreaks like this or I'll eject every one of you," he said, although without much conviction.

"I demand the questions be stricken from the record," Doak said, his voice rising above the noise in the courtroom.

"And I demand Mr. Halleck answer it truthfully," Ted countered.

Judge Downing thought that over. "Is there any proof of such a serious charge other than the testimony of the defendant?" he asked.

"Of course there is. Dr. Erickson can examine Mrs. Halleck."

At that, Little Dickie turned red and sank down in his chair as if wishing he could disappear.

"Dr. Erickson, can you do that? Can you tell if Mrs. Halleck gave birth to that baby?"

"I . . ." Little Dickie began, then faltered. "You see, she's had another child, and this baby was born weeks ago, so it might be hard to tell. I couldn't be sure . . . I never . . ."

"Well, Doctor, have you ever examined a woman who's given birth a few weeks earlier?"

"No, sir. I haven't."

Little Dickie seemed relieved until a woman in the courtroom snickered and said, "It ain't likely any woman here'd go to him for that."

"Then you couldn't tell?" the judge asked.

"I don't know."

Jonas Halleck, who was white with rage, blurted out, "Nobody will touch my wife that way."

"Be quiet, Mr. Halleck," the judge said. Then he turned to Ted. "I have no reason not to order an examination of Mrs. Halleck, but if the doctor says he cannot establish for sure whether she has given birth recently, what good would it do?"

"We can get a doctor from Denver."

The judge shook his head. "This trial has gone on long enough, Mr. Coombs. You should have thought of that before."

"I did not know Mr. Halleck would lie," Ted said. Then he added, "There is another way, of course."

Gracy knew what he would suggest, and she shook her head, but Ted wasn't looking at her.

"And that is?" the judge asked.

"The doctor can examine Josie Halleck. Surely he can tell whether the girl has given birth."

"Dr. Erickson, is that correct?" the judge asked.

"I believe I can," Little Dickie said, looking more confident than he had a moment before.

But the doctor's reply was drowned out by Jonas Halleck. "You touch her, and I'll kill you." Jonas, his face contorted in anger, started toward the doctor, while Edna hurried to him and grabbed at his coat. He slapped away her hand and lunged at Little Dickie. "No man touches my daughter!"

"Not even her father?" Ted put in.

"You go to hell!" Jonas cried, pointing a finger at Ted.

Gracy stood up and tried to get Ted's attention. "No," she said, but Ted didn't hear her.

Instead, he sent her a look of triumph. "We've got him," he mouthed, and then he turned to the judge. "Your Honor, I request that Dr. Erickson examine the girl Josie and bring us his report on Monday."

The judge turned to Doak for his response, but instead, it was Gracy who spoke. "No. You can't do that. I won't let you. It will harm her." Gracy shuddered to think of how bewildered the girl would be if she were subjected to an examination, how humiliated. She had already gone through too much. The examination would destroy her.

"A moment with my client, Your Honor," Ted said, going to Gracy and whispering. "If we can prove she gave birth to the baby, then everything Jonas Halleck said is worthless. No jury would find you guilty."

"I won't allow it," she said.

Ted thought that over. "Then we'll have to put her on the stand. I don't like it. She's not rational, but it's the best we can do."

"Not that, either. She's too fragile. It would ruin her. Leave the girl alone." She knew Ted didn't understand, but she couldn't let Josie testify. That would ruin Josie's life and perhaps the lives of others, too.

"As your lawyer—" Ted began, but Gracy shook her head.

"I will go to prison if I have to, but Dr. Erickson will not touch that girl, and you will not put her on the stand."

Bewildered, Ted stared at Gracy for a moment, then shrugged. "Your Honor, I withdraw my request." Then as if defeated, he said, "I have no further questions for this witness."

The judge glanced up at the clock behind him. Jonas had been on the stand less than an hour, and there was still time for Gracy's testimony. "Your next witness, Mr. Coombs."

"Gracy Brookens," Ted announced. Gracy could feel the rush of excitement in the courtroom.

Gracy shook her head. She couldn't testify. She wished she had talked it over with Ted that morning, but she hadn't. If she didn't take the stand, people would likely believe she was guilty, and she would be sent to jail. But she would have to risk that. She paused, not rising, instead looking up at Ted.

But at that moment the courtroom door opened, and the sheriff stepped in. "Your Honor, I need Gracy Brookens. It's urgent."

The judge looked up and frowned. "What for?"

Gracy was confused. "John?" she mouthed, but the sheriff was looking at the judge.

"What is more urgent than a manslaughter trial, Sheriff Miller?" he asked.

"I'm sorry to interrupt, Judge, but there's been a death."

"A death?" he asked, while Gracy searched her mind. Was it one of her patients? Had someone gone into labor? Maybe there had been an accident or a miscarriage, a hemorrhage perhaps.

"Can't the doctor see to it?" the judge asked.

John shook his head. "Not likely. It's Esther Boyce that's dead, and her boys'll die, too, if Gracy don't get to them."

Eighteen

"Where are the babies?" Gracy asked, as John helped her into the ore wagon.

The judge had declared a recess, not just because he believed that the infants were in danger, but more likely, Ted had said, because he wanted to go hunting that afternoon. Gracy's testimony would wait until Monday, he said. Perhaps she should have told him right then that she would not testify, that as far as she was concerned, the trial was over. But she would wait. Ted would object, and she didn't want to take the time to argue with him. The Boyce boys needed her.

"They're at the trappers' cabin. Ben's taking care of them, I guess. Davy Eastlow came in to tell me about Esther."

"Taking care?" Gracy sniffed. "Closing the door so he won't hear them cry is more like it. But the babies should be all right till we get there. Did he tell you what happened?"

The sheriff slapped the reins on the mules, as Gracy turned to set her medicine bag in the back of the ore wagon. Although she wouldn't be delivering a baby, she never went on a call without it. "I got the borrow of this wagon in case we need to bring the body to town. If there's foul play, Coy Chaney will have to take a look at her, dumb as he is," John explained. He paused. "I don't know what happened. Davy just came in the office and said Esther was dead. 'Died of lead poisoning,' is what he said."

"You mean Ben shot her? Or Davy?"

"It's a confusion. Davy said to fetch you and get out to the place and pick up those babies or they'd die. Then he lit out before I could stop him. Esther already being dead and with the babies still alive, I figured we'd take care of them first. I can find out about Esther when we get there."

"There's other women who can take care of them. Why do they want me?" Gracy asked. She shifted on the board seat, which was not as comfortable as the tufted seat in the buggy or even a saddle.

"I don't know. Is there something queer about the babies?"

Gracy sighed. "Queer enough." She paused a moment, wondering if she should tell. But the sheriff would see for himself when they got there. So she said, "They got different fathers. I can tell such things, you know. One's Ben's. The other's Davy Eastlow's. It's as plain as the wart on your nose. One of the boys is the spit of Davy."

The sheriff whistled. "That's queer all right. I hadn't heard it."

"Maybe I'm the only one that's been to see them. I suppose it will get around now."

"It's not a thing can be kept secret. What do you suppose happened? Did Davy force himself on her?"

Gracy took a deep breath. She was not one to pass along gossip, but the sheriff had a right to know. "She told me she married Ben but ended up wife to both of them." Gracy shook her head at the wonder of it. "Trees aren't all that's warped at timberline. Men, too."

"Everybody said she wouldn't part them two," John said. "But she should have knowed it. She was a whore."

"That doesn't mean she had to be treated like one," Gracy told him. "Whores are women, too."

John gave her an odd look. "Didn't expect that from you," he muttered.

She let the remark pass, and they went on in silence, Gracy shivering a little as they rode under a fir whose branches were bowed to the ground like a tent. It was mid-August, and she could feel fall in the air. There were fewer hummingbirds now. They knew when it was time to move on.

"How'd you know about Esther and them?" John asked after a time.

"She told me. I stopped to check on her. The babies were fine, but Esther . . ." Gracy shook her head. "The men treated her like she wasn't even there, and as for the babies, Ben and Davy gave them no more attention than you would to a baby squirrel. Except maybe to complain about them. I never saw such a sorry woman. I wish I could have helped her. It's pestered me ever since."

"What could you have done?"

"That's the trouble of it. I don't know."

"Well, those boys won't keep the babies. You've got them to raise now."

Gracy looked at the sheriff, startled. "Me? My raising days are over." She gave a woeful laugh. "Besides, how am I going to raise two babies in jail?"

John smiled at her. "You're not going to jail. When you have your say, the jury will believe you. Folks don't like Jonas Halleck nor Little Dickie, either. And they think Coy Chaney is crooked as a gold vein."

"That's just it, John. I'm not going to testify."

John turned to her so quickly that he jerked on the reins, and the mules came to a stop. He slapped the reins on their backs and swore at them, and after they started up, he asked, "Why not?"

"Reasons."

"Anything to do with Nevada? Jeff find out what he was looking for?"

"I don't know what that was. Maybe he didn't, either."

"Gracy, if you don't speak out, folks'll think you're guilty. You could go to jail. What would the women do without you? You're the last midwife on the Tenmile."

"I've thought about all that. But I'm no good at lying, John. You know it. I turn red and my hands itch so much I got to scratch them. That's what set off Jeff."

"What do you have to lie about now?"

"If Elizabeth didn't tell you, I won't." Gracy remembered John's story about communing with his dead wife.

"I never should have told you about her."

"I wish I had somebody like her to tell *me* what to do."

"You don't want to talk about it?"

Gracy shook her head. "I can't even talk about it with Daniel."

"Then it's a plenty grave secret you carry." He slowed the mules as the wagon made its way between aspen trees on either side of the road, trees so close together the wagon could barely fit between them. "This is a lonely spot," he said, easing the wagon through wheel-high underbrush.

"And that cabin is the loneliest place I ever saw. I expect Esther might have died of that loneliness. Those men had no right to treat her worthless."

"You believe one of them shot her?"

Gracy thought that over. "I've been studying on it, but I couldn't say they did. She said everything was fine until the babies came. Then they treated her poor, although they weren't brutes. Just mean."

"You think she tried to run away with the babies and they stopped her?"

"No," Gracy said. "I think they'd be glad if she left."

"Then maybe she should have taken out and left the babies behind."

Gracy thought that over. "She wouldn't have done that unless her mind went queer."

"You think Ben and Davy'll feed them?"

"With what? They're useless." She paused. "The feeding's troublesome. I keep a bottle in my bag along with milk powder, but I don't know if the babies'll take it. Some will, some won't. And there isn't a woman in Swandyke now to be a wet nurse. I might grind up oatmeal and see if they'll eat it."

They were almost to the cabin, Gracy knew, not because she could see it but because she heard the faint cry of the babies.

"Sounds like robins hollering," John observed.

"It does at that. I expect those poor little things are hungry enough to eat worms, too. When did Davy say Esther died?"

"He didn't."

"Those little boys won't have eaten since before then, of course." She reached for her medicine bag and took out a jar. "We'll have to stop and get fresh water. I'll heat it up and mix in the powder and see if they'll drink it."

John pulled the mules to a halt by the spring on the near side of the clearing where the house stood, and Gracy filled the jar. By the time she got back into the wagon, she could see that the two men had come out of the house and were waiting for them.

John stopped the wagon in an aspen grove. A blanket was spread on the ground, and under it, Gracy knew, was the body of Esther Boyce. She'd leave the body to John. The babies were her concern. Without a word, she walked past Ben and Davy and went into the house, where the infants were squalling. She picked up one and crooned to him. He was wet, and she changed him, changed the other one, too. Then with both infants in her arms, she went to the door and told Ben, "I suppose you haven't fed them."

He shrugged. "How'm I supposed to do that? I ain't got me a pair of . . ." He blushed, and Gracy scowled at him.

"Build up the fire, then, and let me heat the water for the milk powder. You better hope your sons take it." Then she muttered, "Your son." She nodded at Tommy, the boy with Ben's coloring.

If Ben heard the distinction, he didn't remark on it, just went inside and shoved kindling into the cookstove and lit it. "There's water," he said, pointing to a bucket with dead mosquitoes in it.

"I got fresh," Gracy told him. She found a clean pan, and poured the jar of water into it, then added the milk powder. She removed a bottle from her medicine bag and fitted a nipple onto it, wishing she'd thought to bring a second bottle. The babies would have to take turns. When the water was warm and the powder dissolved, she dipped her finger into the mixture and put it into Benny's mouth. He sucked on the finger. She wet her finger again and let him taste the milk a second time. Then she took a clean rag from her bag and dipped it into the milk and let the baby suck on it. "You'll have to take satisfaction with that," she told him. "Your brother's littler. He's first." She filled the bottle and attached the nipple, putting it into Tommy's mouth. He pushed it out. Gracy spilled a little of the milk on her finger and let him taste it, felt his little mouth work around her finger, his tiny tongue lick it. Then she dribbled drops of the milk onto his tongue. At last, she put the nipple into the boy's mouth, and he took it, draining the bottle. She filled the bottle again and gave it to Benny, and when that baby was done, Gracy placed both children in the cradle to sleep. She went to the door and leaned against the frame. "They'll be all right," she told John.

"That's a blessing."

"We'll give those boys away if somebody wants them," Davy said. "Me and Ben, how are we going to take care of them?"

"You don't want them, your own flesh and blood?"

Davy looked out at the humps of mountains in the distance, ignoring Gracy's remark. "Me and Ben don't know nothing about babies," he said at last.

"I wouldn't leave them with you," Gracy told him. "I wouldn't want them to grow up to be a pair of fools like you two. The Lord only knows how they'd turn out."

But Gracy knew how they would turn out. She'd seen it before, women dead and their children turned over to an orphan home because the fathers couldn't care for them or didn't want them. Sometimes the children were parceled out to relatives who didn't want them, either. So a boy would run off as soon as he was old enough to be on his own. But a girl would have it harder. She would get pregnant without being married. Then at thirteen or fourteen, too young to give birth, she would die in childbed, crying with the pain and begging Gracy not to tell of her shame. And Gracy would keep the secret. The baby would be given away, and the cycle would begin again. Those mothers were hard to forget, girls who never had a chance to grow up but died while they were still children themselves. She'd seen too many of them, kept too many of their secrets.

"You think poorly of us," Davy said.

"I do."

"Wasn't my fault. Nor Ben's, neither." He kicked at the dirt outside the door with the toe of his boot. "Ben, he thought it'd be handy having Esther around. We wouldn't have to go to that house in Kokomo. Wouldn't have to cook no more, neither. But it didn't work out. She didn't mind what you're thinking. After all, she'd been a whore." He glanced at Gracy then looked away. "It was other things. Her pie crust tasted like it come off a slag heap. She wanted the cabin her way. She'd leave it messy and wouldn't let me clean it up, said she liked it looking lived in. She wanted us to take to her ways, not the other way around. It was our cabin. We built it. She should have made do. It was all right until the babies come. That's when things changed. She never should have had them. The way things turned out was her fault."

"Takes two to make a baby," Gracy said. "And sometimes three."

One of the boys let out a cry, and Gracy glanced at Davy, but he didn't seem to hear the boy. Gracy turned to go inside, but the baby quieted, and she stayed where she was.

"Me and Ben, we never had a fight, not once, until Esther. We could have stood it, but the babies come, and Esther turned peculiar. She'd stay in bed, thought we'd wait on her. Expected us to help with the babies." His voice rose in disgust. "That's woman's work. And there was all that hollering. Me and Ben had to move into the other place, but we could still hear them. Couldn't sleep because of the racket. I reckon we made a mistake."

"It was Esther made the mistake." Gracy looked across the yard to where the dried stems of poppies were blowing in the wind, a few faded petals still attached to them.

Davy followed her gaze. "I planted them for her when she first come. I guess they'll go wild now." He paused. "We tried,

Mrs. Brookens. I know what you think of us, but we give it a try. Ben never should have brought her here. It was wrong."

He stopped talking as John and Ben came up to the door.

"You want to take a look at Mrs. Boyce, Gracy?" The sheriff gestured with his head at the body.

"I do." Gracy followed John to where Esther lay. He lifted the blanket covering her so that Gracy could see the crumpled body of the woman, her chest all but butchered. Beside her was a shotgun.

"We didn't touch her, just covered her up," Ben said.

Gracy knelt beside the body and touched Esther's forehead, brushing the hair from the woman's face as she asked herself what she could have done. Why couldn't she have helped Esther? The woman's eyes were closed, her eyelids as thin as onionskin. Her hands were bloodstained, and when Gracy raised one to touch the gold wedding ring on Esther's finger, blood came off on Gracy's own hands.

"I'd like to keep the ring. It's valuable. It was my mother's," Davy said.

"I don't suppose she'd want to wear it for eternity." Gracy removed the ring and all but threw it at Davy. Then she turned back to Esther. "Poor woman," she said. "What happened?"

"She said she had a yen for rabbit stew. She took the gun and went out, tripped on a root, and shot herself," Ben said. "It was an accident."

Gracy looked at the sheriff, who shrugged. "I don't see no proof otherwise. Who's to say it isn't so?"

"Will you have Coy examine the body?"

"What's the need? It's clear she was shot in the chest. And like I say, there's no proof it wasn't an accident. Ben said they'd bury the body here instead of the cemetery in Swandyke, here under the wildflowers. He said Esther liked them."

"All summer she picked them, put them in a jar on the table," Davy said.

"Told us once she thought the meadow would be a good burying place," Ben added.

"You see any reason she shouldn't be buried now?" John asked Gracy.

The Sagehen stared at the body for a long time. "There's too much misery on the Tenmile already. Those babies will have a hard enough time of it. Why make it worse with them knowing their mother's death might not be an accident? I believe you know your job when you say there's no proof, John. I will back you up."

"I'll help dig the grave," John said. "Gracy, will you clean up Esther a little, maybe put a fresh dress on her? There's a box waiting for her. Ben made it whilst Davy went to fetch me. One of us can say a few words over her."

Gracy nodded and went into the house to find something to wrap around the body. Esther's chest was blown open and wet with blood. She needed a shroud, not a dress. The bed had no sheets, so Gracy found a quilt and took it outside, then held Esther's frail body while she wrapped it in the coverlet. Ben brought the box he'd fashioned into a casket and picked up his wife and placed her inside.

When the grave was dug, the men lowered the coffin into the

hole. Gracy brought the two babies to the gravesite, saying they ought to be there to see their mother buried.

"You want to say something?" John asked Ben, who shook his head. So John bowed his head and repeated a Bible verse. He ended with, "Dust to dust," then picked up a handful of dirt and dropped it on top of the box. Davy did the same, but Ben stood there, staring into the grave, then reached up and wiped away a tear.

The men shoveled dirt on top of the coffin, while Gracy returned to the house and packed up the babies' things. Esther had planned well for her children. She had stitched flannel blankets, knit shirts and stockings, made tiny caps of rabbit fur. Gracy wondered if Esther had shot the rabbits herself. She picked up a china baby cup the color and frailness of a robin's egg and a silver baby spoon with "Esther" engraved on it. There was a framed picture of a woman who looked like Esther, probably her mother, Gracy thought, wrapping the geegaws in one of the small quilts that Gracy and Mittie had made. Maybe if Gracy could find her, the grandmother would raise the babies. Or perhaps there was a sister.

She went outside and asked Ben, "Did Esther have any relations, somebody who could take the infants?"

"None she ever mentioned," he replied.

"What was her name before she married?"

"I never inquired." He patted the mound of dirt with his shovel.

"Got chores to do," Davy said, and the two men turned away.

"What chores?" John muttered.

"Maybe they're grieving. It could be, you know. They're an odd pair, more married to each other than they ever were to Esther. But maybe they've got enough goodness in them to grieve," Gracy replied.

John stared at the grave. "Never even said good-bye to her, neither one of them. What do you think it was like for her in that cabin? Maybe it wasn't any worse than being in a whore-house."

"In the end, the babies were all she had, and they weren't enough."

John brought the wagon to the cabin door, and Gracy put her bag and the burlap sack of baby things into the bed. John loaded the cradle, then held the boys while Gracy climbed onto the wagon seat. He reached them up to her before he settled himself on the seat.

Ben and Davy came out of the barn and stood taciturn, watching.

"You want to see your sons one last time?" Gracy called.

Neither answered, and Ben waved them to the road.

"Poor little fellers," Gracy said, looking at the infants, while John started the mules down the trail toward Swandyke. "Their ma's dead, and their pas don't want them."

"You'll keep them, then?" John asked.

"I'll find somebody to take them. I have an idea already, a woman I know that wants a baby in the worst way. But it'll take some convincing."

They rode without talking, Gracy humming to the infants, who mewled and stretched their tiny arms and legs, then settled down, the rhythm of the wagon rocking them to sleep. "Poor little fellers," she murmured again. Then, "Poor Esther."

"Rabbit stew," John said after a time. "She died 'cause she wanted rabbit stew. Now why couldn't one of the men have gone after a rabbit? That's the question."

"No," Gracy said. "There's another question. Maybe you didn't notice. Why did Esther go hunting wearing her slippers?"

Nineteen

Jeff, Daniel, and Mittie stared as Gracy handed down the babies. Mittie reached for Benny, whose mouth twitched, his tongue going in and out. He grasped her finger in a hand no bigger than a kitten's paw, and Mittie grinned at him. "My, if he don't look like the spit of Davy . . ." Her voice trailed off, and she looked at Gracy, who nodded. Mittie swallowed, then finished, "Like himself, like a perfect baby."

"He is at that." Gracy handed Tommy to Daniel and let Jeff help her down off the wagon.

"I guess you're still taking in strays," he said.

"Jeff," John warned.

But Jeff told him, "I didn't mean anything by it, Mr. Miller. Ma always did have a fondness for other folks' kids. She took in more than one, you know."

"What are you going to do with them?" Mittie asked.

"Well, that's a question, isn't it? I don't know the answer, but right now, they just need to be fed again. I sure could use some help," Gracy said. "You know how to change them, do you, Mittie?"

" 'Course I do. I was the oldest of seven."

"Diapers are in the bag. I got to mix up more milk. It would be a kindness if you'd take care of the babies whilst I fix it—and help me feed them, too. Daniel can see to supper. He does it often enough."

"I brung it, and we all ate, except for you."

Gracy stopped and stared at the young woman. "Well, you are a wonder! How'd I ever manage without you?"

Mittie blushed and set Benny on the bed while she changed him, then placed him in the cradle, which Jeff had carried to the center of the room. She took Tommy from Daniel, put a dry diaper on him, then held him in one arm, while she picked up his brother again. She jiggled the two of them as they mewled their hunger. "They don't look much alike," she said, then added, quickly, "That's a good thing. Who'd want to look just like some-body else?"

Gracy poured water into the teakettle and heated it, then took down her jar of milk powder, glancing at Mittie as she did so. The young woman hummed as she tended the infants. "Poor little things without no mother to love them," Mittie muttered. She turned to Gracy. "Don't their papa want them?"

"Neither of them, neither Ben nor Davy. Those little boys aren't much better than orphans."

"Imagine not wanting these sweet little things." Mittie hugged the babies, and Gracy smiled.

Daniel did, too. He knew what Gracy was thinking. "Come on, Jeff. I need help with the woodpile. Then maybe we'll go to the Nugget to see what they're saying about the trial."

"I need to talk to Ma about something that came up there," Jeff said.

Gracy had a good idea of what he wanted to say and told him, "It can wait, Jeff. Run along with your pa."

Jeff kissed Gracy on her cheek—awkward it was—and said, "You're a good woman, Ma."

"When did you decide that?"

"Oh, I always knew, and I thought about you plenty when I was away."

As she watched her son leave, Gracy shook her head at the wonder of him. He'd never said such a thing before. Nor had he kissed her cheek since he was a boy. He had indeed grown up while he was away. She used the back of her wrist to wipe a tear from her eye. Then she filled two bottles with the warm milk.

"I'm grateful they've taken to a bottle. I'll try them on ground-up oatmeal in a day or two."

"My ma did that. It helps them sleep through the night."

"Would you feed one?" Not waiting for Mittie to reply, Gracy handed her a bottle, taking Benny out of Mittie's arms.

Mittie dropped a little of the milk onto Tommy's tongue, and when he took the nipple and began to suck, she said, "You want me to take them, take them for good, don't you?"

Gracy looked at her in astonishment. The young woman had her figured out all along.

"Is it so obvious? I'm too old, and I don't want to put them in an orphan home. And you wanting a baby so much . . ." She thought a moment, then said, "It won't be easy. Two babies are three times the work. And folks would know how they were sired. If you figured right off that Davy Eastlow was the father of one of them, others will, too."

Mittie brushed off the concerns. "I taken care of a whole house of little ones when Ma was feeling poorly. And as for the fathers, well, ain't nobody's business, and I'd tell that to anybody who says a thing against them. It ain't their fault what their pas did." She glanced down at Tommy, who was stretching his arms and legs. "I wouldn't mind having them for a little while. Henry might go along with it, too. But not forever. I'd know they wasn't mine, and they'd know it, too. Even if I could love them like my own, they wouldn't love me back, not after they knew their ma was somebody else. It's not possible."

"It is possible."

"I saw how Jeff looked at you. He wouldn't do that if he wasn't your own flesh and blood."

Benny pushed the nipple out of his mouth, then cried a little as he tried to find it. Gracy had been staring at Mittie, and now she looked down at the boy in her arms, making sure he'd found the nipple and was taking the milk again. "Yes he could. You see, Jeff isn't really my own flesh and blood," she said quietly, looking up at Mittie and nodding at the truth of what she'd revealed.

Mittie turned to Gracy so fast that she jerked the bottle out of Tommy's mouth, and he began to cry. "You're fooling me. He looks just like Mr. Brookens."

"That's because Daniel's his father."

"You mean . . ." Mittie's voice trailed off.

Gracy nodded. "Daniel and me and John Miller—and now Jeff—know it. And there's others in Nevada that do. But I've never told a soul in Swandyke—until just now."

"You don't have to tell me, Mrs. Brookens."

"Maybe I do, if it'll help these babies," Gracy said. Benny had finished the bottle, and Gracy put him against her shoulder and patted his back. "We'll put the boys down. And after, I'll fix us coffee. I'll eat later."

She laid Benny in the crib, then went to the fireplace and built up the fire to heat the water in the teakettle. She put a handful of beans into a pan and let them brown on the fire, then ground them and dumped the grounds into the coffeepot. After the water boiled, she poured it over the grounds and let them steep. At last, she took down two cups, the china ones she'd used with John Miller, not the tin, and poured coffee into them, setting them on the table beside the sugar bowl.

When Mittie finished with Tommy, she laid him in the cradle beside his brother, then went to the table and sat down on the bench across from Gracy, who pushed a cup toward the woman—the cup that still had a handle. Mittie took a spoon from the spooner and stirred sugar into her coffee. They might have been just two women going through the ritual of making coffee, sitting down for a cup, taking a break in their day to gossip. Mittie looked at Gracy and waited, and Gracy knew the woman would not ask what had happened. She would wait until Gracy told her, would not ask even if Gracy didn't speak of it again.

But now, after all these years, the secret of Jeff's birth didn't matter so much, because Jeff knew. They'd wanted to keep it from him, keep him from the embarrassment, theirs and his. But Jeff had found out. Jeff was the reason they had left Nevada for Colorado, and she and Daniel were the reason he had lit out from Swandyke the year before. They hadn't ever wanted him to know that Gracy wasn't his mother, that his real mother was a whore. And then he'd found out. He'd asked a question, and Gracy had flushed, her hands and face breaking out in a rash, and Daniel had blurted out the truth. They hadn't expected Jeff to react so, to go off like that. But he told them they'd raised him to be honest, and now his whole life was turned upside down because they'd kept the truth from him. He didn't know who he was. How could he when Gracy and Daniel had lied to him since he was a baby? He had to find out the truth of it for himself, had to go to Nevada and learn it. And then maybe he'd still be their son, or maybe not. But he had come back when Gracy needed him, and he still called her Ma, and he acted the way he always had. He might leave again. Gracy wouldn't try to hold him. In fact, it was best that he go elsewhere. But this time when he left, he'd go as their son.

Now Gracy looked at the woman across from her and told her, "It's a confidence."

"I know that," Mittie said, and Gracy believed the girl would not utter a word of what was to be said.

Gracy turned the cup around in her hands, staring into the

coffee. It was bitter—in her hurry, she'd burned the beans a little—and should have sugar stirred into it, but bitter tasted good just then.

"Daniel stepped. It was his nature," she began. "He was easy tempted. Daniel's a lusty man, handsome as a racehorse, and I was just an ordinary-looking woman." That wasn't the reason he stepped, but it eased Gracy to think so. She raised the cup to her lips and sipped, the hot coffee almost scalding her tongue. "He'd done it before, done it before even we left Arkansas. I always knew, and I forgave him. But this time it was different." And then she began.

Gracy had hoped by the time they reached Nevada that Daniel's roving was done with. But there were too many temptations. The bawdy houses drew him, and Gracy could tell, could tell when he came home smelling of the women—their perfume and powder, their sweat, and the woman smell she knew from her years of midwifery. He didn't stray often, and it was usually when he was drunk, but the drinking was worse now. Gracy was hurt, of course. She'd cried into her apron more than once. But she knew she couldn't change Daniel. She could threaten to leave, but she wouldn't, and he knew it. And his infatuations passed in days—weeks at most. They always did. So she was silent about her husband's transgressions and tried to keep her heart from bitterness. She showed Daniel a loving face, for kindness whips the devil, she had been taught. And kindness brought him back.

She knew Nevada had made Daniel a different man. He'd

found very little gold in California, and at times, they had lived on Gracy's earnings. So they'd moved on to Virginia City when they heard the pickings were good there. Daniel worked at it, worked hard, but he fought the rock and lost. Instead of bonanzas, he found *borrasca*. It had been a thin life for them in the gold and silver towns.

And then when they were almost ready to move again, Daniel made a silver strike, a good one, better than they knew when he sold out. "Better to be safe," Gracy had counseled when Daniel asked her if he ought to sell. Besides, where would they get the money to develop the deposit and to fight the lawsuits that were likely to come along? It took a gold mine to operate a silver mine the saying went. They could lose everything.

Gracy's advice was what Daniel said he hoped to hear, because he feared a mining company would sue, claiming the vein apexed on its property, which meant Daniel didn't have the right to mine it. Besides, he wanted money in his pocket. He'd waited too long to be rich. Later, of course, he felt cheated and blamed his wife. Still, he enjoyed the money. He'd always been proud of his appearance and bought a brocade waistcoat, a silk hat, a diamond stickpin, and strutted about Virginia City like a silver king. He still roamed the hills, believing if he'd found one good vein, he could find another, and this time, he wouldn't be foolish enough to sell out. On Saturday nights, he went into the saloons and acted the swell, bought drinks, flirted with the whores, had a fling with one or two of them.

The money changed him in another way. It made him dissatisfied with his life, made him think he deserved better. He bought Gracy a satin dress and an emerald ring, but she hadn't cared about them. Where would she wear a dress with a neckline cut that low? And she couldn't deliver a baby with that ring on her finger. The only jewelry she cared about was the dime she wore around her neck and the thin gold ring Daniel had put on her finger when they married. She wanted Daniel to invest the money in property, buy the house they lived in and another they could rent out, maybe even a commercial building. But what he didn't spend, Daniel invested in mining stocks, and in the end, they turned out to be worthless.

Daniel had always been a happy man, and that changed, too. He became morose, downhearted. He no longer burst through the door at night, ready to share his day with his wife. He was sharp with Gracy, found fault. He complained if she was out delivering a baby and not home in time to fix his dinner, let her know if the meat was tough or the bread burned. Sometimes he'd go to the saloons and not come home until late, or maybe the next day.

The money brought that all about, Gracy thought. They'd been happier when they hadn't had any. The money made Daniel want more. He'd never fretted much when they were poor, but now that there was a little cash, Daniel worried they would lose it. He blamed Gracy for forcing him to sell his discovery. It didn't matter that Daniel had only asked her advice and made the decision himself.

Maybe if she had listened to the hints John and Elizabeth Miller gave her about Daniel—and looking back, she realized they had been aware of what was going on—or had she been more knowledgeable about the world, Gracy would have known. But hers was not a suspicious nature, and so she was ignorant of what Daniel was up to—until the day the letter came.

She had been surprised by that letter, the childish handwriting, Gracy's name misspelled. She thought it might have come from her sister Orlean in Arkansas or perhaps a niece or nephew, and maybe it contained bad news. She let it sit on the table for a time while she fixed herself coffee and sat down to stare at her name. Then she slit the envelope and read the letter, not understanding. Written at the top in the same scrawling hand were the words "read this ladie its your husband." She read the letter again, recognizing Daniel's handwriting in it and frowning as she wondered if he'd written her a letter that had gone astray. But why would he write to her? Besides, the letter was written to Jennie, not Gracy.

And then the truth of it hit her, and she dropped the letter on the table and put her face in her hands. It was a love letter, written by her husband—written to another woman, who had then mailed it to Gracy. Its last words burned into her brain: "I can't stay away from you."

The women Daniel had been with before, it hadn't been like that. Those were infatuations, hot and quick couplings with bawdy-house women that grew cold after a time. Daniel tired of the women soon enough and came back to her. Gracy doubted that he had ever written a letter to one of them. This affair was different, serious, and if the woman had sent the letter on to Gracy, she must have wanted to hurt her, maybe cause Gracy to throw Daniel out. Gracy squeezed tears back into her eyes. Such pretty words, and she had taught them to him, taught him how to write.

She thought to destroy the letter, to add kindling to the stove and build a fire as hot as hell and drop the letter into it and watch the paper curl and blacken in the flames. But she didn't, not yet, because she needed to think. She looked for a place to hide the letter and remembered her medicine bag. But she didn't want it with her when she called on a woman in labor, didn't want to reach into the bag and see it and brood over it, not while she was delivering a baby. So she secreted it in her Bible. Daniel was not a Bible reader and would not come across it there.

Gracy sat at the table all day, neither eating nor preparing dinner. There would be no need for food that night. She would confront Daniel. He would be surprised, because she'd never done so over the other women. And then what? Gracy wondered. Would he leave? Would he force *her* to leave? But that was what the woman wanted. It was the reason she had mailed the letter to Gracy. She needed to ponder more, Gracy decided at last. She would wait until the next day or the next week.

So when Daniel came home that night, Gracy told him she had a hurting in her head and hadn't fixed supper. She was rarely sick, and she wondered if Daniel would bring her soup, maybe feed it to her with his own hand. Instead, he said he'd go uptown for his supper and left.

Not until the second letter came a month later did Gracy confront Daniel. This time, the woman, Jennie, made no notation but only enclosed Daniel's letter in an envelope. Gracy couldn't bear to read it more than once. Daniel had sent the letter to

Jennie with a bouquet of flowers, conservatory roses that cost more than a miner's daily wage. Daniel hadn't brought Gracy flowers since they lived in Arkansas, and then they had been wild daisies that he'd picked himself in a meadow during their courting days. Gracy had loved them, of course, because daisies were her favorite flowers. She had pressed one of them in her Bible and had made a crown of daisies to wear at her wedding.

Gracy knew that this Jennie wasn't like Daniel's other women, and she knew Daniel was in love with her. He'd said so in the letter. Now Gracy understood why he'd grown querulous with her, why he blamed her for his own transgressions, stayed away from her for days at a time, claiming he had been out in the hills with his pick and shovel. But what miner prospected wearing a brocade waistcoat? she thought now.

Daniel's words seared her heart. He'd written how Jennie made him feel young. He praised her golden hair and pale skin, her breasts that were like roses, the softness of her hands. He said he burned for her as he never had for a woman. But that wasn't true, Gracy thought, remembering back to the first days of their marriage when their couplings had shaken the cabin and left them exhausted. Her face was hot with shame that Daniel would say such things. No wonder Gracy couldn't read the letter more than once.

She laid it on the table and sat there all day, staring at it, as if it were a living thing. From time to time she cried or cursed, but mostly, she just sat, feeling numb. She would be there when Daniel came home. He would see the letter, and they would have it out.

Maybe the fault was hers, she thought in those long hours with the letter in front of her. Not all of it, but some. She had been busy with the all the birthings in Virginia City and had let Daniel come home to a cold house too often. Perhaps she should give up her midwifery. It would be hard. She had delivered babies almost all her life and knew it was a gift. She had made Daniel promise before they were married that she could keep on with it. But Daniel mattered more now. He was worth the sacrifice. She would tell him that. She would wear the satin dress and the ring with the green stone, put up her hair in a fashionable twist and go about with him, too, drink a glass of beer in the International Hotel in Virginia City. And she would bring back the days in bed when they exhausted themselves with lovemaking.

Gracy brushed her hair and washed her face. She put on a fresh dress, but the effort made her feel silly. A clean dress wouldn't make much difference when Daniel was in love with another woman. She sat down at the table and waited, and just at evening, Daniel came in.

"Where's supper?" he asked, staring at the cold stove.

"There isn't any," Gracy said.

"You are getting cantankerous. Is it too much for you to fix my supper?"

"It is today."

"I'll go to town for it, then."

Gracy had been staring at the letter, and now she looked up. "Will you?"

"You've grown quarrelsome."

"And you, Daniel, what have you grown?" It was not the

conversation Gracy had wanted. She had hoped they would sit down, talk the way they used to, not argue as they had in the last months.

"God, hell! I won't have a wife who treats me like a common miner."

"And will you have a wife at all?"

Daniel had started for the door, but now he turned back. He stared at Gracy a moment, confused, then glanced down at the table. He didn't pay attention to the letter until Gracy slowly moved her finger toward it. She touched it and drew back her finger as if she had touched a hot stove.

Daniel looked at the letter then, and his face fell. He slumped into a chair. "I didn't mean for you to see it."

Gracy almost laughed. "No, I suppose not."

"Where did you get it?"

"It came in the mail."

"You shouldn't have read it."

"Shouldn't have read it?" Gracy blurted out. "Shouldn't have read it, Danny? You shouldn't have written it, shouldn't have written it at all."

He picked up the letter, read a few words, then turned away, crumpling the letter and dropping it into the cold cookstove. "I'm sorry, Gracy. I never meant to hurt you. It's me. I can't help myself. You know I'm weak."

She hadn't expected the words nor the sorrow in his voice, the tears in his eyes, and she all but forgave him right then and there. Now that he knew how much he had hurt her, he would give up Jennie, would make things up to her. Gracy wouldn't mention the woman again, wouldn't punish Daniel. They would heal together and go on. She leaned forward as if to put her arms around her husband.

And then Daniel said, "You've been a good wife, the best a man could ask for, and it's not your fault. It just happened. This isn't the way I wanted to tell you, but maybe it's for the best." Then he took a deep breath. "She's going to have a baby. It's mine. I know because I'm the only one she sees now. I set her up in her own place. I'll live with her there."

Gracy dropped her arms, her elbows smacking the table, but she didn't feel the hurt because it paled beside the pain in her heart. She looked at Daniel in disbelief.

"I should have told you a long time ago, but I couldn't. I didn't want to hurt you."

"Not hurt me? Then why did you do it, Danny? What did I do wrong?"

Daniel, uncomfortable, rubbed his hand across his eyes. "Nothing," he mumbled. "You never really needed me. She does. Especially now, with the baby coming."

"The baby," Gracy repeated softly. That was where she had failed him. Her babies had been flawed, had died at birth or before. Only little Emma, the child she had raised but not given birth to, had lived, and then she'd passed on barely into girlhood. Gracy had lost that sweet child, and now she was losing Daniel, too.

"You know I've always wanted a son, and now I will have one," Daniel said. "She's healthy, Jennie is, and he will be a strong boy."

Daniel looked almost proud then, and Gracy hated him for it. "And what about me?" She cringed at the whine in her voice.

"You can stay here. You can have the house," he said, as if he did not remember that they hadn't bought the house but only rented it. "You have your work. You could go back to Arkansas if you wanted."

"Go back? A divorced woman?" Gracy remembered the one woman at home who had divorced her husband for beating her and how she was considered not much better than a whore. She couldn't go back. She would never let her family know Daniel had left her. "We could try again," she said, hating the begging in her voice.

Daniel shook his head. "Not with the baby coming. I'm sorry." He reached for her hand, but Gracy snatched it away.

"When will you leave?"

"Now. There's no reason to wait, since you know." He stood up. "I'll get my things."

Like that, just like that. An hour before, she had been a married woman, but in minutes, Gracy would be alone. Daniel had called it deep enough. He hadn't even given her a chance. She watched as her husband stuffed his shirts and pants into a flour sack. Then she got up and took the clothing from him, folding it properly and placing it in the bag, thinking she did not want him to arrive at the woman's house with his clothes rumpled, nearly laughing at the idea of it. Surely no other woman in the world would pack her husband's clothes when he was leaving her.

Daniel reached into his pocket and took out a handful of gold coins, laying them on the table, while Gracy wondered if that was the way he'd paid whores. "I won't let you starve," he said. He laughed. "You'll have to insist the women you attend pay you now."

"But there is plenty of money from the sale of the mine," Gracy said.

"There's not so much money left. But I'll pay for the divorce. You won't have to."

"Divorce?" Gracy asked. She stiffened, thinking she would hold out. "There won't be a divorce. Not yet."

Daniel shrugged. "We'll talk about it later." He picked up his bag and went to the door. "I'm sorry, Gracy. I won't leave you helpless. If you need anything, you let me know."

She didn't reply, only watched as Daniel walked out of the yard and up the hill, watched until he disappeared, thinking she didn't even know where he would live. Where would she go if she needed something from him? But she would never ask. The only thing she needed was Daniel, and he was gone. As she turned from the doorway, she glanced at the stove, where one lid lay on the black stovetop. Daniel had not replaced it when he threw the letter onto the ashes. She removed the crumpled paper, smoothed it, and placed it in her Bible with the first letter. Then she held the Bible to her chest and sobbed, a gaunt, graying woman whose world was *borrasca*. The sin was his, she remembered Nabby warning her. The sin was Daniel's. But why was she the one to suffer so?

Twenty

Mittie stared into her coffee cup as Gracy paused, unable to continue. Mittie said in a low voice, "I been afraid my husband would leave me, too, because I couldn't have a baby."

"That was only part of it, I think. It was an excuse," Gracy said. "Daniel would have left me anyway."

"Did he truly love her?"

Gracy thought that over. "I don't like to think it, but I believe he did. Maybe in a different way than he did me. I believe now that it was because she was young, and she made him feel like the world was ahead of him. But like you say, there was the baby. He wanted a son."

"Well, who would know it now?" Mitt asked hotly. "He treats you like the Queen of Turkey."

"Yes, he does. He does at that," Gracy said. "I've let the coffee get cold." She got up and threw the remains of her coffee out the door and picked up the pot from where it was warming on a trivet in the ashes. "I forgot. We've a can of milk, if you want it. I've been thinking maybe the babies would like that better than the powder. But it's costly, so best if they'll take the powder."

At the mention of the boys, Mittie rose and went to the cradle, staring down at the babies, who were sleeping.

"Their mother must have give them a wash before she went hunting," Mittie said. "She took good care of them." She leaned over and touched the hair on Tommy's head, which wasn't much longer than a day's growth of beard. "You think she killed herself apurpose?"

"We'll never know."

"I can't believe it. Why would she go off and leave them?" Mittie came back to the table and sat. "I don't need milk, but I'd like a bit more of the coffee, if it wouldn't rob you."

Gracy poured the brew into Mittie's cup, and Mittie doctored it with sugar, tasting the coffee, then stirring in a little more sugar.

"I might have a little sweeting myself," Gracy said, pouring her own coffee, then reaching for the spooner. She took out a silver spoon, her best one, with "Mother 1878" engraved on it. Daniel had given it to her.

The two sat quietly for a moment. Then Mittie jumped up. "I forgot about your supper. I'll dish it up for you."

Gracy put out her hand. "Later." She was afraid if she took the time to eat, she wouldn't finish telling Mittie about Virginia City before Daniel and Jeff returned. Darkness was coming on.

"I would like to hear the rest of your story, if it wouldn't trouble you to tell it," Mittie said.

"No, it wouldn't. I just needed to rest my heart for a moment. Like I said, I've never told it to a soul, except to Jeff when he demanded it. But even then, I didn't tell him about my pain."

"He knows."

"I'm not so sure. He's young." But perhaps Jeff did know pain. She hoped he wouldn't say again that he needed to talk to her. Best to leave the past—all of the past—alone.

Gracy picked up her cup, and this time, she drank up the coffee. "Besides, I'm not sure men understand about that kind of heartache." One of the babies cried out, and she glanced at the cradle, but the boy settled down. Gracy began to talk again.

After Daniel left her, Gracy stayed inside the cabin for days, barely eating, not sweeping the floor or tending her garden, rousing herself only when a woman came to her for help. Only in childbirth did she forget her troubles. But they came back to her when the birthings were over, hit her as she walked home carrying her bag. She searched the faces of the women on the streets, wondering if one was Jennie, thinking she would recognize her but knowing she would not.

Weeks later, she passed a saloon and glanced inside to see Daniel sitting at a table with a woman beside him, her back to the street. Gracy stared through the window, hoping the woman would turn around. And then she did for an instant, and Gracy saw that she had hair the pale gold of winter sun and a face that was white and luminous. Gracy touched her own sunburned face with her hand, then felt her coarse hair, and a feeling of despair came over her, for she would never be that woman with Daniel, and never had been. She did not know if she felt better or worse that Jennie was a beauty. She saw Daniel slip his hand to her swollen stomach, and Gracy turned away. The moment was too intimate, too painful. She would not walk that way again.

After that, Gracy looked for the woman in the stores, even at church. She couldn't help herself. Once she saw Daniel and Jennie in the distance, and Gracy turned into a store to avoid them, smiling a little later because it was a tobacco shop, and she had had to busy herself with the pipes and cigars and tobacco pouches until the couple passed by.

Another time, she saw Jennie in a drugstore. The young woman smiled and stepped aside to let Gracy make her purchase first, perhaps knowing who Gracy was, but more likely not. Jennie was buying face cream and powder and a vial of perfume, which she held in her tiny hand, moving it a little so that the clear stone in her ring caught the light and flashed color. But it was not the extravagances—items Gracy herself had never bought—that bothered her as much as seeing Jennie's belly and knowing Daniel's baby grew inside. Jennie would have been seven or eight months along then, and if not for the size of the baby, no one would have known she was pregnant. Her hands and face were still slender, and she had not bloated or grown splotchy as some women did late in pregnancy—as Gracy herself had. Jennie was tiny, not much bigger than a child, and when she spoke, her voice was soft. There was much about her to admire, and Gracy had to admit it was little wonder that Daniel had fallen in love with such a creature.

Gracy encountered Daniel, too. He came to the house on occasion to retrieve something he had left behind or to ask if she was in need. Once he left her a sack of plums, perhaps remembering how she loved them. Other times, she returned home to find money lying on the table and knew he had been there. It wasn't much money, however, and Gracy struggled to pay for her keep. She might not have made it if John Miller hadn't helped, making sure her wood was in, that the windows and doors were tight against the wind, nailing down a carpet he had picked up somewhere. She was grateful, because she knew the winter would be so cold she would dread to sleep alone.

"He's a fool for cutting out, Gracy. He should have governed himself," John told her.

"You judge too harshly," she replied.

"By the living God, you are some woman! Only you could defend such a man," he said. "I find him detestable."

As the days went on and she knew Daniel would not return, Gracy gave thought to how she would keep herself. Elizabeth suggested she could nurse or perhaps take sick miners into her house to convalesce. But Gracy didn't like that idea. What if they had illnesses she could carry to a newborn? Maybe she could sell the herbs that she gathered in the hills and dried. She could ask her sisters in Arkansas to send those that didn't grow in Nevada, order others from a catalogue. After all, she stocked the concoctions that helped a woman get pregnant, those that prevented conception, even the ones that sometimes brought on a miscarriage. Now she could add to her stores, finding herbs to treat catarrh and chilblains and cancer.

She even considered leaving Nevada, going back to California or someplace in the South. Virginia City was harsh and loud, the hillsides ugly with mines and glory holes, and the town was bawdy and godforsaken. But Daniel was there, and for that reason, Gracy could not leave. They might not ever be together again, but there was a bond between them. They had shared so much. He had seen her deliver her first baby, had given her the dime she wore around her neck. They had been young together. They would always be a part of each other. She couldn't break that tie, not yet. And so she stayed on in the little house alone, hoping she would see Daniel when she ventured out—and hoping, too, that she would not, for even a glimpse gave her an overwhelming sense of loss that sent her into days of misery.

Gracy was not aware of time passing. Daniel had left her in the heat of summer, and now the wind was blowing down off the mountains, bringing a chill that settled in Gracy's bones. It surprised her that winter was coming on. Had Daniel been gone that long? She split the wood herself, stacking it beside the door. She pieced quilts, for she had no one to warm her in the nighttime cold. But she no longer made the figured quilts that had brought so much admiration. Instead, she pieced only string quilts from leftover scraps, because the quilts were only for herself.

Food did not matter much, and Gracy grew even thinner and had to force herself to eat. A bowl of oatmeal or a slice of bread toasted over the open flame of the cookstove was enough for a meal and sometimes she didn't eat even that. She'd sit at the table, the food untouched, and stare into the flame of the kerosene lamp until it was time to go to bed.

That night she sat in Daniel's chair looking out the window at the falling snow. The storm was not a pretty one—no soft flakes but instead stringy bits of ice that the wind blew against the glass. It was dusk, the time Daniel had once returned home, but it was her lonely time now, and she brooded. There was a presentiment that night, a sense that something was not right, and Gracy wondered if it was the air, so charged that it seemed to send out sparks. Perhaps a woman was in labor. She stood and walked around the room, trying to shake off the feeling. But it would not go away. When she heard the knock on her door, she thought it was a bitter night to deliver a baby, for why else would someone come in the storm except to call her out. Still, it would be a time of joy, and Gracy needed that just then. She rose, glanced around the room to make sure her bag was in its proper place, and opened the door—to Daniel.

For the few seconds they stared at each other, Gracy thought it was odd that Daniel would visit then, because he usually came to the house when she wasn't there. Surely he had seen the glow of the lamp through the window and knew she was about.

"Daniel?" she said. She did not invite him in, and it occurred to her that he might be drunk, that he could have come to the cabin by mistake.

"Please . . ." he said.

Gracy didn't understand. She moved aside then and gestured for Daniel to come out of the storm. He was disheveled, his hair—graying now, she noted—was mussed, his eyes wild. "What is it?" she asked.

"You have to come." When Gracy only looked confused, he said. "Well, God, Gracy! She'll die!"

"The baby," Gracy said dully, realizing Jennie's time had come.

"Please help her."

"Don't ask it. There are other midwives." Gracy's voice quivered.

"She has one. And a doctor, too. But the baby won't be born. You'll know what to do."

Gracy turned away, a rage inside of her, despair so profound she could hardly look at her husband. "How can you ask it of me, Daniel? How dare you!"

"You're the only hope."

Gracy began to shake, and she sat down on a chair. "No, Daniel. I can't. You ask too much. How could I deliver my own husband's child? The shame of it! Oh, no, I can't." She took hold of herself, swallowed down some of the anger, then said, "It always seems bad with the first one. You don't need me. She'll be all right."

"But she won't. The doctor said she will die if the baby doesn't come. There's so much blood. The midwife, she said to fetch you. She doesn't know what to do. You're the only one."

Gracy closed her eyes. She could not do it. Jennie had stolen Gracy's husband, and now Daniel was begging her to save the woman's life. What if Gracy couldn't? What if Jennie died? Would people say Gracy killed her, murdered her in revenge for taking Daniel? The awfulness of it made her shiver. She shook her head back and forth.

And then Daniel said, "The baby will die, too. You wouldn't let a baby die, would you, Gracy?"

No, she could not. Daniel knew it, and Gracy hated him for using that against her. She couldn't let the baby die, or the mother, either. If she refused to care for Jennie and the woman passed away, Gracy would carry the burden of that death just as she did the deaths of other women. She closed her eyes in pain at the irony of it. But she had no choice. When she opened them, she saw Nabby standing beside her. Nabby had once told her when she balked at attending a woman who had been cruel to her, "Do the righteousness." Now Nabby said again, "Do the righteousness."

"Fetch my bag," Gracy said, rising slowly, shaking herself as if she could shake away the anguish. She took off her slippers and put on her thick shoes, then wrapped her shawl around herself and went out into the storm with Daniel.

"When did the labor pains start?" she asked, as the two hurried along, heads down against the ice that blew into their faces.

"Yesterday. It's been a day and a night and a day."

Thirty-six hours, Gracy thought. That was too long. "Is she conscious?"

"Barely."

Gracy had attended women like this before, women whose labors never seemed to end. Jennie was tiny. Perhaps the birth canal was too small. Or the baby might be turned. She thought of the irony of that. She had met Daniel the day she delivered his mother, Black Mary's, breech baby. Now she might be asked to birth his own breeched child. But she could do that. She had done it often enough before. It was the bleeding that was worrisome. Jennie would be weak from loss of blood, maybe not able to push the baby out. Daniel should have come earlier. But would she have gone with him earlier? Gracy didn't know.

Daniel's house was on the far side of town, a pretty brick structure with white jigsaw trim. Gracy had walked past it before, not knowing that was where Daniel lived, and had admired the roses, which were dead now and covered with snow. The house was far nicer than the cabin she and Daniel had lived in together, the home she occupied alone now. The front door opened to a parlor filled with furniture upholstered in red velvet, pictures in gold frames on the walls. And through a doorway was a dining room with a set of china displayed in a cupboard. Gracy had never had plates that matched, or pictures in gold frames, either. But such things had not mattered to her, and she was never jealous of possessions. She put them out of her mind as Daniel led her into the bedroom.

As she entered the room, Gracy removed her shawl, which had once belonged to Nabby, and threw it over the back of a chair, next to another shawl. The second wrap was new, Persian wool with a design in bright orange, Daniel's favorite color, and Gracy thought he would have bought it for Jennie, bought it along with all the other fripperies in the house. He'd have purchased them with money Gracy might have used to buy food. But that was in the past, and Gracy did not dwell on it.

Instead, she went to the bed, where Jennie lay. She was tiny and white, looking as sweet as water from a spring. The doctor and midwife stood beside her, as if afraid to touch the bones that were fragile as a hummingbird's.

"The baby's turned," the midwife said.

Gracy looked at the woman's hands, which were as big as hams. They could not have reached into the womb and righted the baby.

"We've got to pull it out of her," the doctor added.

"Do that, and you might kill them both," Gracy told him. "Let me see." She set down her bag and accepted the basin of hot water and a bit of soap that Daniel handed to her. She smiled a little as she thought he remembered she always washed her hands before touching a woman.

She put her hand on Jennie's forehead and felt the fever. Then she examined the woman, noting that the baby's shoulder was where the head should have been. But Gracy would turn it. The blood soaking into the bed worried her more. "Jennie, can you hear me?" she asked.

The woman opened her eyes, and Gracy saw the flecks that shone in them like quartz. "Who is it?"

Gracy started to say her name but couldn't. "The Sagehen," she replied. "Now the baby's turned a little, and I'm going to reach in and straighten it. And when I tell you, you push."

"I already tried," she said.

"You'll have to try again."

"I can't."

"Isn't there another way? She's tired, Gracy," Daniel pleaded.

"There's no other way," Gracy snapped, "not if you want them to live."

Daniel went to the head of the bed and brushed Jennie's hair out of her face, then held her hands, talked honeywords to her, and the pain of that love made Gracy look away. She forced herself to think of this as any other birth. She worked on the baby, and when it was turned and a great pain came on Jennie, Gracy ordered, "Push!"

It took twice more, but at last, the baby was born—a boy, just as Daniel had prophesied, Gracy noted as the child let out a cry. Tears ran down her face as she realized her husband had a son, and a healthy one. But not a son she had given him. Methodically, she handed the baby to the first midwife, while she dealt with the afterbirth. She worked quickly, placing the placenta in a basin to be disposed of, then turning back to Jennie. The bleeding had not stopped. Gracy watched the blood run onto the sheet, soak into the mattress. Her own apron was covered with Jennie's blood. Gracy turned to the doctor. He shook his head.

Daniel caught the look between the two of them. "Will she be all right?" he pleaded.

The doctor looked away.

"Gracy?"

Gracy took a deep breath. She had never been one to turn from the truth. Besides, Daniel wouldn't want her to. "I do not believe she will make it. She's lost too much blood, and there's no way to stop it."

"No," Daniel sobbed. He turned to Jennie, who was no longer lucid, and put his head down on the pillow beside hers and cried.

Gracy could not stand to see him like that and busied herself with the baby, taking the infant from the other midwife.

"What will we do with him? I don't know anyone to be a wet nurse," the woman said.

"I'll manage," Gracy told her, and realized it would be up to her to find a home for the baby. It was unlikely Daniel knew of anyone to care for him.

"I'll be going then."

After the woman left, Gracy went to Daniel's side and put her hand on his head. "I'm sorry, Daniel. I'll bring the baby back to the cabin. I've milk powder there to mix up. Maybe he'll take it until I can find a wet nurse."

He turned and hugged her waist. "Stay, Gracy."

She shook her head. "It's your sorrow."

"It's our sorrow," he said, holding her tight, and Gracy, too, wept.

The doctor studied them a moment. "If you're going to stay, Mrs. Brookens—"

"Go. No need for the both of us," she said.

He nodded, and then as he opened the door, he told Daniel, "She saved the boy's life. He'd have died without her. If anybody asks, I'll tell them that."

Gracy was grateful for the words, but she did not think Daniel heard them. She sat down in the rocker in a corner of the bedroom, the baby in her lap, her arms against the smooth wood of the chair. She wondered if Daniel had made it just as he had made a rocker for her years before, when they were expecting their first child. She did not sit there long, however, for death came quickly. Gracy was aware that Jennie had stopped breathing, and she placed the baby in the cradle and went to Daniel and raised his head from the pillow. "She's gone, Danny," Gracy said. And then she held him while he sobbed.

Gracy took the baby home, then waited until after the burying to discuss him with Daniel. She attended the service, not because she wanted to but because she believed the baby ought to be there. She was surprised at the turnout. Many of the women from the row were at the gravesite, because the prostitutes loved a good funeral. It was a chance to honor one of their own with tears and lamentations. They murmured over how angelic Jennie looked, how innocent, her hands folded over her breast, the gold ring with the bright stone on one finger. Best it was buried with her, Gracy thought.

Gracy recognized a few of Daniel's friends, including John and Elizabeth Miller, who moved to either side of Gracy and put their arms around her. She thought Daniel would go off and get drunk after the coffin was lowered into the grave and covered with dirt. But instead, he stood beside the mound until only he and Gracy and the baby were left.

"I will walk home with you," he said, and Gracy nodded. She needed to tell him about the couple she had found who had lost a child of their own and would take the baby. It would be a good fit. He would be their son, but Daniel could see him from time to time. He would be like a grandfather to the boy.

They went into the house together as they had only months before, and Daniel fed wood into the cookstove and built up a fire. He went to the cupboard where he had kept the whiskey, but Gracy shook her head. "I threw it out."

Daniel nodded and sat down at the table, his head between his knees.

"I found a couple who will take the baby. They are good people, who will raise him as their own—"

Gracy stopped when Daniel straightened up and looked at her sharply. "What?"

"I made inquiries. You don't want the baby to go to an orphan home."

"You think I'd give him up?" Daniel looked shocked.

"You're going to raise him?" Gracy had not considered it. How could Daniel care for a baby by himself?

"I won't give away my son." Daniel went to the window and looked out at the gray sky.

"How will you keep him?" Gracy asked. The baby was fussy, and Gracy set him in the cradle that Daniel had made for their own little ones—a cradle she had kept all those years—while she heated water on the stove to make milk. Perhaps Daniel had found a woman who would care for the boy while he worked. Maybe one of the prostitutes had already agreed to move in with him.

"You'll raise him," Daniel said, turning around to face his wife.

Gracy, who held the kettle in her hand, raised her head so abruptly that she spilled water onto the stove, where it sputtered and sent up a wisp of steam. "Me?" She set down the kettle, the baby's milk forgotten.

"Of course. You've always wanted a healthy baby."

Gracy gave a dry laugh that was more like a snort, and said harshly, "You want me to raise my husband's bastard?" She did not like the word, did not like to call an innocent baby such a vile name, but that was the truth of it. "Are you demented?"

"Who better than you?"

"That may be so, but I'll not do it, Daniel. I would look into his face every day and know whose child he was."

"He's my child."

"Yes, and the child of your mistress, a prostitute."

"You would blame him for that?"

"I would blame you." The baby cried, and Gracy hurried to fix his milk, then sat down at the table and gave him the bottle. He was a pretty child, his hair pale like Jennie's, his ears so much like Daniel's. And he was built like Daniel, too. If she had not known before, she would have recognized the moment he was born that Daniel was his father.

"He would be yours, too."

Gracy sighed. "Even if I agreed, how could I raise a baby, a woman alone? I can barely keep myself as it is. I'd have to go on with the birthings, and I couldn't take him with me. No, Daniel, it is impossible."

"I would take care of him then."

"If I could find you. Would you expect me to take him with me while I searched the saloons for you?"

"I'll stop drinking, Gracy. I promise."

"What would people say if I raised him?"

"It's a mining town. Worse things happen here and are forgotten. And when did you ever care what people said?"

"I do now. I do not care to have people think I'm a freak for raising my husband's son by another woman, while likely he is out visiting the fancy houses."

"I won't ever do that again. I promise. I want us to be a family—you and me and the baby. I would move back home and be your husband again."

Gracy stared at him dumbfounded. "And do you think I would take you back?"

Daniel went to where Gracy sat and got down on his knees. "I did a wicked thing, and I broke your heart. I beg you to forgive me, Gracy. I loved her. I won't deny that. But not the way I love you. I knew you before I knew myself. You shaped me, just as I did you. I knew that day in Black Mary's house that we were meant to be together. Jennie, I cared for her because she made me feel like I was somebody. She needed me as you never did. I'll make it up to you if you'll let me come home. I promise I will never step. The baby, he will be our son—your son. We'll raise him together, as our own. We will think of him as a gift."

Daniel had never spoken so earnestly before, and at first, Gracy wondered if this was the plea of a man desperate for someone to raise his child. But Gracy knew him, knew his heart, and after thinking about what he said, she believed him. "If you ever stray, Daniel, I will take the baby and leave. I swear it."

"I'll never give you cause," he said.

It was not an easy time for Gracy, and it took her months, years even, to truly forgive Daniel. And she never forgot. How could she? Sometimes when she looked into her son's face or stroked his pale hair, she saw Jennie, but after a time, Gracy couldn't remember what Jennie looked like, and the boy became just himself.

They named him Jefferson—Jennie's last name; she had chosen it, Daniel said—and called him Jeff. They decided it would be best if he never knew the circumstances of his birth but would grow up believing Gracy was his mother. That was why they had left Virginia City. To keep the secret.

Gracy did indeed love him as her own. She had almost from the moment he was born. Daniel loved him, and Daniel loved her, too, Gracy realized after a time, loved her more than he ever had Jennie. In the beginning, Gracy thought it was gratitude, but she came to realize that Daniel's love was far greater, and she knew that he had never really stopped loving her. The marriage was a good one again, maybe better than before, because they both knew what they had lost and found again. The trials and heartache they had endured strengthened the bond between them.

She came to know all that the day Daniel came home the summer after Jeff was born, with a fistful of daisies. He held them behind his back and presented them to her as if they were gold-plated. "I remember at our wedding . . . your hair . . ." he said, embarrassed. He had kissed her then, kissed her as if they were young together.

That night, Daniel left the pallet on the kitchen floor where he had slept since he'd moved back into the house and slipped into Gracy's bed. She welcomed him. In the morning, she burned his letters to Jennie that she had kept in her Bible.

Twenty-one

Gracy kept the twins overnight, giving the McCauleys time to get their house ready for the infants. On Sunday, she and Daniel helped the new parents move the babies home. Mittie and Henry each carried a boy, while Gracy and Daniel took the cradle and the clothes that Esther had made, along with bottles and milk powder. Gracy didn't know what Mittie had told her husband about the Boyce babies, but when the man saw them, he was as smitten as his wife. "Imagine, yesterday it was just me and Mitt, and today we each got us a baby. Two boys! Ain't that something! Didn't have to wait no nine months, neither." He was as proud as any new father.

"She did the righteousness," Gracy told Daniel, wondering what would have happened if the McCauleys had said no. Surely she and Daniel couldn't have kept the boys themselves. Maybe if the trial ended favorably and they'd been younger, she thought. After all, their happiest years had been raising Jeff. Still, the Boyce boys would be better off with Mittie and Henry.

Ted Coombs was waiting for them when they returned to their cabin. "From the talk around town, I'd say we're doing pretty well. I wouldn't be surprised if tomorrow you'll be a free woman," he said, after Gracy invited him into the cabin and fixed him a plate of flapjacks.

"I told you," Daniel said. "I heard the same thing down to the Nugget, men saying when Gracy testifies, won't anybody believe Jonas Halleck over her."

Ted nodded. He picked up a can of sorghum and poured it on his pancakes. He took a bite and then another, and Gracy was pleased to see Ted wasn't a picky city fellow. He ate like a mountain man. "We ought to go over your testimony," Ted said. "Folks in town already think highly of you, and when I'm done, they'll think you're right up there with the angels in heaven. No matter what Doak asks you on the stand, he won't be able to cast a doubt on you."

Gracy looked down at her plate. She hadn't started on the flapjacks, hadn't even lifted her fork. "That's just it, Ted. I'm not going to testify," she said slowly.

Ted stopped with a bite of pancake halfway to his mouth. Oblivious to the syrup that ran down his fork onto his hand, he said, "You have to, Gracy. Why would you not?"

Gracy glanced at Daniel, then looked away. "Reasons."

"If you don't testify, the jury will think you're guilty."

"Not if they know her," Daniel said hopefully.

"That's not enough. It helps if a jury likes the defendant, but they need more than that to find a person not guilty. I'm not sure you'll get off if you don't testify. If fact, I'd say it's unlikely."

"Then I'll have to take the chance. I don't want to be up there answering questions. I should have told you earlier, but I didn't make up my mind until Friday. I've been thinking about this since before the trial started, and now that I've seen what that prosecutor does, I won't get up there. I don't want to hurt people like Josie Halleck, and I won't lie. Besides, the way I am, folks would know in a minute if I'm not telling the truth."

Ted set down his fork and wiped his hand on his pants. Then he looked Gracy in the face and asked, "What is there for you to lie about?"

Gracy rose, picking up her plate and scraping it into the slop bucket. "Nothing that concerns you," she said after a pause. "I'm just telling you I won't take the stand."

"Then you better start thinking what'll happen to you if you're found guilty." Ted hadn't finished his breakfast, but he handed his plate to Gracy.

"I have." Indeed, once the McCauleys had taken the Boyce babies, Gracy had thought of nothing else.

The lawyer turned to Daniel. "Do you know what this is about?"

Daniel shook his head. "But I can tell you if she says she won't do a thing, she won't do it."

Ted rose. "As your attorney, Gracy, I have to tell you this is a foolish decision, and it may well send you to prison. If you refuse to be questioned, the jury's going to believe you murdered that baby after all." He went to the door and said glumly, "I have to think about how to deal with this."

After Ted left, Daniel stood and put his arm around his wife's waist. "Gracy . . ."

"Don't, Daniel. I know you're going to try to get me to change my mind. But I won't. I can't."

"But why?" He looked confused. Gracy kept her secrets, but this was something she should share with him, he said.

Gracy shook her head. "You're about the last person I'd tell. Now don't bother me."

Daniel pushed back his chair and went outside, where he smacked the washtub hanging on the wall. "Your ma!" he said, when Jeff came outside to join him. "You think you can talk some sense into her?"

Jeff looked bewildered. "I've been trying to talk to her for two days. I want to ask her if that baby was really Josie's and if she thinks Mr. Halleck is the father."

"It sounds to me like that's the way of it. You know the girl?"

"Sure. In school. She was behind me. She was sweet." Jeff thought a moment. "Why would a man do that to his daughter?"

Daniel shrugged. "Why did God make snakes?"

Mittie was not in the courtroom. Gracy knew her friend wouldn't be there, that she'd stay home with her babies, but Gracy was disappointed just the same. She needed all the support she could get, especially now that she would refuse to say a word in her defense. There would be an agitation when folks realized Ted wouldn't call her, and Gracy would have been glad for Mittie's comfort.

It seemed as if most of the rest of Swandyke had decided to attend the trial, however. Gracy had hoped that interest would drop after the first day, but it hadn't. In fact, more people than ever were clamoring to get into the courtroom. Ted escorted Gracy through the crowd, Daniel and Jeff shoving aside people who blocked their way. "They're thicker than crows in a cornfield," Daniel muttered.

A reporter stepped in front of Gracy, his pencil and pad of paper in his hands, and Daniel all but fisted him. "Get away," he growled so fiercely that the man stepped back.

They pushed their way into the room, Gracy and Ted sitting down at a table in front, Daniel and Jeff seating themselves in the chairs behind.

"Why won't Ma change her mind?" Gracy heard Jeff ask.

"She won't say."

"Don't you know?"

Daniel muttered something Gracy couldn't hear, and she turned to look at him.

"Will it go bad for her, then?"

Daniel shrugged. "It might."

"We'll take her to Nevada, won't we, Pa?"

Gracy smiled at that. Jeff was still too young to understand the meanness of the world.

"Even if we could, there'd be a reward, with a hundred men hunting her."

"She's a good woman. People in Nevada still remember her. She birthed a lot of babies."

"Do they remember you, too?"

Jeff nodded. "Some. I went to that place, that whorehouse. A woman there, the cook, she'd been one of the girls . . . back then. She said you were good to her . . . to . . . to my mother. I saw the grave. I put flowers on it."

"She would have liked that. She loved roses." He paused. "Gracy's your ma, your real ma. She raised you," Daniel told Jeff. "You were better off with her than you ever would have been with Jennie."

"I guess I know that now," Jeff replied. "Sitting there, beside the grave, I wondered why Ma took me in. I must have been a trial to her every day."

"She loved you." Daniel paused. "You'll stay on, after this is over?" He glanced at Gracy and saw that she was listening.

The boy sat forward in his chair, his elbows on his knees, his face cupped in his hands. "I haven't decided. There are some things that . . . well, that I wonder about. I guess it depends on what happens with Ma, if she gets off."

"You don't have to stay because of me. But I think your ma would want you to."

Jeff considered that. "It doesn't seem like she does. She says I ought to see the world, the way you did, says there's time enough for me to settle down."

Daniel looked puzzled, as if he had just realized that, indeed, Gracy hadn't said she wanted Jeff to stay on. He glanced at her, a question on his face, but just then, the judge came into the courtroom, followed by the members of the jury, who sat down in the rockers.

Judge Downing looked over the crowd, noting where the reporters were and giving them a slight nod. He made a few preliminary remarks, then turned to Ted. "Sir, I believe it is your turn."

"Thank you, Your Honor. I hope the hunting was good."

"Didn't shoot a blessed thing. Nearly got me a cow, though." He seemed pleased when even the jury laughed. Still, he pounded for silence. "You have a witness, Mr. Coombs?" The judge glanced at Gracy, and Gracy thought he didn't know that she would not testify.

"I have, Your Honor."

Daniel jerked his head up and sent Gracy a questioning look, as if thinking she had changed her mind and not told him. But she was as bewildered as he.

"The defense calls Mrs. Edna Halleck."

Gracy turned and stared at the woman, stunned. Ted must have kept the witness a secret from her for fear Gracy would object. After all, she'd opposed Josie's taking the stand and had refused to testify herself. Ted must be desperate, because what could Edna say except to back up her husband? Before the trial started, Ted had told Gracy that he'd barely had a chance to question Edna and Josie, and then they'd said nothing of importance because Jonas Halleck was in the room.

Daniel and Gracy weren't the only ones who were surprised. Edna Halleck turned white and put her hands over her face, muttering, "No, no."

Jonas jumped up and yelled. "She will not testify. She's my wife, and I say she can't."

"I'm the judge, and I say she can," Judge Downing yelled back. "Sit down, or I'll have you ejected." He paused. "Sir," he added, which reminded everyone in the room—including the jury—that no matter what had come out in the first day of the trial, Jonas Halleck was still a man of consequence.

"I will have satisfaction from you," Jonas told Ted. "It's not right for a wife to testify. The Bible says women are to be quiet."

"And this court says they are required to talk if I say so," the judge said.

"I object." Doak stood up.

"To what?" the judge asked.

"A wife can't testify against her husband. The law says so."

"She's not testifying against Mr. Halleck," Ted countered. "She's testifying in a case against Mrs. Brookens."

"He's right," the judge said.

Edna sat in her chair, weeping, and wouldn't stand until Doak went over to her and said, "There's nothing to worry about, Mrs. Halleck. All you have to do is tell the truth, tell them you saw Mrs. Brookens strangle your baby."

Edna got up, wiping tears from her face with her fingers, and slowly walked to the witness chair. She held up her hand, covered in a lace mitt, and was sworn in, her voice barely audible.

"Now then," Ted began, his voice low and filled with kindness, "you are Mrs. Edna Halleck, wife of Jonas Halleck. Is that correct?"

"Yes," she whispered, looking down at her hands in her lap.

"And you are a God-fearing woman who believes in the Bible. You believe in doing what's right."

She nodded.

"You believe in punishment for wickedness?"

Edna glanced at Gracy, then whispered, "I do."

"And you believe in telling the truth, that the Bible says lying is a sin?"

Edna glanced at her husband, who sat forward in his seat, barely able to stay still.

"Yes, sir."

"So you will tell the truth?"

Doak jumped up then. "Your Honor, is this necessary? The woman has sworn already to tell the truth. The defense doesn't need to badger her."

"Quite right. Mr. Coombs, ask your questions. I don't have all day."

Ted smiled. "It is unlikely that a lady like Mrs. Halleck has testified in a courtroom before. I wanted her to be acquainted with the procedure."

"She is," Judge Downing said. "Move along."

"Josie Halleck is your daughter. Is that correct?"

Edna nodded.

"And the baby who was murdered, he was Josie's son, wasn't he?"

Jonas jumped up and shouted, "I have told you he wasn't. Edna, you will not speak."

Edna blanched, drawing into herself at her husband's words. Jonas made a fist with his hand, so subtle that only Edna saw it—and Gracy. Edna turned to Gracy and shook her head. "I'm sorry," she mouthed.

"It's all right," Gracy whispered back. She couldn't help but feel compassion for the woman.

Edna started to get up, but then she looked at Gracy again. Gracy smiled at her, thinking that jail couldn't be any worse than the life Edna had lived with Jonas Halleck—the terror, the beatings. She knew about them because Edna had come to her for salves to heal the cuts and bruises. "It's all right," Gracy whispered again. "I understand." And she did. Jonas would kill Edna for telling the truth.

But suddenly, Edna said, "It's not right, Gracy." She turned to her husband and said in a voice that was barely audible, "You lied. That baby was Josie's. You know my insides fell out after I lost the baby that came after Josie. You kicked me for it, and I can't have more babies. You know that, Jonas. You told me a hundred times I'm not a woman anymore."

There were gasps in the courtroom and a few muttered words of shame, before the judge called for silence.

"So your husband lied about who bore that child," Ted said.

"He said we had to. He said what will people think of us if Josie has a baby? He said nobody would want her for a wife. So after Josie started to show, we had to stay in the house where nobody would see us. The mercantile delivered our groceries, and I left the laundry outside for the washerwoman. Jonas wouldn't let us go in the garden, even after dark. We were locked up like wild animals."

"Who is the father of the baby?" Ted asked.

"She doesn't know. Josie's mind is mush. You tell them that, Edna," Jonas ordered.

Gracy thought the judge might throw Jonas out of the courtroom then, but perhaps Judge Downing was intrigued enough with what had just happened to ignore the outburst. He might even enjoy seeing the destruction of a man who had been so important.

Edna was silent.

"Mrs. Halleck?" Ted asked.

When Edna wouldn't reply, Ted turned to the judge, who said, "Answer the question, Mrs. Halleck"

"I can't," she said.

"See, I told you she doesn't know," Jonas said. "Doesn't know enough to teach her own daughter to be a decent woman. Josie's not anything but a whore, men coming around sniffing after her like she's a dog in heat."

Edna raised her head and stared at her husband for a long time, before her face turned hard. "If she is a wanton woman, you made her one, Jonas. I've seen you. I've seen you rutting on her, seen how you looked at her ever since she come a woman. First time it happened, she wasn't much more than twelve. I begged you to stop, but you wouldn't. You called her evil and a temptation and went after her with your whip. All I could do was hold that girl after you used her, listen to her cry out her hurt and her shame. You are a fornicator and an adulterer, and with your own daughter. And you made me say I birthed the spawn of your sin." Edna stood and pointed a finger at her husband.

"Shame, Jonas Halleck, shame. You are the devil. The Lord will punish you for your sinfulness."

"Liar! Liar!" Jonas called, while women in the courtroom turned away at the horror of what they had heard, and men, even some employed at the Holy Cross, jumped up, a few making a move toward Jonas, who cringed.

"Your own girl. You'll burn in hell," one man called.

Jonas bolted from his seat. "Let me through," he said, rushing down the aisle toward the door.

But John Miller stepped in front of him and grabbed the man's arms. "You want me to take him to jail?" he asked the judge.

"It can wait. Let's finish the trial," Judge Downing said. "Mr. Halleck, you sit down, and if you don't, I'd be hard-pressed to stop any man in this courtroom from doing violence to you."

John thrust Jonas back into his chair, and two men moved behind him to grab him if he tried again to leave.

When the courtroom quieted, Ted said, "Now, Mrs. Halleck, you have stated that your daughter gave birth to the baby and your own husband is its father. Is that correct?"

Edna nodded once, then put her hands over her face and began to weep. "I didn't protect her. I ask the Almighty to forgive me."

Ted waited until the woman composed herself. Then he asked, "One more question, Mrs. Halleck. Did your husband—did Jonas Halleck—strangle that baby?"

Edna clutched her hands and glanced at Ted. Her face was drawn, and she looked older than the mountains, although she might have been only thirty-five. She hunched in the chair as she continued to stare at Jonas. He rose, but a man behind him shoved him down.

"Mrs. Halleck?" Ted said.

The room was still as death then, and Gracy could hear the sound of a stamp mill on Turnbull Mountain, could hear men talking outside the building, could even hear the buzz of a bee as it flitted through the window into the courtroom. A juror leaned forward in his chair, and his rocker sent out a sound like a crack of thunder. The man reddened and stilled himself, but no one looked at him. Instead, the eyes of the jurors and everyone else in the courtroom were trained on Edna Halleck.

"Mrs. Halleck?" Ted said again.

"Jonas put that baby in a box and stuck it in a hole in the earth, but I wouldn't let him rest easy till he dug it up so we could bury it in blessed ground. He hit me, but I wouldn't let up. Thrown away like that, the baby wouldn't go to heaven. I couldn't let that child spend eternity in hell. I told Jonas I'd dig it up myself if he didn't." She shook her head back and forth.

"Yes, ma'am. Now answer the question," the judge said in a voice that made the woman jump.

"What?" she said, as if coming out of a trance. She turned away from Jonas and looked at the judge.

"Who killed your daughter's baby?" Ted asked.

"Don't make me tell," Edna begged.

"Did your husband—did Jonas Halleck—tie that string around the baby's neck and strangle it?" Ted asked again.

Edna sighed so deeply that her body shook. At last she said, "No."

People in the courtroom sucked in their breath, muttered, and shuffled their feet. Ted sent Gracy a questioning look, but she stared straight ahead, stared at Edna. The courtroom grew absolutely still. Then one by one, people turned to look at Gracy.

"You are under oath," Ted said without much conviction. Daniel shook his head back and forth, as if Ted had made a terrible mistake. By admitting her husband's incest, Edna had made it clear she wouldn't lie. And now, if she said Gracy had murdered the baby, people would believe her. Gracy would be found guilty. Ted must have known that, and he threw up his hands and said he'd withdraw the question.

"Well, I won't," the judge said. "Mrs. Halleck, you can sit here all day until you answer. Who strangled that baby?"

"He was a child of the devil. He had to die," she muttered. She turned to look at the judge, staring at him as if the two of them were the only ones in the courtroom. Then she sighed again and said, "I couldn't let him live, couldn't shame Josie like that. When Gracy left, I saw that spool of thread and . . ." She looked up at the judge. "I killed him."

Twenty-two

Gracy tied the cord of the sweet baby she'd just birthed—a girl who reminded her of Emma—then handed the stork scissors to young Jane. "You cut it," she said.

"Truly?" the girl asked, her eyes wide with excitement and a little apprehension as she took the scissors. She carefully cut through the flesh, then returned the scissors to Gracy. "Did I do it right?"

"Perfect." Gracy wiped the scissors on a soft cloth, then placed them in her bag. She watched as Jane touched the tiny wet cheek with the backs of her fingers. It was clear the girl loved babies.

At fifteen, Jane had promise. She already had helped with three deliveries, and they had gone well. But she'd need seasoning, Gracy knew, before she could tell if the girl really would make a midwife. It remained to be seen whether Jane could cope with a mother dying or a new baby who never took a breath. Gracy had hopes for her, however.

Jane was the daughter of the oldest Richards sister, Martha. Gracy had been surprised when the woman sent for her to deliver her seventh child. But after the trial was over, the Richards sisters and others who had doubted Gracy's innocence had rushed to her side to tell her they'd believed in her all along. And as proof, Martha Richards had sent for Gracy when her time came.

Jane had been at the bedside when her mother delivered that last child, had stood transfixed as her baby brother slid out into Gracy's hands. Jane had held the infant while Gracy cared for the mother, but had kept an eye on what the midwife was doing, too. Later, the girl asked, "You think I could have the learning of this?"

"It takes a love of women and babies," Gracy replied.

Jane nodded. "I have it. Am I too young? I'm fifteen."

"I delivered my first at ten."

"Then I best get started."

So Jane had come to Gracy's cabin during the winter months to learn about herbs and potions, to study Gracy's books, and to talk to the old midwife about childbirth. When Gracy was sure the girl was serious, she took Jane to a lying-in.

The girl had performed well, then and later. She distracted the small children who were bewildered by their mother's cries, rubbed the mother's back, brewed tea for the woman to drink (and for Gracy, too). She seemed to know just which herb or implement Gracy needed before the midwife asked. Maybe Jane would take over for her, just as she had replaced Nabby so many years before. Gracy had once hoped that Mittie McCauley would follow in her footsteps, but Mittie hadn't been interested, especially not now. What with the two boys to care for and a hint that she might look for a girl to adopt one day, Mittie was almost too busy to quilt.

Of course, it would be a while yet before someone else was needed as midwife. Edna Halleck's confession had lifted Gracy's malaise. Gracy had thought her midwifery days were coming to an end. But when the charge against her was dropped, she felt such joy—joy not just that she was no longer accused of killing the Halleck baby but joy that she could return to the work she loved. She had been given a chance to start over. Not that she didn't feel her age these days. Her step was slower now, and her bones ached after standing all night beside a childbirth bed. She would have to give up her work one day. But not yet. If Jane worked out, there would be someone to help her as she grew older and to take her place one day. She wouldn't be the last midwife on the Tenmile.

The birth that day had taken place in Swandyke, and now, the old woman and the young girl walked together through town. May had come on, and the snow had melted, although there would be a heavy, wet storm that bent the willows to the ground before winter truly passed. Still, the winter storms that howled down off the peaks and filled the mountain bowls with silence were done. Already the leaves on the aspen trees were budding and growing things sending up shoots through the earth damp with snowmelt.

"Spring births are the best ones," Gracy told Jane. "The baby will have a chance to grow strong before winter comes on again."

They walked slowly, because Gracy's leg still troubled her, and because the day was too fine to hurry. They passed RICHARD ERICKSON, M.D. painted on a window, and Gracy waved, although she did not know if the doctor was inside. After the trial, Little Dickie had told her stiffly, "I guess I misspoke." It wasn't much of an apology, but Gracy knew what it cost the man to give it. She was a forgiving woman and thought that with a little compassion, he would be a good doctor one day. Swandyke needed someone with book-learned medicine. And so she encouraged young mothers to take their babies to him. He returned the courtesy, sending a pregnant woman to Gracy.

The two went on, Gracy silent as they approached the Halleck house. It was closed up the way it always was, but Gracy knew that no one lived inside anymore. Jonas Halleck had moved to a shack at the Holy Cross and had let it out that the mine was for sale. People said he ought to be in jail, but Ted Coombs told her that what the man had done with his daughter surely was a sin, but he wasn't sure it was against the law. So Halleck hadn't been charged.

Neither had Edna Halleck. Gracy wasn't surprised. Ted had said that after the licking the prosecutor had taken, he wasn't likely to want to go after Edna Halleck, who had the town's sympathy. What's more, folks believed that being married to Jonas Halleck was punishment enough. At winter's end, Edna and Josie moved away from Swandyke, but not before Edna asked for a divorce. She appeared before the same Judge Downing, who gave her a good settlement. Gracy was glad to see them go. There were those who blamed Josie for the baby. It was best the girl was gone, best for everyone. Gracy was relieved.

She and Ted had talked about Edna's confession. Had the woman really strangled the baby? Or had Josie done it and Edna taken the blame to protect her daughter? Ted didn't know. But then, Ted hadn't been convinced that Gracy wasn't the killer. Gracy had seen it on his face when he turned to her after Edna said Jonas Halleck hadn't murdered the boy. Gracy'd seen the questioning look and knew that everybody in the courtroom— everyone but Daniel and Jeff and maybe John—wondered if Gracy were indeed guilty. But she hadn't remarked on it to Ted. It was enough that she was aware that her husband and son knew her heart.

The two midwives reached the trail to Gracy's cabin, and Jane left to return home. "You did finely," Gracy told her, and the girl smiled, happy but a little embarrassed at the praise.

Gracy started up the trail alone. Off in the distance, she saw Daniel with the old dog, Sandy. They had found him on a mine dump years before when Jeff was a boy, and the dog's face now was white with age. Daniel's back was to her and Gracy thought as she had so many years before that it was Daniel's hips. She'd always had a liking for hips. Hips was what she was after, Nabby told her once.

She would miss him when the snows higher up melted and he left her to prospect in the high country. The cabin was warm. The boy Abraham had chinked it before the winter storms. Still, she dreaded to sleep alone. But Daniel would no more give up the search for precious metal than she would midwifery. Come snowmelt, he would tell her he could smell the ore. He'd pack a burro, and Gracy would send him off, holding her tongue, because she knew the summer's work might amount to no more than a few nuggets in the peach can.

Daniel turned and saw her, and his face lit up. He hurried down the trail to his wife, then put his arms around her, right there in the sunlight where anyone might see them. He took her arm, and the two old people continued up the path. They reached the cabin, but they didn't go inside. Instead, they sat on the bench in the light that came through the tree branches.

"There's a letter from Jeff. He's coming home."

Gracy turned to her husband, and the smile lines on her face deepened. "Truly?" she asked.

Daniel nodded. "He doesn't say for good, but he'll be back. I knew he would." He frowned. "You're glad, aren't you?"

"Of course I am."

"But you sent him away after the trial. I think he might have stayed then, but you pushed him out. You told him he'd gone west and that it was time for him to see what was east of the mountains. I never understood it."

Gracy shook her head. "It doesn't matter. There's not a reason now for him to stay away."

"I pondered on it. You must have had a reason then. What was it, Gracy?"

"Best be kept a secret."

"From your husband?"

Gracy thought that over. She picked up a stick and threw it for Sandy, who got up slowly and fetched it. The dog was as old as they were, she thought.

"We don't keep secrets from each other. Haven't for a long time," Daniel said.

Of course they did. Or at least, Gracy did. She kept the secrets told to a midwife. But this secret was different. This wasn't about one of the women.

"If there's a thing to know about our son, you ought not to keep it from me." Daniel had been after her for months asking why she'd encouraged Jeff to leave.

He was right, she thought now. In the years since Jeff was born, the two of them had grown so close that they were a part of each other. If Daniel's heart had stopped beating, Gracy believed hers would, too. She had no right to keep this secret from him, although the knowing of it would pain his soul. She had thought to protect him, but he was right. The secret was his to know.

She watched as a dead aspen leaf drifted in the wind, landing in her lap. She picked it up and smoothed it with her fingers. The leaf had made it through the winter. The veins stood out like a line of fine stitching. It was too brittle to be pressed in her Bible, but she would save it because it had survived, just as she and Daniel had survived. And the leaf would remind her of the day she shared with Daniel the secret that was on her heart.

"Well, God, Gracy?" Daniel said. "Tell me."

She dropped the leaf into her lap and fingered the dime she had worn around her neck for more than fifty years, the coin

Daniel had given her the day she first laid eyes on him. She thought again of Jeff and how she had risked prison rather than let his life be ruined. She remembered the Halleck baby, his strange eyes with bits of amber that shone like quartz, his pale hair the gold of winter sun, the way his ears curled. He was the spit of the baby she had delivered so many years before.

"I couldn't let Jeff stay while Josie was here," she began.

Daniel frowned, then as if he had a presentiment of what his wife was going to say, he reached for Gracy's hand.

"What I couldn't let you know," she said, looking out at a snow skiff on the range. "What Jeff didn't realize until I told him after the trial . . ." She paused for a moment, then turned to her husband. "You know I can always tell who a baby's father is?"

Daniel's eyes narrowed, and he nodded slowly.

Gracy smiled, then pressed her husband's hand. "The Halleck boy was our grandson, Danny. Jeff was the father of Josie's baby."